MUTINY

Clio's eyes snapped up to look at Teeg, standing in the tent door, the perimeter lights glaring behind him.

"Maybe we're gonna make our own rules from now on," Teeg said. "We're a long way from Vanda, Clio. Maybe I like it here. I was hoping you liked it too."

"What are you talking about, Teeg?"

"You ever think about staying?"

"On Niang?" Clio's heart was sinking like an elevator with the cables cut. "No, I never did."

"Maybe you should start."

"Jesus, Teeg. You gotta be kidding. Get a grip. Nobody wants to give up Earth, give up home."

"Posie does. Liu and Meng too. We've talked."

Clio looked at him, scared for the first time. "You're crazy. Think they wouldn't come after us?"

"Think they'd find us?"

Then, from a distance, shouts and then gunfire. Teeg bolted through the tent flap, Clio behind him. She ran for her gun in the crew tent.

Also by Kay Kenyon

LEAP POINT

Coming in Spring 1998 from
Bantam Spectra Books

KAY KENYON

THE SEEDS OF TIME

SPECTRA™
BANTAM BOOKS
New York Toronto London Sydney Auckland

THE SEEDS OF TIME

A Bantam Spectra Book / June 1997

SPECTRA and the portrayal of a boxed "s" are trademarks of Bantam
Books, a division of Bantam Doubleday Dell Publishing Group, Inc.

ISBN 0-553-57681-X

Published simultaneously in the United States and Canada

Bantam Books are published by Bantam Books, a division of Bantam
Doubleday Dell Publishing Group, Inc. Its trademark, consisting of the
words "Bantam Books" and the portrayal of a rooster, is Registered in
U.S. Patent and Trademark Office and in other countries. Marca
Registrada. Bantam Books, 666 Fifth Avenue, New York, New York 10103.

PRINTED IN THE UNITED STATES OF AMERICA

RAD   0 9 8 7 6 5 4 3 2

FOR
THOMAS

CONTENTS

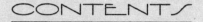

APPENDIX

The telling of this story is dedicated to my husband, Thomas D. Overcast, with love and gratitude. I am especially indebted to my agent, Donald Maass, for his inspired ideas and confidence in me. My special thanks to my editor, Anne Lesley Groell, for her sure footing in literary matters large and small, and to Donald McQuinn and the Pacific Northwest Writers Conference for mentoring and belly laughs . . . and again, to Thomas, for all the long discussions of time travel: maddening, elusive, and exhilarating.

If you can look into the seeds of time,
And say which grain will grow and which will not,
Speak then to me.

—*Macbeth*, I.iii.

BOOK I

GREEN SHIFTING

DIVE TO THE STARS

CHAPTER 1

Clio Finn rested her face against the bulkhead of her cabin, listening to countdown over the intercom, trying not to pass out. She felt a vein in her forehead throbbing against the cool metal of the ship. Minus twelve minutes and counting, ship's voice said. Eleven. She had just popped the last of the pills, and already she was shaking bad, but the ship was primed to go, her metal skin humming, deck throbbing, air charged with static and the hot, sharp smell of engines stoked to burn.

Then the captain was calling her to the bridge, in tones that said, *Now*, Finn.

Clio yanked open the cabin door, jammed down the corridor, nearly colliding with Hillis, chief botanist. He grabbed her arm, stopping her a moment.

"What's up, Clio? You OK?"

"Sure." She flashed him a wide smile, then dropped it. "Maybe this Dive's got me spooked," she said. "Maybe I got a bad feeling about this one."

He pulled her in close to him, looking into her eyes, and whispered, "Jesus, Clio, how many of those things did you take?"

"Just two," she lied, searching his face for some comfort.

He shook his head, released her.

Clio raced for the bridge, taking the ladder to the flight deck two rungs at a time. She emerged onto *Starhawk*'s bridge, now dim for pre-Dive countdown, readouts pulsing on every side. Captain Russo was busy with command central on visual. She nodded at Clio. Clio nodded back, slipped into her chair. Her copilot, Harper Teeg, seated next to her, raised an eyebrow at her.

Clio faced him. "Had to take a pee, OK?"

"I thought you girls had iron bladders."

"You haven't learned anything new about girls since seventh grade, Teeg."

"Just waiting for the right teacher, Miss Finn." His eyes lapped her up in the usual way. Didn't matter they were about to Dive back four hundred thousand years, didn't matter she was sick as hell and the only one on board that could steer this crate. Things like that didn't faze Harper Teeg.

Clio strapped herself in, clipped her headphones on, pushing them into her short, thick auburn hair. She scanned the instrumentation, everything looking good, panels surging to go. Listened to the countdown droning of command central, still coming in clear from Earth's largest space station, Vanda, though eleven thousand kilometers distant from the ship.

On another channel, Captain Russo found time to say, "Lieutenant Finn, you don't leave the bridge during countdown again, you copy?"

Clio turned her head around to her, acknowledging. "Yessir. Sorry, sir." Russo wasn't half bad, Clio thought. Just stiff as hell, a lifer with Biotime. No grey in that short black hair, though. If Russo felt the pressures of command, she buried it deep in her stocky body.

Countdown was looking good, going smooth. Until Ellison Brisher patched in from Vanda Station, his puffy face filling screen number two.

"You got a problem, Ellison?" Russo asked, her voice even, her face scowling at this last-second interference from the company.

"Not at all. You are on track, Captain. Little jumpy aren't we?" He popped a small candy in his mouth, moving his jaw sideways, as though chewing cud.

"Yeah, I'm always jumpy when I take a little trip like this."

Brisher smiled. "Just wondering how Clio's doing."

Russo shook her head. "She's on task, Ellison. You want to talk to her?"

Brisher looked surprised. "No. Not necessary, just backing you up, Captain. Anything you need, just ask."

"Thanks, Biotime, we are ready to fly. No problems." In a tone that said, And keep your goddamn nose off the bridge.

Clio listened to this exchange, her stomach clenching up, a trickle of sweat starting to cut a path down her hairline. Ellison Brisher was out to get her, she figured; whether he had anything on her or not was a question. Didn't want to think about what Biotime's chief operations officer could do to her if he chose.

Screen two blanked out as station systems separated from the ship, leaving them in communications blackout as *Starhawk* gathered speed, reaching for Dive velocity, reaching for their destination, Crippen's Planet.

Clio gripped the chair arms, preparing for Dive. Except there wasn't any way to prepare for Dive. Other Dive pilots had their rituals, customs, superstitions. Clio just dove, letting the time stream take her, fighting the fear, the hallucinations, riding the sheer joy of it. Every other poor bastard on the ship in dreamland, unconscious, depending on her, a Dive pilot with a dozen too many missions, and now with the shakes to prove it.

Russo's voice: "Approaching Dive. Thirty seconds. Finn, you ready?"

"Ready, sir."

Teeg flashed a grin at her. "Night all. Wake me with a kiss, this once, Finn."

"Kiss my ass, Teeg."

"Baby, I been dreaming on it."

Russo again: "Cut the chatter, we're heading into Dive. Helm to you, Finn."

"Yessir." Clio throttled the main engines up to 100 percent, felt the ship lurch and reach for transition speed, threw the pair of switches controlling the time coils. Sensed, then felt, the field envelope the ship, hit the flight deck, take her reeling into the hidden underbelly of the space-time continuum.

And she was Diving. Was Diving down, leaving the common universe, felt her consciousness floating just in front of her forehead, but her thought process, her coordination, they remained normal if she remembered to engage them. The ship lights pulsed way down, cranking up the stars to laser intensity as Clio watched through the viewport. Teeg's head slumped to the side, he was out, they were all out. *Starhawk* was changing dimensions, from space to time, sweeping her up in a slow, rolling wave that for some obscure reason left only a select few conscious and able to fly. And Clio Finn was one. *Used to be,* she thought. *Now I gotta have a little help.*

The dimension change triggered a nasty ripple in space-time. Clio almost thought she could see the ripple fan outward from the ship, but well clear of Earth, got to stay well clear. Ripple or no ripple, you want to avoid your own historical past—avoid changing it, changing yourself. No matter how much you'd like to redo it. No second chances. Just fly by the book, girl.

She leaned forward, cradling her stomach, felt that old warm brick forming there, saw the lights haloed around the control panel, and the air on the bridge turned thick as water at thirty fathoms. *Gotta ride this pony. Going to be fine. Dive fifty-five, going to be fine.*

Clio's eyes flicked over to the comm screen, all static now, picking up only the electromagnetic impulses of the galaxy. The static ebbed and surged, creating patterns if she watched long enough—sometimes faces, a fleeting Rorschach test. Clio yanked her attention back to the control board, trying hard to stay tuned, get the job done.

The right-side controls in front of her were for aerospace, the left for Dive. She jockeyed both sides. The Dive pilot rode the controls through Dive, and, coming up on real space, flew the ship like a normal pilot.

The contrails of the stars striped across the viewport, tracing the bright orbits of their endless paths, as the Milky Way rotated around its center. *Starhawk* was picking up time speed, the past rushing by. Time before she was born, before Mom and Elsie and Petya. Time before the good old U.S. of A. Time before time.

Clio focused her eyes on the chronometer, watched the numbers scroll up, six thousand years, going on seven thousand, now crawling to eight thousand. She scanned the readouts for chunks of matter the galaxy might throw at the ship, hurtling along faster than mere humans were meant to travel. *Gotta stay awake, stay awake.*

Teeg was radiating colors everywhere his skin was exposed. His face had become fuzzy, as though the surface of his skin wasn't always in exactly the same place. His handsome, squarish face had lost its perpetual leer, looking lost and serene. Trusting to wake up in the right time and right place, like a child committing himself to sleep, to the night.

If I should die before I wake . . .

Clio snapped back in a hurry. You were getting a little mesmerized there, old girl. Was not. Were too.

Ran a systems check. What the hell time was it anyway? She laughed out loud at that; heard a voice, high and bell-like. God, was that her laugh? Damn well better be. Don't get spooked now, girl. You got a job to do.

The numbers slipped by the face of the chronometer, counting the years, the thousands, the hundreds of thousands, until time was meaningless, too enormous to matter, to count. There in the blackness of interstellar space, moving back in time meant less about time than it did about space. The solar system, the whole galaxy, was rushing headlong through the universe, while at the same time the galaxy was rotating around its own center. Going back in time, you found yourself surrounded by the stars that had preceded Sol on its swing through the galaxy. Travel to the stars achieved without faster-than-light speed, a simple backdoor approach called time travel. Humanity's only bridge across the monstrous distances of space. A limited bridge, but better than nothing. Vandarthanan's mathematical vision of the mechanics of time had opened up space travel without the need for the speed—or near speed—of light.

A Dive ship was needed. Both a spacecraft and a time-travel device. Send it out far from Earth to avoid paradox risks. Send it back in time, not forward in time—at least not past the Future Ceiling, that current date you left on Vanda. But back in time, in search of an Earthlike planet, one that had once swung by on its immense sweep along the Orion arm of the galaxy. Sometimes Clio thought of it as a merry-go-round, where those rearing horses, nostrils flaring, plunged ahead of her, but only a moment before occupied the very point on the circle, the very point where she and her red-saddled mare now thundered by. Space was like that, a little. Galaxy, solar systems, planets, all thundering by in a headlong, circling rush to nowhere. And with Dive, humanity could hold on and ride . . .

With only a few flaws.

Like the Future Ceiling, forbidding all trespass. Like Dive pilot burnout, where you push a Dive pilot past certain tolerances and neurons burn out, flaring incandescent, leaving your highly trained pilot a few bricks short of a full load. Took twenty-five to thirty Dives, or thereabouts. Then the companies brought in your replacement. . . . Hey, show the fellow around, will you?

She leaned back in her chair, breathing deeply, remembering where she was: *Starhawk, Starhawk,* hawk of the stars, circling, circling, watching for its prey. . . .

Clio jerked up in her chair. She had dozed off. Gods! She had lost it this time, gone over the edge, gone under with the rest of the crew. Jolted awake by the dimension swing. They were stopped dead in space, the chronometer reading steady.

Jesus, how long had they been sitting here, everybody blacked out, no one in charge . . . She punched in visual, scanning the telemetry: and there was a planet—no, a moon. Crippen's moon, by God. Practically a bull's-eye in Dive terms and damn lucky they didn't hit it. Even considering their hopes to get close on the reasonably short Dive, this one was definitely snug on the mark.

Then a shattering Klaxon alarm sounded as a massive object loomed into view, headed directly toward *Starhawk.*

An asteroid, caught in the moon's faint gravity, same as the ship herself. They were about to get acquainted, real fast. Clio hit the thrusters, swinging the ship around, and punched up the engines to full, moving *Starhawk* out of the path, but not before the blast from the ship's jets hit the icy asteroid surface and kicked up a rushing plume of water vapor. The eruption hit the ship, sending a shudder through the cabin. She heard the wrenching of metal down amidships, and then they were plunging toward the large moon itself.

As Clio struggled to bring the ship under control, she heard a groan from Captain Russo, always the first to recover from Dive, then her angry command, "Bring the helm over to Teeg!"

"Teeg's still out, Captain. I'm working this tumble. . . ." *Starhawk* was tumbling headlong toward Crippen's moon, five rotations a second. Clio fought the controls, her hands flying over the board, slowing the tumble, but still they were headed dead-on for the moon, out of control. Voices were screaming over the comm, but Clio rode the ship, shutting them out. *Gotta ride this pony, goddamn it, gotta ride it . . .*

Then she got the nose of the ship up, and they were skimming across the horizon of Crippen's moon, tugged at by the thin gravity, but breaking away in a mad rush for space.

Clio moved them well off from the asteroid, scanned the visual display one more time, saw that they were well clear and safe. Then she leaned into her sick bag and threw up.

"Helm to you, Teeg," the captain was saying as Clio passed out.

In her dreams she could hear the hull resound: metal scraping on metal. Maybe she wasn't dreaming, just delirious, if there was a difference.

She woke up to see Doc Posie leaning over her, taking a blood-pressure reading. Posie was only an RN, but the crew called him Doc; a real doctor wouldn't fuss over a blacked-out Dive pilot.

Clio felt the ship shudder. She pushed up on both elbows. "What's going on, Doc?" Then, putting the situation together, swung off the bed, trying to find the floor with her feet.

Posie pushed her back down. "Just calm yourself, Clio."

"Calm myself? I'm so calm I'm barely breathing. Is that the lander separating? They going ahead with the mission?"

Posie nodded.

"Jesus."

"You don't need to swear."

"I didn't swear, goddamn it." Posie was so squeaky clean, in thought, word, and deed. "How long have I been out?"

"About ten hours."

She swung her feet around again, ran into Posie's thick hands gripping her shoulders, shoving her back onto the pallet.

"You're not going anywhere, so lie still," Posie said. He grabbed her arm harshly, pressing the blood-pressure band against her skin.

"Who says? I'm copilot on this ship, and I'm going to the bridge."

Posie's face zoomed down to fix her with a stare. "Captain says, Finn. So lie still or I'll trank you good." Posie's hands were shaking, his face redder than usual.

"OK, don't have a coronary." She lay back down, deciding to try charm instead of push. "What's the damage, Doc? I gotta know. I feel awful." She worked her face into a knot of anxiety.

Posie sniffed, turned to put the pressure band in a drawer, drawing out the moment. "As much as I've heard, we've got a crunch starboard side as big as a bathtub. No cracks or leaks, but they're still checking."

"Still checking! Jesus Doc, we just launched the lander, and we don't know the full damage to the ship yet? Has Russo lost her mind?"

Posie grabbed his clipboard, stalked to the medlab

door. "You stay here and rest or the captain'll chew you up for dinner, you copy Finn? She doesn't want a pilot with the wobbles on the bridge."

"Goddamn it Posie, you all wobble big time every freeping Dive!"

Posie glared at her and left, slamming the door.

Clio put her head in her hands, smelling her rank uniform, thinking what a mess, an unholy mess she'd made of the mission. A crew out in *Babyhawk*, and *Starhawk* crumpled up amidships, with maybe a lethal crack or systems damage. She heard the final separation of the lander, as it eased out of its position, where it had been nestled into the side of *Starhawk*, its shipside forming a seal against the launch bay opening. Then a rumble as the ship's bay doors closed the gap left by *Babyhawk*.

God, I passed out, passed out in Dive. Rivulets of sweat ran down her sides as she let the thought sink in. God, oh God. Biotime would jerk her back so fast it'd make her head swim. She'd get her retirement real fast, the whole ex-Diver package, a lump sum and maybe a slot as a tech on Vanda Station, so she could hang out near the spacers and shoot the shit with the other old Divers. An unwelcome voice in her head summed it up: *It's 2019, you're twenty-seven years old, and you're finished, sister.*

Or if they weren't feeling generous, she'd go Earthside, and she didn't want to think about that, oh no.

Then she noticed the bandage strip on her arm. *Jesus, a blood draw.* They'd taken her blood while she was passed out, a kind of medical rape. Anger stirred, propelling her off the pallet.

She combed every square inch of the medlab cold hatches. No blood sample. She started to go through the hatches a third time, stopped herself, sat on the bunk, holding herself and trying to stop shaking.

She punched up Hillis' cabin on intercom. "Hill. I'm in medlab. I'm lonely." In a tone of voice that said, I'm horny. You never knew who might be listening, so give them an earful, let them imagine Hillis and her together like a couple of rabbits. She had, many times.

Hillis answered, "You OK?"

"Come find out."

"On my way."

A few minutes later he swung into medlab, leaned against the door. He watched her, a half smile edging the side of his mouth. Hillis was lean without being thin, honed by a high-strung temperament. He was good-looking if you liked high foreheads, sharp features. Clio did. Built for speed was how she thought of Hillis. His wiry, light brown hair was cropped close, like all the crew's, but still it was wavy, or maybe coiled. Bright blue eyes watching Clio with sardonic patience.

"They took a sample. While I was asleep, goddamn it."

"What do you want me to do?'

"Find it. It's not in here. I looked."

He nodded. "OK, I'll look around. Should be easy in all the confusion out there."

"What confusion?"

"One of the launch bay doors is jammed."

Stomach beginning to shred, awash in acid. "Jammed?"

"Dented from the collision, they figure." Her face must have been easy to read. "Don't worry, they'll fix it."

Clio was shaking hard by now. He drew her into his arms. "Those pills are poison, Clio."

"It's not the pills. Just scared to freeping death."

"I'll find the sample. Don't worry."

She called up a fairly steady smile. "Who'll worry if I don't?"

"Nobody. Nobody does it better than you." He turned to go.

"I love you Hillis."

He paused at the door. "I love you too. I'd hate to see you kill yourself with that shit."

"I'm going to quit."

Hillis looked at her a few moments. "We're both out-laws, you know."

"We're only doing what we have to. I need Recon, Hill. I haven't got anything else."

"Those pills aren't going to pull you through. Nobody lasts this long, Clio. Nobody lasts fifty-five Dives."

"Shit. You're counting too. Maybe I'm the exception, Hill, maybe I'll last." She flashed him a grin.

He shrugged. "Maybe you will." Then he was gone.

Clio forced some food down and tried to sleep some more. She ended up lying on her bunk, eyes wide open, wondering how much trouble she was in and how to lie her way out.

Before her watch—way before—came a sharp command over the intercom: "Lieutenant Finn to the bridge, ASAP."

Clio's boots hit the deck. She tore out of her cabin, ran down the corridor, shaking the cobwebs out of her head, her heart pounding.

The captain and Teeg were intent on the monitors, the bluish light from the panels making their faces look sickly.

Russo's voice was raspy. "*Babyhawk*'s turned around, Lieutenant. Aborting mission; we got casualties."

Casualties. God. Clio slid into her chair.

"Helm to you, Finn. Teeg, get off the bridge. You're too damn tired."

He nodded, mock-bowing at Clio, and raking her with those hungry eyes, before swinging himself down the ladder.

"Captain, what's the situation with *Babyhawk*?" Clio was buckling in, noting the approach of the lander, moving in on *Starhawk*.

"An explosion. An hour out toward Crippen. We don't know for sure, but we think there was a leak in a fuel transport line. Got touched off by an electrical spark. Three wounded, sounds like critically. And the bay door is still jammed half open."

The nightmare continued, everything going wrong. Then there was Shaw, *Babyhawk*'s pilot, on comm, moving into docking range.

"Hold your position, *Babyhawk*," Clio told Shaw, "we have a little delay here."

Russo was on the comm, getting tech reports; growling at bad news, barking something about the teleoperator maneuvering system, in case they needed to work on the ship surface. Which techs were saying wasn't needed.

Shaw's voice came crackling into Clio's ears. "You just get your little delay greased up and dumped out, Lieutenant, I got casualties here, and they're getting real quiet. You copy?"

"Roger. We are jumping on it, Commander. We're gonna bring you in."

The earphones crackled again. "You're going to bring us in? That's real good news, *Starhawk*, now I can sleep. What's the goddamn problem out there, Finn? Over."

The captain nodded at her, and Clio answered, "The bay doors won't respond, *Babyhawk*. We're working it. Another five minutes and I'm going out there and rip the damn things open with a crowbar."

Faintly, *Babyhawk* responded. "My God." Then: "I got a man dying here, *Starhawk*. Cut the damn doors off, if you have to."

Clio looked to Russo, got a slow shake of the head.

"Negative, *Babyhawk*, that's last resort. We're working this. Stand by."

Nothing then from Shaw. Clio felt the silence like a fist in her gut.

An hour later they cut the door off after all, with crew hating to use torches, suited up as they were in the unpressurized landing bay. Then *Babyhawk* locked on, and they hauled out the casualties. One man dead, Lieutenant Runnel printed on the breast pocket: a helpful clue since most of his face was blackened with burns. Two biotechs burned real bad, one of them with blisters for eyes, both unconscious. Posie took charge of them, looking like a man in way over his head.

Hillis was there, too. Leaned close to Clio, whispered, "I dumped the blood. It's gone."

Heading home, Clio got *Starhawk* well into Dive, then sat by the two wounded men in medlab. She was patched in by remote to bridge control, listening for any alarms, half hoping for some.

Clio watched the life leak out of her two crewmates. In Dive, you saw things like that. Life exiting like spilled water.

If you die on a Space Recon Dive, deep in the past, the event doesn't set up a paradox. No one in the present is affected. Your children, for instance, don't disappear. Of course, Diving in inhabited space could produce dangerous paradoxes. Anything that you changed would set other changes in motion, in geometric progression, ultimately threatening the very future from which you came. But in the wilderness of space, the Dive was ninety-nine percent safe from encountering human history, from creating paradoxes. So the theory went.

Clio kept her deathwatch. When her crewmates' faces were dim as the pallets they lay on, Clio knew they were dead.

TIME MANAGEMENT

CHAPTER 2

❧

They docked on station deep into Clio's sleep period. She heard the ship whine down into position, the metal on metal of docking, the comm system come alive throughout the ship, footsteps as the crew got ready to off-load.

She grabbed her duffel, already packed, and moved through the airlock behind Teeg. Once in the station corridor, he turned around, blinking against the glaring lights of day period.

"Hey Clio. We're going to have a drink. How about a drink?" Teeg looked tired, but he looked fine, damn if he didn't. Big brown puppy eyes, a sculpted face saved from drop-dead beauty by a nose broken once too often. Still, a handsome dog, and always ready to jump her.

"I'm going to bed, Teeg. See you tomorrow."

"Need any company?"

"I meant sleep. Going to get some sleep." She threw him a big smile, enough to cushion the refusal. Teeg was thin-skinned. She headed down to quarters, feeling Teeg's eyes pull her clothes off as she walked. Truth was, she might like some company. Just not Harper Teeg.

Then she noticed someone waiting for her. Shit. Timeco crew. The competition. Called himself Starfish Void in the quirky way of Divers.

"Hi, Void," Clio said, pumping up a smile.

"Hey, Finn." He scuttled to catch up with her as she strode down the corridor. "Heard you had a bad Dive." He looked up at her, watching for a reaction. "Heard you lost crew. That right?"

"That what you heard?" Clio shook her head, keeping the smile pasted on.

"Heard you got five or six dead, that right?"

"We might of had some trouble. Can't say for sure." She looked at him pointedly. "Wasn't my shift."

Starfish looked hurt. "Don't have to bite my head off, Finn. It's all over station, anyhow."

Clio looked down at him, a full head shorter than she, fidgeting under her gaze. "Sorry, Void. I know you're just worried about me."

"That's right. I was worried. So you're OK, then, huh? Dive fifty-six and still going strong I guess?"

"Dive fifty-six already? Gee, I lost count. You keeping count, Void? Not nervous, are you? You're up to what, thirty or so Dives?"

"Thirty-two."

Clio peeled off to a connecting corridor, turned to wave him off. "You shouldn't keep count, Starfish. It's bad luck." She turned on her heel and left him standing there, looking confused.

Clio unclenched her teeth. Could have told him some juicy details, girl. Could have given him more than a brush-off. Might need a friend or two, come the hearing.

Vandarthanan Station opened up before her as she walked, its giant circle containing a web of inner circles, connecting corridors—and a honeycomb of offices, labs, and crew quarters.

Vanda Station was the new generation of station, catering to ultratech employees, used to the amenities. A scoured refuge from the Sickness gripping Earth. Clean air, a few green pockets, gyms, video centers, and for senior techs, family quarters. You could have sex with a coworker without a scratch test, that was how good the Vanda screening process was. You could drop in on VandaPet to visit the communal pets. Stroke a cat, release tension, lower blood pressure. If you got sick, even a cold, you went into Retreat with full sick leave, and if you recovered you went back to work, no stigma at all.

But what Clio needed right now was a bed. She passed

a cluster of space pilots in HQ Section, a great crossroad where a big spoke to the station's inner rings joined the main corridor. The group, mostly men, stared at her as she passed.

Clio knew what they were thinking: Not a real pilot. But paid three times what a space pilot gets. Even the young ones get premium pay. Eighteen-year-olds, some of them, paid like royalty. Then there's Clio Finn. Thinks she's the Queen of Sheba. Biotime thinks so too. Maybe the Crippen Dive will change all that.

Clio smiled at them, at their guarded faces, pale above their green Recon uniforms. Be good, Clio, she told herself. Don't power up the rivalry. And watch your backside.

One of the women nodded to her, a gesture of sisterhood. Don't snub Clio Finn in front of the men. But Clio knew if she met that pilot in the station bar, she'd stare right past Clio, no mistake.

She passed Quarantine Section, with its heavy doors, windowless walls. You could guess what lay within Quarantine Section: giant, exotic growths, the baobabs of other worlds; or delicate what-passed-for-ferns, or the merest alien fuzz in a petri dish. The universe produced plant life in abundance. Some of it was Earthlike, variations on the themes of leaf and chlorophyll, pistil and stamen. Some of it was a lethal variation. These died a quiet death in Quarantine. And even these were mourned, having traveled down the aeons, down the tracts of space to replenish the greying Earth. You dove for pearls. And some of them you threw back.

She passed the Leery Room, in Free Section. Inside, Clio knew, was housed the biggest catch in Space Recon's twelve-year history. The room itself had become a habitat, with dirt paths winding through a lowland rain forest, both familiar and strange. It was green; it had things that might be called trees, a few soaring almost to the thirty-meter-high ceiling. There were groundcovers, vines and flowers. The flowers were the strangest, their stalks kaleidoscope tubes of color, their tips sprays of leaves.

The haul was from Leery, a planet that had been

discovered three years ago, just ten years after Sri Sarvepalli Vandarthanan had described the mechanics of time travel. Leery was the haul they had dreamed of; when it emerged from quarantine on Vanda Station the previous year, the crew doubled their bonus. Up until Leery, Recon found minor caches on minor planets; this was the jackpot. Leery's planet had passed this way three million years before Earth, and now the vast rotation of the galaxy brought Earth into the vicinity Leery had once known. A ship went back and got the haul. And the crew retired on that bonus— except for the Dive pilot, who couldn't, by contract, retire.

No matter. He burned out two Dives later anyway, in the manner of Dive pilots, brief creatures that they were.

Clio found her assigned cubicle in crew quarters and hit the bed, still dressed. She cut the lights, waited for sleep to take her.

After a few minutes she jabbed at the console, opened the viewport, and watched the stars on nightside. The port window clouded dark as her cabin turned toward the sun, then cleared again to display the nightside stars. Count the cycles, the rotations, lose count, cycle off to sleep.

She lay watching the stars, watching for shooting stars, though none existed here, watching like a child on her back in the grass. Summer nights in North Dakota, when Mom and Elsie finally went to bed and all the house lights were out, you could see those stars plummet down, sometimes in a long swift drive like your best shooter marble racing into the playing circle.

She woke with a start. Ellison Brisher was sitting on the bunk next to hers. Ellison Brisher. Christ.

"Know how to knock?" She struggled up onto an elbow, turned on the light.

"Always a pleasure to see you, Clio. Even when you're in a bad mood." Brisher was wearing a one-piece grey jumpsuit, lending him an elephantine look. He peered at her from tiny eyes.

Clio sat up. "What time is it?"

"Nine. Breakfast is over. You hungry?"

"No. Thanks."

His eyes flicked to the zipper on her togs, where it was pulled down from her throat. She zipped up. Cocked her head at him. Get to the point.

"This Crippen affair is a bad business, Clio, bad business. The Bureau's called a hearing. You're the main witness, I'm afraid. Chocolate fizz?" He pointed a roll of fizzes at her.

"*I'm* the main witness? What about Russo?"

He shrugged, popped a fizz in his mouth. "Ah yes, Captain Russo. We'll question her too. Good idea. You're grounded, by the way." He leaned closer, thrusting out the fizzes. "Sure?"

She stared at his round, tranquil face. "You can't ground me, Ellison. You need me."

"Well, we all have our fantasies, Clio. About being needed, et cetera." He stood slowly, squeezing out a long breath. "I gave up on that fantasy a long time ago. That's why I'm in charge and you're not."

Clio kept her face neutral. "That all?"

"No. We've got a new man on crew. Want you to meet him. Name's Peter vander Zee. Goes by Zee. Astrophysicist. Replacing Ahrens."

"Too bad. I liked Ahrens."

"And you'll like vander Zee. Zee. He's young, and quite brilliant. A prodigy, in fact. Youngest astrophysics graduate ever out of Princeton." Brisher looked down at her a long time, perhaps waiting for her to squirm. She didn't. "Try to watch out for this kid, would you do that?" he said. "The crew likes you, they'll follow your lead. He's young, maybe a bit of a hotshot. Take him under your wing, can you do that?"

"What am I supposed to do, make sure he gets naps?"

Brisher's face grew tight around his eyes. "Whatever it takes."

"If the hearing doesn't go well, guess you'll have to find someone else to baby-sit Zee, huh?"

"You worried Clio? You have a reason to worry?"

"Not if I get justice, Ellison. I had nothing to do with those deaths."

He swayed gently from one foot to the other, thinking. "Ah yes. Justice. I'm sure you'll get your share."

After the door closed Clio lay back on her pillow, drenched in sweat. Brisher would enjoy handing her over to DSDE if the hearing could prove she used illegal meds. He admired DSDE. The Department of Social and Drug Enforcement was cleaning up the country. Queers and drugs are destroying our youth, spreading the epidemic. He'd see her in that light.

They had been clearing the dinner table, she and Mom and Elsie, when it happened. It was Clio's turn to help. Petya was in the living room already back at work on the clock he'd taken apart. Her younger brother liked to fix things. And he could fix anything. Retarded in most ways but that one.

Elsie lit a cigarette and started running water in the dishpan. She always smoked when she did the dishes. And then Mom was standing stock-still. She hissed a warning, and they listened for what she heard, but Clio never knew what it was. Mother swung around, grabbed Clio's elbow, pushing her to the stairs. "Run!" she cried, her face wild, and then at Petya, "Petya, now!" And then she ran for the door and threw the bolt, yanked Petya to his feet, and then there were footsteps on the porch and Clio was already in the spare room upstairs, inside the closet and fumbling at the window.

They always left the window open far enough to get your fingers under it to raise it. A large empty spool of thread kept it open, the sash long since broken, and despite the bitter cold winters they always left it open that far. Clio heard the front door smash, and still she waited for Petya. But finally he was beside her, and she held the window for him and he got onto the roof, all six feet two inches of him, and then into the big blue spruce tree, just like they'd practiced a thousand times.

Now on free time, Clio went hunting for Hillis in his usual hangout, Observation and Mapping, Biological Survey Section. Here, Vanda's great science deck was shared by dozens of science teams and staffed around the clock by clusters of serious, white-shirted analysts seeking knowledge and fodder for their next publication. Monitors hugged the curved outer wall, scrolling and blinking in a hypnotic visual array.

Clio walked through the astronomy section, where screens showed not stars but numbers, a desiccated version of what she saw on every mission. A few techs looked at her, then through her, turning back to their work. Clio put a strut into her walk. Go ahead, stare.

Up ahead, Hillis wasn't alone at his computer station. She'd have to share him today. As she walked up to them, the young man turned and saw her, poked at Hillis, who was bent over the screen. Must be Zee, she guessed. He was tall and slender, as though grown in too little light. Hillis glanced up, waved Clio over, then went back to his keyboard.

"You're Clio. I can tell," the young stranger said.

"How can you tell?"

He pursed his lips. "Subtle clues." And he smiled. A nice smile, helping to soften the impression of his colorless face and ears a little too big. Clio liked him instantly, despite Brisher, despite Ahrens. But she always made up her mind about people instantly, it did no good to analyze, either way you were bound to be wrong half the time.

She smiled back. "Well, they said you were smart."

"Now I can see why they call you the Red Queen." He was looking at her in frank dazzlement.

This time Clio didn't wince at the title, found herself genuinely smiling. Felt good, a real smile. "And you're Golden Boy. Zee, of Princeton." She held out her hand.

He grasped it, released it hurriedly. Clio suppressed a hoot. My God, too hot to handle! The kid's sweet, real sweet.

Hillis looked up at them, taking it all in, looking pointedly at Clio with a knowing smile. Means what, Clio wondered. Jealous? Maybe. But of who?

"They say you're going to prove that Dive pilots don't have to burn out," Zee said. "You're going to be the first."

Clio's mood crashed in a hurry. "Why burn out when you can burn up, I always say. Live fast, Zee. Didn't they teach you anything worthwhile at Princeton?" She took the seat next to Hillis. "How's old Gaia doin'?"

"One day at a time . . ." Hillis was punching the keyboard, shifting the colors on the map screen, deep into the Hillis crusade.

"What's Hillis up to today, Zee? You got it figured out, or is all you care about protons and stuff?"

"Well, technically, most everything has protons, so I like to think of myself as a generalist. But to answer your question, this is forest ecosystem mapping." Zee watched the screen as though it made sense to him, and perhaps it did.

Clio swung back to the screen. Now she could detect the general outline of a northern chunk of South America, with a dark purple artery and veins that must be the Amazon. Well, if it was forest research, that would be the Amazon, of course. The last forest. From space, the last big expanse of green that was visible on Earth.

Hillis had windowed down to a local section. Resolution was poor. He frowned and plunked at the keys irritably.

"I've never been off-planet," Zee said. "Seems kinds of funny."

Clio swung back around. "What does?"

"An astrophysicist nervous about being in space."

"You mean here? Vanda?"

Zee glanced over at the corridor wall. "No. Out there. On mission."

"Well, space is the easy part. It's the Dive that's tough, and you'll be asleep for that part. No sweat."

Hillis chimed in, "And when you wake up, you'll be in a different solar system." He had swung around, joined them. "And that's an astronomer's dream, right?" The computer clicked at him, and he turned back, jabbing a key, blanking the screen.

"Right. All for science," Zee said.

"Shuttle's leaving in a couple hours, Hill," Clio said. "The Bureau's called a hearing."

"I know." Still punching in commands. Always doing two things at once.

"You coming?"

He turned to her. "Think I'd let you go Earthside without me?" He resumed his program. "After the hearing, we'll take a car trip."

"We will?"

"Sure. Have some fun."

Clio watched his profile, intent on his task. How could he worry about the Bureau when he had the whole Earth to worry about?

He glanced quickly over at her. "Hey." Flicked his shoulder, dismissing the Bureau. "Piece of cake."

CHAPTER 3

Earthside, Clio sat on a hard bench outside the hearing room at the BTM, Bureau of Time Management. By now her backside ached in protest. Teeg, next to her, shifted his position again, leaning forward, hands clasped between knees, glancing up at the clock over the hearing-room door.

"It's still four o'clock, Teeg." Clio was sick to death of Teeg after three hours of him.

"Yeah? My watch says four-ten. Here we are at the center of the fucking time universe, and the clock is ten minutes slow."

"Guess you can just hardly wait to testify, huh?"

"Hey. I don't mind. As pilot, I can tell them exactly what happened. They need me. Those other guys? Those retroids weren't on the bridge, they weren't *there*. So they spend all afternoon talking to every freeping crewmate except the man who knows the score. Ain't that the bureaucracy for you?" He shook his head slowly at the palpable idiocy of the thing.

Clio wasn't listening. She concentrated on digesting the last of her stomach. Repeating her story to herself. Practicing surprise at the discussion of her missing blood sample. *But the doc can tell you, sir, we got a sample, all right. Must be there.* Blink innocently.

"Plus, I can put in a good word for you, Clio, if things go bad in there." Teeg glanced to see if he had her attention, pushed on anyway. "They're always trying to pin shit on the pilots. I can tell them you did just fine." He patted her knee. Looked up at her. Withdrew his hand.

"Trouble with you Teeg?" Clio said. "You just don't

get how the Bureau works." The pat on the knee had pushed her over the edge. "See, the Bureau doesn't give a shit what happened, or who was at fault. That don't mean null to them. What they care about is who's the most expendable son of a bitch they can pin this on so they can get rid of some troublemaker, write up a nice report and get out of there before supper. And at your salary, might be you they're ready to retire. Bring in some young hotshot willing to work for half your wage. Yeah, it's probably you that's gonna take the fall."

A deep frown creased Teeg's forehead. "You bloody bitch. You think you don't need anybody, Clio, but someday you're going to need me. Then we'll see how you do, Miss Red."

Clio hoped desperately that Teeg would now shut up. She needed time to worry. It was deep shit this time, no mistake. The Bureau was real touchy about the rules, and it was against the rules to get crew killed. But, damn, that was Russo's fault, not hers. Truth was, she had pulled *Starhawk* out of the trouble she got it into, with only a dent in the side of the ship. But sending the mission out when there might be damage—bad damage as it turned out—that was on Russo or Biotime, no way you could blame the Dive pilot. Except that, as a side matter, they drew blood, and, oh, by the way, pilot, you're busted.

Illegal drugs. They would jump on that. The Bureau liked simple answers, they worked better in the press release.

This was her first hearing at BTM. Could be her last. Here's where her whole story, her whole life, could unravel. Pick a thread and pull. Start with a routine accident investigation, start probing her past, learn about Mom and Elsie, their crimes. And Clio's crime. Get Social and Drug Enforcement on the case. Oh, there was enough to put her away a long, long time. Slam her in a quarry and forget she's there. Her mother's fate.

Despite all the plans and the practice escapes, the quarries waited. Slap the queers and the druggies and the dying in quarantine. Tuck in a few political undesirables. Keep them out of sight of the clean families.

When the door opened, both Clio and Teeg snapped to.

"Antoinette Speery-Hall." Clio got to her feet. Shit. Nobody had called her that since she joined Biotime. No respect.

Teeg looked up at her incredulously. *"Antoinette?"*

Clio threw him a dazzling smile. "As in the French queen, you know?"

Teeg twisted around to watch her disappear through the door. "Didn't they cut off her head?" But the door was already closing behind her.

She entered a shadowy room, cavernous, high-ceilinged, and quiet. Along one wall, narrow, mullioned windows stretched to the ceiling, revealing a rare elm tree outside which was so massive its foliage permitted only a thin gruel of light to enter the room. As Clio moved forward, she saw that the committee sat at a lone table anchoring down a maroon Persian carpet of faded splendor. Over the table, a scar on the ceiling revealed where a heavy chandelier had once filled the room with light.

Around the heavy, dark table sat Russo, Brisher, and the Bureau official, Gerald Meres. Russo was perched on her chair like she had a bad case of hemorrhoids. Clio realized that she had never seen Russo off ship or station, probably because Russo hated being off ship or station. Russo waved her to join them.

Brisher was wedged into his chair so far it might have been growing out of him. He gave her a sober smile, just the right balance of support and sternness.

Meres was rustling with papers, hadn't looked up. When he did, Clio's heart wilted. Out of a pinched, narrow face stared eyes that bored into hers, seeking to ransack her mind. She crumpled into the chair next to Russo.

"Lieutenant Hall," Meres began, looking down at the papers in front of him.

"That's Finn. Lieutenant Clio Finn," Clio said, trying to sound respectful. *I need my name.* At least that much. A privilege of Dive status, to pick your name.

Meres looked up, frowning.

Russo interjected: "Nobody's called her Speery-Hall in years, Gerry. I think we can go along with her on this."

Meres glared at Russo. Eventually he said, "Very well. *Lieutenant Finn*," making it sound like an unsanitary thing.

Clio smiled in relief. Bless Russo's cold little heart. Maybe she underestimated Russo, maybe Russo wasn't ready to hang her.

"You were Dive pilot on *Starhawk* for the Crippen mission, is that right?"

"Yessir."

Meres looked up at her, as though already probing for lies. "I want you to tell me," he continued, "as thoroughly and as accurately as you can recall, what happened as the *Starhawk* came out of Dive on that mission."

Clio swallowed. "Yessir. As *Starhawk* surfaced from Dive, the alarms were sounding, and the screens showed an object in close range bearing down on the ship. I scanned the instrumentation and took evasive action, firing thrusters to bring us around and out of the collision path. When I . . ."

Meres interrupted. "What did the instrumentation show?"

"It showed Crippen's moon, fifteen thousand kilometers below us, and a body approximately three hundred kilometers wide moving in fast on the ship."

"And that's when you took evasive action."

"Yessir."

"Describe what those actions were. If it's not too much trouble, Lieutenant." This last, heavy with sarcasm.

"Yessir. There wasn't time to do more than bring the ship around and hit the engine for a fast burn. The blast struck the asteroid's surface, which was mostly ice, and we got hit with an eruption of superheated water vapor."

"That would have put the ship within thirty or forty meters of the asteroid's surface, is that right, Lieutenant?"

"Yessir."

"Close. I'd call that close. Wouldn't you, Lieutenant Finn?"

"Yessir, pretty close, sir." Clio's tongue was so dry it clicked when she talked.

The sound of Meres' pencil scribbling across his papers filled her ears. He glanced up. "How long would you estimate before the asteroid would have made contact with the ship. From the moment you first observed it?"

"Fifteen seconds, sir." Clio remembered the great ball of ice, hurtling on its path around the moon, ready to mow down *Starhawk* and anything else in its path. Moments before, she had been out cold. She woke to see her impending destruction. She hit the thrusters, her reactions kicking in so fast they left her mind meters behind. Out cold.

Any they can't prove it, she reminded herself.

Meres laid down his pencil and rubbed his eyes, sighing with apparent fatigue. "Do you realize, Lieutenant Finn, how remote, how minuscule, are the chances, on a Dive of four hundred thousand years, that you will come up on a planet, or a moon, or a planetesimal, or an asteroid, or a body of any size, *that close?* Close enough to hit it?" He arched his eyebrows and peered at her.

"Yessir, pretty remote."

"Remote? It's rotting near impossible!"

Clio blurted out, "Well, we *were* aiming for it. Sir." This seemed to her somewhat funny, so that she started to smile, then wiped it.

"There's another explanation, of course." Meres started through his papers again.

Clio waited, cocking her head slightly.

He glanced up. "That *Starhawk* had been sitting in orbit around that moon for quite a while before you woke up."

"That's not how it was, sir."

"Well, what else are you going to say?" Meres snorted, shaking his head.

They don't have anything, Clio thought. *He's just trying to make me squirm. BTM hearings have a reputation to uphold, he's gotta make that bitch squirm.*

Brisher now joined in. "Clio. Lieutenant Finn. Biotime

will support you if you've got a problem. Biotime stands by its own. You know that."

"Yes, Mr. Brisher. And I appreciate that. We all do."

Meres closed his files, keeping out one sheet of paper. "You took a blood or urine sample?" This to Russo.

A trickle of acid eroded down Clio's insides.

"Yes. Standard procedure. That's the lab report, that you have there."

Meres scowled. "Yes, it is, isn't it? And everything looks in order on paper."

Clio kept her face under control with a supreme effort. Lab report? *In order,* did he say?

"That being so, you might not object to drawing a confirming sample." His eyes clicked up to meet Clio's.

Russo's voice was quiet, gracious. "*I'd* object to that."

Meres swung on her. "I don't think I understand what your objection might be, Captain Russo."

"It impugns the good-faith effort Lieutenant Finn has made in cooperating with this investigation. Until there's reason to suspect her veracity, I'd object to the test as giving the appearance of wrongdoing."

"The only effort Lieutenant Finn has made to cooperate with this investigation is to give blood while she was unconscious and show up for this hearing."

"Which is all she's required to do, under her contract," Russo said.

Brisher chimed in. "Technically, that's true, Gerry."

Meres swung his head to look at this attack on his flank.

Russo was busy taking notes, not looking up, most pointedly not looking up.

Clio watched this tableau with astonishment. She was going to win. They were making a stink over the blood test, a simple blood test, that any innocent person would be happy to provide.

Brisher heaved his shoulders up in a shrug. "That's the way of things sometimes, Gerry. Accidents happen. Hard to blame the crew. Just doing their job, you know." Brisher smiled as he said this, always a bad sign.

Then she had it. Brisher was scared. He was so sweet and polite, seemed like his shit didn't stink. Biotime wasn't giving BTM any handholds on the Crippen mission. Everyone was going to stick together, so that nothing stuck to Biotime. Russo too, Russo was in it up to her tits.

Meres tapped his pencil, looking from one to the other. "You may be right, Ellison." He looked at his watch. Then began pulling his papers into a stack. "I'm going to close this file—for now—and I hope I don't see any of you around this table again for a long time." He looked at Russo. "Think you could arrange that, Captain?"

Russo took time to stare blackly at Meres. "Could be arranged. Yes."

"Good." Meres rose. "Time for dinner, I think."

Clio almost laughed out loud, in relief, in disgust. Her ass was saved. But three good men were dead, and nobody was going to own up. And meanwhile, Meres was standing there, shaking hands all the way around, accepting Biotime's gratitude with a smirk of pleasure.

Clio stumbled to her feet. The last light of the day hovered for a moment in the elm tree. The room was so dark she could hardly see. Clio hurried to catch up with the others before they latched the door behind them.

As they all filed out of the hearing room, Teeg jumped up, his face almost falling off. He scrambled to catch up to Clio, already halfway down the hall. "Jesus, Clio, what about my turn?"

Clio shook her head, flashing him her most motherly smile. "Looks like they just forgot you were out here, Teeg."

In the bathroom, Clio bent over the sink, pulling handfuls of cold water to her face until her skin stung. Braced her hands on the sink and stared into the mirror. Short red tendrils of hair clung to her face like seaweed. She flicked the water off her face and made her mouth smile. Ran her fingers quickly through her hair to quiet it down. It was time to head to town.

When she came out, the halls were empty. The bureaucrats had gone home hours ago. But when she hit the street,

Clio saw Teeg waiting for her. Shit. Not going to be easy to sneak off and make a deal; maybe not possible at all. She headed in the opposite direction from him.

Teeg caught up, matching her stride.

"Get lost, Teeg," she said without looking at him.

"What'd they do in there, chew you out?" Teeg was cheerful, eager to talk.

"No, Meres tried coming on to me so I had to slap him around a little."

"Guess you just don't like guys, huh?"

Clio spied a lamppost where she could pick Teeg off, if he didn't watch where he was going.

"If you've got a lady lover, Clio, can I at least watch?"

Clio angled for the lamppost, Teeg went around it, not even noticing her maneuver. She stopped cold, wiping the greasy film of city rain out of her eyes. "I'm meeting Hillis, OK? You're real nice company, Teeg, but will you please get lost?" A gaunt figure out of the crowded sidewalk collided with her, staggered to regain himself, cursing. Clio turned, moving with the press of people. Keep moving in the city, Clio told herself. You don't stop unless you got business—or want trouble. Finally Teeg shrugged and turned back. Clio bit her lip, sorry now to be so rough on him. Teeg wasn't so bad sometimes, and he was desperate for all the things he couldn't have, same as she.

She was headed down Second Avenue, deep into the area called the Regrade. The neon glare of bars, eateries, and chapels wavered in the gross mirrors of the pavement, wet with eighteen hours of rain. Eyes followed her. Hungering, she figured, after her shirt, her boots, her body. A woman with no hair spat on the sidewalk as Clio passed, marking her territory. DSDE couldn't clean up the Regrade; didn't try. Those with the Sickness stayed under cover, Clio knew. And the cops, they pretty much left you alone, as long as you didn't kill somebody on the sidewalk, try to deal drugs.

Up ahead, Clio saw the dancer in the window at Zebra's. He wore a yellow chiffon dress and swayed to the screeching roar of a null pop tune piped out to the sidewalk.

She pushed her way into the crowded bar, through the wall of beery smoke. She grabbed a stool and looked for Zebra. A stranger—a big-boned white woman with mounding curls of iron grey hair—was tending bar, made eye contact. She was wearing a real fur dress, marking her as an anti-Green, and a flower in her hair in what might have been a touch of irony. Clio ordered a beer. She hated beer, but it was safer than water, and she was thirsty.

"Where's Zebra tonight?"

"Gone."

"Gone?"

"You gonna pay for the beer?"

Clio paid. The woman in fur stared at her.

"I had business with Zebra. Personal business."

The big woman smiled, lips parting over teeth way too big for her mouth. "A lotta people had business with Zebra." She got busy, leaving Clio with her mind racing in neutral. What to do? Clio was a foreigner here, a spacer with no networks, no contacts. Zebra was her only link with her pills, her medicine. Clio looked up. Fur woman was grinning at her again, from the other end of the bar. She made the smallest gesture: follow me. Clio swung around on the stool, threaded her way into the pack of regulars. Somebody felt her up. She stuck out her elbows and swung, hoping to cuff somebody. Missed.

Fur woman was waiting for her in the can. She leaned against the door so no one else could come in. "Whatcha lookin' for, hon?"

The acrid smell of urine churned her stomach, unless it was sheer panic. "Where's Zebra?" Clio asked.

"You been gone a long time if you don't know what happened to Zebra." The bartender sized Clio up a moment. "Honey, she got quarried a long time back." She studied her glowing nails. "Dangerous business. Hope you can pay good. Now, whatcha lookin' for?"

Clio countered, "You set me up, I got friends who'll be disappointed, you know?"

The bartender rolled her eyes in mock terror. "Yeah, I

know. So I'm scared. Now whatcha lookin' for, I got bar to tend."

"Dexichloromine. At least fifty tabs."

Fur woman raised one painted eyebrow. "But you'll take what I got, right?" Her lips rolled back off her teeth again, and she dismissed Clio with a wave. "I'll see what I can do."

Clio grabbed her by her fleshy upper arm. "No. It's got to be dexichloromine. You understand me?"

"Well my, my. A discriminating junkie." She pulled her arm free. "You wait in the end stall."

Clio waited a minute, then peered from the door out into the din of the tavern. The bartender had disappeared, but there through the large front window she thought she glimpsed a long, armored van. Jesus, DSDE. Clio ducked back in the can, her mind lurching. She spun around, looking for escape. No windows. Finally she sat in the end stall, shaking, waiting for them.

The bathroom door opened. Then the stall next to hers.

Fur woman's voice came from next door. "I got forty hits. Five hundred dollars. I don't haggle."

"You freeping bitch, you set me up! That's DSDE out there."

A laugh erupted from the next stall. "Yeah? And I'm your father in drag! Godalmighty, that van's the TB wagon, making its fucking rounds. You want the tabs or not?"

"Let's see them," Clio said. From the other side of the partition a doughy white hand extended a blue tab, sealed in glasswrap.

Clio opened the wrap, crushed the tab, smelled it. Like lilacs, yes. She counted out the money, shoved it under the partition.

The rest of the tabs were shoved into a swath of urine by Clio's feet. She grabbed them up, wiped them quickly with toilet paper, then thrust them in her pocket. Slowly opening the stall door, she saw the bartender washing her hands, wiping them on her fur belly. She was shaking her head.

As Clio headed for the door the woman said, "Honey, you better quit. You ain't got the nerves for it."

Out on the street it was raining again, a light, drifting rain that soon coated her face with a greasy film. It was too far to walk to the hotel, but she started moving, hoping for a cab, here in this place where cabs never came. She felt conspicuous. She wore black Chinese cotton pants stuffed into skinny boots, and a black rain jacket. Even these cheap items were drawing stares. People watched her. In particular, one man watched her. He was following her, had been waiting for her outside Zebra's, probably. A man, a trenchcoat, the Regrade: a cartoon setup for DSDE making a nab, making the world a cleaner, safer place.

She turned to confront him, get it over with, scare him off. It was Teeg.

He caught up to her. "I'm not following you, honest. It's just that I've been in a few bars, and now here you are again."

"Yeah, here I am." A ripple of suspicion hit her. She looked into Teeg's boyish face, searching for treachery.

"I thought you were meeting Hillis," he said.

And he kept track of her business, yes. Our boyish Teeg.

A black van moved down the street at a crawl. Paused as it came parallel with Clio and Teeg. Not the TB wagon. DSDE. Its darkened windows stared at the streetscape like the multifaceted eyes of an insect.

What to do. Keep talking to Teeg? Start walking? Clio dragged up a smile for Teeg, pulled on his arm quietly with a trembling hand. Started walking.

Teeg looked at the van, barely reacting, then focused back on Clio. "I know you don't need any company, but this is rough territory. I can walk you to where you're meeting Hillis . . . or I'll just leave. Up to you."

"OK, but it's a long walk." Clio remembered to breathe. It helped.

A flicker of surprise on his face; then he was on her arm, taking command. "This place is getting rough. They'd gut you for the change in your pocket."

Looking around, Clio sized up the cast of characters: the old-timers, the youth, the same kind of eyes in both.

"I'm surprised you're down here alone," he said. "Guess you're pretty fearless, huh?" He gave her arm a friendly hug.

"Yeah, just call me Wonder Woman." The rain had made its way down her neck in rivulets, like Teeg's constant, invasive voice. As they took a turn to Battery, she chanced a look down Second Avenue. No van.

"You think I'm a jerk, I guess. Everything I say is wrong, right?"

"Let's not try to analyze it, Teeg. It's the chemistry. Let's just call our problem chemistry."

"No chemistry," he said, a sigh in his voice. "That's kind of funny. Most women are crazy about me. Women are nuts about me." They walked in silence for a while.

He had been following her, she was certain. But for his own aimless, maybe fixated reason, or for someone else? Was he really that hot for her, just couldn't accept No? Whatever his motive, now that she was really going to meet Hillis, Teeg was a welcome tagalong. Maybe she should try to make friends with him, if men like Teeg had women for friends.

"What you got lined up for leave?" she asked.

He flashed a look toward her, an eager boyishness back on his face. "Resort Reno. The compound, full pass, the whole thing. Me and some friends."

Clio nodded. "Expensive."

"Oh, it'll cost. But they have everything. The games, the shows, good air, even simulated breezes. It's totally enclosed now. The girls are all clean. It's guaranteed."

Or your life back? But Clio was working at a nice conversation. "You going to win anything?"

"I always win. I'm lucky, that's why I go. I win."

"Me, I'm unlucky. Never win at games."

"You gotta be born with it. Nothing against you, but you have to be born with it. I've always been that way. A winner. How I like to look at it, anyways." He was feeling cocky now, he gave her arm a squeeze. "You could come along."

"Busy."

"You sure make it difficult."

"Make what difficult?"

"Us, Clio. I see how you look at me."

"Say again?"

"That look you give me. Drives me nuts."

"You *are* nuts, Teeg." Where did this guy get off? Maybe this little walk wasn't such a hot idea.

They walked in silence a few moments.

Taking another tack, he said, "What do you see in him? Hillis. He's such a Greenie."

"It's the chemistry, I guess."

"I always thought he was a fag."

Clio stopped dead, swung to stare at him.

"Sorry. Always saying the wrong thing. Sorry. That was way out of line. I'm just jealous."

"You go around making accusations like that very often? When you're jealous, or feeling out of sorts?"

"I said I'm sorry. But he's not the man for you, Clio. I can guarantee that."

Clio picked up her pace, maintaining an intense silence.

They mounted the steps to the old Excelsior Hotel. Above the portico, hunching stone gargoyles peered down with what remained of their faces, pecked featureless by the tincture of Northwest rain. In the hotel lobby, Hillis was reading the paper. Or pretending to read. When they walked in he cast down the paper and hurried over to them, frowning at Teeg, then ignoring him. "Jesus, it's past midnight, where the hell have you been?"

Wrong question to lead off with, Hill. Clio smiled sheepishly, said, "Had a drink with friends. Teeg offered me an escort back here." She smiled wider, trying to lock on his eyes with hers. "Were you worried?"

Hillis was still scowling.

Teeg said, "Well, I got her back safe and sound, so no harm done."

"You give up on the hookers, Teeg?" Hillis asked.

A light jumped into Teeg's eyes, and he threw back, "No, I just tired them out. Show you how sometime, if you get bored with your plants."

"Think you could get it up if I watched, Teeg?"

"Cut the crap," Clio said. She tugged on Hillis' arm, trying to snip the thread of conversation before it got worse. "I'm going up. You coming?"

Teeg was shifting his weight from one foot to the other, already in a fury. "You're such a gimp, Hillis. Such a retroid. Someday somebody's going to shove your nose into the back of your head. I'd do it myself, but Clio tells me she's not sick of you yet."

Hillis was already walking away with Clio, toward the elevators.

Teeg said to their backs, "When she is, I'll be waiting."

In the shower, Clio let the stream of water break over her face, pummel her eyelids, roar over her ears. It felt so good she nearly forgot to soap and rinse before the water cut off for the night. The Regrade left its deposits in her hair, a filmy unease in her mind. Zebra was gone, quarried. Could have been me, Clio thought. Then Teeg hitting on her, and damn strange: *I see how you look at me* . . . and what a fantasy that was, the reality being that he was watching *her*. Dripping water onto the mat, she raised her hands before her face, watched as they trembled, a gentle palsy that visited her hands, her stomach, maybe her brain itself. *Stuff is killing me.* Gonna give it up. But just a few more missions, girl. Squeeze out just a few more . . .

The light was still on in the bedroom. Hillis was playing a video game, sitting on the edge of the bed, jacked into the TV screen. She sat down next to him, toweling her hair. Hillis punched at the joystick, thrusting his chin with each squeeze, racking up points. She watched the tension ride across his shoulders, move into his jaw, settle there. She moved behind him and began kneading his shoulders.

"You got a headache?"

He shrugged. That meant yes. She started working the spot just under his left shoulder blade.

She wondered if Hillis had been in the Regrade tonight, if he had found some comfort, some release. *And you can be quarried for that too, no mistake.* The anti-gay laws were tied to Sickness paranoia, so there was no sympathy, no reprieve. Clio worked on his hard, sculptured shoulder. He needed her. Needed her for cover. The hetero façade.

"You pissed at me?"

Hillis punched in a score. "You could have called me after the hearing. For all I knew they could have been ripping your fingernails off in the basement of the Bureau." Snide but cheerful, Hillis was enjoying his game, winning.

Clio smiled at his back. "OK, so next time I'll call. Aren't you even curious what happened? Meres decided the accident couldn't have been prevented, so me and the company both got off, and everyone is happy, even Brish." She started to work on his neck.

"Russo killed three people and everyone's happy," Hillis said, ramming home another score.

"If Russo screwed up, Brisher would have dumped her," Clio said. "I think she was on orders from Biotime, so technically Brisher's at fault."

"And people like Brisher never go down." Hillis jabbed at the stick, missing his prey, racking up a few debits.

"You're such an idealist," she said. Hillis sneered at that. "Yes, you are. You and your Old Green." What was an Old Green, if not an idealist? The old forests, the old savannahs, all the old green places that he wanted to keep, that one percent of the people cared about; what was that if not idealism?

"And you and your New Green," Hillis said. "You really think we're ever going to bring back green from the stars? Green that will save us?"

Clio gave up on his back; it would never unbunch. She sprawled on the bed. "Sure. Better stuff. Stronger stuff. Stuff that can handle a little UV without crapping out. Sure we will."

"Clio, Clio. Why don't we just save what we've got? Too simple for you?"

"What do you want, to put me out of a job?"

"Jesus, Clio." He killed the program, sat staring at the darkening screen.

"Hillis. Somebody doctored up a lab report to show a blood sample for me, from Crippen."

"Looks like you got a friend in high places."

"Yeah, but who?"

"Probably Brish. He needs you to Dive, and besides, he wants into your pants, right?"

"God, Hill. That means he knows I take medicine."

Hillis glanced over at her, frowning. "Maybe some technician phonied up the report. Couldn't find your sample, thought he'd get in trouble, and faked it." He was in a good mood; why ruin it with her worries?

She crept around to sit beside him. "Yeah, maybe. Let's get some sleep. We got a busy day tomorrow."

Clio climbed into bed, suddenly weary. Hillis turned off the computer and the lights and crawled in beside her.

"We'll take Zee with us tomorrow, all right with you?" Hillis asked.

"Zee?"

"He's staying here. Just down the hall."

"Sure. Zee's all right."

Hillis reached out, found her face, and rubbed his fingers into her scalp, tousling her hair. An affectionate gesture, a way to say goodnight, thanks for the backrub.

My pleasure.

CHAPTER 4

&

Clio hit the brakes, almost impaling their rental car on the swordlike fins of the car in front.

"Jesus, Clio." Hillis snapped on his safety belt.

"Sorry. Been a while."

They were crawling along in a tight pack of cars eight lanes wide. Had been for an hour. The traffic panel on the dash showed a block-and-search up ahead.

Off to their left the sun tried unsuccessfully to shoulder up the night sky; an orange blister seemed to swell for a moment on the horizon, then ebb as the curtain of night and pollution sank back into place. Zee was asleep in the backseat of the Ford Green Beret.

"How can he sleep with that much coffee in him?" Clio asked, riding the clutch to another rolling slowdown.

"Astronomers always stay up all night drinking coffee and then sleep all day," Hillis said. He was doodling in his notebook, furiously, as though in a hurry to finish.

They crossed under two decks of freeways, each heading in a different direction, each jammed and moving even more slowly than their own procession. A thin dawn began to soak through the darkness. As if in response, traffic picked up speed, and the knot they had been traveling with dissipated. The panel showed the block-and-search had been lifted up ahead.

Zee's head popped up in the backseat. "Guess they caught them."

"Caught who?"

"The Greenies. Or whoever. Caught them before they executed a few more cars."

They passed a long, low, carrot-orange convertible with a splash of fresh black graffiti across its flank, reading, YOUR CAR, YOUR COFFIN.

"Block-and-searches are illegal," Hillis said. "But nobody cares. We'll just drive ourselves to extinction. Lock the troublemakers up so we can kill ourselves off in peace."

"No politics," Clio said. "We're on vacation."

Four days was all they had. Four days Earthside, then back to Vanda; Biotime was tight on leaves. Can't risk the company property, not Earthside, anyway. Earth was too risky. Simple things like breathing, having sex. Too risky. But they had four days—enough time to see some sights, and, for Hillis, stop by the transition farms east of the city to see how the alien green was doing.

They were well out of the city now, with the day heating up toward ninety-five, and the land spread out in every direction in a broad valley, as though too exhausted to raise itself up. Now and then, a shadow flitted across the fields, a cloud of piranha nymphs. It was the time of year when the fledgling locusts could dine gourmet on the new sprouts of alfalfa, lettuce, and the remaining maple trees.

"Piranhas," Clio said to Hillis. She pointed up as he craned his neck to view them through the car window.

"A small swarm," he reported. And went back to doodling.

Not so small, Clio thought.

Though this was merely spring, already dust lay thick, chalk-like, clouding behind their car and settling on the few remaining roadside grasses and stumpy trees. Once there had been great stands of spruce and Douglas fir along this highway, in cooler times, former times. Their wood had been salvaged long ago, despite all the protests, the outrage at the cutting down of trees. They had conservation and what they called recycling, and people rallied around causes, such as trees. Now people had other things on their minds. They wanted to survive, never mind the old green that could not hang on. They wanted to live. And let the Recon missions find other trees, better trees.

It was a matter of surviving.

To her left, Clio saw a small dog trotting across a field, and she thought, *Target*, and then in the next instant, the swarm descended on the animal so that his yellow fur turned black with piranha nymphs. He raced madly for the cover of trees a hundred meters beyond, but lasted only a fraction of that before crumpling to the ground. The car sped on, out of sight of the kicking animal, but Clio didn't need to stick around to know the outcome.

Hillis had been watching too. "Birds, especially sparrows, were their natural predators. Ask yourself where all the birds have gone."

Clio sighed. "Tell me, Hill, where have all the birds gone?"

He had put down his pencil, and was staring out the window. Softly, he answered: "Gone to graveyards, every one."

They had been running across the field, so hard their lungs seared with pain, and they stopped, bent over, and gasped for breath. Petya was crying, in great quiet sobs. He knew enough not to cry out loud. Clio stood up and looked back. She should never have looked back. The farmhouse was blazing with light, the only light for miles, making it look like the last place left on Earth. Where Mom and Elsie were. And she started walking back, and Petya followed, though he was scared, for they always stayed together.

When they got close enough to hear the screams from the house, they stopped and lay in the grass, holding each other. And Petya covered his ears when he heard it, but Clio just lay frozen in place and stared at the kitchen windows, where shadows passed now and then.

Clio told Petya to stay still, and she made her way to the front of the house, where the DSDE van was parked, to see how many there were. Only one van. And no one outside at all. But then she heard the noise behind her and it was too late, a man stood there, and he had a gun, a strange-looking gun with a thick barrel and loops of wires, with light glinting off it from the front porch light. But the man himself was all darkness, a shadow against the darker night, and he said, "Now what you want to be lying out here in the dirt for, girl?" And he told her to get up, but her legs were so weak with fear that she couldn't move, and so he reached down and yanked her up. Then something crashed down on his head, in a bone-bruising slap, and he toppled. He was a heavy man, and his falling registered loudly. He was groaning, and there stood Petya with a shovel raised up to strike him again.

But the man lunged at Petya's ankles, and they both fell backward, leaving the gun lying next to Clio. She picked it up and walked over to where he was holding Petya down and aimed it at his head. She pressed the trigger button, and though there was no sound, his head was gone, flying off into fragments of bone and blood.

On the outskirts of the transition farm, they came upon a small town announced by a sign reading, NEW HOBART, "CLEAN AND GREEN," POP 3388.

Zee said, "That's kind of catchy. Clean and green."

Hillis groaned.

They passed farms with their dusty, furrowed fields anchored by sagging farmhouses and, here and there, a lone tractor on patrol.

Clio pulled into a gas station, a theme station, painted green, with one cement wall a painted mural of sprouting seeds and rocket ships. Under the long-unused electric-panel section of the station, a table was set up for tourist souvenirs.

A woman in a sunbonnet covering a face like a potato pumped their gas and smiled at them as they stretched their legs. She nodded her head at the souvenir table. "You go ahead and have a look," she said.

Zee took the cue and ambled over to the table.

The woman kept Clio and Hillis in her gaze, pressing home her sales pitch. "We're lots cheaper than the park. Go into the museum, they'll charge you twice what we got." Hillis went off to find the bathroom. Clio smiled at the woman. There was no escaping the pale gnarls of her eyes.

"See you don't have a bumper sticker. If you come to New Hobart, you'll want to have a bumper sticker."

"It's rented. A rental car," Clio said. She felt the need to explain, to be ordinary.

Despite the clear, hot day, a shadow fell across the woman's face. "Where you from, that you got to rent a car?"

Clio opened her mouth, not sure what would come out. But Zee was standing next to her, holding a bumper sticker at arm's length, examining it.

" 'Green Again,' " he announced. "For Hillis. Don't you think?"

"Or we got 'Clean and Green,' you seen that one? That's a good one. We got no Sickness here. We're all families here."

Zee nodded at her, turned back to Clio. "How about you? Buy you a souvenir, Clio? Price is no object."

"No thanks."

Zee's face fell a little.

"Get Hillis that 'Green Again' one," she said. "He'll love it."

"Think so?" Eagerly, he shelled out $10.98 for the thing.

On the road again, Zee drove as Hillis slouched in the backseat looking at his present. "Poor bastards. We're their only hope, you know that? Those fields out there, that genetically altered crap, it doesn't make a good harvest. Look at this place. Christ, it's getting poorer every year. But the feds tell them happy days are here again, that Recon will bring home the bacon."

"The seed," Zee corrected, still cheerful. "The good seed."

"Hell, any seed. Just needs to grow."

"Wait'll they get a hold of Leery seed," Zee said. "Leery's been on the transition farms, what, two years now? Leery's going to make a difference. I heard they've got a grain, vegetables, trees, everything."

"Well if that's right," Hillis said, "we can all retire. Green again. Hallelujah."

Zee looked over at Clio, questioning. Hard to miss Hillis' sarcasm. Clio smiled at him, a pay-no-attention-to-him smile.

As they drove down the main street of the town they saw tourist shops, mostly empty. They passed the Fuji Dollar Store, and the Wayback Café, sporting a homemade sign showing a rocket with a flower in its mouth, like a Spanish dancer. At New Hobart's only traffic light, a church with a picket fence glared bright white in the morning sun. Its neon sign proclaimed, FAMILY VALUES CONQUER DEATH.

Clio felt like an alien, a foreign bee wandered into the wrong hive. If they knew who she was, who Hillis was, the Hobart bees would descend, stinging.

Clio reached back with her hand, rested it on top of the seat, and Hillis covered her hand with his own. "This place scares me," she said.

"Nah," he said. "If they knew who we were, they'd put us in a parade. They're the political bloc that keeps Recon going. Without them, we'd be out of work. You've got to understand, Recon isn't about science. It's about jobs, agriculture. People vote with their pocketbooks. You're their hero."

"Funny," Zee said. "Funny how this place gives you the jitters. An ordinary place like this." He smiled at her.

Gods. He was so young, knew so little. He was like Petya, in a way. Different end of the IQ range, but a lot like Petya. He was absorbed in piecing things together, and he retained an innocence about him. He also seemed perfectly comfortable believing she and Hillis were together, but he still looked at her like a puppy in love. Looked at Hillis like that sometimes, too; desperate, perhaps, for friendship from any quarter. She wondered if Zee would know what to do with a woman. She had a fleeting impulse to teach him.

Outside the town they passed the New Hobart theme park and museum, surrounded by a sprawling, half-empty parking lot. Clio could see a ragtag collection of rides, including a Ferris wheel beckoning with its simple promise, an endless loop of pleasure.

After that, the land, government land, was empty, a buffer zone for the regreenery.

They reached the cutoff to the farm, marked with a sign that said, FEDERAL REGREEN PROJECT, BIOTIME, INC., US WESTERN DIVISION. A spattering of signs reading, NERVE WIRES. EXTREME DANGER.

The first checkpoint took the longest, as the guard scrutinized their IDs, but even that was quick. When he saw their clearances, he waved them through. These were no terrorists. These were from Vanda, these were Space Recon. What it's all about.

They could see the domes up ahead, looking like helmets in the sand, and next to them, the great locust nets tented high above the fields. But Hillis wasn't interested in the domes. He wanted to tour the fields, the real transition crops. Stuff in the domes was still getting hothouse treatment, not ready to go open, to expose itself to the critical eye of a new mother sun. She had been known to kill orphans like these before.

Strangers in the nest.

Out in the fields, the day's heat lay on the land like a hammer. Beneath the wide-brimmed hats they'd been given, their faces prickled with the heat. Clio's skin pumped sweat. The guide was answering Zee's questions: this section was a tuber specimen, the regreen potato, it had to be covered at night, didn't like dew. It was a high-viable, though, it had produced what might be called potatoes, small, very small, but edible.

Zee asked about how Earth bugs liked Leery potatoes, how fertile they were, what mechanism they used to fend off high UV. He seemed to think it was important to ask intelligent questions. Clio used to hate students like that. Showing off with questions the teachers loved.

Hillis was sour and quiet, stewing over being assigned to a guide, as though they were tourists. He trudged down the service paths scarcely looking at the crops. Searching for something, he scanned the fields in the distance. Finally he angled off on an intersecting path, heading away from the group.

Their guide stopped. "Let's all stay together," he called after Hillis. "As a group."

Hillis kept on walking, turning his head to answer. "OK, be right with you, I just want to see something."

The guide left Clio and Zee, trying to rein Hillis in. "There's just a stubble field over there, I don't think we need to waste our time on it, and we really should all stay together." He stopped, but Hillis didn't. The guide turned back, looked at Zee in exasperation, hoping for backup, finding none, then hurried to catch up with Hillis. Clio and Zee followed.

The guide swung around to glare at them. Zee spread his hands, shrugging. "Well, we should all stay together, right?" The man made an ugly frown, squishing his features toward the middle of his face, and tramped over to Hillis.

Hillis was standing at the edge of the stubble field, crouching down to look at the yellowed stalks. "Run into some trouble here, did you?"

"I told you it was a stubble field. There's nothing here. It's been harvested."

"Harvested. Interesting." Hillis walked farther into the patch.

"There's a reason we have guides on these tours. Not all these paths are safe. Some are wired. We can't guarantee security of this farm without touch wires in the paths. You can screw up the whole system by walking off the tour paths, since you don't seem to care." His voice had risen in pitch as his face grew tight with anger.

Hillis stopped and regarded him with surprise. "Wires? You're kidding." He looked down at his feet with a worried expression.

"I'm not kidding," the guide said, backing out, leading Hillis back to safety. Hillis followed him, stepping gingerly. "You've acted very foolishly, Mr. Hillis. We shouldn't even be here."

"No, I can see that. You should have told me. There should be markers."

The guide shook his head. "That would be real stupid, wouldn't it? Mark the paths so terrorists know the safe routes?" He looked at Hillis with contempt.

Hillis put his arm around Clio's waist. "Let's get out of here, honey."

Clio snuggled into his side. "I knew this guy once, got his feet fizzed off by those burn wires. Back when they were legal for home security. And the thing was, it was his own house. He forgot where he buried the wires."

"Jesus," Zee said, eyes wide.

"I'm not kidding." She had just made it up, catching Hillis' mock fear of the paths. He was working hard at seeming ordinary, slow to catch on. She was petty sure this meant he had just caught on to something.

"It looks like a dead bug."

Zee was driving; he liked to drive, and drove easily, carelessly, often looking at Clio and Hillis, not watching the road. He watched Hillis examine the remnant of stalk with fibrous roots, fluttering in the AC draft.

"Can you watch the road, Zee?" Clio leaned forward from the back seat to look at Hillis' stolen weed.

"Rinoculis Leeriatum," Hillis said. He stuffed it into a baggie in his pack.

"So it's from Leery." Neither Hillis nor Clio had been on the Leery mission, had never pulled down a haul like Leery. When Clio thought of Leery it was with both hope and resentment; it was like an Olympic record, beckoning and judging.

"What did they harvest from it?"

"They didn't harvest it. They mowed it down because it was already dead."

Zee was steering, but watching Hillis. "You can't just go stealing things, Hill. We could've got caught."

Hillis shot a contemptuous look at Zee. "Maybe you still don't get it. These saplings were from *Leery*."

Zee and Clio were quiet, letting Hillis vent.

"The fucking famous Leery haul." He twisted the

brown, weedy thing absently between his fingers. "They're dying."

After a long silence, Zee ventured, "I thought Leery plants were going great."

"Advance to the head of the class." The bitterness in Hillis' voice shut Zee up and he turned back to his driving.

The horizon shimmered ahead of them like melted glass. Here and there, motels and gas stations crouched under the sun, sagging and empty-looking. Zee slowed down in front of one of them. The Green Dreams Motel.

"We're camping, Zee," Clio said.

"I have a bad back."

"You think we can just pull in and register, the three of us in one room? Or Mr. and Mrs. Hillis, without a marriage card?" Hillis asked, sarcastic. "Or the two of *us*? We could get Clio her own room, and we could register together. The locals would love that."

Zee accelerated, leaving Green Dreams behind. "They don't lynch people out here," he said. "It's just middle America." Clio watched the back of Zee's head. The westering sun splashed through the windshield, suffusing Zee's ears with a pinkish glow. Sometimes she loved Zee for his worldview, loved the way he said *America*, invoking a land of happy farmers and ordinary, no-questions-asked motels. Part of Zee lived in 1990. Before the gay roundups, before quarries, before DSDE. Before the underground hospices. Before people had to hide to die in peace. Clio thought of her mother and Elsie, and the extra bedroom in their old house where the sick ones could die in peace. If they made it to Mother's house, they could die in peace.

Toward sunset they found a side road, followed it up a narrow valley into the comforting folds of the hills. They ate a meal of sandwiches, using a meat spread that came out of a tube like glue.

"Fine roommates you guys make," Clio said. "Neither of you can cook."

"We're scientists," Zee said.

Hillis laid out his bedroll and stretched out. Above, a few stars stabbed holes in the gathering darkness.

"Give us a science lesson, Zee," Hillis said.

"Not dark enough. Later we'll see something."

They lay side by side, watching the stars gradually revealed. "We've been to some of those," Clio said. "Ages ago." A reverie settled over them, and they lay, struggling to understand what it meant, to have been there, ages ago.

"We travel to the past," Hillis said, "but no one except the mathematicians understand how it's possible. The rest of us poor nulls, we just go along for the ride."

"You've got to have the math," Zee said. "When you look at the math, it's fairly simple. Once Vandarthanan worked it out, it all became so simple. It's like Pomp and Circumstance. Sometimes I think, I could have written that, it's so obvious."

"Somebody still has to break past the Future Ceiling," Hillis said. "You can still make a reputation."

"But you can't get to the future." Clio said. Then, doubtfully, "Can you?"

"Well, no one's worked out the mathematical proof," Zee said, "but theoretically, it's possible. Vandarthanan said that a traveler to the future would exist in a kind of quasi reality. They would be able to witness events, but not take part in them. He even said that this traveler might be invisible to those in the future, and might appear to them as a kind of apparition."

"Ghosts?" Clio asked.

"Well, the theory can be wrong. Experimental proof is missing for so much of Vandarthanan's work. Like traveling to the future and his other work on Cousin Realities."

"The old parallel-universes idea," Clio said. A shooting star, spectacular and brief, plunged across the night sky, connecting the dots of the stars Castor and Pollux in Gemini.

"Not exactly. Vandarthanan's theories suggest that under certain conditions, a parallel universe may spring into being. Only he didn't use the term 'parallel universe.' He called this a Cousin Reality. Because this reality, he says, would exist in the known cosmos, our own known space, side by side with us."

"This is the theory that discredited him," Hillis said. "Poor bastard came up with one last big idea and the establishment pulled the plug on him."

"It wasn't the Cousin Reality concept that people found hard to swallow," Zee said. "It was his ideas of cosmic dissonance. The idea that the two realities would be inimical to each other, setting up a dissonance that would move toward resolution. That one reality would gather strength and the other diminish until the weaker one died out. Toward the end of his life he came to believe that we *did* have a Cousin Reality, and the mess we've made of the planet was evidence that our reality was losing a life-and-death struggle with our Cousin Reality. It's that part that the scientific community rejected. Called it mysticism, not science."

"Called it bad politics," Hillis countered. "Vandarthanan made the mistake of getting quoted in the newspapers instead of just obscure scientific journals."

Clio propped herself up on her elbow. "So they shut him out for criticizing what's wrong with the world?"

"Yes," Zee said. "And for using math to do it."

After that they lay quietly, their high spirits dampened. Finally, Clio struggled out of her sleeping bag. "Gonna go take a pee," she announced. "You guys can continue the science lesson without me."

She made her way into the brush, finding a tissue in the inside breast pocket of her jacket. The night was alive with sounds, the scraping and chittering of insects, the breezes splashing through the trees. Clio squatted down to pee.

When she stood up, pulling up her pants, she heard a noise in front of her, saw a movement of shadow, heard a man say, "Might as well leave them down, girl."

In her surprise, Clio jerked back, hit her head against a tree, and tried to rise with her pants around her knees and her feet struggling to dig in and run. Then the man struck her, with a bruising slap to the side of her face. The blow sent her reeling back against the tree, where she toppled, stunned.

Her ears sang. For an instant she was only conscious of the pain of her body, of her head threatening to crack open and spill all that she knew, all that she was. Then he was smashing her into the ground, and his boots pushed her ankles apart, and she heard noises in the direction of the camp, shouts and trampling feet. His knee was wrenched into her groin, and she cried out in pain as he leaned harder into her, but her shoulders were free as the man fumbled with something, a flashlight.

She twisted her shoulders, punching into his fleshy gut, and screamed with all the breath she could muster, but it sounded like a scream under water. When he flicked on a light, aiming it into her eyes, she stopped screaming and froze as he grabbed at her shirt and clawed his hands across her breasts.

"Pretty, too," he said, with a twist in his face. He pierced her cheek with a needle, no, not a needle, a scratch pack, and in her thrashing it went in deep. She could smell the man's cologne: a sweet, vinegary scent that, crazily, reminded her of her eighth-grade boyfriend, Keith Irving. The man held the scratch pack under the flashlight, watching for the color to turn, and when her smear of blood turned into deep purple, like a bruise, he said, "You're clean," in a friendly voice, "lucky for you. Well, now, let's have us some fun."

Something in the man's words. In her wooziness, Clio heard *Have us some fun, have us some fun,* and she wanted to strike the words from his mouth. Her right arm flew up to his face and she jammed her thumb into his left eye, and for a moment he reeled backward—just in time to receive her foot in his groin. She rolled away from him, onto her hands and knees, scuttling fast for the brush until she felt a fierce pull on her ankle with a strength that dragged her back, back, and she heard him spit out, "Son of a bitch, son of a fucking bitch," and then she felt herself whipped over onto her back.

A voice and a flashlight came from above as someone appeared beside them. "Get off her, Cole, you dickhead."

Another man was standing at their side, shining the flashlight in Clio's eyes.

"You gotta be kidding! At the point I'm at? You can have her next, asshole." He pushed her legs wider apart. The other man lunged at him, toppling him off her. They argued, leaving her on the ground, still aiming the flashlight at her so she couldn't see, but only felt the rocks against her back.

She heard the second man say, "She's Recon, you know that? Biotime for chrissakes."

"I wasn't going to kill her, I was just going to fuck her." He punctuated the word "fuck" with a kick into her ribs. The flashlight switched away from her face as the men moved off. She heard the second man say, "Don't want to hurt the merchandise, shithead."

Clio crawled away from the spot where she had lain, pulling on her clothes, unable to stand. The woods were quiet except for the dry leaves crunching under her hands and knees. She heard a small barking sound. Realized it was coming from her as she emitted short, staccato gasps. She stifled herself, kneeled in the underbrush, and listened for her attackers.

She heard someone call her name. Zee. Zee calling her name. "Here," she said, but it was more of a croak. Then Zee was crashing through the undergrowth and found her, and knelt down and pulled her into his arms, which were shaking harder than she was.

"Did they hurt you?" he asked. "They didn't hurt you did they?"

"Yes, he hurt me. He tried to rape me, but the other one stopped him. But he hurt me, a little."

"My God, my God," Zee kept saying.

An owl hooted in the blackness. "Is Hill OK?" Clio asked.

"He'll be OK. They beat him up, but he'll be OK."

"Have they gone?"

"Yes, I think so." Zee pulled her head deeper into his shoulder, surrounding her with his arms. She burrowed, then pushed away as though suffocating, gasping for breath. Shaking hard.

She pulled on his hand. "Let's go find Hill."

They went back to the camp where Zee had left Hillis covered with a sleeping bag. He was curled up, on his side, holding his stomach, his ribs, where they had beat him. He cursed softly as Clio examined him for broken ribs. "Assholes," he muttered, "fucking Nazis."

"I don't think anything's broken, Hill."

"Sons of bitches kicked the shit out of me."

"They beat me up too, Hill, they . . ."

"Goddamn Nazis stole the Leery sapling, that's what they were after, the plant specimen."

"So they were DSDE."

"No, not DSDE, why would narcs care about a stalk in a baggie? Listen, they were Biotime security; followed us from the farm, the assholes." He winced in pain as he sat up. "You OK?"

"*Biotime* did this?" Clio gaped at him.

"No, she's not OK," Zee was saying, "they tried to rape her, they mauled her. So she's not OK, OK?" He was stuffing their gear into the packs, throwing everything together, sleeping bags, eating utensils, shoving it all together. His voice quavered. "And neither am I. We're getting out of here, let's get this stuff in the car."

They made three trips down the road, then walked Hillis down. "They can't do this," Zee said. "They can't just go beating up people, raping women. This isn't LA, this is America. You can't just take people into the woods and kick the bejesus out of them. We're scientists."

"Shut up, Zee," Hillis said. He was holding Clio in the backseat, brushing her hair with his hand, over and over. "Just drive."

Clio tried to cry, wanted a good cry, but all she could do was shake. She had thought she was going to die, they would rape her and kill her, she thought. They had come back for her, down the years, to avenge their man. She had allowed herself to feel safe, after all the years; the event ripple had spread so far and thin, it hardly registered in the present. But events don't disappear, the future doesn't carry you away from the past. The past is always there, just behind you, and then it reaches out and touches you on the shoulder. You turn, and you face the thing you did, and it leers into your face and drives a needle into your cheek.

It was Petya who got Clio to put down the gun. She had been standing, pointing the weapon at the jacket and trousers of the body, because it had jerked once, even after the head was gone. Clio stared at the collar, still pointing the gun, and Petya had come and pried her fingers loose. And then they were running into the darkness, away from the house, its windows still lit bright. She felt the light on her back, saw herself running across the tall grassy pasture, getting smaller and smaller, she and her brother, like they were entering a new land where everything they had before was dead. It was a dreamland, where Petya was finally all grown up. He took charge, kept her hand grasped in his, ran ahead, leading her to a flight of stairs down into the earth, down past where graves were. And then he closed the doors and they huddled in the darkness until dawn, when old Mr. Reesley came down into his basement and found them, and took them up into the kitchen and gave them soup and Fig Newtons, as though they were children. And Petya cried as he ate, but Clio didn't cry. Her eyes were rigid, made of glass, and the sap of her body pooled way down, in her ankles, her feet.

They drove through the night. The gas tank was nearly full, and they were grateful that they wouldn't need to stop. They felt safe as long as they kept moving. Clio dozed off in Hillis' arms.

Hours later, she became aware that the car had stopped. She fought off the moment of waking, not wanting to remember. It was dawn. Hillis slept next to her, curled tightly into his half of the seat.

"Where are we?"

"We're headed into downtown. Traffic's backed up," Zee said.

"I'll drive for a while."

"Don't bother—since you two are so cozy back there."

"I said I'll drive."

Zee turned around. Traffic was at a dead stall. "Never mind. I've driven this far, I'm going to finish it. Besides, you're not such a hot driver, to tell the truth."

Clio wound up to lob a response back, then stowed it. Something was going on here and not a driving contest, either. Well, it was obvious. Zee was jealous of Hillis.

After a stony silence, Zee managed to say, "Just kidding, OK?" He reached his hand back to find her, other hand on the wheel, inching the car forward in the line. Clio grabbed his hand, feeling tears surging. He cupped his hand around her head, pulling her forward, closer to the front seat, stroking her hair.

Police sirens wound their way past the line of cars. Then the *whup-whup* of a helicopter.

"Something's up," Zee said. "Maybe its a sabotage." It was still too dark to see anything up ahead. Hillis woke, moaning.

"I think he's got a broken rib," Clio said. "We've got to get him to a doctor, could have punctured a lung."

"Why are we stopping?" Hillis asked. "This hurts like hell."

"Police are all over the place. Something up ahead."

Hillis groaned in answer.

Clio leaned forward to see the readout on the dash: no alternative routes available, everything was clogged, with people abandoning the freeway, seeking bypasses. Predicted delay: undetermined. This meant it was an incident.

Zee tuned in the radio, and the broadcast was full of the story. Freeway sabotage, a bombing. Dozens of cars mangled. Old Greens taking credit, claiming another victory against the automobile.

"Hope they shut the fucking freeway down," Hillis said.

"We're driving this freeway too," Clio said hotly. "These folks have as much right as we do to drive."

"Well, we drive once a year, these people practically live in their cars."

"So just blow them up?"

"Just set an example with a few of them."

"Christ, Hillis," Clio said softly.

"Shut up," Zee said. "I'm calling Biotime." He was on the car phone.

"What the hell are you doing?" Hillis demanded.

"I'm invoking some privileges. You've got a serious injury, Clio's been beat up, I've been driving all night, and I'm getting a chopper. Biotime can damn well pay for it and be grateful we don't want anything else."

An hour later the chopper came, in a turbulence of wind and noise. They were herded inside its belly, and it rose over the sea of parked cars, headed toward Boeing Field.

As the chopper banked sharply, Clio looked down, straight into the massive crater that now split the freeway in two. A dozen or so twisted cars were scattered within the crater's puckered lips, some of them still burning.

BEYOND EDEN

CHAPTER 5

❧

Clio ran. There had been no missions, no work to do for six weeks, and she was getting soft, so she ran. Vanda's track was a broad yellow stripe on one side of the main corridor, well-used most day periods; you don't want to lose bone density, or muscle mass. You don't want to lose your mind with the boredom, with being shut in. She veered off to the gym to cool down.

In the middle of her stretches, she looked up to see Brisher standing in front of her. Wearing a baggy saffron business suit.

"How was the run?"

Clio continued stretching. "It was swell."

He watched her stretch for a moment. "You're looking good, Clio."

"Try to."

"This running business. Do you find it pleasurable? Well-being, happiness, that sort of thing?"

Clio worked on her hamstrings. "No."

"Ah. I suppose not. Mind on business, I suppose. Good practice, good practice." He glanced quickly around the gym, then back at her. "I'm sorry, by the way, about what happened."

Clio stopped and gazed at him, her expression fixed.

"About what you went through. With those men." He glanced at her fleetingly, took a roll of fizzes from his breast pocket, squeezed one into his mouth.

"You mean when they beat me up and tried to rape me?"

Brisher looked to one side. A few people in the gym

looked toward Clio. Brisher said, in a lower voice, "Yes, about that. A bad business. I hate to think what might have happened if Hillis and Zee hadn't fought them off."

Clio got up, grabbed her towel, headed for the locker room.

"I can imagine what it must have been like," he said, starting after her. "Just awful, just awful. If you ever need to talk about it . . ."

Clio stopped, turned to face him. "I've talked it out, and I don't want to talk about it anymore." This came out more rudely than she intended. Got to be nice to Brish. She conjured up a really good smile. "Thanks, though, OK?"

"You have to be careful, going Earthside, Clio. Can't just sleep in the woods, these days. Too dangerous. Greenies, kooks, whatnot. Hate to lose a good pilot. Before her time." He took a step closer to her, confiding. "You should be more careful, Clio. You and Hillis. These are dangerous times, even for a Dive pilot. Nobody's immune."

Clio remembered to breathe. "I always try to be careful."

He nodded. "Good. Good practice, being careful."

She made a beeline for the showers. He knew. Something. But how much did he know? There was always a hint behind his words. A warning. An invitation. She let the water sluice over her a long time.

Clio found HIllis in his room, stabbing at the keyboard, running a game. She watched over his shoulder until he won the round.

"Brish is watching us, Hill," she said, "After the episode with stealing the specimen. He may know a lot of things, about you as well as me."

"No. No, he doesn't. All he knows is that I swiped a dead plant from the transition farm, and there's nothing he can do about it, because he can't admit he's got retroids running around beating up people." He punched in another round of Space Ace.

"Jesus, aren't you worried?"

"We haven't done anything yet." Hillis blanked the

screen and swung his chair around to face her. He looked at her a long time, and she grew uneasy.

"What do you mean 'yet'?" She sat on the bunk, with a sinking feeling in her belly.

"We're going to take a Dive. We're going up a couple decades, Clio. You're going to take *Starhawk* to the future."

Clio stared at him a moment. "I'm going to *what*?"

Hillis sprang from his chair, and kneeled in front of her, taking her hands in his. "You're going to take us to the future. Oh Clio, it's possible, possible to see our future!"

"What are you talking about, 'see the future'?"

"Zee broke through. The Future Ceiling. There isn't any ceiling, we can go both ways. Zee did the math. No ceiling."

Clio pulled her hands out of his. He was crazy.

"He's been working on it for weeks," Hillis said. "Turns out, it wasn't that hard."

"You're saying Zee did what Vandarthanan couldn't?"

"No." Hillis sat next to her on the bunk, close, his blue eyes trying to trap her gaze. "I think Vandarthanan did it years ago. And I think we just never heard about it because the powers that be didn't want us to hear about it. Anyhow, he's dead now, so who's to say? Point is, we can get to the future, same as the past. You see what this means?"

"Why would they lie about the Future Ceiling?" She pulled back, yanking her eyes away from his, desperately trying to keep some distance.

"So they can lie about the future. They don't want us to know."

Clio shook her head. "You think I can just jump in *Starhawk*, take her for a little spin? They'd *notice*, Hill. I'd be busted, we'd all be busted."

Hillis sighed, took her hands again. "We're not going to hijack the ship. We're going to change the Dive boards during the next regulation Dive. Next mission."

Clio rolled her eyes. "Oh *that* ought to work! Folks wake up a hundred years from now, and Russo's too dumb to know where the hell she is!"

Hillis put his palms up, trying to quiet her. "Nobody

wakes up. We Dive up for a brief glimpse, then reverse directions and wake up with no one the wiser."

"What if we see the end of the world?" Clio asked. "Is that real, or not? How can we change it?"

"I don't know for sure that we can change it. But suppose the future is a possibility, not a certainty? Maybe we could do something to avert disaster."

"Christ almighty, you guys are playing with theories! It's never been tested. You could kill us all, or worse." She jumped up, headed for the door. "Forget it."

He plunged after her, took her by the arm, stopping her. "Clio. This isn't some college prank. Zee has it all worked out. And it's about saving our future, making sure we *have* one."

"We can't get anywhere near Earth, Hill. At Dive point we'll be out of range of sensors—we won't be able to see a damn thing on Earth except clouds and the bluish tint of water."

"We can still pick up electromagnetic transmissions."

"We won't have *time* to sit there and record radio and TV signals. Folks on the bridge will be awake. And they'll be asking questions." She was facing him, buying into this mad discussion. Goddamn him anyway.

"We don't need time. We'll record decades of broadcasting while we're still *in* Dive."

"We can't do that."

"Why not?"

"You can't use signal receivers in Dive."

Hillis smiled. "Sure you can. Zee . . ."

". . . has figured it out," Clio finished for him. She shook her head. "Why? Why do you have to do this? It's crazy. You're making me crazy." Clio took his face between her hands. "Why?"

Hillis paused a moment. "I don't want to make you crazy, or hurt you. I just have to know. I just have to know if it's all over. If what we're doing here, with Biotime, if it's all a game. We know the Earth is greying, Clio. Every day. I can watch it from the monitors. I know it's greying. I just want to know if it's dying."

Clio looked up at him, thinking, but not saying, *Why do you want to know? We'll get there soon enough, the slow way. Then we'll know. Knowing the future is a curse. You can't hope for things, you can only wait for them, and it's not the same. Not the same at all.*

But she looked up at his face, and said, "I can't think about this anymore. It's too crazy."

"Sure," Hillis said. "Let's just leave it for now." He went over to his desk, started pawing through the stacks of video games. He was pissed, but not showing it.

Then, he turned around, with one of those heart-breaking smiles. "Want to play a vid?"

Clio slowly walked over to the game console. He tossed her Debt Roulette. She lost and lost.

She got two stiff drinks in her at the station bar before Teeg walked in, collected his beer, and plopped himself down at her table.

"Mind if I join you?"

"Yes."

"Well, you don't seem to have a date, so you can hardly refuse."

"I just did refuse, Teeg."

"And I'll buy you a drink." He motioned to the waiter. "You sure got a long face. Booze make you sad? Some people, like me, it makes them happy. Luck of the draw."

He took a long pull on his beer, and gazed silently at her for a few moments. Clio admitted to herself that she liked him better when he wasn't talking. She smiled at him.

"God, you got a pretty smile," he said. A stupid thing to say, but she liked it.

Jesus. Feeling flattered by Harper Teeg. To be that desperate, or that drunk. Change the subject, old girl.

"So where's your date, Teeg?"

"Me? Well it's a very sad story. I'm pretty down on my luck." The waiter brought her drink, and Teeg paid with a large bill, refusing the change. "You like those stricken types, don't you?"

"Yeah, I just love weak men."

"Well, I'm one of those. Stricken." His brown eyes sparkled in mock anguish.

She braced herself for his next move, a half-mocking appeal for some womanly comfort, but he was already getting up, waving at some friends at the bar. He leaned over, grabbing his beer with an easy, muscular reach. "Guess you're feeling quiet tonight. I'll leave you alone. Sometimes I drink alone, too." He moved off, turned around again. "But it's never a good sign." He flashed her a smile.

"Thanks, Teeg," she said, feeling grateful, both for the visit and his departure. He wasn't always so bad, in small doses.

She stared into her drink and thought about the Dive. Hillis' Dive. Hillis and Zee and their science experiment. Just a little variation on the theme of time travel, over in a minute.

Easy. Just tamper with *Starhawk*'s Dive boards, load in an untested program, send ship and crew a hundred outlaw years into the future, take a quick look around and reverse time flow—another untested maneuver—and live to tell about it. Tell about the winner of the Preakness, next president, who dies, who gets rich, fate of the planet. Fate of Mom and Elsie. And Petya.

For better or worse, it's the future. Our future, love it or leave it. If you can.

What if you could change the future, as Hillis thought? Do things differently, change outcomes? What was the future then? An alternate future, not fixed at all, but malleable? Like the ghost of Christmas Future, showing what might be, if you don't shape up?

Clio finished off her drink. She placed the glass carefully on the napkin in front of her, no longer seeing it. Seeing instead what drove Hillis to do this thing. It wasn't that he wanted to know the future. He already knew the future: the bald, grey Earth. But without proof, he was just a fanatic. And impotent to act. Once he knew with certainty, he would do the thing he was born to do. Exactly what, Clio didn't know.

But she was going to help him.

She left the bar and made her way to Hillis' quarters. He'd been on this path for years, but she'd never seen it. Hill was one of those people who cared enough to burn themselves up in a cause. Whereas she never got beyond her own personal horizons. Space Recon, keeping it all together. Mom and Elsie, those losses, always with her. Petya, lost somewhere between Fargo and Minneapolis, always with her. Whereas Hillis could give himself to something larger, something with lasting meaning.

She stood outside Hillis' door. Knocked, walked in. And saw them. Hillis and Zee, sitting and talking on the edge of the bed, neither one wearing a shirt. The bed was a mess, the pillow on the floor, a bottle of wine opened on the desk.

Zee, startled by her entrance, jumped to his feet, met her eyes for an instant, turned away. He walked to the room's only chair, flopped down in it, staring at the floor.

Hillis looked at Clio, very calm. As she stood there dumbly, he raised an eyebrow. Well?

They were lovers. Of course. They were lovers.

"Clio . . ." Hillis said.

She heard herself saying, "You should lock your door."

"Clio, I wanted you to know about Zee, but I never got around to saying it."

"Well, now I know. About you and Zee." She turned, started to leave. Hillis moved fast, reached for her, grabbed her arm, but she yanked away, pulled the door open.

Hillis slammed the door shut in front of her, pushed her against it, pinning her arms. She closed her eyes, not wanting to look at him.

"Goddamn it, Clio, look at me!"

What did she expect? Hillis was her friend, not her lover, he'd never been anything else. Still, she hated him.

"Oh God," Zee was saying, still not looking at her.

She turned to him, this usurper. Started to say something, stopped herself. Zee was too easy, too innocent.

She looked up then at Hillis. Met his gaze, and looking

at him, knew it all. Knew Hill's loneliness, Zee's vulnerability, her own obsession with men who could never love her. She knew it all, and she determined to be a kind, rational adult.

Then she heard herself saying, "You bastard. You goddamn bastard. You could have told me, you could have given me that much!"

Hillis backed off from her then, leaned against the desk, feet crossed, bracing his arms behind him on the desk. His face was neutral again. "I guess the Dive's off, huh?"

A fury built inside her. "Off? You think I care who you screw? You think that's how I make my decisions, like a woman spurned? Maybe you're not the only hero around, Hillis. I came here tonight to tell you I'd do it. The Dive is on. Even though our careers are on the line, even though they can keelhaul us behind Vanda for a few thousand kilometers just for thinking of doing this, much less catching us. Yeah. The Dive's on." She turned to the door, turned back. "But you're still a thoughtless son of a bitch—whether you save the Earth or not."

Clio turned, yanking the door open, leaving it thrown open, made her way back down the narrow passageway, past crew quarters and out into Vanda's main corridor. She walked rapidly, not looking where she was going, not acknowledging a few who nodded at her, not seeing them. Her heart kept feeling betrayal, while her mind kept saying, *Stupid fool bitch*, not his fault that he can't love you, not his fault.

She found herself outside Loading Bay D. Hand on the observer access door, ready to enter. She opened the door, saw Captain Russo standing on the catwalk above the bay, leaning against the railing looking below. Clio almost turned back. But Russo looked up, waved her over. *What the hell.* Clio approached her, boots clacking on the catwalk grating. She stood next to Russo, looking down on the ship.

Starhawk was nested in her bay, massive, black and riveted, a hulking foreign thing, somnolent now, like captured Kong in his hold. Techs were gathered near her belly, dragging hoses to power and fuel her. Preparing for a mission.

"What's up, Captain? We gonna fly?" Clio felt adrenaline sluicing into her veins.

Russo still leaned against the railing, watching the crew. "Thirteen hundred hours. You didn't get a crew call?" Her bulky frame hid her excitement, if she felt any. A little squint around the eyes meant that she saw every move the crew below made. And knew enough to stay out of their way until her command came up.

Three panels lay open on the aft fuselage to receive the power cables. Clio's belly tightened. Looking at the ship gave her a jolt as always, made her yearn. The ship could take her where she wanted to go. Could take her to when. Times she had strapped herself into the pilot's chair, trusting *Starhawk* with her life, her sanity. Times they had gone down that road together, where time and space converge, and only had each other for company, *Starhawk*'s winking control panel and the hum of hydraulics, her only sensory links to the real world.

"Where is it this time?" Clio asked.

"Called Niang"—she pronounced it Ny-Ang, with emphasis on the second syllable.

"Sounds Chinese," Clio said, trying to keep a polite conversation going with the brass.

Russo looked up at her, eyes narrowing. "You look like hell." Clapped her hand on Clio's shoulder. "Go get some sleep, Lieutenant," she said, almost motherly. Russo went back to watching the ship, maybe lost in her own problems.

"Yessir. Thank you sir." Clio left the catwalk, mind racing. Thirteen hundred hours. Planet called Niang. *We're heading out.*

Clio found her way back to her cabin, staggered to the bed and fell on it. She pushed the thought of the mission from her, pushed it hard, her thoughts returning to Hillis, Hillis and Zee. Hillis and her. She rolled over on her stomach, aroused.

Station was growing quiet. Doors shutting, voices in the corridor now and then.

She sat up, pushing her hair back off her face, rubbing her fingers into her scalp. Went to the mirror, used a brush. Her hair crackled.

Charged up tonight, Antoinette. Got to get out.

She headed for the door.

In front of his cabin, she paused. Didn't want to think too much about this. Just get on automatic and do it. What could it hurt?

Knocked. A minute later, a long minute, Teeg opened the door. "Well, Miss Red herself."

"You alone?" she asked.

He looked at her a second or two. "Not anymore." Held open the door, and drew her inside.

Clio's hands were sweating hard as she grabbed the rungs of the flight deck ladder to take her shift. *Dive shift*, it was, and she'd used a few too many little blue pills, for blackout insurance.

A hand on her shoulder. She jumped, nearly striking out at the person behind her. She turned around. It was Zee.

"God, don't sneak up on me like that!"

Zee backed up a step, at the look in Clio's eyes. "Cripes almighty," he said, "you're jumpy, Clio."

"Nah. Calm as a coffin."

This was their first real conversation since that moment in Hillis' cabin. Zee barely met her eyes, shying away, playing hurt puppy. "It'll be fine," he said. "Trust me." He leaned heavily on the word "trust."

Know what irony is, Zee? She waited a beat, wondering how tough to be on him. "Maybe I wasn't born to trust," she said.

"Come on, Clio. What's the worst that can happen?"

She was going to say, *Ship blows up . . . or my career trashed, all-expenses-paid trip to a quarry,* when she saw him smiling. He was joking. She smiled back. "Right," she said, "all for science."

Zee's smile grew, his ears rising slightly as he did. He

moved in closer. "The program's all set. Just transfer it in from science deck. You'll be fine."

Ship's voice started countdown. "Crew to quarters and Dive sequence in fifteen minutes," it said.

Clio turned to climb. Behind her, she heard, "I love you, Clio."

She stopped for a moment, then continued to climb. Zee used these funny words. *Trust. Love.* But who should she trust, and who did he love, really? She left him standing below, and emerged onto the bridge, now dim in pre-Dive mode.

Russo made eye contact. Enough to say, Late again, mister.

As Clio slipped into the pilot seat, Teeg threw her a knowing look. Goddamn. That he could bring *that* up at a time like this. "Get a life, Teeg," she said. A hurt frown dented his forehead. She turned to her work, ignoring him, stomach fluttering like a jellyfish on a stick.

The moment they hit Dive and she could see that Teeg was out of it, she imported Zee's program from lower deck and brought it on line, punching in all the capacity of Zee's jury-rigged memory from science deck, all within six seconds of constant time. And waited while Dive took the ship, and her, straight down to the chasms of time. Eyes blurred as she swung her head to see the chronometer, but she was too slow, as Zee said she would be, to see the flash of numbers *forward*, and by the time her eyes cleared, the ship had reversed, was Diving backward, already a thousand years in past time, heading to two million, give or take. She jabbed the radio receiving toggle off, but no need. The drive was full five hundred years ago.

She looked around her. It was over. Ship still intact. Ran systems checks, yes, ship purring. Checked on Teeg and Russo. Vital signs normal, or as normal as they get in Dive. Checked herself, wondering what normal was. Still alive, by God. And whether they'd gone up a few decades or not—pierced the Future Ceiling or not—was just gravy. Find out soon enough. For now, being alive was enough.

•   •   •

"Play it," Hillis said.

Clio glanced over at Zee's console. "I don't want to hear it, Hill."

Zee's cabin was cluttered with books, stacks of paper, and cast-off underwear. On the desk next to his computer, a plastic carton held partially evaporated soup, a glued-in spoon and a broken pencil.

"I know you don't want to hear it," Hillis said. "But play it anyway."

"Don't try to get me roped into this, Hill. I've already done my part."

He reached out and grasped her arm. "You can't always run from everything, Clio. You can't run forever."

She jerked away. "I'm not running away." But it felt like a lie, with Hillis gazing at her with that long blue stare of his. Plus she couldn't avoid Hillis; they were going to be cooped up together for months, since Dive undershot their Niang target a bit. She was a captive audience.

Hillis nodded at Zee. "Play it."

Zee looked like he hadn't slept for days. Dark half-moons under his eyes and the pallor of too much math. He obeyed Hillis, punching the sequence into the keyboard. "I've enhanced this as much as I can," he said. "It's a continuous, repeating transmission. Hard to tell the year it originated, but my guess is maybe fifty to seventy-five years . . . up."

"How do you . . ." Clio began, but Zee held up his hand for quiet. A static-filled transmission eked out of the speakers.

"Good evening," a male voice began. "I send you greetings. This is my last broadcast. I should be home tonight with my family, as you are. I soon will be, if I manage to slip through the street gangs that have now, it seems, taken over New York City. The recent gallant fight of our city police aided by the National Guard was a last stand against chaos. And futile. Those who have not yet succumbed to the Sickness and cholera—and despair—are either looting their neighbors or barring the doors against the villains. It's come to that. Here, in this formerly great city as elsewhere in the nation and the world."

Clio closed her eyes. Yeah, it was going to be bad.

". . . somehow, with the aid of our brave crew here at the station, we've managed to come to you tonight out of determination to tell you this last story.

"You who are left to listen may be willing to hear what I have to say. If not, then at least I leave this broadcast as a beacon for the future. If our civilization should rise again somehow. If we should have visitors from the vast universe that we had just begun to explore when disaster overtook us. For it is conceivable that the cosmos contains intelligent life—life more intelligent than we ourselves have been. If ever they should look over the ruin of our planet, and our civilizations, I would offer . . . not an explanation—for that is hardly possible—but simply one human being's summation of events. And a last few words for the departed. For Earth.

"In the years when we still had the luxury to argue over who was to blame for ecological disaster, some of us said that the worst had come upon us suddenly. Come upon us in a manner no peoples, no governments, could have prevented. And, in truth, in the last years, one calamity did follow another with unrelenting swiftness: crop failures, civil mayhem, pestilence, UV die-offs, and infestations of every kind.

"Yet, before the final upheavals, we had many decades of tremors. If, in the last years of the twentieth century, some did cry wolf too often, surely the warning cries of the last twenty years were the cries of wisdom.

"Why, then, did we do so little until it was too late? Not because we lacked the scientific understanding to comprehend our environment. Not because of greed—though I don't discount its contribution. Not because we were too busy with other things. Not even—as some have said—that we secretly wished for our own annihilation. It may be the case that the answer is a more basic one. That we could not imagine that the Earth could succumb. It had always been here. It had always been our home, our provider, our enduring world. It would always live and succor us—would it not? So finally, I believe we may have perished from a simple failure of the imagination.

"And the great adventure that was Space Recon? For twenty-five years our hopes rode with these crews. These brave men and women became our ideals, our folk heroes. And a peculiarly American kind of hero worship it was: we were facing the problem head-on, with bravery, technology, drama. No problem that can't be solved with ingenuity and courage. Supply-side reigns, not only on Earth, but in the heavens. They would bring home their treasures, the holds of their ships would be filled with booty. We could continue living as we wished. We didn't need to change. This is what Space Recon allowed us to believe. We needn't change.

"Ultimately, they failed to find viable life. And though we hounded the Service out of existence, much of our anger should have been directed at ourselves. Because our own lives weren't viable. We could not sustain ourselves, our populations, our rampant development, our consumerism, our combustion engines, our sprawling cities. And we could not imagine life without them.

"We could not imagine life without them. What's left is dust. You who may, in future times, come upon this broadcast, take note. We were not always thus. Once we were full of life and promise, a variegated and diverse patchwork of peoples and communities. We nurtured our young, created great art, sought out learning and science, and strove to understand our Creator, and abide by what we perceived was His will. The Earth was lush and green, and filled with creatures, remarkable and thriving.

"These things are gone now. They can be lost. This was our final, most bitter lesson. You who may come upon us here, learn from us. Nurture your world, your habitat well. They are finite gifts. Imagine them lost and you will cherish them the more."

He paused. "Whoever you are, whenever you listen . . . I wish you . . . good fortune. Goodnight."

Clio and Zee stood for a long while without speaking. At last, Clio leaned down to embrace Hillis, who had collapsed into Zee's chair. She sought to comfort him, or to be comforted.

A slight pull of his shoulder, away from her.

Rebuffed by Hillis and stunned by the broadcast, Clio said softly, "Why, why did you want to know?"

He looked up at her bitterly. "Why *didn't* you want to know?"

She sank down onto the bunk. Trying to breathe, trying to process what she'd heard. Trying to deny it. "Maybe there's more than one future," she said.

He glanced up at her.

"Maybe we can change it, maybe it doesn't have to be this way." Her voice trailed off, as he continued to watch her, silently, his eyes like caves of ice.

CHAPTER 6

❧

"Planet Earth, I'd like you to meet your long-lost sister."
Teeg spoke low, catching the tension on the bridge, sub-
duing himself for once. After a journey of three months—all
the while stuck with Harper Teeg on a rig the size of
Starhawk—Clio was ready to pay him to shut up.

She leaned back in her chair, watching Niang's Planet
display itself below. On the planet surface, a great ocean
glided by, as green as the Pacific, with many islands riding
on the waters toward the curved edge of the planet. Niang
was a dazzler, by Earth standards.

The standards that count.

Clio was patched into mid-decks crew station, listening
to the crew deliver the nonstop data on Niang. No artificial
orbiting materials. One moon. Asteroid-type debris in high
orbit. No aircraft sighted; the only radio transmissions
bursts of electrons trapped by the planet's magnetic field
and occasional lightning discharges. And on Niang's nightside, no lights except for, here and there, a forest fire.

No visible civilization.

Got to get that right. Didn't come this far to give the
locals target practice.

A continent crept into view, huge, unbroken, a single
landform. Already the science team referred to it as Gaia.
Clio heard Meng, the botany tech, exclaim over the headphones, "Holy Jesus, look at that color." Blue-green it was,
bordering on turquoise. The colossal forest of Niang,
broken only by the deep clefts of rivers. Rivers so vast they
would consider the Nile a mere tributary. From the infrared

radiation readings, the whole planet was within temperate to tropical temperatures.

"Could be anything living down there. Under that canopy." Estevan, ship's anthropologist. He'd been glued to the monitors for two hours now. "If there are settlements, they don't clear the land for them."

"Incredible." Hillis' voice. "The readings are incredible. They just keep coming in. One-fifth oxygen, boys and girls, and we got a match on CO_2, nitrogen, methane, temperature. It's a match, it's still a match. I'm not getting any adverse indicators. Beautiful. Beautiful. It's like Earth, it's her other face."

On the bridge, Russo took off her headphones. "Finn, you've got the bridge, I'm going mid-deck to conference." Russo heaved herself out of the captain's chair like the world was on her shoulders. Which it was, in a way.

There below them was Niang's Planet. A paradise. Maybe better than Leery. Though nobody wanted to say it, it was underneath their voices, a submerged dream: this is the big one . . . all biota viable . . . the regreening of Earth . . . a billion-dollar find, sweetheart . . . how you gonna spend yours?

Clio climbed into the captain's chair as Russo left the bridge.

"Well goddamn," Teeg said, not turning around, watching the viewport display. "Goddamn anyway."

"Problem, Teeg?"

"Who's senior here, Finn, tell me that?"

"Senior what?"

"Senior what." Teeg was smiling, shaking his head, as he turned in his chair. "Senior pilot. Who's the senior pilot on *Starhawk*?"

"You are. Jesus, Teeg, you hacked about me sitting here?" Clio started to laugh, then thought better of it.

"On the bridge, I'm second in line, that's all," Teeg said. "That bitch knows that."

Clio let out a long, slow breath. Teeg really cared about this little slight. He sat there brooding like a schoolboy. An eight-year-old in a man's body. Jesus. And she had slept with him, sought him out, asked for it. Got it. She was starting to wish she had kept her legs crossed.

"Pilot's job is the main job on this bridge, you know that Teeg." Give the dog a bone, Clio thought.

Teeg looked up at her, warming a notch. "Think so?" His face collapsed from hope into skepticism. "Because I've earned my stripes on this rig. Damn if I haven't. Russo likes to keep power, you notice that?"

When she didn't answer, Teeg drew his eyes down Clio's body, changing gear. "You sure are one gorgeous woman." His tongue flicked at the corner of his mouth. "Far as I'm concerned, you're not wearing one stitch of clothes, sitting there. The way it oughta be, sister."

"Were you born obnoxious, Teeg, or do you take classes?"

"I work at it, same as you, honey." He tapped his chest. "But deep down, I know how you feel."

Clio rolled her eyes and punched a new comm line, listening to crew chatter, drowning him out. Definitely a mistake, that business with Teeg. She'd have to straighten him out real fast. One screw was all it was, was all it would ever be.

Teeg patched into her channel. "You know why Russo's so paranoid?" His voice invaded her ears, nasal and annoying, like a fly buzzing. " 'Cause she's Biotime's little doggy on a leash, that's why. She's ship captain, but she owes her soul to Biotime, the only outfit that'll hire her on. After her little escapade. You remember the story?"

"Yeah, Teeg, we all remember the story."

"How she was the only one got out of that orbiter alive?"

"That was a long time ago, Teeg."

"The oxygen went. And the six of them shared the emergency supply. They huddled around the oxygen packs on the suits and took snorts, until they figured out that they weren't going to make it. Then they drew straws, and Russo won. And she sucked on that air all the way through reentry, and watched them die, man. Watched them die."

"Shut up, Teeg."

He looked startled. "Guess you ladies like to stick together, huh?"

"Just shut the fuck up."

Teeg swung around toward the control panel, and silence reigned on the bridge. Clio glared at the back of his head. *What an asshole.*

Off shift, Clio was sleeping hard. The kind of sleep where you feel like you're lying on the bottom of the ocean with a mile of water holding you down. She was nearing the surface, hearing a knocking sound. It persisted.

"Clio? Clio?"

She woke, rose up on one elbow. Somebody at the cabin door. "Yeah? Come in."

Zee sidled through the door, leaned back against it. "You awake?"

"No."

"Because you need to know what's going on."

Clio staggered over to the water dispenser, swabbed her face, ran her wet hands through her hair in an effort to restrain it, flatten it. It still stuck out in every direction.

"You look great," Zee said.

These days he was anxious to please her, still trying to heal the rift between them. She wanted to turn on him, say, "Look, Zee, I don't care, all right? I just don't care if you slept with Hill. It's over anyhow, right?" But she restrained herself. The kid was in love with her. You had to have a little sympathy.

Clio groaned and lay back down on the bed. "So sit down and tell me what's up."

Zee folded his body down into the desk chair. "Russo's calling for a ground mission."

"So? What we came for, right?"

Zee sprang up. "Not just a ground mission, a camp. She's going to set up a camp!" Zee began pacing. "She can't do this to me, this isn't what I signed on for!"

"Wait a sec. What do you mean, *camp*? Remember, I've been asleep, probably missed something." Clio was starting to track, the mind was warming up, but slowly.

"I'm an astrophysicist, not a soldier. I've never even used a gun before." Zee was waving his arms, pleading with Clio.

"Goddamn it, Zee, sit down and start from the beginning or I'll throw you out."

Zee continued pacing. "Niang's the jackpot, Clio. The science team is so turned on, nobody's slept for a day and a half. It's perfect. It's an Earth clone. Everything looks great from up here, even the elevated CO_2 levels. The atmosphere has heightened methane, the temperature's ideal. And the planet's forest goes on forever. It's a match. It's Big Green on wheels. And Russo's gearing up for a prolonged stay. She's ordered a camp, and nine of us are going down. Nine of us! I'm supposed to help with camp security. Wear a gun!" He crumpled into the chair.

Clio snapped fully awake. "What about me?" She sat up, and swung her feet over the bunk to the floor.

"You're staying aboard. Commander Shaw's in charge of the mission. Hillis, Estevan, Meng, Posie, and Liu and Shannon are the science squad. I'm on security. Teeg'll pilot the shuttle."

"What's Hill say?"

"He's all for it. He's so pumped up, he hasn't left the freeping monitor since last day shift. And he ignores me, completely."

"He's ignoring everybody," Clio said. She stretched her legs to chase the sleep out of them.

"No, I mean he *ignores* me. Like I don't exist."

"Hill doesn't have a lot of room in his life for people, Zee, if you never noticed."

"He had room for me before."

Maybe he wanted something from you, she felt like saying, and didn't.

Zee opened the viewport and gazed out at the local stars, lovely and distant as Zee's hopes for Hillis. After a time he said, "We may never see these stars again. I've just begun my observations. To take me groundside right now is . . ." He turned to plead with Clio. ". . . tragic. I was born to be here, doing what I'm doing. Not mucking about in some screaming jungle."

Clio stood up and headed for the stowage bin to rummage for fresh togs. Peeled off her T-shirt, grabbed a new one. "Zee," she said, "this isn't Princeton. This is Recon, for godsakes."

Zee averted his eyes as she undressed. Clio noted this, pulled the tee over her head with a snap. "Look, it's my quarters. You don't like the view, go find another."

"Clio. It's not that. At all." He looked back up at her.

She swung around, zipping up her suit. "Look. You signed on, Zee. You signed on for whatever comes down, the same as the rest of us. You sign onto Recon, you take what comes." She clipped her belt on, stared at him. "You walk into my cabin, you take what comes."

He nodded slowly, headed for the door, turned. "I wish you were going with us."

"I'll keep the home fires burning."

He smiled, turned, and left, closing the door behind him.

Her irritation faded. Zee was scared, didn't realize they were all scared, to one degree or another. Signed on for it, but didn't mean you weren't scared. But damn if she was going to reassure him. Who was going to reassure her?

Clio sat in the galley nursing a cup of coffee. Estevan and Meng had a game of cards going, trying to waste the last couple hours until the surface mission. Estevan was muscular and abrupt, snapping the cards down and glowering over his hand at Meng, who was well ahead. Meng sweetly called the play: Estevan's three jacks stared balefully at Meng's straight. She swept her earnings into a pile, humming, goading Estevan. She dealt another hand.

Posie was digging in the refrigeration hatch for something to eat, commenting on the rejects. "What's so hard about a ham sandwich? Man wasn't made to eat food from a tube."

Estevan frowned mightily at the hand he had just been

dealt. Without looking at Posie, he said, "Tubes are easier. You just pop off the top and suck."

It began then. The screech of the Klaxon, grabbing the ship and filling it with a metallic howl. Estevan lurched out of his seat and Posie dropped the carbo tubes in his hands.

Ship's voice calmly announced the worst: "CLOSE ALL HATCHES, PRESSURE FAILURE IN LAUNCH BAY."

Clio flung herself up the ladder to the flight-deck hatch, screaming at Posie to shut the third hatch to the galley, the crew-station hatch. Clio grabbed at the flight-deck hatch, pulled the toggle to release it from the ceiling, and cranked it shut. She swung around to check the other hatches. Each one was shut, and guarded now by a crewmate, as though hell itself might barge through those doors. Though the alarms were still screeching, Clio could see Estevan's mouth forming the words *holy shit, holy shit*.

Then, over the Klaxon's blare, Estevan yelled at Meng, "Get your ass in gear, we're ready to blow apart, you bitch!"

Meng, still seated at her cards, stared up at him. As the alarm subsided, Estevan screamed, "You gonna play cards on doomsday?"

In the ensuing quiet, Meng placed her cards facedown. "They must have fixed it," she said.

Clio's eyes were on the crew-deck hatchway, waiting for it to blow if the launch bay did.

Posie was on the intercom, but so were a few other people. Finally Russo's voice piped in: "Posie to medical emergency in the launch bay. We are repressurized. Everyone else, clear the crew-quarter passageway and maintain your stations."

Estevan spun open the hatch lock and made way for Posie, who rushed aft to the launch bay.

Hillis appeared in the same hatchway Posie had just vacated. He swung down the ladder and headed for the coffee spigot.

"What the hell happened?" Clio asked.

"Not much. Shaw was in the launch bay, and the hatch to the landing pod must have failed, or he opened it without checking on the lander's pressure. The room sounded like it was coming apart." He looked at Clio. "So did he."

"Jesus," Estevan said.

The launch bay was the loading area and access point for the landing pod *Babyhawk*, which coupled up to the ship just aft of the crew quarters. *Babyhawk* was the crew's express service from ship to ground and back again. Normally, she rode the ship unpressurized except for prelaunch and when carrying crew.

They heard Shaw then, screaming, as they carried him down the passage to medlab.

Meng stuffed the cards back in their box. "Sounds like he's alive, anyway." She headed up the ladder to crew station.

"Mother of God," Estevan said, after she'd gone. "That witch has no heart, you know?"

"Meng's OK. Just keeps to herself, that all," Hillis said.

"You kidding? That woman wouldn't care if Shaw was wallpaper in launch bay right now."

Hillis poured a cup of coffee from the spigot. "Sure she would. She hates a messy ship."

"No, I'll tell you what she really hates," Estevan said. "It's having her poker game broke up when she's winning. She'll hold it against Shaw, you wait," Estevan said. He followed Meng up to crew station.

Clio moved toward Hillis, and he pulled her close to him. She rested her head on his shoulder. "Think he'll live?"

"Like Meng said, least he's screaming. It's when they're quiet that you worry." He released Clio and started poking around in the refrigeration hatch for something to eat.

Clio watched him, the old Zee thing forgotten. All through the Niang voyage, Hillis had sought Clio out, seemed to want her company more than ever. And Clio wanted that company. Sometimes she and Hillis slept in the same bed, just slept, or talked. He clung to her at first, not talking about future Earth, just clinging to her. And so Clio held him while he talked, talked about Green politics, about his work. About his family and growing up. The East Coast, the fancy schools, the big family with not one close sibling. His father, a remote, depressed federal judge. Hillis looking for meaning among the easy privileges of wealth, finding it, finally, in the early conservation movements, escalating to Green politics, ecowarrior sentiments. Leaving law school for a botany degree. His family's disappointment. Looking at him with strangers' eyes.

Clio would look into Hillis' deep blue eyes, searching for him, but finding instead an absence. A grieving, retreated, Hillis. Until Niang.

Hillis snapped the top off a carbo tube. "We're not going to let this stop us," he said. "Shaw's down, and we need a second pilot on the shuttle. Russo won't send it down without a backup pilot. So that means either her or you." He squeezed half the contents of the tube into his mouth, then threw the tube into the trash.

"Russo won't send me," Clio said. "We've got to Dive to get home. She won't send me."

"Well, it's not going to stop us." He sat in a chair, resting his head on the bulkhead, eyes closed, exhaustion draped over his features. "Turquoise," he said. "The jungle's turquoise. It's as though the plant life has gone beyond green. It's moving down the spectrum of visible light. Like playing scales, in cosmic time. It's the music of evolution, Clio. Music."

Clio looked at him. He had forgotten about Shaw already. Whereas she was still trembling. His long frame was stretched out, one arm thrown back to cushion his head, an unconscious, sensual pose. And he spoke like a man in love; he'd taken one look at Niang, and fallen in love.

"So all of a sudden Recon's OK, huh? Niang's gonna save us?" Clio said.

Hillis shrugged. "You have to ride the winning horse."

"Right. Hope that's what Niang is, Hill, a winning horse." She pulled herself up the ladder and through the hatch to crew station.

Estevan, Meng, and Liu were at workstations, deep into their tasks. One end of the big cabin was rounded, a duplicate of the bridge above them, pressed against the nose of the ship. A circular table in the center of the cabin served as a conferencing place and station for observers like Clio. Computer consoles wrapped around the room, running the onboard experiments and monitoring Niang.

Liu, ship's ecologist, nodded at Clio as she entered, then turned back to his screen, where he was running the geologic survey, in search of rare metals. *Starhawk* wasn't designed to conduct mining operations or haul heavy mining loads, but each mission included a reconnaissance for potential ores. Liu wasn't a geologist, but he ran the programs, doing double duty in his specialties, like most of the *Starhawk* crew. Someday they might have the technology to send out the size ship needed for mining operations. The landing pods would have to be big, the ship itself bigger yet. Vandarthanan's theory related time travel to mass, and attempts to design a mining ship had so far resulted in a ship's mass exceeding the limits for Dive. Someday, when they had the technology, they'd go back for metals. And Biotime would sell their treasure maps for a nice profit.

Meanwhile, they had to travel light. Content themselves with an array of sample plants and, most importantly, seeds. The U.S government paid premium dollars for good seed.

If it grew.

Starhawk's lower deck waited to receive the biological payload. The science deck embodied a two-billion-dollar investment in biological laboratories and a quarantined greenhouse, hermetically sealed. A bulkhead pallet could turn outward, dumping rejects into space. There would be plenty of time to ferret out the rejects. The trip in real space back to Earth would allow three months to conduct onboard analysis of the Niang haul.

Recon missions always required both time and space travel. The Dive only put them in the vicinity of their target. They'd had to travel three hundred thousand kilometers in real space to find Niang, and they had to cover about the same distance to get back, not unusual for a Dive this long. Made the Crippen Dive look like a walk around the block.

Clio sat up straight as Russo entered the cabin.

Estevan, Meng, and Liu turned from their stations, watched the captain as she swung into a chair.

When she had their attention, she began: "Shaw's going to be fine. Got the bends. Posie's got him in a pressure bag. He sustained a concussion. Bruised up pretty bad." She looked at Clio. "He's not going to fly, we know that."

Clio felt her stomach flip over. Got a bad feeling about what was coming down.

"Near as we can piece it together, what happened was that the landing pod in its bay wasn't pressurized. Shaw was in the launch bay, decided to check out *Babyhawk*. I'm not clear what he was doing in there, but he opened the pod doors. Launch bay air pressure crashed in a hurry. He must have half managed to punch the door closure button, but he was yanked across the room and thrown against the half-open pod door. Ship pumped up the pressure real fast. Lucky for him." Russo scanned their faces, looking for questions. Found one.

Estevan asked, "How come the pod wasn't pressurized this close to launch, Captain? I thought we were launching at nine hundred hours."

"We don't know. It's pressured now. We're checking out any leaks. But don't expect to find any. My view of what happened is that the pod was never pressurized to begin with. Shaw assumed it was. Tells you how far your assumptions will take you." Russo stood up. "We're going ahead with the mission. Thirteen hundred hours. Finn, you'll replace Shaw."

There was a stunned silence in the cabin. Meng slid her eyes over to Estevan. A signal for him to speak up. He didn't.

Clio nodded slowly. Russo was risking her Dive pilot. Russo wasn't going on the ground mission. Clio was. Simple as that.

Crew stared at her, a squall settling over their faces. Russo shifted to another foot, watching them, her face hardening. "We don't send out *Babyhawk* with one pilot. That's the rules." She paused, staring them down. Then left the cabin.

Meng looked at Clio. "Looks like the Red Queen is going to chauffeur us down. Lordy, lordy. Going to have to earn your pay this trip, Finn. Same as me."

"No, I never plan to work *that* hard, Meng," Clio said, smiling hard. "I might break a nail."

CHAPTER 7

❧

The landing pod squatted in the middle of a black, circular patch where its thrusters had blasted the ground. Surrounding them for a distance of two hundred meters, a field spread out. Beyond, the jungle loomed. As soon as they debarked they smelled the peculiar fragrance of Niang, the boiled-fruit smell, at first pleasant, then cloying. The 1.1 g seemed to press a sugary glaze onto their skin, half Niang humidity, half human sweat in the ninety-five-degree heat. From all sides came the incessant chittering and creaking of jungle life.

Zee stood with Clio, gazing out at the wall of forest. "We wanted plants; looks like we got them," Zee said. A trickle of sweat zigged down his face.

The dense edge of the forest soared high, defined by huge palmlike growths, taller than Earth trees, that looked like they couldn't possibly stand. Indeed, they appeared to lean on each other at the top where their fibrous heads were woven together in a turquoise canopy, like a crowd of Siamese siblings, joined at the head. A profuse undergrowth thrived below them, but stopped abruptly at the field, where a carpet of thick moss asserted itself.

The crew had moved quickly to set the perimeter wires, a precaution against attack by animals or sentient inhabitants. The tents were clustered around *Babyhawk*: the main tent for meals and conferencing and tents for botany, crew quarters, personal hygiene, and medical. Teeg, as mission leader, had a private tent.

Besides Clio and Teeg, there were seven crew on the ground mission: Hillis, heading up botany and assisted by techs Meng and Shannon; Posie, second-in-command, in charge of medical and zoology; Liu for ecology; Estevan for anthropology and security; and Zee on security.

Clio was standing at the perimeter wire, gazing out at the ring of jungle, when Posie came up beside her.

"Listen to that racket," he said. The forest surged with the cacophony of its local singers. "There's a million eyes staring at us right now, you can be sure of that." He patted the gun, holstered at his side. "Anything comes out of there, I say zap it." His eyes narrowed as he looked at her. "Where's your weapon? You're supposed to wear a weapon."

"Yeah, I was issued one."

"Lot of good it'll do us, in your duffel bag."

Clio was assigned to security. She nodded. "I'll get it. We just got here."

Posie shook his head. "As far as they're concerned," he said, indicating the forest with a movement of his head, "we're invaders. We're little pink men coming out of the sky. They'll shoot first, ask questions later. Right?"

"Who's they, Doc?"

He looked at her, exasperated. "Well, we don't know, now, do we?" He drew his gun, looking down the barrel toward the forest. "Makes it all the more dangerous. Not knowing."

He pressed the trigger. A muffled crash issued from the direction of the burn. Posie holstered the weapon, heading back to camp. "Just a little demonstration of our firepower. Let them know we can defend ourselves."

Deterrence, Clio thought. Twentieth-century foreign policy introduced on Niang. A great beginning.

The only fauna the crew had seen so far were flying insects with colorful, segmented bodies about the size of robins. In fact, Posie initially declared them birds, and grew annoyed as the crew insisted on calling them dragonflies.

One of these was now circling near Clio and settled on the perimeter wire. A wisp of smoke drifted past Clio's nostrils, the remainder of the dragonfly.

Clio thought about the gun in her duffel, and whether she would have to use it. Thinking about what it felt like to kill with a gun. It wasn't impersonal, like they said. You pulled the trigger and there was the bark of the gun, and the recoil, and the heat in the palm of your hand, and the carnage in front of you. Hard, metal violence. Not pretty and easy, like in the movies, where people fell over, clutching their sides and dying silently.

She thought about Russo drawing the long straw on that fatal mission, watching the rest of the crew die. Wondered if they died silently, drifting off to sleep, or fighting for their last breaths, gasping the vacant air. Russo had her reasons for hating the landing pod, for staying shipboard. Clio wondered if maybe one of those reasons was cowardice. By rights, Russo should have commanded the ground mission, not Teeg. And Clio should have stayed on *Starhawk*.

She wandered back toward crew tent to find her duffel. Teeg fell in step beside her. "Where's your weapon, Lieutenant?" he said.

Clio arched an eyebrow. Calling her lieutenant was odd. "Getting it."

"Stay armed. You're on mission now, not playing cards, waiting for Dive on *Starhawk*."

She looked over at him with her best drop-dead look.

"That's an order, Lieutenant."

Holy God, he was serious. "Yessir."

Teeg glared at her. "I've got eight people under my command here, Finn, and probably the most important ground mission in Biotime's history. I need everyone working on the team, playing their role, no questions asked. You understand?"

"Well, I got just one question, Teeg. What am I supposed to shoot? We don't know what might come out of those woods. Could be a hippo, and this is his feeding patch. Could be a delegate from the local chief. Who decides when to shoot?"

"That's two questions. Anyway, first, shoot anything that looks threatening. Second, if I'm not around to give the order to fire, use your judgment, but aim to wound, not kill.

Unless it's charging." He finished peevishly, squirming under Clio's contemptuous gaze.

"That's what I was doing, using my own judgment. What I usually do, you know." She started to peel off, toward the crew tent. Teeg grabbed her elbow.

"Wouldn't mind seeing you in my tent tonight, Clio." He smiled, which looked better on him than the frown it replaced. "Good for the commander's morale."

"I don't think so, Teeg. It's not good for mine." She pulled her arm away and disappeared into the crew tent.

Zee looked up as she stalked through the tent flap. "He bothering you?"

"No, we were just discussing camp morale."

"Because he's getting on everybody's nerves," Zee said. "We've only been on the ground three hours, and already he's so puffed up with himself. Told me to start patrolling the perimeter. Patrolling. Walk around the wires and watch for anything strange. The whole screaming planet is strange. It's blue, for one thing. And those bugs, those dragonflies. What if one lands on me?"

Clio clipped a holster to her belt, dropped the Harmin 317 into it, snapping the cuff over it. "Blow its brains out, I guess," she answered, sweeping her eyes toward his holster.

Zee made a long-suffering face. Then he brightened. "Maybe we could patrol together. Want to?"

Clio grabbed a khaki hat, one of those issued to protect them from the hot sun, and left the tent with Zee. She noticed Teeg watching them from the door flap of his command tent.

"I don't think he likes me," Zee said, conscious of Teeg staring at them. They passed Posie, who was removing a splinter from Estevan's hand in the shade side of the med tent. "And the Doc. He's Teeg's pal, Clio. Ran to tell Teeg that I wasn't wearing my gun. Next thing I know, I'm getting this lecture on camp security from fearless leader."

They walked the ring of wire, on the inside. "He still never talks about it?" Clio asked. "Hillis never talks about the radio transmission?"

"Hillis? No, he never talks about it."

Clio saw movement in the trees. Toward the top, near the overarching canopy, a blur of movement, a dip of a branch. If there was something, it wasn't showing itself.

"Hillis avoids me." A hint of bitterness crept in: "Sometimes it really hurts." And then, more matter-of-fact, he said, "I maybe brought out some feelings in him that he'd rather not know about."

My God, my God, Clio thought. Did Zee think that Hillis was a closet homosexual? That Hillis was as innocent as Zee himself was? She looked up at Zee, the brilliant physicist hopelessly contemplating the puzzle of personal relationships. She didn't like to think that Hillis had toyed with Zee to win his loyalty, to get him to work on the Future Ceiling problem, but there it was. He'd used Zee. And now he was through with him. Not a pleasant thought, that Hillis would use sex that way. That was more Teeg's style. Teeg, who lost a verbal sparring round with her a few minutes ago and immediately wanted to subdue her with sex. Wanted to get on top of the problem, that was Teeg's way. She put him in his place, no mistake.

One screw does not confer a season pass, Teeg.

That night Clio and Estevan shared the watch. Later, Zee and Posie would relieve them. Estevan walked clockwise, Clio counterclockwise around the perimeter, where the floodlights did a fairly good job of illumination except for the dark patches between the widely spaced lights. Estevan got spooked the first time they met on the perimeter, so he concocted a series of notes to whistle as they grew close to each other. After a dozen or so circuits, Estevan was convinced that the birds had picked up the code and were repeating it sometimes. If so, they had just taught the local birds the first bars of "The Star Spangled Banner." After that, they switched codes every other circuit.

The dragonflies were thicker at night. Attracted to the big floodlights, they swooped down on the giant lamps, in a constant game of touch and go. The wires took their toll, with the aroma of cremation drifting on the still night air.

•   •   •

Clio and Petya hid in Walter Reesley's basement for three weeks after the DSDE raid. The old man seemed bemused by their presence, shuffling down the stairs with food and magazines for them, sitting on a crate, watching them eat, rubbing his arms against the cold and muttering. When Clio talked about leaving, the old man would become agitated and wave his hands toward the outside and say it wasn't safe yet, but that they should wait, and he would find "passage" for them. One night he herded them into the back of his Chevy pickup, threw a plastic tarp over them, and drove them to a field where they met a woman with a van. She held Clio at arm's length and studied her face a long while, then patted her cheek, saying, "You're your mother, twenty years ago." She told Clio and Petya to get in the van and lie on the floor, then covered them with a blanket, and drove off. They never got a chance to say goodbye to Walter Reesley, because they didn't realize he wasn't coming along.

They lay in the back as the woman drove most of the night. Once she stopped and gave them sandwiches to eat. Her name was Lena, she said, a friend of their mother and Elsie. By that they knew they were in the hands of the underground.

"What happened to Mom?" Petya asked.

Lena chewed her mouthful of sandwich and looked at Petya for a long minute. "Quarry," she said. "We don't know which one, and don't you ever look." She pinned them with her gaze until they nodded understanding. "Don't ever look. You're underground now."

Several hours later, still on the road, Clio heard Lena talking on the car phone. She told them to stay covered, there was a blockade up ahead. A routine stop-and-search, but for them it was a disaster.

After a few minutes they heard Lena say, "I'm sorry kids, they're going to search us. They're waving me over to do a search. I'm just real sorry. We almost made it." And then the door slid open and the blanket was pulled off their faces, and a man shone a flashlight at them for what seemed a long time. Then he pulled the blanket back over them, and

Clio heard him telling Lena to drive on out. And Lena drove silently a couple miles and took a sharp turn off the road.

She yanked open the door and got them out of the van. She said the policeman had let them go, she didn't know why, but that they were in grave danger and he might change his mind if he looked them up on CrimeNet and found out who they really were, that they had murdered a DSDE agent. She told them to run into Granville, four miles north, and wait by the water tower. She would send someone for them, someone wearing a yellow bandanna tied around the right thigh. And she hugged them both in turn and shooed them into the woods, then drove off, laying rubber.

After that, the police cars came screaming by, hell-bent as they raced down the road after Lena. And then not long after, they come into the field with dogs, and Clio and Petya ran and ran, and finally Clio told Petya they should separate, that maybe the dogs would only catch one of them. She knew she could never run as fast as Petya; he still had a chance. But they ran for five or ten minutes before she could convince Petya, and he cried as he left her, and she said, "Meet me at the water tower." And then he smiled and sprinted off.

By dawn she was hiding in the long grasses under the Granville water tower. And by noon, a man showed up with a yellow bandanna tied around his thigh, and they waited together for several hours there at the water tower, but she never saw Petya again.

The man's name was Kevin Speery-Hall, and she became Antoinette, replacing his daughter, dead at twenty-one of the Sickness but never taken to the quarries to die.

Two years later, when Biotime came through Minneapolis on a big testing drive, on a lark she got tested for Dive tolerance, and they came back into the room with three or four people wearing business suits and talked to her about her plans for the future, and how would she like to learn to be a pilot. And Biotime asked a few perfunctory questions about her past, but in the end they didn't want to know, didn't care what her citizen status was, as long as she

*could Dive. She signed on the dotted line: Antoinette
Speery-Hall.*

Clio's first night on Niang was fitful, with the heat and
humidity a misery. She lay awake listening to the night
songs of the jungle—not lullabies, but the ticking of
mandibles, the shrieks of prey. She slept, finally, when a
light rain on the tent drowned out the alien forest.

In the morning, Clio emerged from the crew tent to find
the world shrouded in mist. A white fog rolled over the
camp in waves, like a sea of perfumed methane. Across the
clearing, the forest could barely be seen, its towering
perimeter trees wavering in the mist. Beneath her fatigues
Clio's undershirt, wet from night sweats, clung to her like
cold seaweed.

Zee approached her with two steaming cups. "Coffee,
my lady?"

She smiled. "Sir vander Zee. My prince."

His reply was cut short by a shout from one of the
tents. Posie emerged from the fog holding up a ten-meter
length of white toilet paper. No, not toilet paper—medical
gauze. "Someone trashed the med tent," he exclaimed,
looking at Clio. "Supplies are missing—place is a mess.
We've been invaded!"

Clio and Zee rushed to the open flap of the med tent
and peered inside. Med kits lay open and disemboweled.
Gauze bandages draped from cot to comm unit and back
again, but no serious damage. Outside, Posie was upbraid-
ing Hillis and Liu, last night's security detail, when Estevan
wandered into the center of the compound and announced
that his shoes were missing. That meant whatever had been
in the camp had been in the crew tent.

After that, everyone went armed. Speculated on the
invader. It had pranked them, done little actual damage.
Maybe it was harmless. Maybe it was an immature animal—with the adults another story.

As Posie and Teeg conferred in the commander's tent,
Estevan prepared camp breakfast in his stocking feet. The
cooking sausage tubes filled the tent with their delicious and

familiar aroma. When the crew gathered around the mess table, the talk centered on the night visitors.

Meng said, "Now at least we know the creatures wear size-eleven-and-a-half shoes and aren't picky about the fragrance." She peered maliciously at Estevan over her cup of green tea.

Estevan whipped egg powder into water. "Next time, Miss Chow Mein, they'll take your fucking hair-goo."

Teeg appeared in the tent door just as Estevan was dishing up.

"OK, folks, we got a serious problem here," he said. "Someone or something has pretty free access to the compound, despite the nerve wires and the patrols. I'm sending out a scouting party this morning to have a look-see. Botany says they're ready to collect a couple samples anyhow, so Hillis, you're on, and then Meng, Finn, and Posie as team leader."

Estevan's mouth dropped open as he stood there holding the pan of eggs. "You're sending Clio? Why do we need to send her? She's our ticket home."

Hillis spoke through a mouthful of scrambled eggs. "That's right, probably you should send Zee. Clio can stay on security at camp here."

Teeg turned calmly to face Hillis. "There's something you all should probably understand before we go any further. We're not making group decisions here. I'm commanding this mission, and I'm making the decisions, like who's on the scouting party. Clio's assigned to security on this mission, and Clio's going on the scouting party. Any more questions?" Posie had come in the tent door behind Teeg, with a Dharhai-8 assault rifle slung over his shoulder.

The crew stared at Posie.

Clio raised her hand, schoolgirl style. "With the commander's permission, I'd like to suggest we bring Estevan into the decision here. He's our anthropologist. Looks like we might have some intelligent life-forms to deal with, and that's why Estevan's on this mission, right?"

Teeg's face hardened. Then he smiled over at Estevan. "You got anything intelligent to say about the invaders,

Estevan?" Estevan began to say something, but Teeg cut him off. "Because if you do, I'd be glad to hear from you in my tent. That's one thing I want you all to remember. I'm always available to hear what you have to say, so I hope you'll share your thoughts with me. At the proper time. Right now, eat up, party will head out in twenty minutes." He slapped the tent flap back, and exited.

Estevan slammed the pan down on the stove. "Hail, Caesar."

Meng pushed her plate of untouched food away. "Somebody has to be in charge, don't they? Me, I'd just as soon have it be someone who's still got their shoes."

Everyone was now looking at Shannon, to see whose side she was on. "Well, he *is* head of the ground mission," she said. "If we have to vote on everything, we'll never get anything done. Besides, Clio's no better than the rest of us." She studiously avoided Clio's eyes. "We're all equal here, and I'm not doing all the grunt work, that's for sure." Shannon was the most junior of the crew, on her first mission.

Clio stared at her plate. She didn't mind the scouting party, but she was starting to think Teeg was more than an asshole. He was a dangerous asshole.

They had been pushing through the forest for almost an hour. The mists had fled under the scouring sun and Clio was hot, but even after she stripped down to a halter top, the trail pack clung to her sweaty back, making her itchy and uncomfortable. The sticky sweet smell of the flora was starting to make her stomach queasy. "Smells like a freeping candy store," she said to Hillis.

"The trees secrete it," Hillis replied. He scraped a small spatula against the flat, nearly translucent trunk of one of the tube trees, as the crew had come to call the smooth stalklike growths. "It's like a resin."

Meng brought out a plastic capsule to hold the resin, and stuffed it into the sample case.

They were in a murky, tented world. The undergrowth formed a barrier on the perimeter of the jungle, but once inside they proceeded quickly, impeded only by the web of vines forming the ropy, uneven floor.

Hillis and Meng were most interested in the trees, and hovered a long while over a recently fallen specimen, with a crown of fleshy leaves stacked thickly upon each other. The seeds were clustered in the lowest layer of leaves, some of them already starting to sprout from the juicy meat of the carrier leaves.

As he went, Hillis described the biota, speaking just loud enough for the patch recorder on his collar to pick up and record. He talked nonstop, and Meng, dutiful assistant, hung on his every word, occasionally adding a comment, and tended to the samples with expert, deft hands.

Clio watched them more than she watched for intruders. This was what Space Recon was all about, she thought. This was the heart of it, this jungle, the sample packs, the science. And Hillis was born for it, totally engrossed, as turned-on as a ten-year-old in a baseball-card factory.

Hillis unstoppered his water flask and drank deeply, then made his way over to Clio to sit next to her on a fallen tree trunk. "I've got a feeling about this place, Clio." He looked at her, his blue eyes verging on turquoise in the steeped jungle sunlight. "This is the real sister planet, the one Earth could have been, without people. It's fecund. Gloriously fecund. It's beyond Eden. The crew is calling it Eden, but it's not. Eden was supposedly created for humans, but this place . . ." He looked around, words petering out. "This place was created for plant life. For the Green."

"For the Turquoise, anyway," Clio said gently. He was so happy, and he was so handsome when he was happy.

A woman's scream. Meng. They jumped up. Meng was pointing into the depths. She had drawn her gun, was pointing it at the jungle.

Posie got to her first. "What is it?"

"Jesus God, a spider! It was this big," she said, throwing her arms apart, almost hitting Clio in the face as she rushed up.

Posie sighted the Dharhai and fired in the general direction Meng was pointing. The report of the gun was swallowed by the thick air.

"Good for you Doc, you got a palm tree, broadside," Clio said. She peered into the woods, but saw nothing.

Meng was shrill with excitement. "It was heading for us, along the ground, real fast. It was dark and hairy, an ugly bastard! And when I screamed, it veered into the woods, over that way."

"Big teeth? Drooling?" Clio asked. Meng glared at her in answer, while Posie swung the barrel of the Dharhai around wildly, expecting to see spiders on every side.

"Christ, Meng," Clio continued, "that creature might have been the president, coming to pay a visit. You made a fine impression."

Meng was still pointing her gun into the jungle. "I don't like spiders," she said, her voice back to its normal soft tone.

"Pack up," Posie said. "We're sitting ducks unless we're on the move."

Hillis shouldered his pack. "Great. A military mind to the rescue."

Posie ignored him. "Keep your weapons drawn. I'll take point; Hillis, you bring up the rear."

"I thought I was on security, Doc," Clio said. "I can take up the rear."

Posie swung around, and the rifle swung with him. "You'll do what you're told, Finn. I said Hillis to the rear. We could be under attack any minute, and I want the women in the middle in case they try to pick us off."

Clio stared at him in open disbelief. She looked over at Meng, who shrugged, pulled on her pack, and got in behind Posie. Clio felt Hillis' hand on her shoulder, warning her against the outburst she was getting ready to hurl at Posie. She turned to Hillis in outrage, saw that he was calmer than she wished he were. "Jesus, Hill," she began.

"Skip it," Hillis said. He urged her to fall in behind Meng and Posie, who had started out.

"The guy is insulting as hell. What is this women and children in the life rafts bullshit?"

"What did you expect? Posie's a churchie kind of guy. The jungle's what he's always thought society was. Now he's got a real jungle, and it's bringing out the worst in him. Forget it."

"Easy for you to say, Tarzan, bringing up the rear."

"Shut up, Clio, and watch for tarantulas."

For Clio the worst part of staying alert for danger was the unceasing chittering and birdcalls of the jungle. She couldn't depend on her ears to detect movement, so she kept her eyes moving, scanning. She saw shadows, nothing more. High above, in the ceiling canopy, the tree crowns seemed to sway now and then, as though giants roamed there, in that rooftop highway. If the spiders existed—and Clio considered it a very good chance that they existed only in Meng's superheated imagination—then they prowled the tops of the trees, not these murky depths.

Toward noon, Posie called a meal break in a large clearing with shallow hills of bare ground. They had to fight their way into the clearing because of the resurgence of undergrowth that flourished in the sunny perimeter of the jungle mass.

Meng ate with her gun on her knee, and her shoes off, sunning her legs. Her toenails were painted bright red. Clio stared at Meng's perfect feet: tawny and lithe, with a high arch. Her red painted nails gleamed in a lusty statement at odds with her Recon uniform. Posie glanced at the feet, nervously. As if fleeing them, he stomped off across the clearing to examine one of the mounds.

"There's snakes in there," Meng said, nodding her head back the way they'd come. "Big ones." She smiled, showing startlingly white teeth. Meng seldom smiled, and when she did, it was never in humor. Meng's humor was dry, ironic, and devastating, as Estevan usually found out when he tried to trade verbal gibes with her.

Clio had seen the snakes, too. Never a whole snake, just glimpses of moving backsides.

Posie called them from the other side of the clearing. Clio and Hillis headed over to him while Meng laced her shoes.

Posie gestured at the mound. "Termite hill," he said.

They looked closer and saw small, segmented insects carrying wood fragments into thousands of portals in the ground.

"That could account for the heightened methane levels on Niang," Hillis said.

"Jungle's probably loaded with termites, or the Niang equivalent," Posie said. "This place looks more familiar all the time. Spiders, snakes, termites, birds. Hard to believe it's not home." He looked at Hillis and shrugged. "Maybe it is Eden."

"No, it's not Eden," Hillis said.

"Well, maybe it could be, with a little work." Posie was looking over at Meng, still bent over her bootlaces.

Clio walked into the brush to relieve herself. Then she pushed through to the jungle tent, and stood for a moment, watching. Crew's voices were shut off here, replaced by the echoing crush of jungle sounds, close and far away into the endless blue-green depths. She was alone. Alone in a way that her crew-centered life seldom allowed. She breathed in, releasing the tension of the three-hour hike with Posie and Meng. A breeze stirred the tops of the trees, dipping the branches, as though Niang breathed too.

A thick vine was spiraled tightly around the tube tree in front of her. Then it moved, became a snake, turquoise and pitted with dark spots, uncoiling meter after meter. Mesmerized, Clio watched it display its fabulous length. After many long moments the splayed end of the creature came into view, completed its downward coil, and disappeared into the jungle floor.

Clio turned back, found Meng standing quietly behind her.

"Did you see that creature?" Clio asked.

"Yes. It was a big one." Meng started to move past Clio.

"Guess you're not interested in animals, huh Meng? Just plants and the botanical ooze?" Clio felt an urge to goad Meng, push her a little to see what came out.

Meng turned. "That's right. Same as Hillis. Plants and

botanical ooze." Her mouth stretched into a sweet smile. "Posie says to fan out. Look for water." She moved away, stepping carefully into the deep humus of the jungle floor.

"Water?" Clio called after her. "We don't need water."

"Posie says look for a stream," Meng said, her voice growing muffled.

"Why?"

Meng's voice was as soft as a whisper in the trees: "In case we need to move camp."

"But we brought all our water on board the lander," Clio said helplessly. She stood thinking hard for a moment, watching Meng disappear into the blue shadows.

When Clio returned to the clearing, Posie was sitting on a rock writing in his notebook. He glanced up at her.

"Next time let someone know where you're going, Finn," Posie said.

"Shall I raise my hand?"

"Just let somebody know, that's all."

"Why do we need water?" Clio asked. "We brought our water."

Posie kept scribbling. "Because we might need more, you never know."

"There a problem with our water supply?"

Posie closed his notebook. "Maybe I like the looks of this campsite better than the one we've got. The clearing is bigger, for one thing. That makes it easier to see anything coming."

"That's nuts. We're leaving in a few days. Not worth it."

Posie stared at her. "Your commanding officers will be the judge of that."

Clio stared back. "Before we move camp, I say we consult with Russo."

"Russo's a long way away."

Hillis came up to them. "We found a stream just over there," he said, waving in the direction he'd searched. "Hack away the vines, you can get down to the edge fairly easy."

The others trickled in, shouldered their packs.

As they headed out, Clio said to Hillis, "Why do we need water, Hill? And why should we move camp?"

"I don't know. In case of emergency, I guess."

They walked in silence for a while.

"Hill, I don't like the way this mission's going. I don't have a good feeling about it. Teeg has completely cut Estevan out of research. And he and Posie are going control-happy."

Hillis shrugged. "I'll grant you Teeg's acting like a generalissimo, but what did you expect from him?"

"Goddamn it, you keep saying 'What do you expect?' You're so cynical about everybody, nothing they do matters or surprises you."

"Clio. There's too much at stake here to worry about the small stuff. Niang's a miracle, Clio. High-viable. I've never seen anything like it. We've got to get through this. Tolerate the assholes long enough to bring this haul back, because this is the big one, you know that? It's the brave new jungle. It tolerates high ultraviolet, warmer temperatures, methane levels, all the indicators. It'll take to Earth like a baby to the breast."

"How do you know? Maybe it'll die, just like the Leery plants did." The moment she said it, she hated herself. Why not give him his hope?

She needn't have worried. Hillis was oblivious. "No Clio," he said, "I don't think so. This flora is too . . . pushy, too lush." He looked over at Clio, pleading. "It's like a gift, Clio. Niang's a gift to us from the universe. A last chance to get it right, to replenish the green, reseed the Earth. Start again." He grabbed her hand. "Nothing else matters, don't you see?"

Clio felt that old Hillis-feeling in her chest, like a wave trying to pass through her. At moments like this she could almost let it out, let it go. "Yeah, baby. I see." He was like a blind man. He didn't see her anymore, not even when he looked at her. She patted his face. "I see."

"No talking," Posie said from on point.

CHAPTER 8

❧

The next morning dawned muted and grey, the sky saturated with the fruit-juice smell of waiting Niang rain. Clio managed a shower in the solar shower tent. As soon as she dried off she was covered with sticky film once again.

The sky lowered and a candy-smelling mist descended.

Clio strolled over to the med tent. Liu occupied one of the cots.

"You OK?" Clio asked him, trying to be nice.

A garbled voice answered her, as Liu tried to speak with his finger stuck in his mouth.

Posie was on the comm set, talking to Russo over a flurry of static. Russo was left nursing Shaw, and Posie checked in with her daily on the only communication rig in camp.

"Keep quiet," Posie said to them, straining to hear the captain.

Clio sat next to Liu, whispered, "Got something wrong with your mouth?"

"Braces," Liu said. "My braces sprang a break. Waiting for Doc to look at it."

Clio peered into Liu's mouth, as he opened for her to look. "Yeah, there's a jagged wire back there. Where's a pair of pliers when you need them?" She smiled at him, and he grimaced. Not funny. Liu didn't like her. He was a foot shorter than she was. Could account for it: men were funny about things like that, Clio thought.

Posie took his headphones off. Looked over at Clio with a frown.

"How's Shaw doing?" Clio asked.

"As well as can be expected." Posie acted busy over the comm unit.

"Poor Shaw. You think he'll be OK?"

"Depends on the kind of care Russo gives him. She's not very handy about these things."

"Well, it's out of her element, that's for sure." Clio treaded carefully, trying to defer to Posie, warm him up a little.

Posie looked at her pointedly. "You in here for medical attention?"

"No. Feel fine. Just wondering about Shaw." Posie continued to stare. "Guess I'll leave. Glad you're keeping a watch on Shaw."

Posie sniffed.

A garbled noise came from the cot, and Posie pushed himself out of his chair, crossed over to Liu. Clio left the tent, thinking about the comm unit, thinking about a chat with Russo. But Posie was usually in med tent. No chance at the unit. Besides, what could she say to Russo? These guys are getting on my nerves?

A clanging sound from the door of the mess tent. Estevan was banging on a pot, announcing breakfast. He had wrapped his feet in canvas secured with twine, making his feet appear enormous.

Meng emerged out of the botany tent. "Well, well," she called back to the recesses of the tent, "it's Daisy Duck. Better come on, Daisy gets peeved if we're late for meals."

Clio was on first watch that night, along with Teeg. They patrolled in opposite directions along the perimeter wire at first. Toward the end of their watch, Teeg fell in step beside her. She wondered if she would be paired with Zee or Estevan anymore. Somehow, she knew her watch partners would be Teeg or Posie from now on. Paranoid, she thought. *It's starting to get to me, too.*

The warm night air was saturated with the songs of the forest. From its turquoise depths, the Niang birds were cranking up the volume, joined by insects and creatures yet unseen. If the tarantulas could sing, they might lead the chorus, or they might be minor players among the Niang cast, the pets of giants who roamed the braided canopy.

Teeg was chatting amiably, in a good mood. She wondered how long it'd take him to bring up sex.

"I still think about that night on station, Clio."

As if on cue.

They walked in silence for a few moments. "We waited so long to be together. Seemed like it was forever. You know, waiting for you."

"Teeg," she began, ready to put a stop to this line of thought.

"No, I mean it," he said, cutting her off. "It seemed like forever. We'd been keeping our distance, sparring like we always do, wanting to be together . . . and then you came to me, like you needed me, really needed me. Man, I never saw anybody so needy. And it was magic, like I knew it would be."

Clio drew away as he put his arm around her. "Look, Teeg. I don't know why I looked you up that night. But it was a mistake for me. You were good to me, but I can't feel anything for you. I'm sorry. It was my fault for starting something, and I'm really sorry for that. But it's over now."

Teeg's face slumped into a frown. "You don't mean that."

"Yes, I mean it. Believe it."

"What about the love letters?"

Clio's stomach tightened. "What love letters?"

"That you write me."

"You think I write you *love letters*?" Her annoyance was rapidly trickling away, to be replaced by a shallow, acid sea. Jesus God.

"The things that you've said to me, Clio. That I'll never forget."

This was crazy; he was delusional. Love letters, for chrissakes? He was fixated on her, and getting worse by the minute. "You need help, Teeg. I've never written you a love letter and I never will. You're sick, you know that?"

He grabbed her swiftly, yanked her close to him. "I know how you feel, Clio. I've always known." He cupped the back of her head and brought her mouth to his, holding her in a grip of iron muscle, parting her clenched teeth with his tongue, covering her face with saliva, moving his other hand down to her buttocks, pressing her into him. He was ox-strong. Clio was a strong woman, but, held as she was, her fighting had as much an effect as a bird fluttering in his hand. It excited him. She forced her knee up to his groin, but he deflected it with his thigh. Grabbing the hair on the back of her head, he pulled her back far enough to slap her face harshly.

Trying a different tactic, Clio fell limp. A mistake. He released his grip only slightly as he prepared to lower himself on top of her, still holding the back of her waist, easing her down to the ground. "I want you, baby," he said. "Tell me you love me."

Clio hung limp, timing her next move. As he released his grip on her hair, she jerked her hip to the side, rolling over and into a crouch, her hand flipping the holster cuff, digging for the Harmin. He swung out his fist, sending her into the dirt as she avoided the punch. He came lunging to his feet, and closed the gap between them. She pointed the gun at his forehead, inches away.

Cocked the hammer.

"I'm going to splatter your brains all over your shirt, Teeg."

She was just informing him, not threatening him. She wanted to kill him.

Teeg recoiled. "Jesus, Clio. Jesus Godalmighty. Don't freep out, point that thing away from me. We're just having a tussle, maybe I got a little excited. Take it easy, OK?" He was still backing up, in a crouch, hand up in front of his face, fending her off.

Clio kept aiming the Harmin. Panting hard. Watching for him to rush her. "Keep your hands over your head. Get on your knees."

Teeg obeyed, but slower now. "Jesus, Clio. You're overheated, lady. Take it easy."

She stood up. Starting to shake. She had a tiger at bay. What would happen when she let him go? Teeg was sick.

Dangerously sick. But she had to play a game with him, or he would have his revenge.

"You're trying to take advantage of me," she whined. "You're commanding the mission, so you think you can have sex on call. Just when I've fought with Hillis, and feel lousy. I trusted you, and you tried to force yourself on me."

Teeg was standing up now. "No, it's not like that Clio. Maybe I was a little rough. I thought you liked that, liked me to be strong with you." Then, in a different tone of voice, "Put the gun away, Clio."

She lowered it a little.

"Put the gun away, and I'll forget it happened. Forget that you drew down on your commanding officer. You were pushed. I admit that. But do it now, before I get mad."

Clio heard the crunch of boots on ground. She holstered the gun.

"Change of the guard," Zee announced cheerfully, from a distance.

Zee walked closer, stopped, eyeing them.

Teeg was gazing intently at Clio, and she, back.

"Carry on," Teeg said to Zee. Then he broke the gaze, and walked off into the shadows toward camp.

Zee hurried over to Clio, pushed the hair away from her face, looking at the bruise. "He hit you, the bastard hit you, didn't he?"

"Where's Posie?"

"Haven't seen him yet. You OK? If he hit you, we're going to report him, aren't we? Because he can't hit you."

"We could report him if we could get to the comm unit in the med tent. If we could get Russo to believe us. Those are pretty big ifs."

Zee nodded. "She might not believe us."

"Right. She might not."

"We can't just let this go by. Teeg hit you."

"Zee. It doesn't matter. We're not in New Jersey now. All the rules have changed, there really aren't any rules anymore. So don't be outraged, just be careful."

He grinned at her. "Me, be careful? Go get some ice on that bruise."

As Clio left the perimeter she met Posie coming on watch.

"Doc," she said, nodding to him as she passed.

He was already past her when he said, "Next time stay on watch until you're relieved."

Clio bit her tongue, headed for the med tent. Found the chemical ice packets, plastered one on the side of her face, which now felt like an overheated tomato. Eyed the comm unit, thinking of Russo. Let it go. She made it to her cot and took off her boots. Slipping her gun under her pillow, she turned on her side, resting against the ice pack, her brain swimming in choppy seas, fending off visions of Teeg, Teeg saying, *What about the love letters?*

After a long while, still wide awake, she got up and laced on her boots. Hillis, Estevan, Meng, and Shannon were asleep. She crept out of crew tent and waited in the heavy night air, listening. Nothing but the jungle. She made her way to the med tent, slipped in, and sat at the comm unit, hands resting on the earphones. Picked them up, reached for the toggle to send. A scape of gravel outside. Clio flew out of the chair and turned to the supply cabinet.

Teeg walked in. She rummaged for a cold pack, hands shaking hard. Found one. He was still watching her.

"What're you doing here?" he asked, his mood dark and blustery.

"Looking for drugs," she said, snapping open the pack.

"Not funny, Clio."

"Sure it is." She pressed the ice against her face.

"That kind of talk can get you in trouble."

"Get me a beating?"

"I didn't hit you that hard."

She sat down on the cot to keep her legs from trembling. Teeg was acting harsh and distant. She had to admit it was better than Teeg the lovesick suitor.

"Look. I'm sorry," he said.

"Sorry's not good enough, Teeg."

He stood silent for a moment. "Maybe it'll have to be."

Her eyes snapped up to look at him, standing in the tent door, the perimeter lights glaring behind him.

"Maybe we're gonna make our own rules from now on," he said.

"Meaning?"

"Meaning, just like I said. Our own rules. We're a long way from Vanda, Clio. Maybe I like it here. I was hoping you liked it too."

"What are you talking about, Teeg?"

"You ever think about staying?"

"On Niang?" Clio's heart was sinking like an elevator with the cables cut. "No, I never did."

"Maybe you should start."

"Jesus, Teeg. You gotta be kidding. Get a grip. Nobody wants to give up Earth, give up home."

"Maybe you haven't been paying attention, Miss Red. Posie does. Liu and Meng too. We've talked."

Clio looked at him, scared for the first time. "You're crazy. Think they wouldn't come after us?"

"Think they'd find us?"

Then, from a distance, shouts and then gunfire. Teeg bolted through the tent flap, Clio behind him. She ran for her gun in the crew tent.

Hillis was just emerging from the crew tent, zipping up his pants. More gunfire from the perimeter.

Liu came by on a dead run, shouting, "Rally at the lander! They'll go for the lander!" He spied Clio. "Something's on the perimeter, come on!" And he was gone.

Automatic weapons fire stuttered as Clio raced toward the sound, nearly colliding with Shannon, who was headed in the opposite direction toward *Babyhawk*. "We're supposed to guard the lander," she shouted, waving Clio to join her. Clio ignored her, noting that the gunfire had stopped for the moment. The perimeter lights were still functioning.

Up ahead she saw Teeg and Posie huddled together and Meng close by, saying, "Holy shit, you got one. Holy shit."

Meng grabbed Clio by the arm as she went by. "Don't look. It's an ugly son of a bitch."

Clio shook loose, peered over Posie's shoulder, saw a

mass of furry legs and a round body the size of a volley ball. Whatever it was, it was dead.

Teeg nudged the creature with his boot, flipping it over. A set of capable teeth ringed a mouth in the center of the body. Its six legs were jointed once, ending in round pads like feet. Its black hair was close and shiny, like a jaguar's.

"At least eight of them," Posie was saying. "They came from all sides, at once. I lay down a curtain of fire, atomized three, at least, maybe four. Then this one leaped the wire and was coming for me, and Zee was right behind it, so I had to use my pistol, or I would have blown Zee away. One round put the spider down. Must have been a lucky shot."

Estevan was crouching by the remains, probing it with a stick. "Doesn't look like an insect to me," he said.

Teeg noticed Clio. "You and Zee keep a look out. This could be a diversion. Estevan, you and Meng take the Dharhai and post yourselves at the lander. Where the hell is Hillis?"

As Clio and Zee moved off from the group she asked, "What happened, what did you see?"

Zee's voice was high-pitched, spring-loaded. "I didn't really see anything. I heard the Dharhai erupt, and came running in time to see Posie screaming at this huge bug that was bounding over the perimeter wire. Posie shouted at me to duck, and I heard a pistol shot so loud I thought I'd been hit. Then Posie swings back to the perimeter and starts blasting away. To tell you the truth, I was most afraid of a stray round from Posie, he was swinging that gun from side to side like a crazy man, laying down fire at the thin air."

They stared across the clearing toward the brush, watching for movement. The chittering of the forest continued unabated. At a sound behind them, Zee swung around with a short gasp.

Meng stood there, looking at Clio. In her soft, lilting voice she said, "I told you there were spiders."

She turned and walked back toward the center of camp. Zee stared after her. "She gives me the spooks."

They walked in silence for a time. Then Clio took a detour off her perimeter walk to check on Hillis.

He was standing in the door of the botany tent, holding the tent flap open, staring out toward the jungle edge. He was just a black silhouette against the light from the tent, but his lean form was unmistakable. "All clear?" he asked.

"Yeah. Posie mowed down a visit from the spiders. They were unarmed, but he figured it was an invasion."

Hillis had already turned into the tent, busy with some boxes.

She followed him in. "Looks like you were packing."

"No need to, now." He began pulling sample packs and specimens out of a box. "I could have saved at least some of these. If it comes to evacuation, we've got to save what we can."

"It doesn't look like much."

Hillis looked up at her with a half smile. "Doesn't have to be much. Seeds, mostly. We take the whole plant if we can, to see how it fares, but what we really need to preserve are the seeds."

"They got one of the spiders. To dissect."

"What I'm really hoping for is to transplant a few saplings from the tube trees. But I've got the seeds in any case."

"They might be intelligent."

Hillis turned to face her, cocking his head. "The trees?"

Clio grinned. "No, the spiders."

"Sorry. Guess I'm preoccupied."

"Yeah, you're preoccupied."

"Pretty bad, huh?" He leaned against the lab table, arms folded. The harsh lantern light made his face gaunt.

Clio looked at him, started to talk, stopped. She had nothing to say to him. Teeg had assaulted her, was planning a mutiny, the camp just got its first native visitors. And she had nothing to say. She faced him, empty. She tried to call up the usual knot in her stomach, the rush of pleasure when she looked at him, the keen image of Hillis as the rebel, the cast-out, the ecowarrior. But now he seemed none of those things. Only tired, strung-out Hillis, leaning against his boxes. They'd had all the conversations they would ever have, all the relationship they would ever have. Maybe all the relationship she ever wanted, for that matter. Pick the ones that don't care, so you don't have to care. Pick the ones that don't listen, so you don't have to tell them anything, don't have to tell them how you feel.

Hillis, we could all die, here, on Niang, she wanted to say. Hillis, I could have loved you. Did love you in my own way. Why couldn't you love me?

"Guess I'll try to get some sleep," she said. Turned to go.

"Clio."

She turned back, weary.

"Clio. If something happens, make sure you protect yourself. Get yourself on that lander, no matter what. You're the Dive pilot, you're the one that'll get us home." He waved at the boxes. "Don't worry about this stuff. It's extra. I've already got samples stowed in the lander. They'll be enough, if we have to leave in a hurry, which I hope to God we won't." He put his hands on her shoulder, tenderly. "Just be careful."

"Right. That's me, careful."

Hillis' eyes narrowed. "I'm counting on you, Clio."

She nodded. No words left.

"Just get us home, baby."

CHAPTER 9

Posie came out of the med tent, pulling off his surgical gloves. "It's a mammal," he announced. The crew had been gathered there most of the morning, speculating on the carcass and what it meant for the mission.

"Probably arboreal. The legs are incredibly muscular, which accounts for the bounding movements we observed."

"Hell, we didn't see a thing, Doc. You were the only one that saw the invasion." Estevan was sulking for not being allowed to watch the dissection.

"What does it eat?" Meng asked.

Posie sniffed. "It's an herbivore."

"Mother of God," Estevan said, "then its some kind of monkey-like creature. You killed a bunch of monkeys."

Scattered laughter at this. Posie whirled on Estevan. "This one charged me. They have to learn they can't overrun the camp, breaking the perimeter defenses and stealing equipment. I had to kill it."

Estevan glared at him. "Maybe this was their way of sending a welcoming gesture, man. Maybe we could have made a gesture to them, when we first knew they'd paid us a visit. If they wanted to kill us, they could have done it that first night, you know? Maybe they came openly across that field right at you because they figured you had great night vision and could see them coming, and when you didn't shoot at first, they figured they were welcome."

"Right," Posie spat, "and maybe this one was trying to jump up and kiss me hello. If this is your anthropological contribution, maybe you'd better stick to making tacos."

Estevan lunged forward, but Clio restrained him. Posie recoiled, backing up into the tent door.

Meng broke in cheerfully: "Well, the important thing is that the tarantulas are harmless. Maybe we can all relax a little now."

"Monkeys," Clio said, releasing her grip on Estevan.

Teeg and the scouting party were gathering in the center of the compound, and all eyes moved in that direction. Teeg had Shannon, Liu, and Zee decked out with armament. He carried the Dharhai and a backpack comm unit.

"Next thing we know, he'll be calling in air strikes," Clio muttered to Estevan.

Teeg's party headed their way. Above the crisscrossed ammo straps on his chest, Zee's face looked forlorn.

Meng piped up, "They're monkeys, Commander. Herbivores."

Hillis approached the group from the direction of botany tent, his face anxious. "Commander," he said to Teeg, "I hope you won't need Shannon now. That's a pretty big scouting party, and the threat seems to be easing off. I need Shannon here. Sir."

Shannon brightened at that, looking hopefully at Teeg.

Teeg sighed with elaborate patience. "I won't be needing your advice, Lieutenant. But if I ever do, I'll be sure to let you know. Crew, we are headed out. Glad to hear the . . . monkeys are harmless, so you can all get on with your work and keep your minds on your jobs." He patted the comm unit on his back. "I'll stay in touch with the major, here," he said, indicating Posie. "Anything happens, he'll call an alert, and I expect you all to fall into a defensive posture. Otherwise, expect us toward the end of the day." He surveyed his three recruits. "We're going to take us a little hike."

"Just be careful," Clio said. "We can't afford to lose anybody." She looked up at him with a hint of worry sketched on her face.

Teeg's eyes snapped over at her. "We're not going to lose anybody. We're all in this together. From now on."

The party headed out, ducking under the perimeter

wire, as Meng blanked it for an instant from the controls in med tent.

Hillis looked at Posie. "Did he say 'major'?"

"Teeg will be colonel from now on." Posie stared them all down. "Until the crisis passes."

Hillis turned a stupefied look on Posie. "What crisis?"

Clio elbowed Hillis, glaring at him. Turning to Posie, she said, "I don't think Hill understands what we've been going through, sir. He's been holed up there in botany too long."

Posie held her gaze, then nodded, disappearing back into med tent. Estevan stared at the ground.

Clio shrugged her shoulders. "I suggest we all get back to work. Like the colonel said."

As the group dissipated, Estevan kept staring at his feet. "Mary, Mother of God. Mother of God."

Clio hissed at him, "Snap out of it! Don't you freep out on me, too. Listen up. It's worse than you know. Teeg's thinking of staying on Niang. He doesn't want to go home."

Estevan looked up at her, his eyes black and deep. "I'm ready to put his ass in stir, good and ready, you know? We don't need to contact Russo, don't need to get her permission, man. That won't mean null to Teeg, long as he has the Dharhai. I say, let's get Posie and have a little surprise for Teeg when he gets back."

"That's fine if we can catch Posie off guard, but the man is armed and jumpy as hell. If we expose ourselves and fail, then we don't get another chance. And we don't know where Shannon and Liu stand on this. If it's Teeg, Posie, and Meng so far, against all the rest of us, then we might have a chance. Or else we need the Dharhai." She locked her eyes onto Estevan's. "That'd tip the balance."

"Where does Hillis stand?" Estevan looked suspiciously at the botany tent.

"He's with us. Whatever gets the mission back safely. That's what he wants."

"I'll get the Dharhai. Leave it to me." Estevan's words came out slowly, stabbing the silence between them.

"Then tonight," Clio said. "I'll take care of Posie. You take on Teeg. After dinner. Soon as it's dark."

He started to move off, turned. "How far do we go?"

Clio had been asking herself that for days. "I don't know. Do what you have to do. But remember, we have to answer for our actions when we get back to Vanda."

"Vanda," Estevan said. "That's a long ways away, man."

No kidding.

Clio lay on her cot in the empty crew tent, hoping for sleep. She was desperately tired, but the nervous roll of her stomach kept her eyes wide open. They would have to face a hearing; it would be one story pitted against the next. She and Zee and Estevan and Hillis. Four against five. Four grunts against five others, including the senior officers. And she would be seen as the ringleader. She could go down this time. Go down real bad. Whoever was covering for her at Biotime, if it was the Biotime top brass themselves, could drop her. One mess too many, even if it is a Dive pilot.

Can't have many more Dives left anyhow. Dump her.

Depending on how big a mess Niang turned out to be. If someone got killed, for instance, there could be probes into crew's background. Questions about Antoinette Speery-Hall, alias Clio Finn, alias that long-ago name that linked her with the underground, with the murdered DSDE agent, with Mom and Elsie. Clio allowed herself to fantasize that she would be sent to the same quarry. She would see them again. They might keep families together. Yes, they would keep her with Mom and Elsie. She would be home again. No need to run.

Home again.

Mother had planned everything down to the last detail. The window, the closet, the day pack. The escape.

Every once in a while they'd have a drill. "Fire drill!" Mother would shout suddenly, in the middle of dinner as she passed the sweet potatoes; it could happen anytime. And then she and Petya would dash upstairs to the room with the secret closet. "Come on, Elsie!" Petya would shout.

Elsie would laugh and hold her ground. "I can't fit through that window anyhow," she'd say, snapping the black ten on the red jack, her solitaire hand played out before her, evidence of her power over games of chance.

Petya usually won the race, and would be the first through the loose panel in the back of the walk-in closet, and into the closet on the other side, where an unused bedroom would never miss its closet, drywalled over and painted. And then through the window with the broken sash, the heavy window poised over their heads like a guillotine.

It was all a game to Petya, and even to Clio, those drills played out in the stark North Dakota nights, when losing the race to the window meant you did the dishes by yourself for a couple of days. When, straddling the window-sill for a moment, and gazing into the thick black ether, you knew with certainty how flying is only a matter of believing, and for an instant you felt your arms tremble in readiness.

But toward the last, the drills got more serious. Mother grew jittery, frowning at everything, and Elsie got quiet. Clio would work on her high-school themes at the kitchen table, with Elsie across from her, drinking coffee, smoking and advising. Mother would do the bills at the desk in the corner, swearing like a farmer, and Petya would be at his repairs. Clocks, lamps, hair driers, even cameras and microwaves.

One evening she was writing on the assigned topic of "Why I'm Grateful for Church and Country." Clio had trouble with writing themes. She was trying to say how she was thankful that in America, if you were caught speeding, they didn't shoot you like in Guatemala.

"What's the speed limit in Guatemala?"

"Whatever the secret police are doing, plus ten," Elsie answered.

Mother frowned at Elsie's sarcasm. She put down her ledger book. "What's the subject of your theme?"

When Clio told her, Mother exchanged glances with

Elsie. Elsie raised an eyebrow, was all. Mother sighed, through her nose, like she was too weary to open her mouth.

"Give me the damn notebook," Elsie blurted out. She reached for Clio's theme book, grinding her cigarette out with a vengeance. Clio leapt up to sharpen her pencil, handing it over to Elsie before the moment passed.

Elsie looked her in the eye. "We're gonna write you a humdinger." For a long time Mom watched Elsie perform this act of cheating. There was no sound in the kitchen except the scratch of Elsie's pencil and Petya's quiet tinkering. Mother's face was perfectly blank. Spooky in a way. She, of so many scruples. It was as if her conflicting emotions had just canceled each other out.

Clio was in the living room with Petya, watching TV, when Mother went upstairs to bed. "Be sure to turn the lights out," she said, though the only light was the pale strobing of the TV screen.

That night, past one o'clock, Clio heard Elsie come up the stairs, so slowly the stairs seemed to last forever. Clio fell asleep before Elsie got to the top.

The scouting party returned at dusk. Clio had just made another pass by the med tent, eyeing the comm unit and hoping for fifteen minutes alone with it, when she spied the group emerging from the forest edge.

Teeg and Shannon were in the lead. As they crossed the field, Clio saw that Zee and Liu were carrying something strapped to a pole, either end of which was supported on their shoulders.

At a shout from Estevan, on watch, the crew emerged from tents and rushed over to the perimeter wire to watch them approach. The body of a four-legged animal hung from the pole, its head lolling back exposing a mottled yellow throat stained with blood. Zee and Liu trudged toward camp, struggling under the weight of the Saint Bernard-sized beast. A garland of flowers drooped in a wilted circlet on Shannon's head.

Teeg raised his rifle in a cheery wave. "Dinner!" he called. Then, as they entered the perimeter, "We'll have a barbecue and tell our hunting story. Doc, you skin the thing."

At Posie's look of surprise, Teeg clapped him on the back. "You're the zoologist, you might find it interesting." To Estevan, he said, "Think you could get this thing on a spit and get the crew a real meal? Anybody you need to help you, just put them to work. We've been eating out of tubes too long." Teeg's face took on a frankly eager expression. "I want this to be a kind of celebration for the crew. It's been all work and no play. I'd appreciate anything you could do to make up a nice meal."

Estevan shrugged. "No sweat." Then a big chumpy smile. "Colonel."

Clio winced. Estevan was laying it on a bit thick. And Teeg was settling into his colonel routine: indulging the troops, savoring his love letters, and dreaming of Shangri-la.

Meng eyed their dinner. "Meat. God, all of a sudden, I could kill for some good, red meat."

Liu was trudging off to the hygiene tent. "And I could kill for a shower."

Zee warned Clio off with his eyes, and headed for crew tent.

Teeg and Posie dragged the kill to the shade side of the med tent, Clio following. "Who brought it down?" she asked.

Teeg slapped the rifle slung over his shoulder. "It practically ran into us, grazing. Shot it right between the eyes." A sheepish grin flickered for a moment on his face. "Not much of a war story."

Clio smiled back. "Well, it's results that count." She sauntered away, brooding hard about the Dharhai slung over Teeg's right shoulder.

Late in the afternoon, Estevan built a fire and let it burn down to coals. Fashioning a crude rotisserie, he and Liu hoisted the bloody carcass over the fire pit to begin cooking. Before long the smell of roasted flesh pervaded the camp.

Toward sunset the crew pulled up makeshift seats. Meng and Shannon were giggling. They had prepared what they called hors d'oeuvres, and passed among the crew urging tastes and flirting with the men.

Teeg slapped Estevan on the back, relieving him for a few minutes on the task of turning the spit. The Dharhai was still slung over his shoulder. Estevan bustled back to the meal tent for the rest of the food, catching Clio's eyes in passing, the smile melting off his face like wax.

Posie unbuttoned his shirt a few notches, watching Meng's every move. She had removed her shoes, tied her shirt to expose her midriff, which seemed a scandalous thing: tummy and feet against the sober green of the Recon uniform. She wore her gun at her hip, as they all did.

Clio went over the plan in her mind. She would take Posie, Estevan was on Teeg, and Zee on Meng. Clio would take on Liu if she could, disarm him, after she had tied Posie. Estevan would watch for Shannon, who was possibly unaligned, and a lightweight in any case. Hillis was on his own. Clio didn't tell him their plans. A painful deception. He would support her in a pinch, but he might not like the plans, and right now Clio didn't want any vacillation.

The Niang mission was going to abort. Get to *Starhawk* with as few injuries as possible. Get home. *Got to get the job done, sister.*

Zee was poking at the coals with a stick, not doing well in party mode. Clio slipped her arm about his waist. "You're kinda cute, what's your name, honey?" Clio asked loud enough to bring snickers from some of the crew.

Zee looked up with a fine attempt at a smile. "Just call me professor."

"Ohhh." Clio cooed. "A professor. I just love intelligent men." She swept the group with mocking eyes. "They're so rare." Liu hooted, enjoying the banter.

Teeg watched her with growing interest, a wry and wondering light in his eyes, all the while talking to Shannon, turning the meat spit, and retelling the story of the kill. A man who wanted badly to believe this fantasy; to enact it, in fact.

Estevan dished out the feast as the last of the light slipped from their patch of sky. The meat caused something of a sensation, dark and stringy as it was, but it was meat, basted and barbecued. It was meat without tubes. The crew turned serious in their eating.

After some time Shannon left her plate at her seat and slipped away, promising to come back. When she did, they stopped eating to stare at her. She wore the bandanna again as a halter. A man's shirt was converted to a short draped skirt, slit up the side nearly to her hips. She was barefoot and her skin glistened with oil.

"Kind of hard to dance without music." She spread her arms, presenting herself. The crew beat forks on plates, whistled.

Teeg was grinning. "Hey, Estevan, how about some of those Latin rhythms? Use a couple of sticks, man. Let's see this lady dance!"

Estevan didn't move. Clio jumped up and searched the clearing for a couple of likely sticks, hurried over to Estevan, joking and prodding him. Catching his eye.

He stared at her a second, then grinned, and started the beat.

And Shannon moved. Closing her eyes, she swayed in place, her hips and shoulders catching the rhythm first, spreading across and down her body, moving outward along her arms. Slowly she turned to the fire, undulating her hips, where all eyes went. Then, gathering confidence, she began to move around the dying coals, twisting her body and coiling her arms to the cadence of Estevan's percussion as though possessed. Amid shouts from the group, Liu jumped up to dance with her, but Posie jerked him back to the applause of the men. This was a solo performance. Shannon had the stage, and she knew it.

Clio waited for the bandanna to come off. Shannon must have that much planned at least. She watched the crew as they watched the dancer. They were entranced, the fire-light glittering in their eyes. They were waiting for the bandanna too. When Shannon threw it off she actually tossed it to Teeg.

He caught it. Then he leaned over to Estevan and stopped the drumming. Standing up, he started the applause for Shannon, which came with shouts of approval, Meng and Clio vying with the men in showing appreciation.

Shannon bowed, deeply flushed, suddenly at loose ends, as to whether she should cover herself or not, leave the campfire. Teeg settled that question. He walked slowly up to her, put his arm around her waist, and pulled her close, covering her face with his own. The crew watched this demonstration with quiet stares until he took her by the elbow and steered her toward his tent.

"You kids are on your own. I got business to attend to." He looked pointedly at Clio as he passed.

It positively hurt her to stifle the sneer he deserved.

Meng got up from her seat by the fire, and glided toward Posie, who seemed frozen to his seat, watching her approach. She stood in front of him, her eyes locked on his as if daring him to touch her. He finally reached out his hand toward her, a trembling, tentative clutch at her midriff, but at that, she turned and started to walk out of the circle, twisting her head around to see if he was following. He was.

Then Clio was on Zee, choosing before she was chosen, trying to ignore Hillis' bewildered glances, trying to maneuver herself out of the campfire circle. She caught Estevan's eyes, nodded almost imperceptibly. He nodded back. He was ready.

Liu watched Clio and Zee heading into the dark of the camp. "Hey Professor," he called, "you should share her." Clio clutched Zee's arm, urging him onward, not to respond. "There's only three women, Zee. Just remember that!"

"My God," Zee was saying, "my God, what's happening to us? We're scientists, don't they remember that? What about the mission, doesn't anybody remember that?" He looked at her in distress. "What would Captain Russo say?"

Clio muttered under her breath, "Russo would be pissed. More to the point, *I'm* pissed." She led Zee into the crew tent, turned to see if they'd been followed. Nobody.

"Posie and Meng are in the med tent. Probably doing it

on the cot right now. Let's go." She checked her gun, jammed it back in the holster.

"My God," Zee said again. At her stare, he checked his own gun, nodded he was ready.

"I'll go in first, get them facedown on the floor. You watch my back. When I call you, come in and cover me while I tie them up. Then I'll find Liu and disarm him."

"I'll take care of Liu."

"No. He'll be happier to see me, less on guard. Now hurry."

They checked outside before leaving the crew tent. Estevan was nowhere in sight. Several figures were still sitting around the campfire some forty meters away. That would be Hill and Liu.

Zee went ahead, Clio following, taking the long way around to med tent, then crouching down outside it, listening for Posie and Meng. Clio bent low, ear to the tent. Nothing. No sound from inside. Zee looked up at her, started to whisper, but she put her hand to his lips, urging silence. The noise from the jungle was loud in their ears, and Posie might be a quiet lover. Minutes stretched out, marked only by the thumping of their hearts.

A slight movement to Clio's left. She turned. And there it was, it's eyes only slightly lower than hers, a monkey creature, its eyes focused upon hers. A membrane slipped over its eyes, retracted. Slowly, Clio put her hand on Zee's shoulder, turned him around to look, covering his mouth just in case. No use. Zee cried out, jumping back and falling against the tent. Cursing, Clio jumped up and ran for the tent door, flung herself inside, gun drawn. Posie was standing naked beside the bed, trousers in one hand, trying to get a leg in. Meng was sprawled on the cot, grabbing at the covers.

"Get down," Clio said, louder than she meant to, "get down on the floor, facedown. Now, goddamn it!" Finally Posie was moving, and then Meng, dragging the covers with her, modest even now. "Drop the covers," Clio hissed. "Lie down on your face."

Zee was standing behind her. "Get their guns," she

said, trying to scan the med tent for weapons other than their pistols. Zee jumped to it, retrieving the weapons. He rummaged for bandages, found them, and hurriedly bound Posie's hands behind his back. In the midst of this they heard two rounds of gunfire, close, somewhere in camp.

"What's going on here, Finn," Posie said, twisting his head to the side, his voice quavering.

Clio began backing up toward the door to look out, hoping to hell Estevan hadn't botched the job. And then Liu was standing there, and his gun was against the side of her head.

"Drop your gun," he said.

Clio let her gun slip to the ground. At that moment, something small and dark came scampering away from the side of the tent, coming within a meter of Liu, who turned his weapon toward it and fired. Then someone was rushing up from the dark center of camp, hair flying, and as Liu swung the gun around and squeezed off another round, Clio saw that it was Shannon, heard Shannon saying, "He's dead! Dead!" Before she could say more, Liu had shot her full in the chest.

As Liu screamed, Clio rushed over to Shannon, knelt down beside her where she lay. "Who's dead, Shannon, who?"

Shannon looked up at her with a kind of smile. "Estevan," she said. The name blurted out on a pulse of blood from her mouth.

Liu stood fixed in place, emitting a series of cries, staring at the remains of Shannon's chest. Meng had rushed out of the tent, stark naked, and was now screaming at Clio, "I'll kill you, I'll kill you!" She grabbed the pistol from Liu and fired at Clio, missing. Then Hillis was standing on the edge of the scene. He stalked toward Meng, took the gun from her hand, and struck her, sending her reeling into the tent.

Clio's thoughts slowed to leaden pace. *Fast, think fast,* she told herself.

Zee was still armed. He stood in the tent doorway, staring at Shannon's body, as they all were. "Let's get out of here," Clio said. When he hesitated, she added, "I think Estevan's dead, and Teeg'll be looking for us. Let's get the hell out of here."

Zee urged Meng up with the toe of his boot. Clio grabbed Hillis' arm, said, "We tried to jump Teeg and Posie. We got Posie tied up, but I think Teeg's on the loose." Hillis was holding the gun as though it were a dead rat. Clio gently took it.

Hillis grabbed her by the shoulders. "Stop it, Clio," he said. "We need to stop this. Shannon's dead. We need to talk this out, not shoot it out. Don't you see what you're doing? This doesn't need to be a gunfight. We don't have to kill each other, we need to talk to each other."

"You still don't get it. Open your eyes someday, Hill." She backed away, watching the shadows behind him, watching for Teeg. Then she turned and bolted after Zee.

They herded Meng and Liu behind the meal tent where Zee bound and gagged them, using the roll of bandages he had tied Posie with.

When they had finished this task, she and Zee stared at each other a moment. A shiver clawed its way up Clio's back. "Now what?" she said for both of them. "He's got the Dharhai. We've got hostages, but he's got the Dharhai." Clio turned to gaze out toward the jungle clearing. Close enough to touch, the perimeter nerve wires now had the disadvantage of fencing them in, prohibiting their retreat to the forest.

Zee noted her look. "I blanked the wires from med tent."

Clio threw her arms around his neck, hugged him. "Only good man in the group," she said. Pulled away. Got to concentrate. "Let's go." She started to climb through the fence wires.

And then Teeg was standing there. The Dharhai was pointing at them. "Nobody move," he said. "I don't want to kill you, so just nobody move. Throw your weapons aside, real slow. Real, real slow."

Clio began to shake. Her hand wouldn't obey. Her arm fluttered like a ruined wing.

"Now, you bitch. Throw out the gun now."

Clio finally managed to put her hand on the gun, and pitch it to the side.

Blackness swarmed over them. The night flooded in on all sides as every light in the camp winked out. She hurled herself through the fence and ran. Ran hard, wanting to shout for Zee to run, but afraid to draw fire with her voice. Sprinting toward the jungle wall, not knowing how close she was, but running with the power of terror, hearing the Dharhai thumping out rounds, ripping the night air with its metal stitches. Crying under her breath for Zee, Zee, Zee.

She hit the brush at the jungle edge, dove into it, burrowing like a rabbit fleeing a wolf. She clawed her way through the barrier of undergrowth, and emerged finally into the humming, black nest of the forest.

CHAPTER 10

Ever since first light the Niang monkeys began dropping onto the jungle floor. They lowered themselves on the vines, slowly, methodically. Some vines were solid with monkeys as they streamed down from the tree canopy, forming a pillar of black, glistening movement.

The Niang monkeys kept their distance from her at first, intent upon their foraging. After a time, some approached her, observing her from close range, making tentative moves toward her, then away. They lacked faces, which made it hard to think of them as mammals. Their two eyes protruded from the hump between their six legs. Their mouths were beneath their bodies so that their normal feeding stance was raised up on two legs, braced against a plant with two more, and pulling food to their mouths with their forward legs.

The sun was up full, lighting the jungle floor with a submerged glow. Like the bottom of a shallow sea, the Niang forest was a world apart, touched by sunlight deeply stained with turquoise. The voices of the forest depths filled her ears with alien cries. Small clouds of flying insects swam in formation through the murky spaces, while dragonflies swooped to feed on them, wings glinting.

Clio tried once again to plan her next move. Through the night she had stayed close to the forest edge. After the first few hours, she crawled to the edge of the clearing and saw that the camp lights had come back up; there was no sign of Zee. When she heard Teeg calling nearby, she had fled into the jungle, fearing him and fearing the game that they played: he the hunter, she the prey; he, the wronged lover, she the mocking woman. And Teeg was angry, no doubt about that. Maybe crazy, too.

Hunger began to gnaw at her. Finally she ate part of a succulent leaf she saw the Niang monkeys eat. It was too coarse to swallow, but she sucked the sugar from it and her stomach felt a little appeased.

She began following what looked like a path, a narrow indentation in the matted floor. Behind her, Teeg's voice was faint now, growing fainter. At last his voice was subsumed by the jungle, though from time to time she thought she heard her name, as though the Niang chorus had learned it from Teeg. Perhaps Estevan was right. The Niang birds repeated what they heard.

By the slant of the sun, Clio calculated she was moving away from camp. She turned off the path at a right angle and headed in the direction she called north, thinking to circle back to camp, coming upon it at a different point on the perimeter. That was the best scenario. The worst was that she was already lost.

She trudged on, drenched in morning dew and her own sweat. The rankness of her uniform was cloaked with the heavy sweetness of the forest, especially the trees, their trunks slick as water slides with their oozing stream of sugars. She stopped for a minute, listening for Teeg, her limbs trembling. The old shakes got to her even here, reminding her of all the ways her body had betrayed her, had given her Dive flights and then taken them away. *Tried* to take them away. She pushed on.

When she rested again it was in a clearing where a slight breeze lifted the dampness from her clothes. She filled her lungs, leaned against an overgrown rock, and stared into the clearing, unseeing.

She must have been gazing at the shape for a quarter of an hour before her brain clicked in. Dazed, Clio stood up. Before her in the clearing lay a streamlined mass about twenty meters long and fifteen wide. She circled it, heart thudding. Though completely covered with jungle growth, it appeared symmetrical. It had the look of a gigantic racing car, draped with a heavy cloth.

After several minutes of probing, she found an opening in the thing, covered with a drape of vines. She peered inside. In the gloom, she saw a passageway leading back into the interior. She pushed through the vines. In the dim light from the entryway she saw that the walls, floor and ceiling, every surface and protuberance, were covered with brocades of plant life. Small eruptions of flowers and woody stalks of mature vines ran rampant along with a pervasive turquoise moss.

Deeper in, a muted light beckoned her, and she came upon a circular room with slanting panels at the height where instrumentation should be. The sun trickled through a hole in the bulkhead, revealing panels padded with airy ferns. To Clio, the room was unmistakable. It was a cockpit or flight deck. And it was an alien ship. Must be, since no Earth ship had ever been here. No Earthly craft. She rested her hand on the bulky form of the pilot's chair, then cautiously sat down. Who had sat there before her, and died there, she wondered. A Niang pilot? Or some unlucky visitor, unlucky as she herself?

She rose and turned to a ledge on the opposite bulkhead. Here, the odd colors of tan and white lay untouched by biotic growth. Barely visible tracery showed what Clio immediately recognized as star charts. She bent close to examine the lines and runes, but the dim light revealed little except, here and there, what might be a number. *A recognizable number.* Her eyes must be making things up. Too dim to be sure. She lifted the page and found others beneath it, but the top one crumbled, littering the next sheet with debris.

She turned to the instrumentation again, poking at the console, peeling a layer of moss from a small section. Her hand shook slightly as the thought took root. *There are explorers in the universe. Like us. At least a little like us.* Using her small utility knife, she dug into the panel itself, which gave way like the soft threads of banana skins. Beneath, green fuzzy wires looped methodically through a series of small, corrugated sections. As she scraped at them, clear, faceted protrusions sparkled. Though everything supported its growth of plant life, each ship component was strangely intact, each wire separately coated in Niang turquoise.

At last she made her way back down the corridor and pushed into another doorway leading into a large room where most of one bulkhead had caved in. The bulkheads curved to meet floor and ceiling, scrupulously avoiding strict right angles. A platform to Clio's left was about the right length for a bed. She sat on it, and examined the blanket still covering the pallet. The coverlet was turquoise green and flexible, as though made of delicate, low-growing ground cover. She pulled at it to tear, couldn't.

Then the thought that had been growing for the last few minutes formed clearly: the ship was not overgrown with plants. It was *replaced* by plants. Each thing retained its shape, and sometimes its function, but the metal of the ship and its other materials had not rusted and decomposed, but had transformed. The star charts were the only things that were not metamorphosed. Those, and the crystal-like studs under the instrumentation console.

The ship had crashed. That was obvious from its major structural damage. Its occupants had fled, or died. And Niang had moved in. Eating the ship, eating its metal. And mimicking it.

A chill flitted across Clio's neck. She quickly glanced up, nervous all of a sudden. Nervous about this unearthly place, about Teeg finding her and cornering her here. She found the outside hatchway and quickly moved out of the ship, heading toward the cover of the forest.

Pausing at the edge of the clearing, she looked back at the ship. "So, you've got a flaw, Niang," she said. The ship lay heavily in its green nest, all vine and wood and moss. "You like to play with metal. I don't think Biotime's gonna like that."

She turned from the clearing and stepped into the jungle canopy. As she pushed on, she practiced ways to tell Hillis, to tell him Niang's secret flaw.

Each time, she stopped, seeing the look in his eyes.

The forest brightened up ahead. Moving toward the light, Clio emerged out of the canyon of trees onto the edge of a rock wall, its sheer face dropping out of sight below her. The sunlight stabbed into her eyes, and she sat abruptly, holding her head, trying to catch her wits. When her eyes adjusted, she looked out over an awesome vista. Thousands of feet of vertical cliff below her, the turquoise crown of the jungle spread out before her in a 180-degree panorama stretching to the world's end. Far below, burrowing into the forest mass, a river wound away from the cliff face. After gaping at this sight for several minutes, Clio noticed a muted, rumbling sound off to her left, and headed in that direction, picking her way along the edge of the cliff.

She came upon the source of the noise, a waterfall, and stood on the rocks beside it, watching it plunge over the edge. A rainbow had formed some twenty feet below her, and the water cascaded through its prismed bow. Clio reached for a drink of water, but it was too far away. She lay on a flat rock nearest the spray, her arm stretched out. The sun was hot on her back. She was exhausted. She slept.

She drank from the canteen, gulping the water, even if it was warm and brackish. Finally the man pulled it away.

"That's enough for now," he said.

She came fully awake, and saw that it was Teeg, unmistakably, Teeg. Her stomach plummeted.

He wore a bandanna around his forehead. That and a day's growth of beard gave him a pirate look. A rifle was slung over his shoulder; his pistol was in a holster at his side.

Anger swept over her. "Lieutenant Harper Teeg," Clio said. "Look at you. Turned a science mission into a war movie. Hunt down the gooks. Get those women rounded up. Hasn't this gone a bit far?" She reached again for the canteen.

He held it back, over his shoulder, out of her reach. Then a smile cracked over his face. "Now that's the old Clio. Don't try to fool me, ever again. Because I can tell. I can always tell when you're lying." He stood up, pressed the toe of his boot into her side. "Get up."

She pulled herself to her feet. "I want to go back and have this out with the rest of the crew, Teeg. We've got a real mess here, and we need to figure out what to do." She looked him in the eyes. No good. Not getting through.

"Start walking, Clio. Just keep to the edge of the cliff. I'll be right behind you."

"Teeg, let's go back. I want to go back to camp."

"You do, huh? Well, maybe I'll let you, but for now, I got something else in mind." He grabbed her by the arm, and pulled her along with him, moving so fast she stumbled, and the bushes clawed at the shreds of her flight togs.

They were headed into the sun along the lip of the rock face. Teeg was pulling hard on her arm. Clio hurried to keep up, unable now to talk because of the exertion, and judging it best to keep silent until she figured out what he was up to.

They came to a place where the cliff face was deeply fissured and formed a series of ledges. Teeg pushed her on, and they descended the shallow, steplike indentations. The rock here was deeply pink, as though baked to a rosy glow in the hot sun. At last the terraces broadened out into a huge lip of rock, jutting out into yet another river whose own waterfall could be heard farther down the streambed. The river rushed below them, close enough to jump into and swim, which she thought about, hard. Teeg was at her elbow, between her and the river. She stumbled on.

Within a dozen meters they stood in front of a gaping dark hole, the opening to a large cave. Here, the jungle was kept at bay by the massive rock formation and the river beside it.

Teeg unslung his rifle and sat against a boulder in the sunlight, leaning his head back against the rock. He closed his eyes, as though he had forgotten about her.

Clio sat opposite him in the shade, on the other side of the cave opening. She realized, as he must have, that running was useless. He was bigger, faster, meaner. The law of the jungle. Now it was a matter of wits; she tried to summon hers, but her brain was warm and spongy.

"The cave is huge," he said, eyes still closed. "I don't know how far back it goes, but must be hundreds of meters. There's water trickling back there, too. So there'll be running water right inside our house."

God. Clio almost groaned, but her throat was too dry.

"There's room for all of us," he said. "It's secure. It's warm at night, but cooler than the forest during the day. It gets light in the morning and through half the day. We got the river, where there's probably fish. We got rock at our back and water at our front. Nothing can get to us that we don't see first. And it's paradise, see. No people, no cars, no pollution, no bureaucrats to tell us what we can and can't do. And it's beautiful. Jesus, but it's beautiful."

His eyes were open now. He looked at Clio. "I don't want you as a prisoner, Clio. God knows I don't want that."

"Then let me go, Teeg. I want to go home. I don't want to be here."

"You think you don't want to be here. That'll change. People can get used to all kinds of things they thought they couldn't stand. Like me and Recon, the Service. I love to fly, but I hated to take crap from people. The rules and regs, the yessirs. Watching stupid people give orders. But I got used to it, so it was a way of life. Same as this, it's a way of life. Take some getting used to, that's all." He paused, as though expecting a rebuttal.

Then he continued. "See, the thing is—and you don't know this yet—it's not safe for you, back there, Clio. You never knew it, but you were a marked woman in Recon." He grinned, seeing her eyebrow flick up.

"Brisher was on to you, woman. Could have hauled you in at any time, but I talked him out of it. He thought you were a menace. You and your pills, jeopardizing the missions. Yes, pills. Your little secret just wasn't very secret, you know? You were watched every minute. Brisher made sure of that. He didn't like you, Clio, if you didn't know. But I spoke up for you. Me. And Biotime held off. See, I've been watching you. Biotime's had me watching you for two, nearly three years now. It's just a little something extra I do for them. They figured I was the only one on the crew they could trust to keep an eye on you. Russo's too dumb. Hillis, biased, of course. Posie, too obvious. They needed somebody neutral, somebody sharp. And I enjoyed it. You've sort of been my hobby for a long time. And

Brisher paid me real good. Of course, it's not Biotime that cares what you do, so long as you can Dive. It's DSDE cares what you do. That night you went to Zebra's? Pretty stupid. DSDE picked Zebra up last time you saw her. DSDE has got hold of lots of people through you. See, I watch you and report to Brisher, and he reports to DSDE. Biotime and DSDE are scratching each other's backs. DSDE let Biotime keep you on the theory that eventually you'd lead them to your friends. They know you're no lesbo, no underground freak. But they know your family was. Sooner or later you were bound to make contact. But damned if I ever saw when you did. Maybe I'm just a lousy spy. Or maybe you were innocent. Anyways. Doesn't matter now."

He clambered up, walked to the edge of the rock shelf, and took a long piss into the river.

Nausea welled up into Clio's throat. DSDE was watching her. Had been, all these years. She started to shake. *Get a grip, girl. Now, more than ever, get a grip.* She eyed the rifle where Teeg had left it. Teeg turned around, buttoning up, and laughed a little.

"Go for it, girl. I'm just waiting for you to give me a good workout. I don't want to hurt you. But if you give me a reason, see, I'll beat the shit out of you. Pay you back for a few things. I should pay you back anyway. But I'm not that kind of guy. I don't enjoy hurting women. But I'll do it if I have to, by God."

Teeg walked back to the rifle. He leaned against the rock, stared off at a point above Clio's head, summoning up his story, her story, the rest of it.

As bad as the story was, the thing Clio hated the most was hearing it from Teeg. Hated his calm, storytelling voice, shredding up her life. Hated hearing it from Harper Teeg.

And he went on: "Your father, Kevin Speery-Hall— who wasn't really your father, as we all know—took you in, gave you his daughter's name. So your name isn't Antoinette Speery-Hall. They never told me what your real name is. Anyway, this Kevin is just null. A minor player. Doesn't know anybody. But your mother, now. She was a ringleader."

He paused long enough to a make her look him in the eye. He wanted her to watch him while he said the next part, Clio knew, which is why she avoided looking at him. To prevent him from saying it. But finally, she had to look at him, had to hear.

He nodded at her. "Oh, yeah, we know all about your mother. And what-was-her-name, her lesbo lover. Elsie. In a way I feel sorry for you, growing up in that kind of place. They killed hundreds of people, you realize that? They spread the Sickness with every fugitive they brought in. Those people belonged in quarries. Only thing that keeps the epidemic under control. You get all those infected people scurrying through the underground, contacting dozens of people along the way . . . it just spreads it everywhere. And you thought they were heroes."

Clio's eyes were locked on his now, waiting for the words to keep coming out, for the story to spill out. The whole story. Now she would know the whole story. God, even if it was from Teeg, she wanted to know.

"They're dead, Clio."

Clio was shaking her head, even as the words came out of his mouth.

"Yes, and they deserved it. You might of loved them, but they betrayed you."

A lie. Now he would say any monstrous thing. She was shaking her head. No.

"That night that you killed the DSDE agent—or your brother did, they never figured out which of you—that night, they killed Elsie and your mother. They tortured them to get information, and they spilled everything they knew, eventually. They betrayed you, they betrayed everyone they could think of. And when DSDE was finished, they killed them. That was a mistake. Because it later turned out they gave made-up names, and it all led nowhere. And then it took four years for DSDE to find you, after they lost you that night in the field outside of Granville. Well, when you signed up with Biotime, they were on to you from the beginning. Waiting for you to lead them to bigger fish. Which you never have, Clio. A big disappointment. So after this mission, Brisher was going to hand you over. You're burned out, girl. You were dog meat, after this mission."

Clio turned toward the rock wall, the tears coming fast now, gritting her teeth to cry silently. "And Petya?" she asked.

"Your brother? The half-wit? That's the funny part. He's the only one that got away. They never found him. That I know of."

He left her alone then. She curled up into a ball on the warm rock shelf and let Teeg's story sink in. The further in it sank, the more pain she uncovered, and the more her tears welled up from her chest. She cried until her throat was sore, cried as though it was twenty-seven years of crying all coming at once, which maybe it was. Finally, when her body was empty of moisture, she curled tighter into a ball and hid her face in the shadow of the rock.

An hour might have passed. Teeg was sitting beside her, his arm over her back. She stirred, and he offered her his canteen. Then he left the rock shelf for a few minutes. When he returned, he had taken off his shirt, and carried it in a bunch in his hands. It was wet. He began cleaning off her face, pressing the cool cloth against her eyes, rubbing her neck and bare arms. She let herself be bathed.

Teeg spoke gently. "That world is gone now, Clio. DSDE will never follow you here. You're not worth it, not to them. That world and its sickness, its ugliness, its rules and little games they made us play, they can't control us anymore, babe. We're free. We're in charge here. This is our world. You can be a queen if you want to. I'll treat you like a queen. And the others, Posie, Meng, and the others, they'll do what you say, because they'll do what *I* say."

He spread out his shirt to dry. "We lost Shannon. That's really tragic. Now we've just got two women. I could kill Liu for that. He deserves to die. But we need everybody we've got. You and Meng, you'll be treated like queens. Your babies will be the most important things in the world. Literally. They'll be the start of a new people, a new society. We won't need DSDE or Biotime or any other bureaucracy, just ourselves. Like it was meant to be."

Clio got up and walked into the cave to shut off the

spewing of Teeg's words. Within a few yards the light bled away, leaving her sightless in the dark. It felt good. Like pulling the covers over your head when the world pressed too close, when senses were too keen, when your brain picked up the static of events, when the world just kept on grating inside your head.

Here it was cool and black. She turned her back on the bright gash of the cave opening, faced the dark. Teeg had said the cave went far back, farther than he knew. You could walk a long way back, perhaps down as well. They said that rivers carved caves like this, wending their paths through stone, pulled by forces of the planet. Stand still enough and you feel it yourself, tugging at your limbs, pulling you downward. A destiny of sorts. It was gravity that Clio felt now, standing in the great cave. A force of the natural world, the prime force, or one of them. In the face of that, her own motives hardly mattered, were, in fact, puny. Had chased her all her life. Hide. Hide, they told her. Hide what you are. We'll hide the window in the closet, hide the closet door behind the great chest of drawers, hide the sick ones, hide their graves.

The night they buried Lenny Holt, and Petya had finished off the grave with pebbles and brush, Elsie cried. Lenny had only been with them for three weeks, but Elsie cried like she always did. And Mother, like always, didn't. Quiet, Mother always was at the burials. She never believed in the afterlife. There was nothing after life. Pie in the sky bye and bye, was what Mother had to say about religion. So she was quiet most buryings.

But as they stood over Lenny's grave, watching Petya make it invisible, she said, looking at Clio, "Don't put me in the ground. Just scatter me somewheres. It'll be up to you, someday. Just don't put me in the ground."

This was the closest Mother ever came to admitting that anything mattered, after death. She looked over at her mother, where the moonlight brightened half her face. Clio felt like saying, But if you're dead, you won't care, right? Then she caught Elsie's quick look. She aimed an impish smile at Clio, saying clearly, Leave it be, leave it be. Clio smiled back.

Then Petya said, "Nobody can tell, can they?" And he stepped back and looked at the secret, rocky ground.

Clio turned back to the hole of light, squinting. She didn't have to go out there, to Teeg, to his vision of the world. She could turn and walk now, follow the cave back into the womb of the world where it was quiet, dark, embracing. Buried from view. The third choice, after DSDE and Teeg's world. It was still death, like the other two choices, but it had the advantage of immediacy. And it was clean, like gravity.

But she had assisted at too many burials to add her own. Something about the ease of it, the giving in. Not her heritage, giving in. Mom and Elsie, they had their secrets, but they kept on fighting. Going underground was about resistance, not running. All these years it was their lesson, the one they never spoke, and it had taken her this long to learn it.

She walked out onto the hot shelf of rock.

Teeg looked startled to see her. "I was just getting worried about you. Try to get out the back way?"

"Yes," Clio said. "There isn't any."

He raised his eyebrows. "How far back did you go?"

"Pretty far."

He watched her a while, frowning. "Well, I should be upset with you. Trying to escape."

Clio held his gaze, feeling calm, utterly calm.

"But you came back. So I give you credit for that."

"Yes. I'm back."

He looked at her, watching for something. Tears, perhaps.

"Well, let's get going, then. We're going back for the others." He stopped, still watching her. His eyes narrowed. "You ready?"

A small smile edged at the sides of her mouth. Small, but genuine. "Yeah, Teeg. I'm ready," she said.

CHAPTER 11

A heavy mist sifted down around Clio and Teeg as they thrust their way along a narrow animal path winding through the forest. From the jungle crown, water streamed down the ropy vines in fast-motion stalactites. The rain on the canopy set up a roaring percussion that reverberated around them, as though the forest itself were a vast drum.

There was no talking over that noise, not even for Teeg. This gave Clio a chance to think. To plan her strategy. The one stupid thing Teeg had done was to bring his guns. He didn't need them. But she did. Getting those guns became her sole purpose. Get them before they arrived in camp. Do it soon, in the jungle; maybe her only chance. Of course, he would expect her to try to escape. He would be alert, paranoid as hell, every minute.

Paranoid. Clio knew what that was like. Before every Dive. Your eyes so wide open, it feels like your eyelids are torn off. Clio's hand went to her vest pocket. They were still there. Her pills. Make you paranoid as hell.

She patted her vest pocket again.

The decision was easy. The most important decisions of her life, she had always made spur of the moment.

"I'm hungry, Teeg."

"Don't lie to me, Clio. I can tell when you lie."

"I haven't eaten since last night. I'm hungry."

He looked at her a few moments, searching her face for lies. Finally, he said, "OK, then. Food for the lady."

Teeg slipped the pack off his back and rummaged.

"Water," Clio said, holding out her hand for the canteen.

He tossed it. Then he pulled out some meat tubes and his knife, concentrating on his task.

Clio took a long gulp of water, her heart jumping in her chest. This would be her last drink of water for a long while. She slung the canteen strap over her shoulder and stood up.

Teeg looked up at her.

"Need to pee."

He nodded, went back to his work.

She moved away a few paces and squatted.

Clio had twelve tabs in her inside vest pocket. *Never keep them in just one place. Spread out your stash, make sure they're always close to hand.* She took six of them and tried pulverizing them between her fingers, but they were too hard. Finally she ground them between the canteen cap and the container and dropped them in, shaking the canteen. As she walked back, Teeg was watching her, so she raised the canteen to her lips and pretended to drink.

"God, I'm thirsty. Maybe I don't feel so good," she said.

"Try this," Teeg said. He handed her one of Estevan's tortillas, spread with meat paste and rolled.

As Clio reached for it her hand trembled so hard she almost dropped it. "I don't feel so good," she said. She sat down, back against a tree, hoping now for delay. Stretch the time out, head home slowly. She chewed on the rolled tortilla, thinking of Estevan, wanting to ask about him, but not wanting to remind Teeg of the failed coup. *Drink, you bastard,* she thought. *Drink.*

"We'll make the transition gradually," Teeg was saying. "Start with a few treks to the cave, to carry supplies. Get everybody used to the jungle. Start cleaning the cave up. We'll need to see what kind of building materials these trees make. For tables, chairs, stuff like that. Carry as much as we can from the ship, before the monkeys get it."

He reached for the canteen, unscrewed the cap, waved the canteen at the forest crown. "Estevan's boots are up there in some nest. Probably they'll have the whole camp dismantled within a day or two, once we're gone." He looked back at Clio, his eyes narrow. "That was another stupid thing you did."

When she didn't answer, he snorted at her, then took a long swig of water. "Sent a man after me with no boots. Pretty stupid."

Clio remembered to chew. She had barely been breathing. The food stuck to the roof of her mouth.

"It's hot," she said, slumping further down against the tree trunk. "Too damn hot." She reached for the canteen, put it to her lips, tilted her head back, swallowed the spit in her mouth. "And you call this a paradise." Better not be too nice to Teeg. Stay in character. She offered the open canteen to him. He took it, drank again, stoppered it.

"Let's go." He wiped off his hands on his togs, hoisted the pack onto his back and the rifle over one shoulder.

Their progress was slow. Teeg had made cuts on the trees as he followed her into the forest. Now they retraced that path, searching for marked trees, along Clio's original, wandering path. An hour or more passed as time dissolved in the jungle's humid grasp. The rain eased off, met by a resurgence of the buzzing, chittering, and screaming of the local creatures.

"The noise," Clio finally said. "It's just the damn noise. Gets on my nerves, you know? Can't tell if anything's coming. Can't tell if something's right behind you, even."

"That's what this is for," Teeg said. He patted the rifle. "But you don't get a gun, honey. Gonna be a long time—if ever—before you carry a gun. If that's what you're leading up to, save your breath."

Teeg's mood had soured. That talk of Estevan. He pushed her on ahead of him, steering her from time to time with a shove of his hand in her back.

She picked her way carefully along the vine-threaded jungle floor, shying at times from imaginary movements on either side, playing on the spikes of noise that occasionally pierced the sound of rain.

"Goddamn, you're jumpy." Teeg had been quiet for a long time.

"Sorry. But can't you feel it? Like there's things out

there we can't see? I just got this bad feeling, Teeg. I'm not saying I want a gun. Just you be ready, that's all."

She opened the canteen, faked a drink, handed it to him.

He was watching her, watching her closely, even as he drank. "You think your retroid friends are coming to rescue you, you got a big disappointment, girl. Estevan ain't going nowhere. Zee—we got him trussed up like a turkey."

"What about Hillis?"

Teeg wiped his face with his sleeve. "Think I'm that dumb? He's in the brig too."

"Come on, Teeg, Hillis never gave anybody any problem. He wasn't in on the mutiny. Never even knew what was going down."

"Yeah. Right." Teeg capped the canteen, handed it back. He sneered. Something about the way he looked at her. Hostile. He was counting up his grievances, Clio was sure. Instead of directing his anxiety at the murky surroundings, Teeg was focusing on Clio. He continued to stare at her, the sneer taking over his whole face. Clio froze, afraid to move. This wasn't in the plan.

"You got a lot of men dancing to your tune, don't you, Miss Red?"

God, Clio thought, *here he goes.*

"And you think you got me dangling by a string, too, isn't that right?" When she didn't respond, he pushed her. "Isn't that right?"

Clio staggered back. "What do you want me to say, Teeg? You seem to have all the answers, so what am I supposed to say?"

He lunged forward, pushing her again. "Just say that you ran a fucking tease number on every man on crew. Just say that, Clio. Say it!"

She scrambled backward, tripping on some roots, fell. "You shouldn't hurt me, Teeg. You need every woman you've got, remember that."

He towered over her. Paused. Stepped back, wiping his face with his hand. He seemed to reel, lose focus. Then he snapped upright, slapping his rifle, as though making sure it was still there.

"Right." He frowned, looking at her sprawled there in front of him. "Get up."

They pushed on, following the gash marks in the trees. The rain had slacked off, and the jungle brightened. The sunlight glazed the wet surfaces everywhere with a bluish glow. Bird and insect sounds rushed back to claim the airwaves. Monkeys were skittering down every vine in sight, sending Teeg spinning to cover each new assault. Twice he fired off a round, shooting wide, but calling forth a surge of screams as though he had hit something—perhaps the jungle itself, registered in a billion mouths.

Up ahead, brighter still, the forest edge. The end of their trek. Clio would march into camp behind Teeg's gun, a hunter's trophy.

No. Not her heritage. She tried her last maneuver.

"The crew isn't with you, Teeg," she said. "They think you've gone too far. I'm just warning you, not everyone you count on is a friend."

"So now you're my friend, is that right?"

"I'm just trying to save your life. Because the crew wants to go home, Teeg, and they're armed too."

"Your friends aren't armed. Mine are."

"But Liu is with us. And Meng is just going along with you to save her skin. She wants to go home. And Posie, he'll do anything for Meng. She leads him by the nose."

"You're lying. Posie's with me. They're all with me."

They had come upon the perimeter undergrowth. Here the light was brighter. Teeg's face rippled now and then with nervous tremors. His eyes shifted constantly, but always came back to Clio. "You're lying," he said again.

"Then just walk out there, Teeg. Just walk out there and trust your fate to Posie. You think he wants to share Meng with you? Man, he wants to take her home and live in comfort, not in some ugly, stinking jungle!"

Teeg lunged at her, gripping her arms, shaking her. "You lying bitch, you fucking lying bitch." He pushed her hard in the chest, and she fell into the wet cushion of the undergrowth. He unslung his rifle, pointing it at her. "I'll kill you, if you lie to me, I'll kill you."

"I'm not lying! I'm trying to save your life. I don't want a bloodbath, Teeg. I don't want us all to kill each other. But you're in charge, you decide what you want to do, Teeg. You've got the gun, just remember that. I can't hurt you. I want to help you. But you got to decide."

Teeg swung the rifle around, stared toward camp. He reached down and grabbed her arm, yanking her up. "Move," he snarled. Then he plunged her into the dense undergrowth, pushing her headlong through the bushes. Clio shielded her face with her forearm, staggering and tripping, moving just ahead of Teeg's rifle butt. When they reached the edge of the clearing, Teeg pulled her down into a crouch.

Someone was walking along the perimeter. Looked like Liu. From beside her, Teeg's breathing was hard and ragged. "You go out there and tell Posie to come out and talk to me." When Clio hesitated, he thrust her out with a shove. "Go! You just don't go more than halfway into the clearing. Tell Posie I want him to come out and talk. And if you run, Clio, so help me, I'll shoot you down. Now go!"

Clio started walking. She folded her arms behind her head, like a prisoner, and started walking toward the perimeter wires. The figure they had seen was walking away from her, so she called out, "Liu! Hey, Liu, it's me, Clio!" He came running to the wire. "Teeg's willing to talk," she shouted. "This doesn't need to be a fight. He's willing to talk, but only to Posie. I'll wait right here." Clio's only weapon now was confusion. To spread confusion, distrust. And she thought hard about running. Teeg was strung out, shaky. Maybe couldn't hit a moving target.

After a few minutes Posie was walking toward her, across the clearing. He moved toward her, pistol drawn, as though she were a horse that he walked into the pasture to put down.

Everything now depended on convincing this man who hated her that she was telling the truth, that Teeg had gone crazy, that Posie and she now had to align to survive.

He was standing in front of her.

"Doc."

He stared at her, hard, gun directed at her belly.

"Doc. Teeg is in those bushes, with a rifle aimed at us. He tracked me down, then he took me to the big cave by the river and started raving. Said we're all against him. Me, you, everybody. Said you want to kill him and take over. Doc. He's cracked up. I think he's going to kill you."

Posie looked at her contemptuously. "Why should I trust you? Maybe Teeg isn't there. Maybe you killed him."

"He's there. Want me to call out to him? But meanwhile you have to figure what you're gonna do if he answers. 'Cause he's got a bead on your forehead right this second, and he's gonna put you down, and then me too, probably."

Posie's eyes were shifting rapidly across the expanse of the jungle wall, then flicking back to Clio, searching for the enemy. Weighing her story.

"Get down on your knees, hands behind your head." He gestured toward the ground with the gun.

Clio sank down, arms folded against the back of her head. They shoot prisoners this way, Clio thought. *God, I'm going to die.* She looked up at Posie to catch his eye. But he was looking at the turquoise surge across the clearing.

"Teeg!" he shouted. "You out there, Colonel? You out there?"

A few beats. Then: "Yeah, I'm here."

"This bitch says we got a problem, you and me. That makes her a liar, I figure. We had our plans, and we've still got those plans, right Teeg?"

Clio blurted out, "Oh God, Doc, you called him Teeg. That makes him real mad, you gotta call him colonel. God, he's going to kill us all. Why do you think he's hiding out there Doc? He's not afraid of *me*, he's afraid of *you*. Can't you see that?"

"Shut up!" Posie was still watching the jungle wall. He'd made the mistake of keeping his gun drawn. Teeg would notice that, for sure.

"Let's talk, Posie!" came the shout from the undergrowth. "Come over here, and bring her with you!"

Posie's tongue flicked at the sides of his mouth. He was hesitating.

"God, don't go, Doc," Clio said. "He said he's going to make sure he doesn't have any rivals. You're the only one smart enough to be his rival, for me, for Meng. You're a dead man."

"Shut up!" Posie said, not looking at her. His feet were still rooted in place. God, he was hesitating.

One thing Clio was sure of. She wasn't going back. If Posie walked toward Teeg, she was going to bolt. Nothing to gain by letting Posie and Teeg parlay.

"You come out, Colonel. We don't need to hide from each other. That's not how we work together, is it? You come out, I'll meet you halfway."

Then, from the thicket, Teeg's voice came, a misshapen growl: "Hell you say, Posie! I'm your commanding officer! We're not bargaining over *orders*, or *are we?*"

"Colonel! You could be in the hands of an enemy. How do I know? If you come out here, then I know you're safe."

"Fucking hell!" Teeg was plunging out of the bushes, and Clio lurched to her feet, screaming, charging up the scene with a high-pitched warning: *"Run, run now! For your life, Doc, for your life."* And Posie was falling backward, his hand thrown up over his head, his gun sailing out behind him, turning over and over in the air.

Clio was up and sprinting before Posie hit the ground, before the crack of the rifle split the air, before Posie's scream mingled with her own.

It was a long run to the perimeter. Her sluggish body lurched across the clearing, and she shouted, "Don't shoot, Liu, help me!" Others were gathered there, guns were drawn. The thud of rifle fire filled her ears as the clearing erupted into a lead-infested kill zone.

In the last few yards, Clio dove into the grass, skidding within inches of the wires. "Blank the wires!" she called out.

Behind the perimeter, a few feet away, she heard Liu say, "It's blanked, you can come in, Clio."

She dove through. Behind her, gunfire still. In front of her, Liu and Meng, crouched behind the hygiene stall. "Teeg's gone crazy," Clio said. "He's going to kill us."

Liu was staring, slack-mouthed, out toward the clearing. "Posie's down," he said. "Posie's down. Teeg shot him. God, we're all going to die."

Meng said, "Christ, what a fool. You're stupid, so you probably *will* die." She looked at Clio, who was still lying belly-down in the dirt. "What the hell happened out there?"

Clio elbowed herself over to them, got into a crouch. "He just lost it, broke down. Started to rave. He thinks you want to kill him, like a coup. He's completely berserk. And he's armed."

Meng squatted down, cocked her rifle, bracing it on her knee, facing the wires. "He comes through that line, he's hamburger."

Liu said, "I don't see anybody. Where is he?"

"Get Zee and Hillis out here," Clio said. "Give them guns, and we'll have a better chance of holding him off."

Liu gaped at her, looked over at Meng.

"Do it," Meng said, not moving from her position. Meng unclipped her sidearm, tossed it to Clio.

"They're all in crew tent," Liu said. "Guns are in med tent, under the comm unit."

Clio raced toward the crew tent, opened the tent flap, plunged in. Hillis and Zee were tied back-to-back and gagged. Estevan was lying on a cot, hands tied in front of him.

Clio tore off their gags, then began fumbling at the knots of their bonds.

"Clio," Hillis said. "You're alive."

"Don't ask me how," she said, finally working the ropes loose.

Zee pulled her close, hugging her face against his. "Clio . . ." he said, barely a whisper. Hillis was there too, his arms around them both.

Clio pushed away. "No time to talk. Teeg's strung out

on my Dive meds. I got him suspicious of Posie and everyone so he shot Posie when we came to the clearing. Liu and Meng are scared of Teeg, they're lying in wait for him at the perimeter." She moved over to Estevan, bent down to untie him. "How is he? Thought he was dead."

"He'll live," Hillis said. "Took a slug in his left lung."

Estevan opened his eyes, managed a crack of a smile at Clio. "I screwed up. I really screwed up, you know?"

"Yeah, we all did. Now we're going for a rematch," Clio said. "Can you walk?"

Estevan shook his head. "Naw. I'm useless."

"Then we carry you."

Hillis grinned. "The lander. We're getting the hell out of here, right?"

"To *Babyhawk*," Clio said. "Vacation's over."

"Cripes, you think they're just going to let us walk out of here?" Zee asked.

"Maybe not without a fight. Somebody get a couple more guns in med tent—under the comm unit—and some extra ammunition." She looked at Zee. "Meet us at the lander."

Hillis put up a hand. "No. I'll go."

"Goddamn it, Hill," Clio said. "No stops. No stops at botany. We're getting out of here, fast."

"OK, OK, no stops." And he was out of the tent, running.

Zee and Clio got Estevan out of bed and pulled his arms around their necks.

"What about the others?" Zee asked. "What about Meng and Liu?"

"We'll wait for them. But we'll wait in *Babyhawk*. Let's go."

They dragged Estevan, groaning, out of the tent. The gauze of rain had separated around the sun's disk. Steam rose from the ground, whisked away by a light breeze. The odor of crushed fruit too long ripening rode the air. The camp was still, submerged in the din from the world jungle.

Zee bore most of Estevan's weight on himself,

allowing Clio to hold on to her gun, and attempt to cover their flight.

Up ahead, *Babyhawk* loomed like a riveted metal insect. The bolted, grey, hexagonal body crouched on segmented struts, ready to leap at the sky and take them back to the mother ship.

Clio caught movement to their left, swiveled, saw Hillis, his arms full of weapons. A few clattered to the ground. He left them, running to catch up.

"Get Estevan into the ship," Clio told Zee, and he obeyed, pulling the big man by his armpits, sliding him up the ramp. The door whooshed open, and then the world stopped.

"Hold it, everybody. Move and you're dead."

Teeg stood there, some thirty meters off, with Hillis halfway between him and the lander. Zee paused on the ramp.

Clio's gun was aimed right at Teeg's head. But she wasn't that good a shot, and right now the best target in sight was Hillis.

Teeg stood in back of Liu and Meng. No telling whether they were with him as allies or prisoners.

"Zee, you come on down now," Teeg said.

Clio spoke under her breath. "Don't move, Zee. Anything happens, you get in there and power up the lander. Hear me?" He nodded.

Clio shouted, "I've got a gun, Teeg, and I'll kill you if you make a move toward us. I swear I'll kill you."

Hillis was frozen in place. His arms were full of the weapons of the camp, yet not one was available, in his hand. He said, "Get in the lander, Clio."

"Hillis." Clio tried to pull him toward her with her eyes, tried to imagine how to get him just fifteen meters closer.

"Get in the lander, Clio, you stubborn bitch," Hillis said. "Don't get yourself killed on my account. I never cared for you. We were friends for a while, no big deal. Now go."

Clio's eyes were so blurry, she couldn't see Teeg and

the others. Furiously, she wicked the tears away with her sleeve. "Meng, you staying?" Clio asked. "You gonna be Teeg's baby machine? Bear him a dozen kids and die when you're forty? You crazy, woman? You gonna take orders from Liu and Teeg for the rest of your life? That your idea of Eden?"

Clio was backing up the ramp. "Just start walking, Hill, just slowly come toward us."

Hillis remained stock-still.

Teeg shouted, "I don't want to kill you, Clio, but I will. Just stop where you are. Please."

"Teeg, get this straight. I'm leaving. You can come too, but I'm leaving. We all need each other. We're crew, damn it, we're human. We're not going to kill each other. We're going home."

Teeg started moving in, keeping behind Hillis, shoving Meng and Liu along with him. "Stay here with me, baby," he said, his voice cracking. "I love you. I always loved you." He was crying. "Don't leave me here alone, baby."

The lander powered up. Clio was at the door.

"Then come with me," Clio said, crying too, looking at Hillis, looking into his eyes across those fifteen meters.

"Baby, I can't do that," Teeg said. "I'm up for hanging, if I go home. They'd hang me, you know they would."

"Just start walking, Hill," Clio said.

And Hillis was walking toward her after all, still carrying the guns. He was at the bottom of the ramp.

"No, baby," Teeg said. "You can't have him. I can't have you. Neither can he."

Clio staggered a few steps down the ramp, pushing her hands out as if to stop him. "God, Teeg! Hillis and I aren't lovers, we were never lovers!" She saw that Teeg wasn't listening, that he was just fixed on Hillis, who stood there, still frozen, he and his armload of guns. "We faked it all these years. God, we faked it!"

Hillis took a step onto the ramp and then the shot crackled and Hillis fell, fell slowly, first to his knees, though the back of his head was gone, then full on the ground, and Meng was running, ducking and running as more gunfire laced the ground. Clio felt herself yanked back into the lander, saw Meng fall on the ramp.

"Get in the pilot chair and climb," Zee was shouting at her.

Meng was crawling up the ramp, and her body jerked as it was hit again, and she was screaming as Zee hauled her through the lock.

"Close the hatch!" Zee shouted.

Clio hit the Close toggle. The door shifted shut as a staccato pulse of rifle fire clanged against the hull. Clio stared at the control panel, hands limp in her lap.

"Gun it," Zee said.

Clio looked up at him. "Hillis is dead." The blinking of the deck lights strobed over Zee's face, making him Hillis, then Zee, then Hillis.

"Yes," Zee said, "Hillis is dead. Now take us out of here. It's what he wanted you to do. Take us home, baby."

Clio punched in ignition and the lander roared to life, making that great jump up from camp into the calm Niang sky.

METAL FUTURES

CHAPTER 12

Meng shuffled the deck of cards again, arching the cards and making them flutter, like a trapped bird.

"Pretty good for one hand, huh?" Her broken arm was in a cast, but her right arm was itching to play poker. Crew station display screens glowed with readouts that no one cared to read. Only Zee sat at his station, face lit with greenish light, hunched over his keyboard. The other chairs—for Estevan, Liu, Shannon . . . Hillis—were empty.

Clio sat at the crew conference table with Meng, staring at the one-handed shuffle.

"You folks are a lot of laughs," Meng said, "but you're just a few plates short of a picnic."

"Why don't you play with yourself, Meng, and we'll just watch," Clio said. Meng had been egging her on ever since Captain Russo and Commander Shaw left the crew cabin. *Meng. Miss Chameleon, Miss Main Chance. Watches who's winning and then chooses sides.*

"Nasty, nasty," she said. Meng laid down a row of cards. "Could have been a royal flush, except for the eight." She flicked her eyes up at Zee. "Science never sleeps. Guess you missed your astronomy down there with all those bugs and guns, hey Zee?"

Clio started to respond, got interrupted.

"Yes, I really did," Zee said, not turning around. "Clear, rational science. I feel like I'm in heaven. Not a plant in sight, and the stars at my fingertips."

A smile curled at the side of Meng's mouth. "Yes, rational science. It sure got us out of a jam down there."

Over Zee's head. Clio felt her face frozen into a

smirk as she struggled to keep from shoving the cards into Meng's face.

Captain Russo had been on the flight deck for over an hour, conferencing with Shaw, after grueling individual sessions with Clio, Estevan, Zee, and Meng.

Clio had told the truth about the mutiny, withholding her personal story, her family's story, and the matter of the overgrown crashed ship, the Niang fatal flaw. Meng, no doubt, had told her own side of it, making Clio out as an unstable, hysterical female, the bringer of doom. One moment charming and flirtatious, the next moment rampaging through camp with gun drawn.

She wondered if Meng had ever intended to play Eve to Posie's Adam. And if she did, she would never forget that it was Clio who expelled them from the garden. For her own part, Clio trusted Meng like she would a shark in home waters.

"Who knows, maybe we'll get a bonus," Meng was saying. "Despite everything, we got a haul. Looks like the best stuff ever. Maybe it was worth a few lives."

Clio was across the table before Meng could snap down the card in her hand. "I'm gonna break your other arm, you slimeball. Which way you want it pointing?" She had grabbed Meng's arm behind her back and forced her down to the floor on her knees. Zee flew out of his chair and yanked Clio off Meng, hauling her upright. Meng was huddled on the floor.

"Holy smoke," Zee said, "take it easy. Haven't we had enough fighting?"

Clio pulled away from Zee and crouched down by Meng again, grabbing her gently by the collar. "I'm only going to say this once, Meng. My best friend died down there. Shannon and Posie are dead. All murdered by the men you were sucking up to. So you got to figure some of them might still be alive if it wasn't for you, if you'd worked with us to bring the mission home instead of wagging your ass at the quarterback. So if you don't go to jail, it's going to be a gross miscarriage of justice, and I'll personally see to it that something really bad happens to you.

Like breaking your fingers so you'll have to use your teeth to shuffle the goddamn cards. You understand me?"

"Get out of my face." Meng's eyes were as bland as eggs.

Clio released her, stood up. Zee put his arm around Clio's shoulder. "Let's go get something to eat."

"What about your experiment?"

"Fuck science."

Clio laughed out loud, grabbed his arm, hugging it as they made their way through the galley hatch. "Don't ever say that, Zee. You don't have to say that for me."

He shrugged. "It was easy."

They had just filled their cups with galley coffee when Shaw came down the hatch ladder.

"You, Finn," he said, "captain wants to see you, top deck." Shaw narrowed his eyes when he spoke to her, as though trying to squeeze belief, or clarity, or something from his picture of her. Something that would explain what happened, how men lose their wits and hunt each other down and the women are possibly both the cause and the victims. How Clio's story could possibly be the only rational story, and the worst story at the same time.

Clio followed him up to the flight deck.

The lights were dim on the bridge, the flight deck consoles pulsing spots of light, systems ready to jump into action. Russo sat in the captain's chair, watched the screen at her side. Niang filled the monitor.

Shaw motioned Clio into the pilot's chair, took the copilot seat himself. That was a good sign. The chairs on the bridge assigned status; you get your chair, you still got your rank. Clio swung her chair around, watched Russo's profile. It was quiet up here, the hydraulics soughing away, like the sound of the captain's thinking. Now and then the ping of metal, reminding them of the metal skull that held them together, physically, psychologically.

Russo swung to face them. Looked at Clio. All her years crouched in her face, pasty against her black hair. "Shaw says we go down and bring them back," she said. "What do you say, Lieutenant?"

"I say ask them. They've got a comm unit."

"No, Shaw says we take them home for trial. We go after them."

"Begging your pardon, sir, but that's nuts. They've got a jungle to hide in. We'd never find them." Clio remembered Teeg, standing in the med-tent door, a black shape against the glare of floodlights outside, saying, *Think they'd ever find us?*

Russo glanced up at Shaw.

"These men have killed three people," he said. "We need to make an effort to bring them to trial. It's our duty."

This prissy, do-your-duty stance was a load of crap, after what they'd been through. Clio turned to him. "We did make an effort. We tried to get them to come back, that's why Meng is here."

Shaw bristled at her tone. "And Liu?"

Clio shrugged. "He was Teeg's ally. I don't know if he would come willingly."

Russo grimaced. "I know. I talked to him." She turned back to the monitor, where the blue surface of Niang wheeled ponderously by. A serene galaxy-like swirl over the ocean marked a hurricane. "I've been talking to them for over an hour. He's solid with Teeg. Or seems to be. I believe him."

"And Posie's dead, sir? Confirmed dead?"

"Yes, dead."

Clio closed her eyes. She had seen him sailing backward, struck hard by rifle fire. And she had lured him into the field, broke up his alliance with Teeg, brought him to his death. She helped to kill him. It felt lousy, even if it was self-defense.

Shaw cleared his throat. "They're criminals. We should bring them home." He looked pointedly at Russo. "Hear their story."

Russo frowned mightily. "I've heard their story. And they're lying."

"Excuse me, sir, but that's for a court to decide." Shaw's face was earnest, proper.

"Ideally, yes. But here and now, I'm the court." Russo

was quiet for a long while. "Lieutenant, in your opinion, Teeg and Liu would fight us, if we went down?"

"Teeg would, yessir."

"And in your opinion, he is mentally unstable?"

"He planned to commandeer the whole mission, dismantle the lander, kidnap at least three crew members, force them to have sex and procreate. He murdered Hillis and Posie. He threatened to kill me, tried to kill Meng." Clio paused, staring at them. "I'd say he's unstable. I'd say he's freeping out of his mind."

Russo looked up at Shaw. He held her gaze for a long while, then broke contact. She swung around to stare at Niang. Russo didn't like ambiguity, Clio knew. By-the-book Russo just had to hate looking at that wild turquoise swamp below her, hiding the crew members who decided to break all the rules, and in doing so, just broke her career in Space Recon, once and for all.

Dive countdown droned on. Clio looked at the control panel. Left side for time, right side for space. As though they were separate, like gates at a bus terminal, and not actually the same, a continuum. The mind wanders off, thinking of it, loses hold. So you split the control panel in two, keep things in their places.

The Dive panel displayed its controls in a bank of lights and touchscreens, toggles and switches, giving the mystery of time the outward semblance of common mechanical function. You press buttons, visit the past, return to the present.

At this moment, Clio had her last vestige of real power. She sat at the Dive controls. Pointed them home-time. A fantasy occurred to her, that she could Dive back a week and find Hillis alive on Niang. It was a way of overcoming death, mind-bending and lethal in its own way, of course. But to see Hillis again . . . There would be no other chances. This was the last Dive.

The paradox, though. No one had ever traveled to the past within one's "sphere of causality"—one's own history. But the theories were frighteningly clear: if she saved

Hillis' life, she would create an unresolvable paradox. For starters, there were at least six people who saw him die. This could not exist side by side with the same six people who saw him survive. The universe, Vandarthanan said, would not tolerate such a profound time paradox. No one knew the result. It was an experiment, he said, that must never be conducted.

She left the program intact. Headed home-time.

"Helm to you, Finn," Russo was saying.

Clio nodded. "Yessir."

Shaw cinched in his lap belt, leaned back, eyes closed.

She said her goodbyes to them all again, before Dive hit. *I never meant to leave you. I would have scattered your ashes, if I could. If they buried you, Mother, I hope you never knew.*

Clio eased the ship into motion, firing thrusters at half power to bring them to transition speed. *Starhawk* was headed out, gathering speed, rushing toward Dive, zooming in for their Dive point. Caught it. Niang's system, its hot, blue star, flicked off the screen in an instant. The cabin air closed in around her, pressing the weight of time against her face, squeezing liquid out of her eyes.

And she was sick this time, very sick. Kept to her chair and fought for consciousness. Needed water. Knew she wouldn't want it if she got it. Ran systems checks. Routine preserves sanity. Ran them again.

When her stomach was under control, she went aft to medlab. Estevan lay on a pallet, breathing noisily. His face flickered a wan light, like a bulb giving out. She took his blood pressure. Not bad for a man on one lung. His hands were cold, and she rubbed them, thinking of the journey home.

They had taken the specimens out of the lander, transferring them to the science deck. The seed packets with Hillis' writing on them, the seedlings and growths in clear specimen bags, cloudy with the moisture of transpiration. There was little enough of the Niang haul. Meng bemoaned the cache left behind, in the botany tent. Crew treated the haul with feverish respect. Something good had come of the Niang disaster, they told themselves that. Something good.

Clio looked at the floor in medlab. Beneath her, on science deck, the Niang green, in strict quarantine.

She thought of the alien crash site she found on Niang, the deserted ship tucked into the botanical maze. How long had that ship been in the jungle; how long does metamorphosis take? How long before computer circuit boards gave up their metal fragments to the thin, blue tendrils?

How long before the first pinpoint holes in *Starhawk*'s hull?

Clio looked back at Estevan. His life pulsed under his skin, keeping faith. "We'll make it," Clio told him. "We've come this far, we're gonna make it."

Zee coaxed Clio into the chair and brought Mars into fine resolution on the screen. In the great rift valley of Vallis Marineris, the stupendous northern cliff faces were cloaked in shadow. *Starhawk* was still in good position to observe Mars, though the craft had entered home-time midway between Earth and Mars and was now hurtling away from it. Zee had been studying Mars for days, trying to interest Clio, wooing her with pictures, and stories of the world that humanity had still only seen close up on monitors, never on foot.

Zee shook his head. "I should have been born fifty years ago, when there was still such a thing as pure science."

"You're an astrophysicist. What's that, if not pure science?"

"Yes, but, in the end, what am I accomplishing? Biotime was the only job I could get, you know. Otherwise, why do you think I'm with Recon and not in a research lab?"

Clio watched the red planet with a kind of nostalgia, thinking that the Niang seed, Earth's salvation, meant, perhaps, the end of spaceflight, of all flight of metal. And as for pure research. Well.

Zee was still talking. "I was just born in the latter days, that's all. The days when we came close to planetary death."

"What did we hear, then, on the radio transmission? If it wasn't planetary death, what was it?"

"A possibility. The ghost of Christmas Future paid us a little call."

"And we would have done anything it took to avoid that future, right? No price too high?"

Zee looked at her, paying attention now. "I suppose not. No price too high."

"Even pure science?"

Zee crumpled his lower lip, thinking.

Clio persisted. "If it came to that choice, would it be worth it? No price too high?"

"Are you thinking of Hillis again, Clio? That price?"

"No. I'm thinking of you, Zee. What price would you pay?"

He drew a deep breath, weighing her words. "Well then, I would say, against the whole body and history and future of humanity, even pure science could be given over. But how human we would be without it, I'm not sure. So no, no price too high."

Clio was watching him intently. He laid his hand on her arm, questioning.

She nodded. "Thanks. I thought that's what you'd say."

Beneath them, on lower deck, the Niang seedlings settled into Meng's watchful care.

CHAPTER 13

❦

Two weeks in-system, *Starhawk* began heating up. Cabin temperature was eighty-one degrees, crew were in T-shirts. Russo assigned Shaw to investigate the coolant system.

Meng noticed it first, and cooled down the science deck to keep the biota within ideal range. After twenty-four hours the cooling system strained its capacity, heating up the other decks to over ninety degrees, endangering the onboard electronics.

Shaw spent hours on lower deck checking out the water pumps and heat-exchanger system. A by-product of *Starhawk*'s electrical system was water. Oxygen and hydrogen were mixed chemically in fuel cells, creating twenty pounds of water every hour. This was fed to a series of pipes used for the galley and to pipes that would dump heat through the freon radiators in the equipment bay doors.

Clio and Zee were on the crew station, checking out systems, when Meng leaned her head in from the galley hatchway.

"Time to strip, boys and girls," she said. "I need to bring the temp down another notch or our plants aren't going to be happy. That means crew deck heats up a notch. I'm going on flight deck to tell the captain. Hope you can take the heat. You can always come down and do some real work on science deck, instead of staring at the scenery." As she ducked her head back out and headed up the galley ladder to the bridge, her voice trailed off: "I've seen better pictures of Mars in *National Geographic*."

Zee stared after her. "She really works at being unpleasant, doesn't she?"

Clio wiped the sweat off her face with the back of her hand. Cabin temperature was rivaling Niang's and the air smelled even worse. "I think she misses Estevan," Clio said. "He could take her on. It's being ignored that she hates."

"He's not doing so hot, is he," Zee said.

"No. Looks like he's got pneumonia."

Zee nodded, glum. Turned back to the screen. "Meng's right about one thing. The pictures are lousy. We've been losing definition for days now."

"Makes sense to me. We're getting farther away all the time."

"Right, but not at that fast a rate, to account for the interference." Zee settled into his task at the controls, his arms glistening with sweat, looking better than Clio imagined he would without his shirt on.

Clio walked over to watch what he was doing.

"So what do you think it is?"

"Don't know, but I'm working on it."

"But what do you think it is?"

Zee was deep into the computer program, searching for something, working the keyboard. "Actually, I think the computer is affected. I think the program is failing." He caught Clio's eye. "I know. Not good."

A little knot had begun to form in Clio's stomach. Six weeks out from home. So close, so close.

Zee didn't speak for a long time, fingers clicking away at the keyboard, deep into the ship's systems, on a mission to find something. Then: "Holy shit."

Clio sat bolt upright, leaned closer to the monitor. Zee was in the file showing capacity of the water storage tank, where the excess water not diverted to galley or freon radiators was stored, then dumped if not needed.

"Holy shit." Zee said again. "We're dumping one hundred sixty-five pounds of water overboard right this minute."

"But we're always dumping excess water overboard. We never can use all the water by-product, Zee."

"That's right, but this is way too much. Way too

much." He swung around and headed out the hatchway. "I'm going to get Shaw. He should take a look at this."

Minutes later, Shaw came scowling into the crew station, flushed with exertion, grease on his face.

Clio relinquished her seat to Zee, as Shaw sat down at the terminal.

Shaw looked at the numbers, began calling up the thermal system into visual. A schematic onscreen showed the water output. "How can we be producing that much water?"

Zee said, "Maybe we're not. Maybe we're not using it up as fast as we used to."

Shaw stopped dead. Looked at Zee. "That's it."

Zee was nodding.

"What's it?" Clio asked.

Shaw punched at the keyboard, and there it was. Thermal systems had shut down the freon radiators' water supply by thirty percent. They weren't dumping their excess heat, they were conserving it.

Shaw hit the comm switch. "Captain, sir, we've found the problem . . . it's the thermal-system computer program. It's been diverting water out of the coolant system and storing it in the tanks belowdecks. We've been heated up by those tanks for days now." Shaw listened a moment longer, then swung around to face Zee. "She'll do a manual override. From now on, we monitor the thermal system, operate it manually if we have to. Zee, you're on that one."

"Yessir."

Shaw nodded at him. "Good work." Then he ducked through the hatch, heading for the flight deck.

Zee swung around in his chair, face beaming. "We did it."

Clio brought up a big smile. "Yes, we did it." All the while her stomach was sinking rapidly. It might be just a glitch in the program, an isolated event. Clio tried hard to believe it, and failed. "Zee," she said. "Could you run some systems checks? Electrical, air system, pressurization, water. We should do a complete run-through."

"Sure. Easy." He shrugged.

"Manually."

"Manually. That'd take a while." He cocked his head. A question. Why?

"If the computer screwed up once, we need to double-check, that's all," Clio said.

"That would be true if we had a pattern of failures. But we don't."

She could do it herself. Not as fast as Zee, but she could do it. "OK. Maybe you're right." She headed to the galley hatch. "I'm going to clean up." She grabbed a cup of coffee on her way through and climbed the ladder to crew deck, heading for her cabin. Heard Zee on the ladder behind her. She turned to face him.

"What's going on, Clio?" Zee asked.

She laughed. "A cup of coffee and a shower. Not a lot."

He held her gaze. "You're suspicious about something. The coolant-system failure. What about it?"

"Nothing about it. Made me nervous, that's all."

"So you're not going to tell me."

"Tell you what?"

Zee gazed at her steady. "If you don't trust me, Clio, who do you have? You going to keep stuff to yourself, never let anybody in?"

Clio looked away, started to prepare some excuse.

He stopped her before she could answer. "What am I to you? Some useful sidekick you can use like Hillis used me? Because if that's what I am, you can keep your stupid secrets, I don't even want to know." He caught her gaze for a moment, then turned to go.

"Zee . . ." she began.

He swung around. "No!" He was shaking his head, words building up inside but not yet ready to come out. Then: "Keep your Red Queen magic away from me." He was backing away. "Just keep away from me."

Clio strode to catch up to him. "Zee," she said, "listen to me. I don't know much about trust, you're right. But this is the biggest deal I've ever faced. I'm scared to death to trust. Help me." She wanted to tell him, wanted desperately to tell him, she realized. To share the decision with another human being. And of everyone on board, in fact, of everyone she knew, Zee would be her choice. All these years she thought it was best to trust to silence, but silence didn't always save you. DSDE, for example, had other ways of knowing. She had to trust Zee, now.

He shook his head, a dark look falling over his face. "You've got to help yourself, Clio. I'm here for you, but you've got to take the plunge."

She nodded her head, licking her dry lips. *Time to take the plunge.* "Let's talk in my cabin," she said.

They walked down the corridor of empty crew cabins. Russo's and Shaw's quarters, senior-officer quarters, were off the flight deck. Here, there were only Zee, Meng, and Clio. And Estevan in medlab. Names were still on empty cabins: JON HILLIS, HARPER TEEG, ROBERT POSIE, SHANNON RESSMEYER, WONG LIU.

She held open the door that read CLIO FINN, motioned Zee through.

Clio sat on the bed, put her untouched coffee on the desk. Zee perched on the chair, quiet. A patient man. She felt grateful to have a minute to find the thread of her story.

"You're right. I don't trust many people. Guess I've got too many secrets. My whole life is composed of secrets. I'm used to them."

"They're safe with me," he said.

"Zee. The biota we took on. It has a flaw."

He waited. He was going to make her do all the work.

"It eats metal," she said, flat out.

"Jesus."

"Maybe plastic, too. I'm not sure."

"How do you mean, eats? Corrodes it?"

"No, it takes over, replaces metal. It replicates the shape, like minerals replace wood in a fossil. Except I have no idea what the process is. I only know it happens." She told him then. Told him of the crashed ship, the Niang intrusion. How Niang erases technology.

Zee listened intently, absorbing her words. And Clio talked, told him every detail. It felt so good to talk, to let all the words out. Give it to another human being, hold nothing back.

His eyes would sometimes flick to the left, a sign he was thinking hard. Yes, Clio thought, yes Zee. Think. It's what you do so well. And I'm so tired of thinking.

"So you think the Niang biota is contaminating the ship," Zee said.

"Yes. Question is, how is it spreading. All specimens are in quarantine."

"But how effective is our quarantine? Maybe the pollen, or spores or whatever, have eaten through the metal, like acid through silk. And their first effects are being felt in the most delicate metal parts on board. The computer circuits." Zee paused. "If we tell the captain, she'll dump the plants."

Clio nodded.

"And we can't let her do that. Can't tell her what's going on." His forehead wrinkled in a confused frown.

He was learning the necessity of secrets. All they could do now was keep watch, nurse *Starhawk* home. But to bring it to Earth, that was the issue. She waited for Zee to say it.

"So when you asked me if I would give up science for the regreening, this is what you meant." He looked at Clio wistfully. As someone who had been happier not knowing. He got up and washed his face in the sink, toweled it dry. "Not just science. This is Western civilization. Buildings, electricity, transportation, hospitals, communications. Telescopes. Printing press. Computers."

"Right," Clio said. "And paper clips and lawn mowers. But people will survive."

"How do you know?"

"The Niang monkeys. The animal life. It exists."

Zee shook his head. "But it's had millions of years to adapt. Niang could hit Earth like measles hit Hawaii."

"Yeah. It's a risk."

"Clio. Niang will never make it through Vanda quarantine. It's a bust."

"We have to help it through quarantine."

Zee stared at her.

"We smuggle it, Zee. Only way it's going to survive."

He sat down, towel still in hand. "Holy cow."

Clio leaned forward. "Because it's at least a chance. It's maybe regreening with a vengeance, but it's regreening. Without it, the future is a bust. The big die-off, Zee. So, the way I figure it, we don't have much choice."

They sat for a long while, not speaking. He had to work it out, take it step by step in his own mind, like she had. Zee had more to lose. He had his career. He had no quarrel with DSDE, had no sentence hanging over his head. The rising star, still ascending. Peter vander Zee, boy wonder, welcome home. So his choices were harder than hers. She gave him time.

Finally he stood up. Ran his hand through his hair, massaging his scalp after too much thinking. "Guess I'll go run those systems checks."

Clio got up, walked over to him. "You're really something, you know?"

Zee smiled, a tentative, probing look in his eyes. "So are you."

She moved toward him, put her arms around him, as he wrapped his around her. It was only a hug, but it felt safe, even if only for the moment.

CHAPTER 14

❧

The transmission from Vanda was weak, crackling and flickering. Say again, Starhawk. Say again, Vanda requested, as though they had trouble hearing, trouble believing, what they heard.

Then, within the hour, though it was two A.M. on Vanda, Brisher was on visual. Even through the snow on the screen, he looked bad. Doughy, creased.

His face filled the screen. "Not good news, Captain," he said. "Not good at all. I'm disappointed." He looked to his right, then back at them. "Folks here tell me five crew are dead, one more critically injured. You are down to five able-bodied crew? Over."

Russo's face was as blank as Clio had ever seen it. Her voice flat, captain-like. "No, we have three dead, two missing. Another man with a collapsed lung, stable but critical. We're covered for essential ship functions. No ship damage. Over."

"What in the name of hell happened?"

"Landing crew mutinied. Led by Lieutenant Harper Teeg, aided by Posie and Liu. Finn, Hillis, vander Zee, and Estevan resisted. In the conflict Hillis was killed, as well as Posie and Shannon Ressmeyer. Estevan took a bullet in his left lung, and we need to talk with a doctor on that."

"You'll talk to a doctor when I'm damn good and ready. What the hell were you doing during this shoot-out, Captain Russo? How did Shaw let the ground mission get out of control? Put Shaw on."

"No need, sir," Russo said. "Shaw wasn't on ground mission. Teeg was in charge. Because Shaw was injured, from an accidental depressurization in launch bay. Which might have been sabotage on Teeg's part."

"Well, you've got conspiracies all over the place, don't you, Captain?"

She let it slide, her face stiff as the clipboard she was holding.

"Lieutenant Finn, you there?" Brisher asked.

"Here, sir."

"What happened down on Niang? You got a believable story? I sure hope you've got one hell of a believable story."

"It's the same story Zee and Estevan have, sir. Teeg didn't want to come home. He saw Niang as some kind of paradise. Where he could be leader. It was a chance to live a great adventure, to test himself against the planet. Only he needed us all with him, to survive. For company. Said he hated Biotime, sir. Always hated to take orders. When we wouldn't go along, he clamped down on us, abandoned the mission. We tried to disarm him—Zee and Estevan and me. That's when Estevan got shot. By the time the shooting was over, Hillis was dead. And Shannon and Posie. We got the lander back, but we barely escaped."

"You're saying we got five, maybe six crew lost because Harper Teeg wanted to play Robinson Crusoe?"

"Yeah. I guess so. Sir."

"And why weren't you on that ground mission, Russo? What was our Dive pilot doing on a ground mission?"

"It seemed the best assignment at the time. My place was to captain this ship."

"Better think of a different answer, Captain." Brisher's face stared out from the screen, across seventy-two million kilometers. "I'm going back to bed. All I can say is, it's sure going to be one sweet hearing at the Bureau."

Then Vanda botany staff wanted to talk to Meng, and Shaw patched them through to science deck.

Clio was the first to break the silence in the cabin. "I think he enjoyed that," she said.

Shaw glanced over at her. "What did you expect, a medal?"

"He's sadistic, petty, and banal. But if he wants to give me a medal, I wouldn't turn it down," Clio said.

Shaw's mouth was hanging open a notch. "That'll do, Lieutenant," he said. "You will observe protocols, you understand?"

"Yessir. Sorry sir."

Russo was looking at Clio, a smile appearing for a moment around her eyes. "You're relieved, Commander," she said to Shaw. "Go get some sleep." He hauled himself out of his chair, and headed back to the officers' cabins.

Clio ran systems checks, running through automatic checks first, for something to do, giving Russo some privacy. Russo was dead meat, and knew it. Brisher had washed his hands of her. This was one mission they needed to blame on a live body, and the captain would do nicely. Russo was finished in Recon. It couldn't be a surprise to her, but now, clearly, Brisher had taken a stance. You're dead meat, he said between the words.

"I'm going to run a manual check on reaction-control system for rotation, Captain," Clio said, asking permission. Took the silence for an OK. Clio grasped the hand control and gently moved it forward and backward, adjusting the pitch of the ship, then twisted the control left and right to adjust for yaw. The ship responded. The screen showed *Starhawk* rotating along its X/Y axis.

"Excuse me, sir," Clio said after a time. "But can I ask you a personal question?"

Russo hadn't spoken since the Vanda transmission. She blinked over at Clio. Nodded.

"Do you have family, sir?"

A pause. "No. No family. Just Biotime, I suppose." After a few moments: "How about you? Your father's still in the Midwest—Minneapolis, isn't that right?"

"Yessir. You know sir, I'm real sorry for what's coming down. I got the feeling I'm never going to Dive again. Tell you the truth, I'm starting to get the shakes anyway. Truth is, I get them pretty bad. So I figure I'm done, one way or another. But I'm sorry you're in trouble. Biotime ought to keep you, sir."

"Well, the mission was my responsibility. If it had been successful, I would have had the glory. Now I get the blame. It goes with the stripes. Don't fret about it, Lieutenant. It's a good system. I'm not sorry."

"What do you think they'll do to you?"

"Quick retirement. Terms depend on the outcome of the hearing. No matter what the outcome, I'll never fly again."

"Me neither."

"Oh, you've still got a few Dives left."

"No, Captain. I'm starting to lose it. I never could admit it. But now, I'm retiring. I want to tell Brisher that first, before he yanks my pilot bars."

Russo met her gaze, nodded slowly. "You have my permission to do just that, Lieutenant." A pause. "I didn't know."

"Nosir. But I wanted you to know now, since we're in for it with Biotime. I just want you to know, I don't have a lot to lose. So I don't feel like taking a lot of shit from Ellison Brisher. It's not worth it."

Russo was smiling broadly now. "That's the spirit, Lieutenant." She raised an eyebrow. "Just observe the protocols. It's more dignified."

Clio nodded, smiling back. "Yessir." She turned back to the instrument panel, not seeing it, feeling light-headed, in the dazed way of one who has finally told a long-suppressed truth. The spoken words seemed still to hang in the air between her and Russo: *I'm losing it. I get the shakes, so I figure I'm done. Get them pretty bad, to tell you the truth.* Sucking in a breath deep into her chest, Clio knew why people talk of getting something off your chest, when you have something important to say, and you finally say it. The breath filled her rib cage.

Doctors on Vanda were patched into medlab talking to Zee. He was the only crew available for more or less constant watch over Estevan, since Meng was in charge of the botany deck and Russo, Shaw, and Clio were on constant rotation schedules on the bridge.

Clio listened in. Estevan was bad, real bad. And they were still two weeks out from station.

Over the last eight weeks Estevan had lost forty pounds, and most of his muscle tone. In the last week he stopped playing cards, much to Meng's disgust.

"Only goddamn thing that keeps him alive," Meng said. "Losing at cards makes him mad, gives him a reason to live."

Clio thought she might be right.

Clio's shift was up, a twelve-hour marathon. She was dog-tired, and headed down to crew deck, passed medlab, ducked her head in. Zee was sitting with his patient. He put his finger to his lips, indicating Estevan, asleep.

She nodded, swung back into the corridor, headed for bed. Passed Hillis' cabin, paused. Then pushed his door open.

The bedcovers were tucked, the desk was clean. Someone had bagged his stuff, stacked it against the starboard bulkhead. Idly, Clio opened his desk drawers, one by one. Clean.

She started on the bags then, peering into the contents, trying to find evidence of his life, to find something personal. This one had folded shirts, togs, underwear, belt, shoes. She ran her hands over these items, waiting to cry, feeling her face swell up, then, knowing she wouldn't cry; that release was too easy, it was too much to hope for.

Another bag held game disks, prescription headache medicine, notebooks filled with plant sketches and scientific notes, an audiotape, a stack of photographs. Clio started through the photographs: vistas of Earth, forests, trees, nameless plants. No people in them, and worse, no pictures of Hillis, no picture of Hillis and Clio, no people at all.

"I told her, Hillis," she said. "I told Russo I'm burned out. But, anyway, DSDE knows, they've known for a long time, so I told Russo. I expected it to be hard to tell her, but it wasn't. It felt like coming out of the closet. It doesn't feel good, but it doesn't feel that bad either, not as bad as my nightmares."

She put the pictures back into the box. "I'm going to

jail, or worse. So it's really all over. You got out just in time, Hill." She saw him inching toward the shuttle, a dozen weapons in his arms, a look of amusement on his face, as though it were all a game, as though he knew Teeg would never let him walk up that ramp. Tears jumped out of her eyes. The picture of Hill was so clear in her mind. As she closed her eyes against the tears, the picture was even sharper, in memory.

She picked up the audiotape. A slight clutch in her stomach. In Hillis' scrawl, the label read "A Short History of the Future." She tucked it back in the bag, cinched it up, stacked it back against the bulkhead.

Clio shut Hillis' door behind her, turned to head down to her cabin when the emergency bells slammed into life.

"DON PORTABLE OXYGEN SYSTEM. DON PORTABLE OXYGEN SYSTEM," Clio heard ship's voice say.

She lunged for the nearest cabin door, Hillis' cabin, grabbed the oxygen pack from the wall, pulled the mask over her face, sucked in a breath. Got to be fast when air systems go. You got two minutes without oxygen, then you're out cold, and in four minutes your brain starts to die. Worse if it's a toxic gas. Could kill you in seconds. Clio leaned against the wall a moment trying to get calm, stopped gulping air. Heart still pumping hard, she stepped back into the corridor, and reeled. Dizzy. The pack wasn't working. She pushed against Posie's cabin door, yanked the oxygen pack off the wall, sucked in hard. Nothing.

Back in the hall, gasping, she chanced breathing, hauling in a ragged breath. It didn't kill her, but it was thin, very thin. She heard herself inhale with a desperate, sucking sound. She steadied herself with one hand against the bulkhead. *Fall down and hit your head, and you've just hung it up, girl.* She lunged for Shannon's door, tore the pack off the wall, collapsed with it to a sitting position, flipped the mask over her mouth and nose.

Pulled in sweet, breathable air.

She struggled back to her feet, and checked out Liu's and her own cabin's packs. Hers worked. She dashed back into the corridor and ran down to medlab. Zee was sprawled on the floor. Estevan had managed to climb out of his cot, and was crouched on the floor next to Zee. As Clio hurried over to them, Estevan put his oxygen pack over Zee's mouth.

"Can you share your pack with him?" she asked him. He nodded yes, brought the pack up to his own face, alternating. Zee was coming around, struggled to get up. Clio pressed him into the floor. "You lie here until you're OK, I'm going up to flight deck to check on the captain," she said, and was already racing through the door. In the corridor the alarms were still sounding. Where was everybody? Clio slammed through the hatchway and took the ladder rungs three at a time down to the galley. Shaw lay at the foot of the flight-deck ladder, the galley oxygen pack lying uselessly at his side. Clio charged through the hatch into the forward crew deck, pulled down every pack in the room, testing them. One usable pack. Better than nothing. She rushed back to Shaw and slapped the mask over his mouth. As soon as he made a small movement, she left him, and started up to the flight deck.

Russo was attempting to get out of her chair, staggered back, saw Clio, waved her mask at her. "Air," she said. Clio put her own mask over Russo's mouth for a moment. Then took it back, sucked in a long breath, gave it back to Russo, and charged back down the ladder, fueled by one breath, praying for a usable pack on the science deck. All decks were accessed from the galley, making it a short run to science deck. Within twenty seconds, Clio was in the botany lab. No one in sight.

She ran to the intercom in the quarantine doors and shouted Meng's name.

"I'm here," came Meng's voice.

"Meng, open up, I got no air."

A long pause.

"Meng! Goddamn it, open up."

"If there's poison out there, I'm not opening the door."

"Meng, there's no poison! I'm OK but the air packs are ruined. Now open the door!"

"Why should I trust you?"

"Meng! I'm going to die out here. Help me." Clio banged on the door with her fist. She was dizzy, starting to lose it. Clio pushed away from the quarantine doors and grabbed the nearest oxygen pack. Dead. Ran to the next station, found another dead one. Rushing back to the intercom, she jabbed the button. "Please, Meng! Open the door! I can't breathe."

"I'm sorry, Clio. Whatever's killing you could kill these seedlings too. You don't want it all to be for nothing, do you?"

"Meng, you murdering bitch. Open the damn doors." That last a hoarse whisper.

She was starting to black out, heard Meng say, "Now, that wasn't very nice, Clio. . . ."

She leaned into the quarantine wall, fighting to stand up, but finding herself starting to slip down the long, long wall into the void.

The sounds of the carnival jammed the air. Clio was standing in front of Amazon River House, where a gaping hole swallowed one car after another. From deep inside came muffled screams. Clio handed her ticket to the man. The orange scrap of paper stuck to her fingers for a moment, from the paste of sweat. He looked at her funny, as though she had passed him an unsanitary thing. Sweat couldn't hurt him, you'd think he'd know. But bodily fluids were bad manners these days.

The line of fun-seekers was emptying itself into the waiting cars. A young man up ahead turned around, searching the line for someone. He looked right at Clio a moment, and smiled. Then he climbed into a car. His T-shirt stuck to his back; a line of sweat down his backbone molded the cotton to his workman's muscles.

Clio shared a car with a teenage girl who screamed on cue at every snake, bat, panther that the Amazon House threw at them. Clio thought of the young man up ahead of her, riding alone. She wondered if he knew that the Amazon House used to be the Tunnel of Love, and she longed for some of the sweet, silent darkness of that old-time ride, imagined the darkness spreading over her like a lover bending close, blocking the sun. But you couldn't have Tunnels of Love these days. A bad influence on the teenagers, who everyone hoped were practicing abstinence. So they converted it to other uses.

The sunlight hit her face suddenly as the ride ended, hurting her eyes. She saw the young man in the T-shirt standing in line for cotton candy. Amazon Man. She looked for the smile again but he didn't see her.

She was walking rapidly now, trying to spy Petya. It was time to get home for dinner. Mom and Elsie made a big deal out of meals together. He was supposed to wait for her by the ticket booth. Then she saw him in line for the Big Top. Her heart sank. The performance in the Big Top was an hour at least. She'd never get him out of line. Petya could be stubborn. She produced a big smile and approached him. "Big Top, huh?"

"Yes. There's going to be elephants?"

Clio could hear the choir tuning up inside. She doubted the elephants; sounded more like a revival. "Maybe there'll only be singing and such."

A frown flickered on his forehead.

"Want to come with me?" she asked. "Maybe we'll get some cotton candy."

"You have to stand in line to see the show?" He turned to watch the front of the line, still hoping for elephants. At twenty he still had never seen one.

"You might be disappointed," she said.

"That's OK."

Clio was resigned. He wanted to see inside the Big Top, elephants or not. He had lived through a longer childhood than most, had seen a million promises broken. But as long as he stood in line, at least for that long, he had elephants.

"I'll be out here waiting. Then we'll go, OK?" she said.

Petya nodded happily, turned to shuffle forward in the line.

When Clio turned she saw Amazon Man leaning against the Chair-o-Plane railing, eating the last of his cotton candy, watching her. He wasn't bothering with subtlety. She found herself walking toward him, and wishing she wasn't.

His face was well worn from the sun, his eyes so soft blue she wanted to cup her hands across his brow to shade them. But you don't touch people you've just met, she scolded herself. We have formalities. Before we touch.

He broke the silence with a smile. "Hi."

They did the Tilt-a-Wheel, then the Rocket. When the Rocket pitched into its headlong dive, Clio dug her fingers into his forearm, and he brought his arm closer around her. She had let him pay for the rides, so it was almost like a date. She let herself pretend he was her boyfriend instead of a man she'd just picked up at a traveling circus in a vacant lot outside of town.

They found a storage tent on the outskirts of the carnival. They'd gone looking without deciding in words, just turned away from the middle of things to find a sheltered place.

The tent cast a yellow glow on them as they sank down together, first to their knees, like some kind of nuptials. She pulled back and put her hand out between them, palm out. He reached into his jeans pocket and drew out the small scratch pack, broke it in half and pricked her finger. Nothing happened. "Don't be shy," he said, coaxing her in the ritual. She squeezed her finger, hard, until a glistening red pearl welled on her fingertip. He pressed it into the paper, where it turned the right shade of purple, certifying her clean. Then he held out his left hand to her, all the while stroking the back of her neck with his other hand. She scratched him hurriedly, watching it turn purple. Then she pulled him down on top of her, casting his shadow over her face.

Zee was looking down at her, his face contorted, saying something, she couldn't quite make out what.

She tried to sit up. She was on the floor. Why was Zee shouting?

"What's up?" Clio asked. Zee was usually so calm.

He was pressing the air pack over her mouth and nose.

She sucked in a deep breath, remembering. Finally, she pushed the mask away. "What's the situation, we got air?"

"Yes. Take a deep breath, these packs have more oxygen than ship's air, and right now you need it."

Meng stepped into view, hovering next to Zee. She was out of her arm cast, and looking fit. The expression of sisterly concern was laughable. "I guess I was a little slow in getting the doors open."

Clio stared hard at Meng until the woman broke the gaze. Meng looked over at Zee, said, "I think she's still woozy. Let's take her to her cabin."

Zee and Meng each grabbed an arm, hauled Clio to a standing position. Clio slowly withdrew her arm from Meng, leaning on Zee. "Thanks for the help, Meng," she said sweetly. Meng smiled tentatively, a question on her face. Clio smiled back, a big one. Best to keep her off guard. Confront her, accuse her, and Meng was at her best; now Clio would see how Meng did with a little bit of ambiguity. "Thanks for everything," she said. Said it nice.

Zee helped her up to crew deck, to her cabin. Made her lie down on her bunk. "You feeling OK?"

"Yeah."

Zee just kept looking at her. Scientific skepticism, maybe.

"No," she said.

Zee pulled a blanket up to cover her. "Just rest."

But Clio's mind was racing. "However the biota spreads, spores, or whatever, it's in the air system. And it's hungry."

"I wish you wouldn't put it that way. It isn't a monster. It's just plant life."

Clio let that one lie. "But it's undermining small metal parts."

"It's not attacking the liquid oxygen or the nitrogen tanks," Zee said. "Or the valves. Too big. Maybe it's going after the sensors monitoring the oxygen content of the cabin atmosphere; those are more vulnerable. We'd better take those off auto and go manual."

Clio was silent a long while. Lying there, staring at the ceiling, staring at the panels with their stitches of metal rivets. "Two weeks. We got two more weeks, Zee. Hope this bucket can hold on a few more days."

"Captain says Vanda is sending out a rescue ship."

Clio raised an eyebrow. "I'm surprised Brisher would go to that expense."

"Captain says the company likes what they've heard about our samples. Got a whole flock of botanists lined up to talk to Meng. They figure Niang may be important."

"They got that one right." She pulled the blanket up under her chin, suddenly drowsy. "That should cut our time on *Starhawk* in half. So we got one week to go."

"One week," Zee said. "Ship can at least hold together one week, huh?"

Clio looked up at the rivets in the ceiling. "Shit, yes. Made in the U.S.A., man."

CHAPTER 15

❧

Estevan lay dying. Clio sat beside him, had been, for three hours. Then she called Russo down, when she saw that he was going down fast. His breathing filled the room, pulling her own breath into the labor of it, as though she could show him how. But he was succumbing to pneumonia, had long ago given up his color, most of his consciousness, all of the fight.

Russo bent close to him. "Aurelio," she said. "Is there anything you want me to do for you. Or say to your family?"

Estevan lay still, not responding. Finally, Russo left, leaving him in Clio's care.

He opened his eyes, looked at Clio. There was a thin light in them as he moved his lips. Clio bent nearer.

"Shaw's an asshole," he whispered.

She nodded. That was true enough.

"Don't let him be the one. Don't let him sit with me, man."

Shaw's medlab shift didn't come up again for another hour. Estevan wouldn't last that long. "I won't let him. No assholes in medlab. New rule."

Estevan let out three coughing gasps, the dregs of a laugh. His hand groped on the blanket next to him, and Clio brought up her hand. He gripped it with surprising force. "You know, I always liked you." His voice was a harsh whisper, and Clio leaned close to hear him. "You're OK. Got balls, you really do. Just don't turn into one of them, like Shaw, like Posie. Meng. They're crazy, man. No heart. You know?" He gripped her hand and shook it, looking at her with bright eyes.

"Know what you mean, man."

"Something else." He closed his eyes for so long she thought he had gone under, but he opened them again. "My share. I want you to have part of my share of the haul. Niang is the best haul. It's like Hillis said, its regreen on wheels. Make Leery haul look like hothouse tomatoes, man." He grinned in an awful way. "Except for you, none of us would have made it. So you can all retire, man, you'll be farting through silk. And Shaw and Posie and all the rest can just stuff it." He laughed again, looking at some scene on the ceiling. "And Meng too, that bitch." His voice had grown so soft, Clio could hardly make out what he was saying. He closed his eyes.

Clio's hand had grown as cool as Estevan's. She placed her other, warmer, hand over his, and waited with him. He fell into a deep sleep then, his breath rattling in his throat. He never woke up again.

The whole crew assembled on science deck for the funeral. The whole crew was now just four people, five, if you counted Shaw, who was patched into the ceremony from the flight deck. Besides Clio, the mourners were the captain, Zee, and Meng.

Estevan lay in a shroud on a lab table. It was silver-colored, with a zipper from head to foot, and a green and yellow Biotime logo emblazoned across the chest, as though Estevan were a specimen from a foreign world.

Meng's eyes were red, and she kept dabbing at her nose with an embroidered hanky. This, Clio found hard to believe, both that Meng gave a damn about Estevan and that she actually had a handkerchief, with lace, no less. Russo swung her eyes in Meng's direction, hearing her snuffling, but didn't quite make eye contact. Probably Russo couldn't believe it either.

Russo swept them all quickly with her gaze and began: "Aurelio Estevan wasn't a religious man, but he'd want a few words said at least. Aurelio was a scientist, and a fine one. He was a father and husband, as much as anyone can be who joins Space Recon. He was a man who loved his work, stood by his crewmates, and took his injury bravely. Some of us standing here owe our lives to his strength of character. Space Recon is a dangerous service. Aurelio accepted that, as we all do, and I believe he wouldn't have chosen any other way to die than in service. I'll miss him." Russo grimaced, looked up at the others. "Anyone want to say anything more?"

In the ensuing silence, Zee and Clio rolled the table over to the extravehicular instrument pallet, and shifted Estevan's body onto the platform.

Meng let out a loud scraping sob and buried her nose into her hanky.

Clio found herself patting Meng's shoulder.

Meng jerked away. "Leave me alone."

"I feel as bad as you do, Meng."

"Oh no you don't." Meng backed up, away from the group. She waved the balled-up hanky at Estevan. "You think I'm crying for that crock of shit? Is that what you think? I'll tell you, he was such a loser. He was chauvinistic, boorish, and jealous of anybody better than him. He was a lousy shot and he cheated at cards. That's why he's dead, and not me."

Russo's face had crumpled into a livid scowl. "Meng," she said, "you are out of order. Pull yourself together."

"I'll tell you why I'm crying," Meng went on. "It's the haul. It's a crock of shit!" She spun around to face the quarantine doors, gesturing at them. "The stuff's no good, not viable. Not one goddamn little plant. I'll tell you what's wrecking the ship, it's this haul! It's invading ship's systems. It's a bust, boys and girls. A bust!"

Clio panicked. "You're hysterical. You always were crazy, Meng, always crack under a little pressure. We oughta trank you good."

"You will go to your quarters, Specialist Meng, or I'll have Lieutenant vander Zee drag you there," Russo said, barely moving her mouth.

Shaw's voice on intercom: "You need help down there, Captain?"

"*I'm* crazy? *I'm* crazy?" Meng shrieked at Clio. "You're the one that goes running through camp armed to your gills, getting everyone to choose sides until everybody kills everybody!" Meng was sobbing now, sunk down on a chair, her arm draped on the pallet, bumping up against the corpse's feet. "It's all a crock of shit," she kept whimpering. "Every single goddamn plant."

Clio wanted to shut her up. Wanted to bad.

"Might as well dump the whole fucking tray of plants out the door with Estevan. . . ." Meng waved an arm in the direction of the pallet.

Russo nodded to Zee. He walked over to Meng, took her by the arm, and pulled her to her feet. She let him take her up the ladder off science deck without a protest.

Left alone with Russo, Clio stared at her feet. *Damn Meng, damn her anyway.* The whole game was up, the whole damn game.

Eventually, Zee came back down the ladder. The captain nodded to him and he keyed in the rotation of the instrument pallet, and it rolled slowly around, releasing Estevan's body to its spacey grave.

Hell of a way to hold a funeral. Clio poured herself another drink, shook her head. Hell of a way. The scotch wasn't half bad, tasted all the better for being contraband on ship. She raised her glass. "To you, buddy, brave-hearted and true." Shit, she was stupid sentimental already, after only two drinks. But two stiff drinks, no doubt about that.

She wanted not to think, hoped the scotch would help. Wanted not to think about the whole disastrous trip, spiraling down to calamity. The mission had its chance, up until an hour ago, had its chance to redeem everything, regreen on wheels, bring that sweet green Eden back to Earth. Maybe a long shot, but a chance. Give Hillis' work, his death, a meaning, maybe. And her little trip to the quarry, a meaning for that too. *I did my share, Mom. Went down fighting.* Shit, really sloshed by now. She poured another drink.

Thing was, she wasn't finished with this mess yet.

Couldn't just get ripped and let the chips fall where they might. *Starhawk* still carried the Niang payload. It was still down on science deck, sprouting away, wafting its spoorish messengers all over the ship, still blue-green and growing. Still viable, in the ultimate sense. And she was its protector, its only chance to make it. Call it a slim chance, damn slim. Clio pictured herself taking the captain aside, spilling the whole truth, convincing her to bring it home. Convincing her to sneak it through Vanda quarantine, keep the whole thing quiet, put the fear of God into Meng and Shaw . . . Clio put her glass against her forehead, squinted her eyes to drive off the pounding in her skull. *Fucking hopeless.*

Somebody was knocking on the cabin door. Zee. He came in, all worried. Saw the bottle, eyebrows arching way up.

"It's Estevan's," she said. "Told me a few secrets before he died." She held out the bottle. "Get another cup."

"No. Rather not."

Oh damn, he was going to stay sober and ruin her party. He sat down next to her, looking miserable. He really did need a stiff drink.

"Captain and Meng are up on the bridge, talking it out."

"Figures."

"Meng sounds pretty sure of herself. She must have found something."

"Right."

"It doesn't look good."

"Nope."

As if in answer, the lights surged a moment, then dimmed low.

Zee's face dropped another notch. "Electrical surges again."

"Shit. Can't see my own drink in front of my face."

Zee expelled a long breath. Fumbled for a chair, brought it over by her bunk. "They're going to dump it, Clio. They might dump it."

"We can't let them do that, Zee. Can't let them dump Niang. We gotta talk them out of it."

"How? The stuff is eating us alive. Biotime won't let it anywhere near Vanda. They'll flashburn the ship if they have to. It's Russo's duty to dump it before it ruins the ship."

"Well it's *not* ruining the ship. We've got some computer malfunctions, that's all. It could be a virus, sabotage of some kind. And Meng is unreliable. She's just a tech. She's hysterical. Her behavior on Niang proved that." Clio took a drink, looked up at Zee over the edge of her glass. "Sound convincing?"

"No."

"Well, what's your plan, then? You got a better idea?" He was starting to get on her nerves. Why was it always up to her to solve things?

"Clio, maybe they *should* dump it. There'll be other planets; Niang isn't our last chance. Space Recon doesn't end with this mission, we'll keep looking. . . ." His voice faded, seeing the expression on her face.

"We've *been* looking, and now we've found it. Hillis said that Niang was a gift, a gift from the universe. I think it's our last chance. I'm not giving up." She could see that he didn't understand. Shit, why should he understand? He was young, had his career, didn't know what desperate meant, didn't know about nothing left to lose. "Zee," she said. "I'll tell you a thing. Tell you what drives me. You want to know?" He nodded, slowly. And she launched into it, telling him how Biotime and DSDE were waiting to snap her up, waiting to yank her pilot patch and slap her hands, slap them hard. How they knew about her medicine, long time back. Connived together to clear her in the Crippen affair, to keep their doggy running on the track just a little longer. Then Zee was sitting on the bunk next to her, looking pretty blurry by now, but holding her hand as she talked. And she spun out the rest of the story, all the way back to the night Mother heard the noises on the front porch and sent her and Petya running upstairs to the secret closet with the window. And Teeg's story of the ending of it all.

And then they were lying together, and Zee's arms were around her, and when she looked at him, she thought he might be crying, but it was hard to tell. She was, for sure. *Damn booze.*

She heard him saying, somewhere next to her, "I'm with you, Clio, whatever you need to do, I'm with you."

She recognized that for a nice sentiment. But right then she was wondering about getting it on, it had been a long while, and he was ready, no doubt about that. She stretched out against him, then realized that moving was not a good idea, tended to make the room wobble like it was losing a tire at fifty miles an hour. He held her tighter, and it seemed to quiet things down while she fell into an undulating sleep.

She cranked the volume control up, listening to them argue. The crews' voices were hard to distinguish over the headset, and sent spikes of pain through her forehead.

Clio was on flight duty, patched into crew station, where Russo was holding her powwow. Meng was spinning her theories, fending off questions by asking other questions. "So you think the photohormones are conventional?" Zee was doing his best to shoot holes, but the others were damn quiet.

Meng's theory wasn't much, so far. Some, or all, of the plants manufactured hormones that caused the plants to release unicell particles of some sort that inoculated certain metals—maybe *all* metal, and plastic as well. The action might be similar to how pathogens react with host plants. The first intrusions were into small computer parts and lightweight plastic hoses that could be easily penetrated by the enzymes that the particles released. Meng had examined the defective portable oxygen packs and found microscopic evidence of invasive plant-cell growth in the plastic hoses. She thought the vehicle of transmission of the particles was the ship's air-circulation system.

Clio took off her headphones, rested her forehead in her hand. The VDT screens pulsed in her eyes, driving in the nail a little deeper. They were buying it. They were all tired, all scared shitless. Gods, they could throw it all away. She put the phones on again.

"You son of a bitch," Meng was saying. "You just can't stand to be told anything by a woman, can you. Just can't stand not to have all the answers yourself. Hysterical woman is your last resort. Mr. Science shows his true colors."

"That's a tad harsh," Zee said.

"You'll keep your temper, Meng, or you're off this deck," Shaw said.

Zee said, "I do feel that Specialist Meng's tests should be replicated by others. Test her hypothesis. Way of science, that's all."

"Meanwhile, we slowly turn to confetti." Meng's voice.

"Commander, what's your scope on this?" That from Russo.

Shaw answered, "I'm tempted to believe Meng. We're having simultaneous systems failures, and generally in the computer systems where the metal circuits could be the most vulnerable. I say let Meng have a look at some of the circuit boards."

"Do that. Lieutenant vander Zee, you will assist Specialist Meng. Meanwhile I'll talk to Vanda about this. Meng, you will prepare for possible evacuation of the Niang cargo on science deck."

"Little late for that, isn't it, Captain?" Meng asked.

"You still follow orders on this ship, Meng?"

"Yes, sir."

"I'm glad to hear that. Two things I don't like. Hysteria and a smartass. So I won't be seeing either one around here, will I?"

"No sir."

"You can dismiss the crew, Commander. I'm going to the bridge."

CHAPTER 16

❧

"They've eaten the microscopes," Meng announced. "Fuckers have eaten my equipment." Meng was half in, half out of the crew-station hatchway. On her way to whine to the captain, no doubt.

Clio cringed, hearing her voice. Kept a calm façade, said: "That's a bit melodramatic, isn't it? Did you try using the On button?"

Meng's parting shot was lost as she scrambled out of the hatch, heading for flight deck. Clio swung back to the console, where she completed the cabin pressurization check. Pressure was at 12.9 psi, lower than it should be, but OK for now, best they could do. She had taken readings on all decks, part of the her assigned rounds this shift, since two of the main onboard computers went down. She had been awake twenty-six hours.

Damn poor timing to lose the computers. Everybody with the jitters, and now the life-support computers, controlling air and water, give up, putting everybody on double duty, pushing tempers over the edge. They could get by without the crew-deck main computers, but it meant everything done manual, done once, then done again, keep checking oxygen, nitrogen, carbon-dioxide levels, pressure, electrical. And on the rounds, you just hoped like hell the rest of the hardware, the valves and switches, the bolts, and, good God, the hull itself were uncontaminated. Three computers were operating, those on flight deck, those farthest, Meng pointed out, from the science deck. These three controlled navigation, communications, and Dive. Meanwhile,

Russo was sending messages every hour to Vanda, and no answer.

Clio moved down the access ladder to the lower deck. Rolled up her sleeves, opened her shirt button at the neck; damn warm here, amid the guts of the ship. She didn't quite need to duck low as she walked, but felt like it with pipes twined across the upper bulkhead, centimeters from her head. Bright colors marked the canisters for oxygen, nitrogen, and water; grey for mere equipment lockers. The hum of the ship was close here; hydraulics sighed. Crew didn't like lower deck. Didn't like the reminder, thank you, of the mere machinery holding their little pocket of life against the cold deep of space. Liked the upper decks with their normalcy, lulling you to forget you were seventy million kilometers away from the nearest post office. She found the access panels and checked on the liquid-oxygen tanks and the heat exchangers that warmed the gas on its way through the system's regulator. Pressure inside the tanks was 847 psi, within tolerances. She closed the panel, stood up, suddenly dizzy. Crouched down, head low. *Get a grip, girl.* Her skin was clammy, her face hot. Damn lower deck, too dark, too close. Funny noises. She moved on to the nitrogen tanks, finished her checks, turned around, nearly bumped into Shaw.

Could've said something, announced his presence. Not his style.

"You got call to be on lower deck, Lieutenant?" He was standing too close, looming large, larger than brass usually did.

Clio backed up a step. "Yessir, duty roster has me checking cabin pressure, atmosphere tanks." Always nice to know the answers when Shaw asked the questions, to be able to tell the truth. Nothing to hide, so he could damn well stand aside.

"We've got too much work to be slacking off, Lieutenant, you copy?"

"Yessir. Not slacking off, sir."

His eyes flicked down to the oxygen access panels.

"What's your reading on oxygen pressure?"

"Eight hundred forties. Within range, sir."

He nodded slowly, looking about, not really hearing her. Jerked his eyes back to her. "You heard the captain call you to crew deck a while back?"

"Nosir. I didn't hear anything, sir." *Jesus, so that's it. And he waits long enough to tell me, stringing it out, wondering what I was up to in storage, what was so important I let the captain sit waiting.*

"Intercom work down here, Lieutenant?"

"Don't know, sir. Guess not, sir."

He nodded again, squinting at her, trying to see past her yessirs, nosirs.

"Captain want to see me, sir?"

"Did. Never mind now." He turned, walked toward the hatchway ladder. Turned again. At a distance, his voice came floating to her, tinny and severed from his body. "Captain announced we're dumping the Niang haul. Danger to the ship. Thought you'd want to know."

Then his boots were echoing up the ladder.

She listened to him climb, her insides jumping around like they wanted out. *What he said, can't do that. Nosir, we can't do that.* She was climbing the ladder after him, but when she climbed through the hatchway to science deck, he was gone. Zee stood there.

"Clio, Captain says . . ."

"Yeah, I heard. I'm going to see Russo." She met his eyes, saw he was as jumpy as she was. He looked behind him toward quarantine, said, "I'll hold Meng off as long as I can. I'm supposed to help her." He wiped his hands on his jumpsuit.

"Do anything you have to. Slow her down." Clio was up the ladder to galley and on up to the bridge.

Shaw was talking to Russo on the flight deck. He turned to look at her. Russo glanced up, eyebrow raised.

"Permission to talk with the captain, sir."

"What's on your mind, Lieutenant?"

"The plants, Captain. Can I ask why? Because I thought we were waiting for further tests before deciding to dump." Clio knew better than to show emotion. Kept her face calm.

Shaw took a breath to say something; captain raised her hand slightly, cutting him off. "You can ask. I'll tell you what I told the rest. We've just lost two main onboards. Communications went down an hour ago. We're running the ship on manual with half a crew, cut off from Vanda. I'm trying to save navigations, not to mention five people and a three-hundred-billion-dollar ship, what's left of it." She turned back to the console, punched up a new screen, eyes flickering down the columns of numbers. "Anything more, Lieutenant?"

Clio sucked in a breath, pushed out the words: "Yessir."

This time Russo swung full around. Dark pools under her eyes, her face a wall.

"Ship is deteriorating, we know that, but we don't know why. We got no proof it's our haul, sir. We can't just kill them, if we're wrong, we kill off maybe the best haul Recon's ever done, we kill off this mission, once and for good." She took another breath, *control that pitch, girl, don't go too far.*

"I know how you feel, Lieutenant. We're all disappointed. But science deck is nearly shut down and I can't wait for tests on Vanda. I've got lives under my command. I've lost half of them. I'm bringing the rest home, by God. I've made my decision."

"Yessir. Can I ask what Vanda says, sir?"

Shaw looked at Russo, itching to break in, but hesitating.

"We've lost all contact. And last thing we got from the rescue ship was they were turning around. They don't have the quarantine facilities. We're on our own until we reach station." Russo closed her eyes a moment. She opened them, looked at Clio with a faint shade of life, of recognition. "A Dive pilot doesn't last forever, I know that Lieutenant. We all wish this mission could have been the big one. I wish I could do more. I'm left with my duty. That doesn't mean I like it. But I will do it." She nodded at Shaw.

"You are dismissed, Lieutenant," he said.

"Yessir." Her feet stuck to the deck. Finally she turned, got her body walking in the right direction. *Don't want to think about what comes next, just do it, girl. Nothing left to lose.* At the hatchway, turned. "Commander, sir, there's just one thing. . . ."

"You have been dismissed, Finn."

"Yessir, but there's something on lower deck. Probably minor, but I've been thinking about the oxygen valves. I'd like you to take a look at them, if you would, sir."

Shaw paused a moment, nodded. Followed her out.

Her hands left sweat on the ladder. Leaving tracks. Her brain yammering at her, couldn't shut it down. Wishing she could talk to Zee, wishing it didn't come to this, wishing she had stayed on Niang; Eden couldn't be as bad as this, even Teeg's Eden.

They were on lower deck, Shaw staring at her. She knelt down, drew back the deck panel. And then he was kneeling down, head lowered, reaching down to turn the valve, and she had her hand on the long wrench, the one they used if the valves were irky, and he was saying, I don't see anything, and she was swinging back her hand and brought the wrench down on his head. A thudding noise, and he fell forward, clattering against the open panels. She knelt by him, rifled him for ship's keys, hands shaking bad. Found them in his breast pocket. Took them, stood up, and considered how to tie him up. Could use his belt, but maybe time was more important now. They were going to dump the haul, maybe getting ready to dump it now. She raced up the ladder. Emerged onto science deck, nobody in sight, headed up to crew deck.

Down the corridor past crew cabins to the lockers next to launch bay. Her shoes on the deck echoing off the bulkheads. Looking around her, spooked, but who could be here? Shaw was down; Russo on flight deck; Zee and Meng on science deck. The jitters for sure. Just attacked ship's officer, that's good for five years, if he's not dead. But tack that on to the rest, she was dog meat anyway. Still, it made her crazy, a little crazy, to hit the commander, take him down.

No time for angst, girl, you gotta finish what you started. She had most of the ordnance cleared out by now, guns, rifles, ammo clips. Ducked in to her cabin, grabbed an empty duffel, stuffed the weapons in, all but two small pistols, stuffed those in her belt, hoisted the sack over her shoulder, jammed down the corridor toward science deck.

She managed to wrestle the duffel bag down to science, threw it on the deck, against the bulkhead. Place was empty, that meant Zee and Meng were in quarantine section. She hurried to the intercom, jabbed it, wondering what she was going to say.

Meng answered.

Clio swallowed, forcing her voice normal. "Hey, sorry about this dump, you guys. Captain sent me down to help."

A pause. Then: "Put on an exposure suit. They're in stowage by the instrument pallet."

Clio glanced over at the hatch down to lower decks. Shaw could come to anytime. Should've tied him up. She dragged the bag of weapons over to the farthest workstation, shoved it underneath and behind a chair. Grabbed an exposure suit from stowage and shoved herself into it, feet first, snagging her boots on the damn thing, fumbling the zipper, fastening the soft helmet onto the suit body; all the while, a hard stare at the hatchway. Finally suited up, there was the matter of the pistols. No pockets, no belt. Held them behind her back, punched the intercom. "Coming through."

Clio unlatched the door to the airlock, a space about six meters square, waited while it vented its air, refilled. Saw Meng—probably it was Meng, hard to tell through the helmets—looking through the clear plastic window; then the inner door unsealed, started to open. Clio stood back, let them open the door for her, saw two suited figures, one tall, one short, aimed both guns at the short one.

"I'm gonna kill you if you try anything, Meng," she said through the faceplate. "Put your hands behind your head and kneel down."

Meng didn't budge.

"Do it now, Meng."

She began to move, got onto her knees.

Clio pulled off her helmet, looked over at Zee.

"Holy shit," he said, the words muffled behind his helmet. "These are the captain's orders, Clio."

"Jesus, Zee, you think I care? Didn't you know it might come to this? Don't give me that captain's orders bullshit. You in or out?"

He pulled off his helmet, brushed the hair back off his forehead, started to zip down the quarry suit. "I'm with you," he said stepping out of the suit.

"Look me in the eyes, then."

His head snapped up, angry. "I said I'm with you."

She handed him the other gun. "Watch the door." To Meng: "Get out of that suit. Hurry." Meng peeled it off, looking cowed, obedient. Made Clio nervous.

"Just don't shoot, Clio," Meng said. "I know I've made some mistakes, but I don't deserve to die for them. You kill me, it's like taking the law into your own hands, it'd be murder. You're not that type, I don't think, Clio. I just . . ."

"Shut up. Don't give me a reason to shoot, Meng, if you're worried." She got Meng lying on her stomach, belt off, hands behind her back. Clio tied her hands, threaded the belt through a bulkhead pipe. Stood up, looked around. Every specimen had been loaded onto trays. Plastic bags bulged with seed boxes. It had been close.

Zee saw her looking at the trays. "Only reason we weren't done by now is, I got her talking about each specimen. She likes to talk about her plants."

Clio moved over to him, rested her head on his shoulder. "Thanks." She looked up at him. "I should've known you'd hold her off. I rushed here so fast I didn't take time to tie Shaw up."

"Oh my God. You were going to tie Commander Shaw up?"

"When he comes to, he'll be pretty mad. I left him on lower deck."

"Oh my God. You knocked him out." Zee scraped his fingers back through his hair. "Cripes almighty."

Clio plunged through the quarantine airlock, out the other side, Zee following. Science deck was still empty. She pulled out the duffel bag. "Let's dump this. It's got every weapon on the ship except for our two."

Zee carried it over to the extravehicular instrument pallet, hauled it up on the platform. He punched up the command, and the pallet turned slowly and stopped. Zee hit the rotate key again. The pallet whined, now caught in a quarter-turn position.

"Stuck," Clio said.

"Maybe stuck, maybe not hearing the command." He hit Reset on the function keys, tried again. Still nothing.

Clio was hovering over him, reached past him, hit the Rotate key five times in a row. The pallet began turning again, humming smoothly. She turned to Zee, shrugged. Outer panel opened, from the sound of it. Weapons dumped out.

Zee was visibly shaking. He crossed his arms in front of him, rubbing his hands on his upper arms.

Clio nodded. "I know. Deep shit. Really deep shit this time, babe."

"What are we going to do about the commander?"

"I could go back down and tie him up."

"Unless he woke up," Zee said. "Then he'll be waiting for you. And he would have alerted the captain."

Clio bit her lip, trying to get her brain on line. "But maybe he's still out cold. I hit him pretty hard. Damn. Should've tied him up. Probably waiting for me with a wrench."

"You never called me babe before." Zee was still looking at her, no longer shaking.

She grinned, shrugged. "Yeah."

Zee let it lie. He pointed to the quarantine doors. "We should stow these doors. Make it easier to watch both the hatchway here and the emergency hatch on the far end of the deck."

Good. That was clear thinking. But she was stuck on something.

Zee talked as he thumbed the controls at the

workstation. "We're in a siege mode now. We have a hostage, we're in a secure position. They have to come and get us."

Clio's head came up, finally locking on to the thought. "Except I got to get up to crew deck." She slapped her thigh. "I got to get up there."

Zee's face showed what he thought of the idea. "We should stay put. They could be waiting for us up there."

"Listen. Sooner or later we're going to lose the Niang haul. If not today, then at Vanda, once they analyze it. We need some supporters, somebody like the captain, who carries some weight."

"I'm not sure how much weight the captain carries with a thing like this, Clio. She may not be very persuasive."

"She doesn't have to be persuasive. She just needs to get some seeds through quarantine."

Zee shook his head incredulously. "Clio, how you going to persuade the captain to break the law?"

A pause. "Play her the tape."

It took Zee a while to realize what tape. "You've got the transmission," Zee said.

"Yeah."

"Where is it?"

"Hillis' cabin."

She watched him expel a long, slow breath. "I'll go with you."

"No, somebody's got to watch our hostage."

"Then I'll go."

"I don't know which is worse, Zee. Staying here or going up deck." She shrugged. "Either way, they could come after us. Besides, I know exactly where Hillis hid it, you don't."

He nodded glumly. Struggled to say something. "Be careful" was all that managed to get out.

She flashed a smile. Drew her pistol and climbed the ladder.

CHAPTER 17

Clio pushed open the hatch door fast, sweeping her eyes through the galley. Nobody, not within sight. Coffee cups and the remnants of a meal still cluttered the mess table. She climbed slowly through, flicking her gaze to the crew station and bridge hatchways. She scrambled up the ladder to the crew deck, her back prickling.

Crew quarters were empty. The long corridor stretched down to launch bay, looking spooky. Pick a door, any door. Something waiting for you behind one.

First cabin was medlab. Estevan's ghost there, urging her on. *Come on, man, you can do it.* Clio slid by, walking softly—nobody ever walked so softly—gun drawn, heart making a clanging noise in her ears. Pushed open Hillis' door. No ghost here, only emptiness. The more you long for ghosts, the less you see of them—Murphy's law, or something, Clio reckoned.

She fished inside the duffel and found the tape. Then she walked over to the console, paused. The captain might not wait to hear this, might send Shaw after her, straight to the cabin where the transmission originated. But if she ran the tape from science deck, she'd have to get back there first. Also a risk.

She powered up the console and slid in the tape plus an extra. Copied it. Tucked one disk into her vest pocket and thumbed the keyboard to send the transmission to all stations. Put it on hold, went to the intercom.

"Captain, this is Finn, you read?"

A long wait. "I read you, Lieutenant."

"How's Shaw?"

"Never mind how he is. What the holy hell is going on? You cracking up?"

"All I ask is that you listen to the transmission coming through. That's all I ask. All you got to know is that Zee broke the Future Ceiling, and we programmed *Starhawk* on the Dive out to Niang to take a little detour to the future. This is what they found. You can believe that or not, up to you." She switched off. Now they knew where she was; time to hurry. She punched in Send and left the cabin, double time down the corridor. They'd be confused for a minute, probably at least punch up to receive the transmission. And they'd figure she was still in the cabin. Wrong. She was in the galley, still empty, then down to science, closing the hatch behind her.

Zee stepped out from the wall he had been pressed against, watching the hatchway for Shaw or Russo.

Clio nodded at him. "It's running."

He punched up the program. The recorded broadcast was under way, with the announcer saying, ". . . the luxury to argue over who was to blame. . . ."

They listened again as Harding described the end, the end of life as humanity had known it, listened as he spoke his few last words for the departed, the late, great . . .

Zee sat at the console, Clio standing next to him, not wanting to listen but listening anyway.

And then it was done. Zee switched it off, sat quietly staring at the console. "On the way out to Niang, after the Dive, I stopped by Hill's cabin one night after my shift. Hillis was lying on his bunk, staring at the ceiling, listening to the tape. I tried to speak to him, but he was far away, deep inside himself, not even listening, I don't think. He was grieving." Zee paused. "For me, maybe for you, the whole thing was too big to think about, but Hillis took it inside and grieved. I think he felt things more than most people . . . at least about this. Maybe he couldn't express himself, but he felt the death of Earth in ways the rest of us never could. That's why he loved Niang so much." He looked up at Clio from where he was sitting in front of the terminal. "You know?"

Her voice cracked, answering him. "I know." She leaned down, embraced him, wiping her tears on his shirt. Zee wrapped his arms around her waist, brought her onto his lap, rubbing her shoulder. He held her, crumpled against him, for a long while, then slid his hand onto the back of Clio's head, into her thicket of red hair, rubbing her scalp for a moment, then pulled her face down to his, finding her lips with his own.

After a moment he stood up, holding her so that she stood with him, and turned her body to face his. *Stronger than he looks, by damn,* she thought. "Got to keep watch, Zee."

"I am watching," he said, as he buried his face in her neck, moving his hand up her sides to touch her breasts with his thumbs, pulling her closer to him at the same time.

The man's on a mission, for sure. Clio flicked her eyes toward the hatch, then felt Zee's hand on her chin, bringing her face back to look at him.

"They're going to do what they're going to do," he said. "We've done all we can. My guess is that they're going to sleep on it." He pulled her down to the floor. He had that single-minded intensity that seemed to come over men but that eluded her, with her mind still on the hatchway and on Meng, tied up over there but turned the other way, and Shaw and Russo on the bridge, or where the hell were they. Then Zee's hands were getting real personal, and this brought her attention back to the moment, and she sighed, raggedly.

He put his forehead on hers, paused, said, "Let yourself go, sweetheart. Just let yourself go."

God, how long had it been? Found herself counting back the months, then those thoughts vanished as he pulled the zipper of her suit down to her navel, and she arched herself out of the thing. He held the fabric of the arms down and she pulled free, folding her arms around the back of his neck, pulling him closer, feeling him wanting her, suddenly quite clear about whether she wanted him.

"Zee, Zee," she said. "Just don't think I'm promising

you anything, OK? Don't stop, but don't expect anything, OK?"

"Just shut up for once, Clio," he said, tenderly.

Later, they raided the emergency tubes of food in quarantine section, fed themselves and Meng, let her wash up and relieve herself, then tied her back up, settled themselves down as best they could on the floor with chair cushions, and slept.

And Clio dreamed that she was running, running . . . The grass spiked up her skirt as she ran, jabbing her hard. She kept her eyes fixed on the ground in front of her, despite the shouts and the blare of horns behind her. Petya was running by her side. "Go," she urged him, "go, Petya, don't wait for me." He was over six feet and strong, a much faster runner, and dressed in running togs. He put his arm around her and lifted her forward at a faster pace, but it was no good, her gown caught on the brambles, and now her high heels broke off and she was running barefoot. Why was she wearing a ball gown? DSDE was getting closer, the sounds of dogs barking and the horns, the awful horns, that sound was worse than anything . . .

Zee was pulling her up, saying something. She was on science deck, and the emergency bell was clanging, deafeningly. "HULL BREACH IMMINENT. TWO MINUTES TO HULL BREACH. CLOSE SCIENCE DECK AND PROCEED IMMEDIATELY TO DECKS TWO AND THREE."

Jesus, hull breach, did it say?

She stumbled to her feet. Zee was already on the terminal, querying.

"It's the extravehicular instrument pallet," he shouted. "It's going to blow."

Intercom crackled. Russo: "Move onto mid-decks, I'm going to lock the hatches. You copy?"

Clio swung to look at Zee. "We've got to take the samples with us." She started toward the far end of the deck where the trays were still loaded with Niang specimens.

"We don't have time to load out the haul, Clio!" He was unfastening Meng.

Clio glanced at the pallet. Looked normal, but it was failing. Her eyes focused on the quarantine doors, folded back against the bulkheads. She dashed for one side, unfastened the door, and pulled, shouting, "Zee, help me with these! We'll section off quarantine, load up from there, and exit out the emergency hatch to equipment bay."

"Clio, we don't have time!"

Meng was dashing for the hatchway. Zee grabbed her.

Clio punched on the intercom. "Captain, pressurize the equipment bay, we're coming through that way, you copy?"

"Goddamn it, Finn, that'll take three minutes. You've only got two."

"We're fastening the quarantine doors to buy time. Do it, Captain. Out."

"You're fucking crazy," Meng screamed. "This place is going to tear apart!" She bolted for the hatchway, but Zee grabbed her, yanking her back. Drew his pistol.

"Pull the doors," he ordered her.

"SIXTY SECONDS TO HULL BREACH, SCIENCE DECK."

Meng flew to the starboard-side doors and yanked them across to meet the others, secured the latches. Zee activated the seals, and they pressed into place with a long hissing sound, barely audible in the clanging of the bells.

Clio hauled trays over to the emergency hatch and ran back for more. She glared at Meng. "Move it! Because we're not leaving this deck until we get every sample." Meng grabbed a seedling tray and raced for the hatch.

Clio charged over to the hatch with a tray, colliding with Zee as he stood up from where he had crouched to set down his load. Soil flew in every direction, the seedlings trampled underfoot as they stumbled to regain their footing. Clio looked in dismay at the precious semigreen shoots.

"Leave it!" Zee shouted, and ran for another load.

The clanging was replaced by a screeching horn. "HULL BREACH. HULL BREACH. SECURE SCIENCE DECK HATCHES." An explosive crack shook the deck, followed by a great roar. Crashing sounds from beyond the sealed doors mingled with the roar as Clio shouted into the intercom, "Bay pressurized?"

In the deafening noise, the captain was shouting. "Yes, you are clear. Get the hell out of there!"

Zee threw the hatch lever, swung himself through. Meng handed the trays to him recklessly now, as she watched the quarantine doors shudder from the giant vacuum behind them.

Clio shouted to Zee, "Take some of the trays on up to the launch bay. Quarantine's going to blow, and might take this hatch with it." Zee nodded and disappeared up the ladder to launch bay, balancing a box under one arm.

The trays and samples were all through. Meng climbed through the hatchway, with Clio right behind her, and then the hatch closed hard on Clio's leg, and Meng was pushing her back into quarantine with a fierce strength. Clio lost her balance and fell, but her leg hooked over the hatch-way. Meng was prying her leg up, shoving it, while Clio struggled to stand on one leg. She flailed for the wall grip, hooked it with her left hand and smashed through the hatch opening with her right hand, grabbing Meng's arm.

The quarantine doors blew.

One half sailed away from its moorings and smacked into the gaping hole where the pallet had been. Every loose item on the deck shot toward the hole. With the hatchway door wide open, Meng plunged through headfirst, sucked into the ferocious vacuum. Clio was still holding on to the wall grip and clutched at Meng, grabbing on to her hair. Meng was screaming without sound. Then the piece of quarantine wall that had been temporarily plugging the hole in the bulkhead folded in on itself and flew out, and Clio's grip weakened. Meng clawed onto Clio's outstretched arm. The cloth tore free, and Clio's fingers uncurled from Meng's hair, their strength gone. And Meng was flying through the cabin. She slammed against the gap in the bulk-head, where equipment had formed a plug. Then the detritus shuddered and she was wedged between a loose computer monitor and a lab table, queuing up for ejection. She flailed wildly for a grip on the bulkhead, her face frozen in a kind of surprise, as though she were losing at poker, and then the detritus made a pulsing, sphincter-like movement and she disappeared out the hole.

Zee was pulling Clio back through the hatchway. The reason, she realized, that she had lost her grip on Meng. He slammed the hatch shut.

Clio slumped to the floor, put her hands to her ears where a warm liquid was trickling out. She gasped for breath as the cabin atmosphere normalized. Zee crouched down beside her, folded his arms around her.

Shaw's voice was on intercom, shouting something. They let him shout for a while; then Zee got to his feet and hit the switch. "We're in equipment bay. Me and Clio." He looked at Clio; she quickly formed "Meng" with her mouth. "And Meng," he said. "We're going up to launch bay and through to crew deck. Is the launch bay pressurized?"

"Yes," came Shaw's voice. "You're OK to come through. This ship is now crippled, Lieutenant. I hold you and Finn personally responsible. If any harm comes to Specialist Meng, I'll add murder to your account. You understand me?"

"Yes, sir," Zee said. "I see what you mean. We're heading up now. I suggest you and the captain stay off crew deck. Just to avoid any misunderstandings. Out."

Clio forced herself to stand up, took a box of seeds underarm, and started climbing the interdeck ladder. Shaw'd be pissed when he realized they'd brought the Niang plants with them. But, for sure, he was going to be real upset anyway.

She and Zee carried what was left of the Niang specimens up to the launch bay. Here, the lander slept out the long ride home, its convex side bulging into the bay in its usual nesting position. *Babyhawk* was the ship's partner in the Recon enterprise, and its life raft. In some ways the lander was more complicated than *Starhawk* herself, and almost as expensive, with its maneuverability and atmospheric flight capabilities. Clio cocked her head, thinking about *Babyhawk*. Life raft, that was a funny concept. They had never conceived that *Starhawk* would need a life raft.

Zee and Clio looked at each other.

"You're bleeding from the ears," he said.

"Has it stopped?"

"Looks like. You OK?"

"Could be worse." She looked down at the trays. "We could leave the specimens in the bay here."

"And then they can dump them at will."

"Think they'd sacrifice *Babyhawk* to junk this stuff?"

"In a minute. Sure they would."

Clio nodded.

Zee said, "So let's take them through to crew deck."

Clio smiled at him. "You've become very protective of our little demons, haven't you?"

Zee grinned. "Like a mother hen."

Clio unfastened the hatch, reaching for the gun in her belt. Gone. Probably halfway to Mars by now. Zee saw her movement, stepped forward, his own gun drawn, and opened the hatch. He stepped through, eyeing the cabin doors of crew deck. Clio stepped through, after him.

"Zee." Clio touched his arm. He turned to face her. "That time on Vanda. When you slept with Hillis . . ."

A frown dented his forehead. He nodded, as if to say, I wondered when we'd get around to that one. But he remained silent, waiting for her question.

In truth, what was there to say? But Clio wanted something said. She decided on, "Well . . . was it love? Or what?"

"How many people could I be in love with at one time, right?"

"Something like that."

He sighed, sat down on a large carton of seed packets. Clio winced. He noticed, slid off the carton onto the floor, back against the bulkhead.

Clio crouched down, facing him. "Is it so hard to answer?"

"Yes. Depending on how important the answer is to you."

"Well, there's only one answer to give, right? The truth. That's all I'm asking for."

"That's a lot sometimes." He looked past her, at the opposite wall, thinking. Then turned back to her. "OK, Clio, I loved him. I loved you both. I know that's hard to understand. Sometimes I don't understand it myself."

Clio moved in closer to him, embraced him, pressing her face against his. "That's what I hoped you'd say." She smiled. "It's better than any other explanation. Only . . ."

He raised an eyebrow.

"Only, I'm not sure he loved you. You know? I could almost guarantee that. Or me either. Didn't love me either."

"His loss."

"Yeah, on both counts." She wiped her face on her sleeve, stood up. "Not sure what that settled, but I feel better." Zee nodded slowly; maybe he felt better too. "I'm going up to the bridge, Zee. Alone. I'm gonna tell them about Meng. And see where we stand. 'Cause we're not headed in a very good direction; looks like the tape didn't make a big impact on Russo. Shaw neither, obviously. We're about at the end of our rope, I figure."

"That's what I figure, too."

"So I'm going up to parlay."

"We've got nothing left to parlay, Clio."

"Maybe not." A smile pulled at the corners of her mouth. "Don't hurt to talk."

Zee stood up, handed over his gun. Clio shook her head. "Nah. I'll never get on the flight deck if I'm armed."

He slid his arm around her back, kissed her.

She walked down the corridor toward the bridge. By the mid-decks hatchway she hit the intercom.

"Captain Russo, this is Lieutenant Finn. Permission to come to the bridge. Truce, OK?"

Clio waited, tapping her fingers on the metal intercom box. The housing was still hard as nails. Maybe someday, she thought, in the way distant future, nobody would know what that meant, hard as nails.

"Captain, we got to talk. I'm unarmed."

Shaw's voice then: "You can come up, Lieutenant. Come up real slow, hands over head."

How can I climb the freeping hatch ladder with my hands over my head, you jackass? Clio climbed through to the galley and up the ladder to the flight deck. Shaw hovered over the open hatchway, a length of pipe in his hand. As Clio emerged through the opening, he jerked her arm, forcing her to her knees.

"Lie on your stomach."

Clio lay on the deck while Shaw searched her, searched her good.

"That's enough, Commander." Russo's voice.

Shaw backed off. Clio stood on the bridge. Stood there again after what seemed like a hundred years. The curved bank of instrumentation nestled against the inside nose of the ship, sparkling with light. Russo sat in the captain's chair, enthroned in metal technology. The room glowed, blurring. Clio bit her tongue, hard. Couldn't speak.

Russo held the silence.

Finally, Shaw said, "You going to talk, or do I have to beat it out of you?" His head was wrapped with a bandage, headband style.

"I got to report, sir, that Meng is dead." She flicked her eyes to Russo, then back to Shaw. No reaction. "She got blown off science deck. I tried to grab her, but I couldn't hold on. I told you she was OK because we thought if you knew it was only me and Zee you'd shunt us out of launch bay."

Shaw nodded. "Yeah. Maybe we would have. Good idea. Now you've got the contaminants on crew deck, is that right?"

"Yessir."

Shaw looked at Russo, clenched his mouth. Had to let the captain speak on this one.

She didn't speak. A ripple of uncertainty made its way over Shaw's face. He took the lead. "You got five minutes' truce, Finn. Then if you're still here, I'm going to disable you with the only weapon I have." The pipe twitched in his hand.

Clio registered the threat in her stomach. Backed up a step. Looked at Russo.

"What I came to say is that I had information that you didn't, sir. Information about a threat to our country, our planet. I acted on that, knowing it might sacrifice the ship."

Shaw charged in: "That damn *haul* is the threat, Lieutenant! You just don't get it, do you?"

"I get it sir. I get it that the Niang haul eats metal. And also that we got no future at all without it." She turned back to Russo, who was still silent, eyes turned in Clio's direction but bordering on vacant. "I'm asking you to bring this haul home, Captain. That's what I came to say. I came to say that we can Dive back a day or two, and take *Babyhawk* in for a landing, Earthside. Plant the Niang seedlings. See if maybe we have an alternate future. That's what I came to say."

A burst of air erupted from Shaw. "You really *are* crazy. Crazy as Meng said, crazy as Teeg said. You're paranoid as shit, Lieutenant. You ran amok in camp, and then you ran amok on this ship. You're disaster on two legs, just like they said." He had come closer with each statement, shouting at her, shouting louder the closer he got. It was the animal sound of his voice that scared Clio. She backed up a pace, avoiding looking in his eyes. He was losing it.

"Back off, Commander." This from Russo.

Shaw pushed Clio in the chest, lightly, like a street fighter warming up. "You want to drive this reeking hulk back to Earth, do you?" He pushed her in the chest again. "That right? You want to come off ship, guns blazing, that right?"

"Knock it off, Commander."

"You want to bring this plague onto station, that it?" He was screaming at her, his spittle hitting her in the face. "You want to perform a Dive in local space and risk a paradox that could kill us all?"

Clio was backed into the console now, saying, "Nosir, nosir. That's not it. We sneak in under cover of night, aim for a wilderness area. One-day Dive, two days max. No paradoxes."

"No paradoxes," he sneered. "What if we burn up on reentry? What if we land in the Hudson River? No paradoxes? You're out of your bloody mind."

She looked him in the eye, dead on. "OK, there's danger. But we're all dead anyway—us, Earth, everybody, right? Time's up, Shaw, don't you get it?"

He yanked her arm, swinging her around, bringing her close to his face. "You're a danger, Clio Finn. A danger to this ship and your country, even your planet."

"Release her, Commander, or I'll fire."

He turned, still gripping Clio's arm, face quickly draining. Russo stood there, a pistol aimed at his chest. He released Clio, staring hard at the gun.

"You forget the captain always keeps a gun?" Her voice was calm and flat. "Now I'm going to tell you what's coming down. Drop the pipe, Commander." He did so, scowling. Russo looked at Clio, looked at her cold. "So you want to Dive the ship back a few days, sneak in before the shit hits the fan, eh? Cast your seeds before Vanda sanitizes the whole load?" Russo hadn't moved. Gun still pointed at Shaw. That was a good sign, so far, Clio thought, in what little mind remained at her command.

"Tell you this much, Finn. I've been thinking it over the last twenty-four hours. And what I decided is, you might be right. But I just couldn't do it. My career may be over, but I'm no criminal."

Shaw nodded, started to move to the pilot chair.

Russo swung the pistol to match his movement. "Stay where you are, Shaw."

He looked at her, his mouth frozen half-open. Backed up.

"That was my decision. Was. Until now. Tell you why, if you care." Clio and Shaw both stared hard at her.

The radio crackled with an incoming. Russo backed up a pace, hit the radio receiver switch, killing the transmission. She leaned against the console, short arms crossed in front of her, gun drooping slightly toward the deck.

"Twenty years with Biotime. Nearly a quarter of a century. That's how long I've been in service. That's worth something, by God. Now they send this . . . welcome-home committee. Think I don't know what a Class M warship looks like?" She caught the reaction on Shaw's face. "Oh yes, Commander, a warship, the *Eisenhower*. Heading straight in on an intersect trajectory. And not a word from Vanda, not a peep. So we're the target. The warship's going to take on the *Starhawk* mess, and going to take care of us at the same time.

"Why? That's what I've been thinking on all night. Why? But the way I figure it, it's cleaner this way. Think of the investigation. The bad publicity for Recon. Biotime screws up royally. Everybody looks bad. And that right there is the crux: looking bad. Because, as we learned from Hillis' tape, Recon's a bust. Never worked so far, never will. You think the Bureau doesn't know that? You think Zee's the only one ever cracked the Future Ceiling?" She shook her head, smiled crookedly at Clio. "He's good, honey, but he's not *that* good. The government, the Bureau, Biotime—they all know we're headed for disaster. And not a goddamn thing they can do about it. Except give the common folk a pat on the head, keep them quiet while the ship goes down. Keep the top brass in power a few years longer. Maybe the agreement is, the government pretends the problem can be solved, and companies like Biotime pretend they're on the verge of solving it. Meanwhile, it's business as usual. The bureaucrats keep their privileges, Biotime gets fat, and the masses stay quiet. Everybody's comfortable."

The lights dimmed overhead, then winked out.

Shaw threw himself into Russo, and Clio heard the gun skidding down the deck. Clio dove for Shaw, but got a boot in her face. The lights pulsed once, twice. Clio saw the pistol against the hatchway door. Shaw saw it too. They scrambled for it. Shaw reached it a split second sooner, turned it on Clio. A shadow behind him. The crack of metal against bone, and he was pitching forward. Shaw moaned into the deck.

"Find a lamp, Lieutenant," Russo said.

Clio fumbled along the bulkhead panels until she found

the storage locker. Groped inside, found a lamp, and snapped it on. Shaw was leaning against the console, head in hands. Russo stood poised in the middle of the flight deck, commanding the bridge with fifteen inches of steel tubing.

"Find the gun, Clio."

Clio washed the deck with light. Found the pistol.

"You and Zee load up *Babyhawk*. Depending on how close they get before they strike, we might not have much time. I'll give these boys a call and act my part."

Clio hesitated. "About the paradoxes, Captain . . ."

Russo waved her hand. "We calibrate for a couple days only. Land in the jungle. Amazon, I figure."

"But it's still a risk. Nobody's ever tried a Dive this close to local space. I just want to say that."

"So noted."

"And the *Eisenhower* . . ."

"We'll blip out on their screens. Just blip out. And at this distance the event ripple will nudge them a bit, but won't scratch the paint job. Not that I wouldn't mind giving them a little bounce."

Clio smiled. Felt like her face cracking open. Felt good. "Thank you, sir."

"Cut the 'sir,' Clio. That stuff's over now." Russo nodded quickly. "Run now, we've got work to do."

Clio ran.

CHAPTER 18

❧

Zee cranked open *Babyhawk's* main hatchway entrance, releasing a sigh from the interior, like a ghost escaping. He plunged on through, arms loaded with seed boxes.

Clio was behind him, cradling a botany tray in her arms. First thing she saw was the blood on the deck. Dried stains of blood. Estevan's, or Meng's. She remembered both of them moaning, lying on the deck, no time to strap in. Clio crying so hard she could hardly fly, Zee by her side, coaching her on, reminding her how to pilot, convincing her she could make it, they were counting on her. Hillis was dead, no going back. *Five minutes ago, he was alive, but no going back.*

Clio secured the botany tray in the stowage bin. "How about you finish loading," she said to Zee. " 'Cause I better get Dive started, up on the flight deck."

He took her arm. "Clio. You better let me calibrate the Dive."

"I can do it."

Zee frowned. "Maybe, but you've got to trade off time accuracy versus place accuracy. We need to be sure it's a very short dive, and still be sure we don't end up in Vanda's lap. Can't program both aspects accurately. The Vandarthanan Uncertainty Principle."

Clio raised an eyebrow. "Yes, Professor."

"But Clio . . ."

She gently pulled her arm away. "It's gonna be uncertain. One way or the other."

"I'm not saying you can't handle it. I'm just worried about you. What if you pass out during Dive?"

"I took an extra hit of my medicine," she said, and walked to the hatchway, where she turned back to him. "We'll do the best we can, Zee. It's gotta be good enough." She saw him sigh. Perhaps letting go of math, of certainty.

Finally he nodded. "I love you Clio."

"Right," she said. Slipped out of the hatchway and jammed through the launch bay to crew deck. In the galley, she grabbed a tube of meat paste and a tortilla, made herself squeeze the meat out, roll the tortilla. *Gotta eat, or I will pass out. Don't want to die in your sleep, girl.* She stormed up the hatchway ladder to flight deck, chewing on the damn thing.

Russo saw her, nodded quickly, turned back to the console. Countdown had started.

Clio's stomach lurched. Countdown started, and she wasn't even strapped in.

Russo had tied Shaw into the copilot's chair.

Clio gestured at him. "What's the deal?"

"He's staying. I invited him to join us, but he's staying with the ship. Acting like an officer, I guess. Problem is, once we take the lander, he needs to be free to pilot the ship. So, when you're out of Dive, you loosen those bonds just a bit so he can work his way out of them. Then you get down to *Babyhawk*, double time."

"Yessir." Corrected herself: "Right." She slipped into the chair next to Shaw. Gagged, he still could muster a pretty good glare.

Clio strapped in, chewing on the tortilla, which tasted like boot polish in a sock. Ship was accelerating fast, heading for Dive. She wiped her hands on her flight suit, trying to bring some blood into them. Shivered.

"Going to make it, Clio?"

Clio looked into Russo's well-lined face. "I figure."

The captain smiled. "Then let's get this operation under way."

Console showed three minutes to Dive.

Russo noted Clio's look. "We're programmed for a forty-eight-hour Dive. We'll see where we end up."

"Cut it kind of close, didn't you?"

"Had to. The *Eisenhower* isn't talking to me. Figure they're busy lining up one of those missiles. Got our name on it." She patted Clio on the shoulder. "We're punched up to transition speed. Let's get the hell out of here." She disappeared down the hatchway.

Clio grabbed her headset, switched on the receiver, scanning the channels. Nothing. Cleared her throat, switched over to Send. "This is *Starhawk*, over." Paused just long enough. "*Eisenhower*, we are not receiving you. We are sending on all channels, *Eisenhower*. We have a top-priority message for Ellison Brisher. *Eisenhower*, *Starhawk*'s condition has completely stabilized, and we must report our situation to Mr. Brisher as planned."

Just get them confused. Clio saw the blip on her screen. The Class M shape unmistakable, ultrafast and equipped with smart missiles that could take them out even at this distance, even with evasive maneuvers.

"Situation has played out as ordered, *Eisenhower*," she said. "This top-priority message to Ellison Brisher, as follows, stand by to patch through to Vanda Station."

Fifteen seconds to Dive, her stomach registering the passage of seconds. At six seconds, Clio said: "Sayonara, Brish, you freeping Nazi. I quit."

The last three seconds took a long, long time to count off, with Clio wondering if ship could even pull off a Dive with the computers disintegrating like snow in the rain.

Then the VDT blurred and stretched in front of her, the lights of flight deck pulling out like taffy, across the minutes, the hours. Clio pressed her head into the headrest, clenched her fists. This was going to be a short ride, damn short, but maybe no easier for that.

Clio's stomach felt like it was climbing up her throat. She twisted in her chair, ended up facing Shaw. His eyes were open.

Open?

Her startle reflex almost threw her out of her chair. Shaw was looking straight at her, eyes twitching like a fish flopping on sand. Clio staggered back from her chair, heard herself saying, "No, no . . . ," felt herself slam into the console behind her.

He turned his chair slightly to watch her, managing the maneuver by lurching his body against the pilot's chair.

She was losing it this time for real, hallucinating. *Never look at people's faces when you Dive, they don't look good, you know that.* She'd never even looked in a mirror during Dive, much less looked into anyone else's open eyes—especially somebody like Shaw. Shaw was struggling to get his gag off, working his jaw to loosen it, when the deck shuddered, throwing Clio against the captain's chair. They had come up out of Dive.

Shaw passed out. Clio regained her balance, stared back at him. Somewhere, somewhere, Clio had seen that look before, that crazed, hyped look in Shaw's eyes. Then she remembered. Christ. Just like Teeg. Just like Teeg when she'd given him her meds in the jungle, that was Shaw, without a doubt. He'd found her pills. But for a non-Diver, he must have taken a shitload to get through Dive. Might have killed himself with that dose; might have. Just like she'd been doing all these years.

Klaxon was blaring on flight deck, all over the ship, echoing through the hull. Ship's warning voice was saying something. She struggled to bring her mind together. Remembered she was supposed to be somewhere. Where was the captain?

Then ship's voice: "ELECTRICAL FAILURE, ALL DECKS, BACKUP SYSTEM FAILING, DON PORTABLE LIFE-SUPPORT SYSTEMS. SIX MINUTES TO SYSTEMS FAILURE. ALL DECKS . . ."

Clio jerked her head up, noticed Shaw tied to the pilot's chair, remembered, then: supposed to run for the lander, supposed to untie Shaw, supposed to meet Zee at the lander. She hauled herself to her feet. The ship lurched, and she fell again, as a great shudder passed through *Starhawk.* "EQUIPMENT BAY BREACH, EQUIPMENT BAY BREACH, SEALING ALL HATCHES IN NINETY SECONDS. DON PORTABLE LIFE-SUPPORT SYSTEMS

AND PREPARE TO ABANDON SHIP. DON PORTABLE LIFE-SUPPORT SYSTEMS."

Clio's mind clicked into gear. *Sealing all hatches, oh Jesus.* She scrambled over to Shaw, untied him. Spun around and headed for the hatchway, feeling like she was in slow motion, swinging down the ladder, feet hitting the deck in the galley. Horns screaming, and ship trembling like it faced death, and feared it. Pulled herself up the ladder to crew deck, cranked on the closed hatchway. Nothing. *God! Got to have more time, got to open, got to open.* She cranked harder. Ship's voice blaring, "SEALING ALL HATCHES IN SIXTY SECONDS, FIFTY NINE . . ."

Clio beat on the hatch door, crying. Then swearing: Jesus God, no! She was turning the crank the *wrong way*, it was counterclockwise to open, God, not clockwise! She yanked it counterclockwise with all her strength. Then again. It turned. She spun the crank, threw open the hatch and hauled herself onto crew deck. Sprinted down the longest corridor in the universe. Slammed into the aft hatchway to the launch bay, cranked the hatch, as the ship quaked and rolled. "FORTY-FOUR, FORTY-THREE, FORTY-TWO . . ."

She grasped the hatch holds to pull herself through when she felt herself jerked back, thrown back into crew deck, slammed against the bulkhead. Facing Shaw. His face contorted as he screamed at her, she couldn't hear what. The ship's voice was deafening, the deck rumbling under their feet. Spittle flew from his mouth as his hands closed around her throat.

Clio brought her knee up to his groin. His hands loosened their grip, and he bent forward at the waist as Clio brought her clasped hands down hard on the back of his neck, sending him crashing to the deck. She spun around, clambered through the hatch, then felt Shaw yanking her foot, clinging to her from the other side of the hatch.

"ABANDON SHIP. ABANDON SHIP. TWENTY SECONDS TO HULL BREACH."

Clio screamed in rage, screamed to drown out the ship's voice, the horns, screamed to yank her foot across that hatchway. Did it. Bringing Shaw's arm with her, just as the ship slammed the hatch shut, locking it. The arm compressed into the juncture, pinched off in a slow, soundless amputation.

Then Zee was pulling her into *Babyhawk*, half dragging, half carrying her into the lander, and the ship was patiently droning, "THIRTEEN, TWELVE, ELEVEN . . ." And he threw her to the deck, covering her body with his own, and Russo was screaming something at him, something about closing the hatch. And he was off of Clio and, a moment later, back holding her as *Babyhawk* separated from *Starhawk* with a jolt and the blaring of the ship cut off. They were thrown into the lander bulkhead as Russo hit the thrusters.

Babyhawk rolled as the first wave hit them—probably the launch bay exploding—and Clio and Zee hit another bulkhead. Clio saw Russo punching up full power, held on as *Babyhawk* accelerated to the max.

"Take it easy!" Clio shouted at Russo. *She's gonna break up the lander, by God, just can't punch this crate up to speed so fast. . . .*

Russo shouted back: "Ship's going to blow any second!"

Clio looked at the viewscreen. As if on cue, *Starhawk*'s lower decks flew apart, then upper decks, in a one-two explosion that roiled toward them, took the lander, and tossed it like a leaf in a hurricane.

CHAPTER 19

Below *Babyhawk*, in the south Indian Ocean, lightning flared in bright patches against the clouds. Clio watched from the viewport as the lightning pulsed in sequence over thousands of kilometers, like neurons firing across a vast cerebral cortex.

She pushed away from the viewport, floating in zero g, and turned to survey the lander's cabin. The usual metallic tidiness of grids, panels, and switches was disrupted by an array of escaped Niang organisms: seeds roaming in schools, and tiny seedlings moving with air currents through the cabin like jellyfish, their roots floating beneath them. The smell of oil and warm electronics mixed with the deep, sweet smell of decay and life. Clio grasped at a seed as it floated by her face. Thrust it into her breast pocket, but it rose up and free as she tried to button the flap down.

Russo was at the controls, Zee asleep in a crew chair. They were preparing for atmospheric entry and a landing half a world away in the jungles of Brazil. Keeping to the southern hemisphere would lessen their chances of arousing defensive military systems. Soon they would cross into night over western Africa. Fifty-five minutes to touchdown.

The peace of the moment surrounded her like a warm bath: the silent Earth turning below them, the noiseless lander, Zee asleep, Russo piloting, and Clio at rest. Dive had shifted them smack into Earth orbit, the first stroke of amazing good luck Clio could remember in her short life—if luck was what it was. Zee said something about the relation of mass and Dive and the action of gravity on the Dive parameters. Which was why he'd been worried about coming out of Dive in a hard reentry burn. But no such thing. The Dive was exactly forty-eight hours back. Back just far enough to sneak up on a slumbering Earth. Easy enough, with military defense systems focused on low-tech third-world revolts, and clueless that Niang was about to pay a visit—a permanent visit.

They'd done it. Brought the seeds home, escaped the *Eisenhower*, Dived back a brief two days and lived to tell about it.

How could it be, though, she'd once asked Zee. How can we be in orbit and back out in space, all at once, repeating these two days ... Zee grabbed his notebook and started sketching, quick, arcane diagrams that soon became math, as easily as ice cubes melting in water. Finally he'd said: It's a function of distance. We live these three days over again, but outside of our prior time stream. No one completely understands how it works; but every time we Dive, we're Diving past our own lives, we're two places at once.

She tried hard to concentrate. So there are two Clios? One back on the *Starhawk*, one in orbit?

He took his pencil up again. Then laid it down. Yes, he said.

So if I met the other Clio, we'd get a beaucoup paradox.

But you're not going to meet her.

She nodded. It's a function of distance.

He smiled. It's math.

Turning away from the viewport, she gently touched Zee's shoulder to waken him. He jerked upright, startled. Clio pressed him gently back into the chair. "We're here."

"Where's here?"

"Earth, three hundred twenty kilometers above the Indian Ocean."

"One of my favorite spots." He pulled her down toward him, kissed her.

As he unbuckled his seat belt, the clasp separated at the hinge, and the belt floated away into the cabin, clunking against other bits of hardware chewed loose by the

Niang growths and slammed out of place by the *Starhawk* explosion.

"Come look at the lightning," Clio said.

They pulled themselves over to the viewport, grabbing on to the bulkhead struts. Zee looked out. "Nothing but the African Waste," he said.

Clio pushed past him to see. They had left the ocean and its lightnings behind, and were coming over the savannahs of Kenya and the Masai Steppe, into the shadow of night, but even so Clio could see the vast stretch of brown marking the ruin of central Africa that stretched through the Congo Basin, Nigeria, and Ghana, devouring the tropical forests and abundant plains in one, great, overarching Sahara.

The craft lurched.

"Strap in," Russo said. "I'm going for deorbit burn." Russo had insisted on piloting the lander. Clio was exhausted from Dive, and Russo was eager to fly. Landing in the tropical forest was a tough maneuver for a woman who hadn't flown in a long time, Clio argued. But Russo stared her down, so Clio relented, figuring it was going to take more luck than skill anyhow to land *Babyhawk* in her present condition.

Before Clio was secured in her chair, the lander began shaking again, as it had off and on over the last four hours, then subsided. A swarm of Niang seeds drifted past Clio's face. *Whole damn lander is leaky,* Clio thought. *Reentry's gonna be hell on us.*

In a few minutes it was.

"I'm on descent trajectory; beginning descent," Russo said. "Heat building on exterior. Five hundred degrees centigrade."

Clio found a chair with seat belt intact, cinched in, and held her breath. *Just a few more kilometers, baby, just a few more.* She patted the armrest, reassuring *Babyhawk*, reassuring herself, as g force kicked in and the lander began to rattle and groan.

Within thirty minutes Babyhawk had descended to 120 kilometers, blazing down over the south Atlantic, coming in hard, the roar of their swath through the atmosphere filling their ears.

Perspiration streamed down Clio's face as the exterior climbed to sixteen hundred degrees centigrade. She looked at Zee in the chair next to her, saw him gripping the chair, eyes squeezed shut, then he opened them, managed a kind of smile, reached for her hand. Clio met his grasp and they rode the descent together in the shaking, screaming lander, like being in the throat of a roaring animal.

"Damn it to hell!" Russo shouted.

Clio saw Russo struggling with the controls.

"We're losing control!" Russo said. "Can't get response from her. She's freezing up, freezing up."

Clio pressed forward against the 1.5 g's. "What's freezing up?"

"The control stick," Russo shouted above the din. "I'm barely controlling this ship!"

"Jesus, Captain, switch to auxiliary."

"I tried. We're off course. Off course. Coming in too fast. I'm going for a water landing."

Clio unclipped her harness, struggling forward. "No! No water landing!"

"No choice. We're going to crash."

Trying to heave herself out of her chair, Clio failed and fell back into it, pinned down by the crushing gravity. Heard Zee shouting at her, heard her own despair: "My plants," she said. "My plants."

"Buckle in!" Russo was shouting. "We're going down fast."

Clio grabbed for the harness, her arms in slow motion, fighting, fighting to snap the buckle, finally sliding it into place, and letting herself give in to the insupportable weight of g and fate.

She turned to Zee, mouthing the words, "My plants . . ."

His face mirrored her own distress. "Hold on. I love you," she thought he said, though holding on could not possibly matter anymore, and love couldn't matter, not if the ocean took the seeds and drowned all their hopes.

All the while g was increasing, bearing down hard. And then her body was coming apart, her bones, her skull, pressing through her skin, and all around her the thundering of the hull.

Then the hull screamed, as impact concussed the lander. Clio's body dug hard against the restraints, until she thought she'd slice in two. *We hit water, we hit water, we're plunging* . . . The thundering went on and on. They were diving deep, deep into the ocean, and *Babyhawk* was reeling from the impact, while outside the awful rumble of the ocean boiled against the hull. *Babyhawk* was shuddering hard, rivets flew across the cabin, white-hot bullets of steel, and Clio closed her eyes, hoping for one in the head, to get it over with fast. She didn't want to drown, had never planned to die in water. A bad way to die, she figured, not that there were any good ways. There seemed no end to their dive; they plunged on and on, until it seemed they'd be so deep the ocean would crush them in her jaws. But at last Clio felt a different sensation, a surcease of noise, and a return of normal g force, and the feeling of riding an elevator up, up. And water trickled in through the seams of the craft, and Clio spiraled down into blackness.

Zee was bending over her, holding her face between his hands.

She looked up at him, seeing double. Closed her eyes. "Hell of a landing," she said. "Never did like water landings." She opened her eyes, seeing two of him still. They smiled at her.

"Clio, we made it, we really made it. We're down. We're home." He helped her unbuckle. Then the consoles blanked out, leaving them in darkness.

Zee fumbled in the bulkhead lockers for a flashlight, found one, switched it on. Wincing hard, Clio pushed herself out of her chair and went to Russo's side, putting her hand on Russo's shoulder. "It's OK, we're down. We're OK."

Russo didn't answer, didn't move.

"Captain?" Clio asked. Still no movement. "You did good, Captain," Clio said. "You got us down, and we're alive. Floating just perfect, right about where we planned to be. You did good."

"We're taking on water pretty fast," Zee said from behind her.

Russo said, "It's what we all decided on, right?" She looked up at Clio, her eyes childlike. "We drew straws so one person could live. We decided together, and no matter who won, that person had to keep the air. No matter what." She kept looking at Clio, waiting for an answer.

Clio took a deep breath. "I know," she said. "It was fair. You all decided, fair and square. Otherwise, everyone would have died. It was the right decision."

"So you don't mind being dead?" Russo looked at her hopefully.

Clio paused. "No," she said. "I don't mind. It was fair."

Russo nodded slowly, released the control stick.

Zee gripped Clio's shoulder. "Clio, we got water coming in from every . . ."

One of the hatches blew. The ocean pulsed in.

"The raft!" Zee shouted.

Zee and Clio ripped open the panel housing the raft and struggled to haul it out.

"Grab the seeds," Clio shouted. She bolted over to the stowage hatch, yanking at it.

Zee pulled her around. "No time! Help me get this raft up the ladder! Russo's useless. Hurry!"

Clio jerked the stowage door open, grabbing boxes of seeds, then dropped them as Zee hauled her away. "God-damn it, Clio, we're sinking!"

Zee opened the escape hatch, then helped Clio drag the raft up the ladder.

Outside, the ocean came at them in a moderate chop. As *Babyhawk* lurched in the waves, Zee managed to slit open the raft casing, and the craft inflated. Clio clambered down into the lander and helped Russo to climb up to the open hatch, where the cold ocean air swept over them in sheets. She and Russo jumped in. By the moon's sallow light, Clio could see Zee perched on the edge of *Babyhawk*, waiting for the raft to swing closer. Across a million years of space, and now a few meters left to go. Zee hesitated.

"Jump!" Clio yelled.

He jumped, and landed heavily in one end of the raft, bringing a spray of salt water over the bow.

"We made it," Zee said, triumphant.

Clio lay in the bottom of the craft, no longer caring.

In the morning they surveyed their surroundings. The raft floated easily in the calm, blue sea. The salt air burned Clio's lungs, the sunlight crushed against her eyes, as though she were an alien, accustomed to fluorescent lights and stale air—as indeed she was. The tranquil blue Atlantic Ocean stretched away to the edge of vision on every side. *Babyhawk* was nowhere to be seen.

"So where the hell do you suppose we are?" Clio asked.

"Somewhere off the eastern coast of South America," Zee said.

"That narrows it down."

Russo squinted against the hot white sun. "Should be somewhere near French Guiana," she said. "Maybe the northern tip of Brazil. If the readouts were OK."

Clio watched Russo scan the horizon. She was back to business.

Clio looked out at the sea, turned north. North America was only a few thousand miles away, but as far from her in a practical sense as Niang had been for *Starhawk*. She would never see it again. Unless captured, she would never see it again. The thought struck her with more force than she expected. But it wasn't the U.S. in particular that came to mind, it was North Dakota, and a little town called Upham, halfway between Buffalo Lodge Lake and the Canadian border. She closed her eyes and saw Petya walking through the wheat field, his arms outstretched, the grain up to his waist. From a distance he appeared to be surrounded by an undulating, yellow sea. He laughed and pointed at her, and she stretched out her arms in the field and walked like a goddess through the waves. "We're swimming!" Petya shouted. "We're swimming!"

Zee put his hand on Clio's shoulder. "Some plants— Earth plants—floated across seas, and lived to grow on new islands," he said. "Maybe some of the Niang plants made it out. Maybe the sea will be a good mother."

Clio turned toward him, put her face against his chest. "Goddamn it all, anyway. We were so close, so close." She looked at Zee. "You know? We fought so hard to bring them home. We lost everything. Everyone died." She was crying hard now, giving in to it. The rising sun was behind Zee's head, backlighting his ears, his light hair, giving him a sunny halo.

"You did the best you could, Clio. Like you told Russo, you did good. You did real good."

Clio looked at him, tried to smile. Failed.

They set their course by the sun, and took turns rowing southwest toward what they hoped was a relatively unpopulated tract of northern Brazil.

Between her turns at rowing Clio flopped in the stern of the raft under the tent of blanket they had rigged to fend off the sun. The glare of the water and the heat blasted all thought, melding each minute to the next, making a circular progression of misery. Clio's light skin took a sunburn within a half hour, despite the hat she had fashioned.

When at last Zee sighted land, she tore her mouth with a smile. It was a long way, appearing as a mere line on the horizon, but suddenly they rowed with renewed strength.

By nightfall they were still far off shore, but doggedly rowed on by the light of a crescent moon.

"What happens when we get there?" Zee asked.

"We sleep," Russo said. She slapped the water with the oars again, taking her full turns despite the protests of the others. She wasn't in the best shape for fifty-one, but, as she pointed out, neither were Clio and Zee after months aboard *Starhawk*.

"But I mean, after we sleep, in the morning." He looked at Clio. "When we meet any people."

"I don't know," Clio said. "Think three white folks dressed in rags, without passports, will attract much attention?"

"Guess we give it a try and see what happens," Russo said. She pulled on the oars again. "And we stick together. If they pick us up . . ." She pulled on the oars again, rested them on the gunwales. "No regrets."

Zee took Clio's hand. "No regrets," Clio said.

An hour later they pulled the raft up onto a small beach, half-encircled by the rocky arms of a headland. A black primeval forest stood before them, its hot, fecund breath whispering to them at the edge of the beach. They dragged the craft into the undergrowth, deflated it, and buried it in a shallow hole. It would be a long time before Biotime, before DSDE found it, if ever, Clio thought. *Buried things often stay buried. The earth can keep secrets, sometimes forever.*

They laid their blankets out on the ground and fell on them, asleep instantly.

In the morning Clio woke to find a stranger staring at her.

A little girl, hardly more than six years old, dark-skinned, with black hair cut bluntly across her forehead, leaned on a staff watching them. She was naked except for a short cloth with a Mickey Mouse pattern tied around her hips.

Startled, Clio stared a moment, then said, "Hello. What's your name?"

The child backed off a few paces into the jungle. She moved behind a tree and disappeared.

Clio lay back down, watching the morning sun spray through the forest, lighting their nest of blankets as well as the fifty-meter tops of the trees. She allowed herself, for a moment, to pretend that the Earth was a forest, from sea to sea. That giant trees like these ruled, and humans lived among them, small, two-legged, and frail. And for a moment, the jungle took on a turquoise tinge.

Zee was sitting behind her, slid his arms around her waist. "Thought I heard you say something."

"There was a little girl in a Mickey Mouse skirt."

Russo was up, folding blankets. Raised an eyebrow.

They found a trail leading deeper into the forest and followed it, carrying their blankets and empty canteens. They drank water from the cups of flowers where dew had collected, and looked for food. When Clio came upon the man standing just off the path, she almost stumbled into him, so intent was she on finding something edible.

Clio regained her footing, stood stock-still, watching him. He wore only a loincloth and several necklaces of bead and bone. The little girl was behind him. Clio kneeled down, took off her watch, held it out to the child. The girl came forward, reached out toward Clio, touching her hair. She smiled, a sudden splash of white teeth and lively dark eyes. Then she took the watch, moving back behind her elder.

He spoke a few words in his language and motioned for them to follow him. The three went with the natives deeper into the brush until they came upon a tiny encampment of twig huts, where cooking fires burned and some thirty natives crowded around them.

Here they were fed and helped to wash. One of the women dressed Clio's sunburn with a sticky ointment, and offered her a bed where she rested, then slept, as did Zee and Russo.

In midafternoon Clio awoke as the camp broke up and the group prepared to move on. One of the natives brought Clio a woven bag, showing her how to carry it slung over her shoulders. It seemed they were being given permission to travel with this small tribal group. Clio looked at Zee and Russo. They also had hefted up their carrying bags onto their backs. Clio walked over to them. "This isn't going to be easy," she said.

"You got a better idea?" Zee asked. Somehow, he managed to seem cheerful. That counts a lot when you're in deep shit, thought Clio. She smiled at him. *Damn, if it doesn't count a lot.*

Russo was already moving off, following the others.

"I'll be right back," Clio said. She walked to the edge

of the former encampment, moving into the undergrowth. Here she removed a small packet of seeds from her breast pocket, tore open the thick plastic, and knelt down in the moist soil. She pressed the seeds in, one at a time, patting the black earth over them.

She crawled on her hands and knees, continuing her planting until the seeds were gone. They were safe. These few seeds, at least, had a fighting chance. All you can ask for. In a few more hours the *Eisenhower* would confront *Starhawk*, Brisher would get her resignation message, and *Starhawk* would disappear in front of them. That was as far as her predictions could go.

Clio saw the young native girl standing before her, silently watching. She wore Clio's watch tied closely around her throat. It was 2:15.

Time to leave. Clio brushed the soil from her knees and followed the girl into the forest.

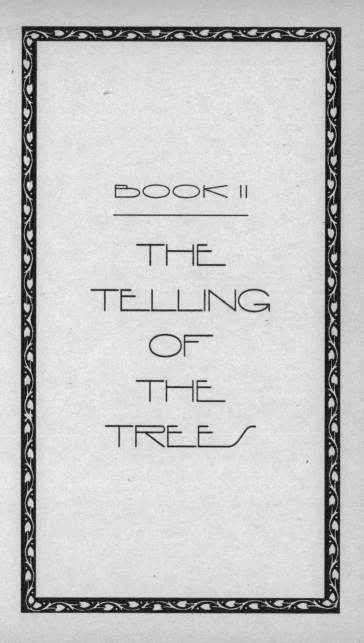

BOOK II

THE
TELLING
OF
THE
TREES

TREASONOUS
SEEDS

CHAPTER 20

Amid the ruins of the abandoned Earth camp, the lander from the Dive ship *Pilgrim* perched on its jointed mechanical legs. The jet housings creaked and groaned as they cooled, answered in symphonic measure by the alien jungle. Beyond the perimeter wire and a short clearing surrounding it stood the spindly, vanguard trees of the world forest, bulging toward the camp as though pushed from behind by rampant vegetation. One of the tall, opaque trees lay fallen across the clearing, its frondy top just short of the nerve wire. It seemed to be pointing right at the lander, right at Corporal Janacek, as he pressed his nose against the viewport.

Someone grabbed Janacek's arm. "Time to head out."

He wiped the imprint of his nose off the plasiglass, then turned to follow Sergeant Fraley down the middeck, joined by the rest of the platoon, their heavy boots rattling the deck plates and echoing off the bulkheads.

Whiteout fell in beside him. "Ho, daddy, we are going to breathe some gen-uuu-ine air. Ain't that a boot in the butt?" He slapped Janacek on the ass. "After these canned goods, it likely to kill me, no shit. One toke, my eyes be fizzin'. Two tokes, pop 'em right out of their sockets." He clamped his hands around his neck and bulged his eyes. "Think you could still love me, boy-o. I look like this?"

"Shut up, Whiteout." Janacek felt jumpy, wanted some quiet, standing there waiting for his turn to cycle through the hatchway, watching it swallow one crew member after another. Not his first mission, not as though he'd never been off-world or clutched a pulse rifle waiting for trouble.

Janacek scrambled down the ladder from the ship, into a plastic quarantine cell reeking of chemical sprays. Here, everybody's face took on a blue-green glow from the jungle scene that climbed the walls and bent toward the top of the cell. Whiteout did the self-strangulation number again, bluish tongue sticking out.

"Keep moving," came the sergeant's order. They ducked, one at a time, through the flexible hatch door. Janacek followed Whiteout into the blasting light of Niang.

His nostrils and lungs filled with hot, verdant air. Whiteout was right, it was hellish—and wonderful. Janacek gasped, filling his lungs again with the thick soup of real atmosphere, smelling of sweet citrus. *Maybe this is how real air smells. Three months on the* Pilgrim, *living on recycled army farts, and now we gag on the real thing. If you could call this the real thing, two million years from Earth.*

Beyond the camp remnants and perimeter wire, they were surrounded by open field for thirty meters before the jungle massed up. From its tight nest, bedlam: screaming, hooting, chirring, and buzzing in a nonstop caterwauling that made you want to hit something.

The platoon fanned out into the abandoned camp. Signs of the firefight were everywhere. On sergeant's orders, the platoon walked with pulse rifles at the ready, sweeping the encampment for signs of the mutineers, the crazy remnants of the old science team, who killed off their crewmates, the ones who wouldn't stay.

The med tent was in shreds. Must've taken at least fifty rounds to slice it up like that. Through the tears, Janacek could see cots overturned, bandages festooned from floor to roof, med kits cracked open and gutted. Whiteout ducked inside. "Hey, Janacek, get a load of this," came his voice from the tent.

Janacek pushed inside through the tattered flap.

Whiteout stood there, shit-eating grin on his face, with an opened bottle of whiteout. He took a hit, offered it to Janacek. "How sweet it isssss," he said.

"You null, I thought you said you were out."

"Emergency stash, man." He offered the little black and white bottle to Janacek again.

Janacek waved him off. "You must have been one of those glue sniffers when you were little, huh?"

Whiteout shrugged, grinning.

"Jesus, grow up." Janacek pushed out of the tent, squinting against the piercing light. Above his head, the local star burned hard, swallowing his shadow. In his mind the bloody scene played out, of crew killing crew, the cries of the women, the raving of Harper Teeg as he swung the machine gun wildly through camp. Harper Teeg. Kill him on sight. His co-conspirator, Liu, kill him as well. Before they kill us. Freeping crazy they must be by now, trapped in the endless turquoise jungle, their dreams of a new paradise smashed when the lander escaped with the women, the blossoms of their imagined empire.

The platoon set up a new perimeter wire tight around the lander, a good hot one. With that, Sergeant Fraley led half the platoon plus three science crew into the clearing, stopping just short of the jungle mass.

"You heard it before, but I'm tellin' you again, so listen up," Fraley said. "Somewhere in this damn blue swamp is a ship. It's covered with plants, so you won't see it like a ship, but that's what it is. You find it, you tone me out, and state your position. Me and the science team will join you. You encounter the mutineers . . . take them out." He looked each soldier in the face, waiting for nods. "I know it sounds simple. Those are the missions that usually fuck up. Anybody here going to fuck up?" Again, he looked for nods, found a few. "Whiteout, you nod your head yes every time I ask you a question?"

"Yessir."

The sergeant stared at him a couple seconds, sighed through his nose, scowling. "Janacek, you and Whiteout pair off, head southeast along the jungle perimeter. You catch him snorting from a little bottle, you shoot him on the spot. Got that?"

Janacek nodded. "Yessir."

Fraley looked at the two of them. Shook his head.

"Rest of you in your teams, fan out. Check in on the half hour. Meet back here in two hours. Any questions?" Without waiting for an answer, he said, "OK, get moving."

One by one the teams dove into the wall of under-growth flourishing under the jungle canopy. Engorged leaves parted before them with soft slaps, leaving their rem-nant of dew on fatigues and exposed skin. Janacek and Whiteout peeled off southeast, and fought their way through the steaming thicket with knee and forearm until, moving deeper into the woods, they found clearer passage where shade limited growth.

Here, under the dusky skirts of the trees, hairy vines swayed from their distant anchors in the canopy. Janacek looked up to the treetop ceiling, where, they said, most of Niang's creatures lived.

Whiteout followed his gaze. "Think those fanged mon-keys live up there, man?"

"That's what they say."

"Think they come sliding down those vines like firefighters?"

"Yeah. With fire axes."

Janacek tried to be gruff to ward off the queasy feeling in his gut. It started with the wrecked camp, grew worse in the jungle, the feeling of being watched. Maybe space-case crazy Harper Teeg. Maybe leopards, crocodiles, whatever the Niang equivalent was. Whatever crouched unmoving in the maze could watch, undetected, whatever moved. And *they* were moving. To make matters worse, the screaming of the forest masked the sound of anything approaching. You heard everything at once, and so you heard nothing. Janacek held his gun at the ready, and trooped on, setting each foot-step carefully in the bluish webbing of the forest floor.

At first they walked past the ship without recognizing it. They had been walking down a long, fifty-meter-wide clearing when Janacek referred to it as a corridor. He and Whiteout looked at each other. A straight-as-an-arrow runway through the forest.

They went back and looked at the burly mass tucked half in, half out of the jungle. The ship was cloaked, like the sergeant said. Moss clung to the contours of the ship in a turquoise fur, transforming it into a mere boulder, unless you were looking for it.

Looking for a ship. A starship.

"Well, Jesus H. Christ, looky this." Whiteout circled around to the other side. "Ain't no lander, this size," came his voice. "Could be we won the jackpot, or what?"

Janacek stared at the massive hulk, heart racing. No wings, but an overall cylindrical shape, bulges for cockpit and thrusters, opposite ends. Indentations in the moss that might define a hatchway. Looked like. The queasy wobble in his stomach ran up his torso, through his face. Not Bio-time. Not Earth. Alien. And stranger yet, the fleshy growths of flowers blooming from its sides like hands reaching through a blanket.

He swung his rifle around to the jungle. Shit almighty. Not paying attention. Way to get killed. He remembered his comm unit, unclipped it from his belt. "This is Janacek, Sergeant."

He waited. Tried again, hit buttons. Nothing.

Now his stomach was turning over like a rotisserie. Hadn't heard anything from Whiteout from the other side of the ship, either. Jesus, in how long? He approached the ship, back against the mossy side, inched along it in the direction Whiteout had taken. Something screamed, louder than monkeys, but maybe a monkey. Janacek gripped the rifle harder, to make it stop trembling, and shook the sweat out of his eyes.

As he came around the cockpit, he saw the boots first, then Whiteout lying there, still as a fallen tree, his face frozen in horror, his shirt ripped open. Oddly, no blood, no trauma, but shirt half blown apart. Janacek swung his rifle back and forth, trying to see through the sweat streaming over his eyes. He kicked at the body. "Whiteout? You son of a bitch. You lazy son of a bitch." His voice sounded like somebody crying. He knelt beside his buddy, heart lurching. Realized he was too near the turn at the end of the ship. Staggered backward for cover. Pivoted to cover his backside.

A man, a soldier, was standing there. Dressed in a brownish green jumpsuit. A leathery vest studded with bright stones or buttons. Handgun drawn, pointed at Janacek's head. His own rifle useless at these close quarters. Janacek fell backward. "Please," he said.

Another of them appeared at Janacek's back. He swung his head around to face this new one. Same fancy vest, clean shaven, very young. Too young to kill.

The young one slapped his rifle away, pinned his arms down.

The first one bent close, pushed his hand into Janacek's chest. The fabric split, the hand disappeared up to the wrist, and as his ribs cracked the pain began. A pain that a body couldn't hold. Janacek looked down at the hand in his chest. No blood.

The stranger's hand closed around his heart.

Janacek opened his mouth to scream, and all the jungle screamed with him.

CHAPTER 21

❧

Clio Finn approached the overgrown alien ship. She parted the curtain of vines fallen over the hatchway and thrust her way in with her boot and knee. Oh, dark in here.

Have you turned on your belt lamp?

Turned on her belt lamp, unhooked it, peered into the gloom. She was in a narrow passageway. Light screwed its way in via a collapsed section of bulkhead down to her left. She turned that way. The inside of the ship was a garden, flowers growing from the bulkheads, a bluish moss cushioning her steps. Niang everywhere, the ship turning to plants and soil in an effusive decay. Door handles like mushrooms. Funny things. Follow the white rabbit.

And then you find the flight deck. Tell us about this, Clio.

And then the bridge. Unmistakable beneath the layer of Niang. A semicircular bridge. Control panels. Seats for crew. Storage hatches. Sat in the pilot's chair. Dreamed of who had sat there, what had sat there. And what happened to them. Sat in the green-blue, brocaded chair, thinking, not alone. Not alone in the universe. Someone is out there, someone who's been in this chair. . . .

I'd like to hear about the instrumentation, Clio.

Instrumentation. The layout was strange. Holes and indentations where knobs and levers should be. The console wrapped completely around the deck, more like a diving bell than a spacecraft. Took out a utility knife, scraped at the panels. Hard to tell where the overgrowths ended and the instrumentation began. Peeled back a whole panel section. Gave way in shreds, like banana peels. Underneath, conduits looping still. Everything covered in turquoise, but not exactly rotted. Not yet collapsed into pulpy slime. Niang slime, has a certain ring. Niannnng sliiimmme.

Clio. Clio. You told us before about the star charts. What else do you remember?

Star charts intact, some of them. Fibrous pages, so thin, like pressed leaves. Crumbled in my hand . . .

But some don't crumble.

Some don't. Some that shouldn't have been there, were there. Don't recognize them. Not Earth, not Niang.

Think hard about the charts, Clio. Which stars?

Other charts, other pages, turning and turning, stars upon stars.

What regions, Clio? What quadrants? Think.

Not an astronomer, goddamn it.

But think.

Charts. Not familiar. Crumble to my touch. Crumble like old leaves. End of report. Sir!

She's useless beyond this point. This is as far as she gets.

Not a damn astronomer. A Dive pilot. Damn good one too. Thirty-one missions, world record. Now retired. Too tired.

Bloody hell. Wake her up.

Clio staggered against the guard as he hauled her across the quarry main yard. She saw two lines of patients fanned out for noon meal, two guards on her arm, two suns, everything double. Tears streamed from her eyes, cut a cold course down her cheeks in the brisk autumn air.

"Keep moving, bitch, or I'll drop you here, let you crawl back."

She swayed in place as the guard shook her shoulders. He smelled of sweat and aftershave and onions. Over his shoulder, a portly man in the grey quarry garb stood in the meal line. A new quarantine acquisition. Soon lose that fat. He looked away from her, the way they all did. Don't look the guards in the eye, draw attention to yourself. Don't look a distressed fellow-prisoner in the eye, share their sorrow. You've got enough of your own.

Clio allowed herself to be propelled onward by the ill-smelling youngster in the guard uniform. Her body didn't respond to the command to move legs. She didn't care. Her quarry sandals toed the dirt. If he dropped her, she would break her face on the main yard grounds. Didn't care. No joy in being the only survivor, so let him freeping well drop her in the dirt.

As the morning fog waned, it revealed the brownish eye of the sun, glaring through fathoms of smog. The lines of patients queuing up for meds emerged and receded behind the vapors like apparitions. The dead calling the near-dead. *I'm coming. Save me a place in line. I'm coming.*

Always there were the lines for the Sick and lines for the Clean, giving the lie to DSDE's contention that all who came here were Sick. The patients sorted themselves out, enacting the eternal quest for hierarchy, here where the last difference among them all was merely life itself. In the Sick line, parents kept their children in tow, though often the children were Clean. Children of Sick parents carried the family's stigma, of weakness, death, and sexual deviance. Not welcome in the Clean lines, no. As Clio and the guard moved haltingly through the main yard, a small cluster of children shadowed them, drawn by Clio's apparent collapse from the Sickness. A rumpled, towheaded child of about eight dangled a long insect larva in front of his lolling tongue. His eyes rolled; then he swallowed the thing, to the cheers of the others who chanted, *The worms crawl in, the worms crawl out, the worms play pinochle on your snout, boo hoo, boo hoo.* The guard glared at them, and they scattered.

She felt herself being hauled up the four steps to her barracks. The guard pushed her against the doorjamb, leaned in to her, close. His double head began to melt into one. She was starting to track again.

He cupped her breast and squeezed. "This is my first day in your lovely quarry. Initiate me." He spun her around, thrust her ahead of him through the door.

Heads turned as they crashed through the door. Twelve bunk beds held down the floor of a spare, cold room, still wobbling from the drug. He dragged her toward an unoccupied bed in the corner.

"This your boudoir?"

"Yes, this is my boudoir." Clio sat on the lower bunk, looking up at this boy in a brown guard uniform. Her chest was cold and tight, not from fear but hate. Didn't get a chance all that often to call up a grand cold surge of feeling. It was upon her now.

"Take off your clothes," he said, standing there, looking down at her.

Pitiful, Christ, so pitiful. So fucking predictable. What desire can do to you. Power came from not wanting anything; if you don't want anything, you become superhuman. Nice thing to know. Now that it was too late. Clio unbuttoned her shirt rather more slowly than she had to. Pulled it back off her shoulders, sleeves still on, exposing her breasts, leaning back on her arms, arching her chest a bit. "Come here, soldier," she said. She pulled on his belt, until he was kneeling in front of her. She kissed him, long and expertly.

When she pushed him away, his eyes were leaking all their desire.

"Here's how it works," she began, trying to punch up her voice into the feeling range.

"I can give you what you want. Everything you want, and some things you never knew you wanted." She ran her hands down his torso to his crotch, and leaned forward to flick her tongue at his mouth. Leaned back. Pushed him gently back as he leaned in toward her.

"But not today." Her voice dropped its sensual cloak, hardened. "See, today is Monday. Monday is the captain's day. He likes me clean for him, so you don't want your initiation today." She looked into his eyes and smiled. "Trust me."

"Tuesday is A Shift, those that don't piss off Ferris. He's lead worker. Wednesday is B Shift, Niemeyer takes care of that lineup. You beginning to catch the pattern here?" The rolling cold wave had passed through her chest and was moving up through her throat, making her spew out her words as sweetly spiteful as she could. "Thursday is the captain's office staff. Friday the maintenance crew. The shifts don't think much of the cleaning grunts getting me, but I like to keep things fair. Saturday is lottery day, they do a gambling pool, one winner, he spends the night. Or she, if so inclined."

Clio started buttoning her shirt. "You're C Shift. So you get your turn on Wednesday." She lay down on the bed, the grip of spite passing from her suddenly, leaving her tired, unimaginably tired.

The guard's face was struggling to find an expression. Disappointment won out. "What about Sunday?" he asked, looking down at her long, perfect body.

"Day off."

He watched her another moment, then turned to go.

"Oh, one more thing," Clio said.

He turned back. Behind him, Clio's scrawny roommates didn't bother to suppress their delighted sneers.

"You bring me a gift. When you come on Wednesday. I'm in the mood for a half-pound bag of powdered milk. And, since it's your first time, a blanket." She closed her eyes, dismissing him.

He shuffled to the door.

"Oh, about the blanket."

He stopped a moment, not turning around.

"Make sure it's clean."

When she heard the door creak shut, Clio knew he'd gone.

"Fucking A," someone said in the gloom.

A baby began to cry. Clio turned over toward the wall, her chest now empty of bile. *So, I am still alive. God-damn, anyway.*

A hand on her shoulder. "Clio." It was Loren. "Clio, God, Clio thank you." He rested his forehead on her shoulder.

"How's the baby doing?"

"He's not doing so good. Rita still doesn't have her milk. The baby won't suck."

"Maybe the powdered milk is helping."

"Helping?" Loren gripped her shoulder as he pulled his head back. "It's the only thing that's keeping him alive."

"We'll have more on Wednesday."

"Clio." Here a long pause. "I wish . . . Rita and I wish you didn't have to do this. We don't expect it. It's hellish, a nightmare. But we owe you the baby's life. I'd do anything for you, Clio, anything. I'd die for you, just ask." His voice wavered into tears.

Clio propped herself up on her elbows. Pinned him with her gaze. "Get real, Loren. I'm not doing this for you or the damn baby. I don't know anything about kids or babies. You think I'm going to turn myself into a fucking machine for a guy who's too dumb to get his politics right?" Loren winced at the foul language. "Tell you why I do this, you think I want to be hauled out of here on some crazed asshole's whim and raped and beaten? Think I want to get gang-banged in the guards' quarters, with the dummies cheering the sadists on?" Clio watched as Loren's face became more and more horrified. She softened a bit, but not much. It was the truth, let him hear it. You get too soft, you die. You love somebody, they're ransom against you. He didn't need to love her. Love was a liability where they were. *Toughen up, Loren. Learn how it is.* "Think I can let some pimply eighteen-year-old guard control my body, control me? I may not have much left, but what I got, I'm keeping."

Loren's eyes were moist and a faint smile tugged at his lips. The baby's squalls cranked up in volume.

Clio managed a scowl, and pushed him away. "Jesus, can't you stop that brat from screaming?"

Loren squeezed her arm and stood up, moved back to his cot.

The screams pierced her aching head like nails. She closed her eyes, saw it again. The Amazon jungle bush looming up before her as she and Russo and Zee crashed through it, the drumming whacks of helicopters beating the air, villagers screaming as the gases seared their lungs. The smell, the smell that burned her face, ripped her nose, throat. Tripping, elbows in the wet mush of jungle floor, mud clinging to her hands in clumps, and she, staggering on with monkeys joining the chorus of screams. Heard her own sobs, "God, oh God, you bastards, you killing bastards. . . ."

Opened her eyes on a plate of cheese, part of an apple. Loren sat next to her, his large brown eyes urging her to eat.

Clio turned her face, her stomach squirming. "Got some of that tea? The stuff that smells like raspberries?"

Loren bustled off. On the next bunk, Ed Coombs stared at the plate of cheese with a baleful eye. Clio put the plate of cheese on the floor between them.

"I can't reach," he said, his voice spun thin as the throat cancer invaded his esophagus.

"You gotta make some effort, Ed. You look like you're giving up, sometimes."

Ed leaned over. His hand stopped in midreach as a pale larva dropped from the ceiling onto the plate. Ed watched it inch its way toward the cheese. "I can't," he said.

Clio leaned over and flicked the grub away.

Ed looked queasy. "Piranha larva," he said.

"They gotta live too," Clio said.

"Live? They'll outlive us all. Few years, they're all that's left."

"Come on, Ed."

"It's true. It's all part of the food chain. First the trees went. Without their habitat, the birds go. Without their predators, the insects reign. Insects are the only ones that are adapting. The rest of us poor bastards . . ."

". . . are going to kick ass on these bugs," Clio finished. She flicked another grub away as it dropped onto the plate from a nest in the ceiling.

Ed snorted. "Yeah. And the world is flat. And angels dance on the heads of pins. And UV radiation isn't cooking us to death . . ." He broke off, coughing.

Clio saw Loren coming back and snatched two pieces of cheese, pressing them into Ed's fist. Ed swung slowly over to protect the cheese from Loren with his back.

Loren's brow was creased. "Clio, it's a waste. It's a

waste to give food to those people." He picked the plate up and laid it on the bed beside Clio, sat next to her.

"Ed hasn't been hungry for days. I'm gonna tell him no?" She stared up at the upper bunk, arm under her head. "He used to be a computer programmer. For Nintendo. In the time before. Raised—what do you call them—dahlias, won contests even. Drove an antique, some rare GM car, forget which. Always hunting the junkyard for parts. Found a kid living in one of those junked shells one time, took him home, they lived like father and son until DSDE came. His neighbors turned him in for Section Three, Deviant Lifestyle. Social and Drug Enforcement brought him here, along with the kid and his life partner. The kid died in a main-yard fight last month."

Loren sighed, looking at the floor where the plate had been. "I know, Clio, but we're all struggling to make it. Some of us are starving. Who's going to live?"

"Not up to me to decide. Not up to you."

Loren handed over a cup of cold herb tea.

Clio slurped at it. "Used to hate shit like this. Too healthy, no punch." She inhaled the fragrance, raspberries, it was, with a faint dream holdover of ammonia and sulfur.

Loren watched her expression. "Not exactly the Sorrento. I'll speak to the help." Loren always called the barracks the Sorrento. Posh hotel, an outrageous wedding-night splurge.

"Yeah, do that. For what we pay, service sucks."

He chuckled. Easy to amuse, was Loren. She looked down at the two remaining pieces of orange cheese. Took one, chewed it a long time. Need some go-power for tonight, girl. Chewed another. Pushed the plate away. "Not hungry."

Loren pushed it back. "Eat anyway."

"Son of a bitch, not hungry, OK?"

"No, not OK." His motherly stance was ludicrous. Urging her on so she could work her night shift for him, for all of them in her barracks. Feeding the mule, and oh, the mule was tired.

"Cheese gives me bad breath."

"That's what the apple's for."

She ate the apple slice.

"Thanks."

Loren beamed. "Compliments of the house."

The barracks door slammed open. The pimply guard. Loren rolled his eyeballs, retreated to his cot.

The youngster stood in the doorway, staring down the occupants, daring someone to look at him. No one did. He strode over to Clio's corner. Thrust a plastic grocery bag at her, twist-tied shut. Powdered milk, lots of it.

"Here's your present." He rocked back and forth on his heels, mouth set in a pout.

Clio took the bag, set it down on the bed without looking at it.

"I want you now," he said.

"You're early."

"I can't wait until Wednesday."

Clio took a long sigh. "Today's the captain's. Told you."

"He won't know."

"Yeah, he can tell."

"Depends on how we do it."

Clio shook her head. "He has spies." She looked around the room. "Maybe even some of these. Probably are. Quarried folk who get special favors for ratting." She smiled up at him. "Get lost, honey."

He dove at her, smothering her with himself, his rancid breath. Yanked on her thick, short hair, trying to find her lips.

Clio murmured in his ear. "Want to know what happened last time somebody moved in on the captain? They used a nerve probe on his member. Heard the guy screaming all the way across the yard."

He stopped thrashing on top of her. Tried thrusting at her a few more times. "Shit." He swung his legs over the bunk. Raised his hand to strike, found himself firmly blocked by Clio's grip.

"Bruises are off-limits too." She raised her chin at him. "Captain likes his dates pretty."

He nodded silently at her, over and over, like a windup mechanism. Finally said, "I'll get you for this."

"No, mister, you won't get me for this. You're going to be real nice. Learn the rules, learn some manners. Point here is, you want *me* to be nice to *you*. I can take you real high. But I got to be in a good mood." She scowled at him. "Right now, I ain't in a good mood. Now get the hell out of here."

He pushed off the cot and fairly raced for the door. Crashed down the stairs outside.

Quiet sat in the room. A listening, waiting quiet.

A voice from the upper bunks said, "You go too far, Clio Finn."

She snorted. *Too far? You can't even imagine where I already been.*

Night sucked off the day, as the quarry grew dusky, then black. Moans and racking coughs pierced the dark barracks, marking the fatal course of the Sickness, while those who were uninfected cursed the disruptions of their sleep, cursed the baby's cries. Clio strained to listen for the captain's footsteps.

As the moon rose, the windows emitted a cool light. Clio stood by one, pressing her temple against the woodwork, squinting to see the prison yard through years of grime. Her nose grew cold near the glass. The temperature in the uninsulated barracks plunged.

At thirty degrees below it was too cold to snow. Three months of snow mounded around the backyard, disguising rocks, abandoned toys, frozen shrubs in a world of exotic alabaster. The day's brief moments of sun had melted the thin top layer of snow, which, quick-frozen in the evening, now gleamed in the moonlight. Inspired by the beauty and fantastical landscape, Clio broke off a four-foot icicle dagger from the low eaves.

"On guard!" she screamed at Petya, lunging forward with her sword, free hand waving behind and overhead like in the movies.

Petya turned slowly, arms piled high with firewood. His eyes grew round in surprise.

"Release that maiden, or I shall skewer you through and through!" She brandished the ice sword at his face.

"Huh?"

"Release her, I say, or DIE!"

Petya carefully set the wood on the ground. He looked down at Clio from his six-foot height, prompting Clio to stand on tiptoe and raise the icicle high.

"Mom will be mad if I don't bring in the wood," he said.

Clio snorted. "So many have said, yet few have lived to repeat it! Make your prayers to your God and prepare to die, coward!"

Finally, Petya began to get it. They were playing, this was going to be a fun game. "Head them off at the pass," he shouted loudly, but without expression.

Clio grimaced. Wrong movie. "With this Sword of Power," Clio declaimed, "I will vanquish all my lord's enemies, and free the poor . . . and punish the rich. And you, my evil magician," she said, advancing, icicle pointed at Petya's chest, "shall be the first to DIE!" Petya's arms flew up in surrender.

Clio lowered her voice in an aside. "You can run, or something, because you're really scared of me," she said. Petya loved to play, but sometimes, in his serious childishness, he needed a little prompting. "First to DIE," she repeated, menacing him.

Petya's hand came down on the sword, breaking it like it was an uncooked spaghetti noodle.

They looked down on the shattered Sword of Power.

"You weren't supposed to do that," Clio said softly.

Petya's face grew hangdog. "Maybe I can fix it."

Clio looked up at his stricken face. "That's OK." She gazed around at the old backyard, with its mud-stomped snow, and the shingles missing from the house, and at Petya's bulky form, enormous in his secondhand plaid coat.

"It's OK. Let's bring in the wood."

•   •   •

She lay back down on the bunk. Captain was late. Usually not late. Hurry up, you old fool. Gotta get some damn sleep. The moon moved out of the window, passed over the horizon.

Rita woke Clio. It was morning. Loren stood behind his wife, holding the baby over one shoulder. "Wake up, Clio." Clio tried to push the hand away, damn annoying. "Wake up, Clio."

"It's morning meal, Clio," she said. "Everybody's already in line."

Clio snapped awake. Oh God. Breakfast. No captain last night. Not good, not good. Don't want to change the routine, no. She pushed herself up, shuffled to the john, headed out to join Loren and Rita at the end of the soup line. A breeze came in off the Issaquah hills, bearing its quota of brown pine needles, spattering her face like sand.

"How's the brat?" Clio asked.

"He's getting stronger, I think," Rita said. She smiled tentatively, looking for confirmation from Loren.

Loren leaned in toward Clio. "There's news, Clio. New quarry captain." His face was somber, eyes dark. "His name's Beecher. Got the guards nervous."

"So what's he like, this Beecher?"

"Don't know. But got the guards real nervous. They rang the meal bell before dawn, rousted everybody up. Been waiting here for forty-five minutes, and the line isn't moving." He licked dryly at his lips. He saw the look in Clio's eyes. "Probably they just need to make a show for him. First day. Making a show."

Clio sighted down the soup line, saw the mess crew standing by the soup pots, but no one dishing out. Beyond the soup tables were barracks eight and nine, then the high nerve-wire fence, bent in on top. In the distance the pine trees in shades of brown clung to the hills like scabs. Rita elbowed her. A motion of brown uniforms out in the yard. A man stepped forward. Dressed in a clean, pressed uniform with smart leather jacket. The captain.

"Bring the soup," he commanded. The servers looked

at each other for a moment, then, prodded by supervisors, brought out the huge pots.

"Dump it."

The servers dumped the pots out, moving back from the captain to avoid his feet. A lake of yellowish soup soon lay upon the main yard.

"This is your breakfast," the captain barked. "This may be your lunch. You'll find out at noon. It all depends. Depends on what?" He began pacing, skirting the lake, eyeing the line of quarry-mates. "Depends on discipline and your behavior."

Clio smirked. It was over. She knew it all, the whole picture, like you realize things sometimes without thinking. It had been too good to last. The queen of hell, she had been, now heading to be deposed. Her breath left her lungs, like the last drop of mediocre wine. Don't care if it lasts. Never cared, you asshole, never cared.

Captain Beecher continued: "You've all been cheating, and that's going to stop. Nobody works, nobody obeys, nobody earns their soup." His chest seemed to swell as his voice reached out, "This is a quarantined facility of the U.S. government, Department of Social and Drug Enforcement! A DSDE quarantine facility to protect the health and welfare of the greater community. This is NOT a summer camp! Not a place to cheat and steal. And this WILL stop.

"Clio Finn, come forward."

"Oh my God," moaned Rita. Loren clutched his wife in his arms.

Yes. It was over. Clio Finn come forward, no different than the DSDE boot through her Mother's front door, no different than Harper Teeg revealing himself as a DSDE spy, her whole front exposed. Had always been exposed. They knew, they always knew. They always catch you in the end. Clio stepped out.

"Further," Beecher ordered.

She walked to the middle of the yard, entered the soup lake. Fearless, she was. Empty. Stopped in front of Beecher.

"Turn around," he said for her ears only. She did so.

"This is a patient with special privileges," he bellowed.

"This is a fellow-quarry-member with six blankets on her bed, extra rations—not only of soup, but also of cheese and fruit and even pastries. Excused from all work. Why? Tell them why, Finn."

Clio looked over the heads of the patients to the sky in the distance, blue for once.

"Greed, sir," she answered.

"How does it feel to cheat your quarry-mates, Miss Finn?"

"I laughed at them for being so stupid."

"And who brought you the blankets and pastries?"

Clio paused. What the hell. "A few corrupt guards, sir."

"And how did you persuade them to do this?"

"By seducing them. Sir."

A blow to the back of her head sent her to her knees. Wet. Chopped carrots in the soup, some still with hair on the peels. And floating everywhere, the brown needles of the sagging trees.

"You liar. They are as degraded as you are."

Clio moved away from herself, saw herself kneeling there, a tall, scrawny woman with a mass of short red hair. A woman in a grey tunic and pants getting ready to die. The captain was still barking at them, her ears were still ringing from the blow. His voice came to her from far away, tinny and incoherent.

An hour might have passed, but still she didn't move. Movement in the yard, lines of people, a soft buzzing.

Someone pulled her to her feet, threw her in line. People surged away from her. The new quarry-mate, the fat man, sneered, "Pastries and cheese." Someone kicked her.

After a time she heard a buzzing noise. It went on and on. The woman in front of her turned around, her face tight with worry. "They're cutting off our hair," she said. She wore a little lipstick, her eyebrows were plucked into neat arches. She seemed to wait for Clio to answer. Clio looked to the head of the line.

Two guards were shaving the head of an old man whose hair was already clipped close. Bits of hair dispersed on the breeze like pollen. The woman in front of Clio whimpered. "Not my hair," she said. She touched the lustrous brown coil of her hair, drawn up into a roll so carefully that the hairpins didn't show. She tucked in an errant wisp. She pleaded with Clio again, "Not my hair." Clio looked her in the eye, feeling nothing. When the woman's turn came, she quieted, kneeled with head bowed. They pulled the bun down and cut it off with scissors in three strokes, threw it, hairpins and all in the great pile of hair, now growing large behind the guards.

Clio watched her own turn come up. She kneeled, neck exposed. They started at the nape, the fearful buzzing right behind her ears, sheared up the back and over to her forehead. The auburn chunks sparkled in the sun. Her head was cold as she stood up, naked in a shameful way. Again, she looked down on herself, this time seeing a prisoner like every other. No difference. Makes no difference. To one side, a huge pile of hair, guards using shovels to stuff it into large plastic bags.

Then the pimply guard was at her elbow, yanking her back to the barracks, and people were crying. Or was that her. No couldn't be her, no tears left.

The next events came swiftly upon each other. Several guards in the barracks swinging pistols, hitting people. In the clamor, Clio was jerked back into herself, forced to listen, watch. The young guard was taunting her, had his bag of powdered milk. He slit it with his knife, swung it around in circles, white powder everywhere, the smell of gluey milk in her nose. Clio stared at her tormentor vacantly, though he was shouting. This seemed to enrage him. He looked quickly about the room. People hid on their bunks—those that were not already involved in the fray— everyone was covering their heads, newly shaved, newly vulnerable. He found Loren and Rita, pulled on the baby's wrap, and Loren sheltered the child with his shoulder, Rita shouting next to him.

Then he was struggling with Loren, the baby on the floor, the guard propelled backward by a mighty fist from the diminutive Loren, and all was silent in the room but for the baby's cries. Even the other guards stepped back, waiting for their fellow-guard to react. In another moment he did, drawing his pistol, marching forward, raising it to Loren's head and pulling the trigger. A small round hole appeared in Loren's forehead as he tipped backward against the wall, dead before he hit the floor. Amid Rita's screaming, Clio felt her body move, full of a strange heat. She pivoted to her left, grabbing the rifle strap from the guard next to her and kicking him in the side, pushing him away, swung the rifle to bear on Loren's killer, who now had the baby by the arm, lolling at his side as he silenced Rita with a blow to her face. Good. Very good. Both his hands were weaponless.

"Freeze!" Clio screamed.

He did, his face amazed.

"I'll kill him before you can kill me," she shouted for the benefit of the other guards. "Tell them to back off," she ordered him.

"Don't shoot her, you might miss," he told them. He brought the baby up in front of his chest. "You gonna kill us both?"

"Yes." Clio cocked the rifle, adjusted her aim.

"Hey," he said backing up, hitting the bunk behind him, "you're crazy. You kill me, you're dead too."

"I don't give a shit, soldier." She was smiling now, exhilarated. Kill this bad ass, then go down to death and taunt him there, too. All gonna die now. 'Bout time.

Rita ran forward to grab at her son. They struggled. Clio fired into the ceiling. They froze in a tableau, baby between them. "Let the kid go, maybe you'll live."

Rita swiped the child from his grasp, retreated to the far corner. Clio circled around, joining her there. Kneeled down behind the far bunk, gun sighted.

"Get out of here, all of you. Get out!" The guards hesitated, then backed from the room. The young one started toward the door. "You stay," she said. He stopped.

She lifted her face to the top bunks. "The rest of you, get out too." Her barracks-mates moved down from the bunks and hurried for the door.

Clio turned to Rita. "You can go or stay. Either way,

you're dead, you and that baby." She held Rita's gaze. "Maybe you're better off out there. Try your luck. I'm not your savior, just get that straight. This is where we all die. I can't fix this one, it's gonna happen. So you make your own decisions." Rita slunk back into the deep corner behind Clio, fussing over the baby's hysterical cries, her eyes deep in their sockets. Loren's body was just to their left, slumped along the wall.

"You," she said, raising her voice, "take the body over to the bunk by the door. Lay him out on it."

The guard did so.

"Cover his face."

When the guard finished, Clio said, "Go back where you were and kneel, facing the door."

Clio was shaking. *Gonna die. Come so close so many times. This is it, though, this time, this is it.*

She sat a long time, head vacant as a windy plain. Even the baby quieted. A cockroach stalked across her shoe, disappearing into the shadows near the wall.

Then a bullhorn outside. "Clio Finn. This is Captain Beecher. Let that young man go. He's a murderer and will be dealt with. Don't you commit the same crime. Come out, and you and the woman will be treated fairly."

Clio rested her chin on the bunk, rifle by her ear, one arm resting beside it, finger on the trigger. Shaking hard now. Not afraid of death, no. When everything's gone, nothing left to lose. Family, oh, gone long time back. Petya, disappeared so long ago it was hard to remember him now. Big, he was. Tall, hulking, still a boy, always a boy. Eternal childhood. Not like her, an old woman now, aiming the gun at the man's head. Old at twenty-eight. She had seen too much death, seen her quota, time to die. Earth was old too, had its quota of autumns, dying too. No springs now, no regreening. Now that her seeds were dead. Scorched in the remnants of the Amazon coast, her last stand for the fading Earth. Should have died then, a good death it would have been, all at once, not in pieces as over the last months. *Make up for it now, I guess.*

She held on to the rifle. The barracks door opened.

A man entered. Opened the screen door, closed it behind him, turning to do so, stood casually before her, arms at his sides. About five-foot-ten, a trim man, with sandy brown hair combed carefully into a small wave at his temple with too much gel. Maybe fifty years old. Dressed in U.S. Army khaki. From the distance of five meters, Clio couldn't read his insignia, but he was brass, high brass. He stood before her, looking straight down the barrel of the rifle. His face pleasant, a small smile tugging at one corner of his mouth.

"You'll be Clio Finn, then," he said.

"You'll be dead if you move closer."

His expression didn't change. He held out his arms, palms out, and slowly turned. Short sleeves, looked unarmed. Could have a gun strapped to his ankle.

He looked down at Loren's body. "That shouldn't have happened." He looked past Clio into the corner. "I'm deeply sorry, Mrs. Scally."

Clio remained kneeling, rigid. "Go fuck yourself."

His lips pursed. "I don't blame you for your cynicism. The quarantine facilities are hard places. Those that come here, come here to die. People are desperate—and dangerous. The quarantine captains must use harsh means occasionally to keep order; sometimes they go too far. It's a hard balance. I wouldn't want the job."

She was starting to feel sleepy, bored by his gentle droning. Snapped her head up.

"You're tired, I'm sure. Let me get to the point." He gestured to the bunk across from her. "May I sit down?"

Clio didn't move. Couldn't decide what to do next.

He moved to the bunk on the other side of hers, sat, hands clasped between his knees.

"Now that you've got me, I think you can let this youngster go." His voice was sonorous, amiable. Threw her off. She swung the rifle up to aim at his head. Too cramped a position. She moved back to join Rita against the wall, braced the rifle on her knee.

He turned to the kneeling guard. "Move out, mister."

He looked intently into Clio's eyes. The guard gathered himself up, moved carefully, slothlike, to the door. He was gone.

Clio surveyed the man's bars. A colonel. Yes, high-brass military. That old enemy. Came after her Dive ship, limping home with Niang riddling the bulkheads, came after the ship with surviving crew, going to gun it down. Kill the Niang seeds and every man and woman aboard. Reward for bringing home the green. Kill it before it spreads. Reward for surviving the jungle and Harper Teeg tracking her down, reward for escaping the camp massacre. Welcome home.

"You got a gun?" Clio asked. Her heart, a flat stone.

He spread his hands.

"Get a gun." Once you make up your mind, the rest is easy. Life isn't always the best thing, despite what they say.

She waved the rifle barrel toward the door.

He hesitated, sighing.

"A pistol, fully loaded."

He went to the door, talked a moment with someone outside, came back with a .45.

"Put it on the bed," she ordered, indicating with her eyes the bunk in front of her. He did so. She crawled forward and took it. Heavy, a .45. She slid the rifle down and pushed it against the wall. Rita whimpered.

"You can kill me with the rifle, but it's rather hard to kill yourself with one, isn't it?" he said. "But it's not necessary, Clio. I've come to take you out of here. Out of the quarry."

Clio heard him, but as in a movie, a scene from someone else's life.

"That's a hard way to go," he said. "A forty-five puts a big hole in you. And not necessary, Clio." He smiled: a brief, jabbing pull at his lips. "You'll have trouble trusting me, of course. And I'm not telling you you're off scot-free. You are a criminal, from any viewpoint. But I'm offering you a chance for recompense, for rehabilitation. A chance not many people get, Clio."

Clio moaned. A tiny stab in her chest, an unwelcome twinge. Something returning to her, a dread twinge of hope. She cocked the gun. Get it over with, damn stupid bitch.

Swung the gun to her temple. No more of this, no more of that rattling voice, no more promises, no more goddamn hope.

"Clio, I'm going to stand up now and come over to you, and I'm going to take that gun from your hand. And you can kill me or kill yourself, either way. But that's what I'm going to do. You don't have to do anything, decide anything. I'm going to decide for you, because right now you are too tired and scared to decide anything, too tired and scared. I'm going to protect you. Nothing will hurt you now. If you let me come sit by you. So easy . . . I just come and sit by you."

He stood up and started walking toward her. She saw his trousers walking, saw his shoes, spit-shiny black like right out of the box. He took the gun. Knelt down beside her, an arm around her shoulder.

"Get out," he said to Rita.

A shuffling, and then the door shut behind her. He settled down on the floor, back against the wall, arm tucked around Clio.

They stared off into the end of the barracks while her life slowly, oh so slowly, crept back to her.

CHAPTER 22

&

He wrapped a rough barracks blanket around her shoulders and slowly led her outside. In the brightness, Clio saw the world in all its parts: people, buildings, ground, trees and sky in a strange mixture of acuity and peace. They crossed the main yard, all silent around them. The smell of vegetable broth mixed with mud. A car waited, black, sleek. She allowed herself to be helped into the backseat.

The colonel took a seat in the front with the driver, leaving Clio alone in the backseat with its buttery brown leather and her reeking blanket. She clutched the blanket around her. The gates opened, guards looking after them, and they sped away from the Issaquah Quarry, the car running smooth as flight.

Through the shaded windows she watched the outside world slide by. Ordinary things had been out here all the while as hellish things had worked their course inside the quarry. That was the way of things. Chaos and peace both commanded their realms without troubling, even, to contend with each other. And no one cares, the world doesn't care. Case in point: the Issaquah Quarry and this creamy smooth limousine.

The suburban countryside sped past the window at her elbow: gas-station signs perched on hundred-meter poles, freeway lane upon freeway lane bearing long, finned cars. Brown-tipped evergreens sagging under the invisible UV glare, sere grasses on vacant lots with signs to rent, build, buy, make hay while the sun shines. And as an antidote, perhaps, banners on homes proclaiming religious messages, and lavender-fuzzy in the distance, a church with its neon cross, proclaiming a better world in the next.

The car stopped, idling. Then the motor stopped. Clio tried the button on the window. Didn't respond. A blur directly outside her window resolved itself into a grasshopper, resting on the lip of the window ledge. Its glistening, black body looked like it was struck from metal. Not a grasshopper. A piranha nymph. A fly that took the wrong moment to inspect the remains of an insect on the window was snatched up in an instant. The nymph's mandibles twitched. Then, leveraging with its huge hind legs, it jumped into the air and disappeared.

"Could call in a chopper, sir," the driver said.

"No, Lieutenant. They're a target, too easy. Better to melt into the crowd, eh?"

Eventually, a tap at the window. DSDE stop-and-search. The window rolled down.

"Driver's license, health certificates," the man said, while his eyes swept the inside of the car.

The lieutenant pulled down the visor, slipped out a card. "U.S. Army Command," he said.

The DSDE agent scrutinized the card, and frowned at Clio. "And her?"

The colonel leaned into the conversation. "My custody."

The agent's gaze took in the rank insignia. "Yessir. And we'll want her ID, just for the record." Looked back at Clio.

The colonel smiled, the briefest of stabbing smiles. "Negative, Agent . . . Kern. National security. Check with your HQ, then I'll expect clearance to jump this queue." The colonel handed forward his own ID card.

Clio saw the agent's name sewn over his breast pocket. Saw his deep scowl of uncertainty. Saw Kern looking at her shaven head, dirty blanket. She smiled at him. A quiver on the edge of his mouth, then. He pulled back from the window, stood up and disappeared past their window, striding toward the cluster of roadblock cars with that blackshirted DSDE swagger.

•   •   •

Clio and Petya pressed forward against Dee Dee
Mullen and her husband, craning their necks to see the procession, just now passing Third and Maple. Dee Dee looked
down at Clio, brought her arm around Clio's shoulders.
"Here, honey," she said, nudging her forward, curbside.

Clio squinted against the metallic glare of sun and the
simmering asphalt. No one could remember a hotter April,
never had Easter morning boiled the ladies' flowered hats
as this year, or browned the planting strips on Maple. Clio
slid off her sandals and buried her toes in the grass where
her body cast a noon shadow. Across the street, Kevin
Reiner's snow cone fell onto his chest in a raspberry cascade as he tipped it back for a hit of ice. Mrs. Reiner yanked
on his ear, but his cry was lost as the crowd's voice, in a
rolling wave of sound, surged their way, breaking finally
into many individual murmurs and shouts.

Now Clio could see four DSDE blackshirts striding
behind two naked men, stumbling along in front. No, not
naked, wearing boxer shorts and holding hands, except, as
they neared, Clio could see that their wrists were tied
together on one side. One man had crew-cut red hair, same
color as Clio's. With a small jerk in her stomach, she saw
that it was Neil Kiepe, the fifth-grade teacher at Sherwood
Elementary. The other man was John Crivello from down at
AA Rentals. Mr. Kiepe saw her and for a moment she stood
alone, with time stopped the way it does when you have to
stand in front of everyone and answer the question, but you
don't know the answer. The sunlight surrounded her in a
nimbus, broiling the surface veins in her skin, and still she
looked at him and wished for an earthquake or tornado to
disrupt this moment, but the peaceful, hot noon stayed and
stayed.

Then time started up again with Dee Dee's voice:
"Look at that," she said, "in their shorts." From the other
side of the street, Kevin threw the funneled snow cone cup at
John Crivello. As he missed, his father glared at him. Kevin
was usually a better shot than that.

"They'll get sunburned, sis," Petya said.

Dee Dee's brow folded in the middle, like it always did when Petya said something stupid.

Clio elbowed her brother to be quiet. "Shut up," she said, her voice attempting harshness, but coming out in shreds. Dee Dee had been watching them, but now turned back to the procession.

As the group passed, folks in back of Clio surged forward, pressing her into the road, rolling over her sandals, leaving her barefooted on the asphalt. The bottoms of her feet screamed. She stepped in the red footprints of one of the prisoners.

She tried swimming back to the curb, pushing her brother sideways, and finally cutting a path with him as pilot ship. She sat on the grass and rubbed the soles of her fevered feet. Petya brought her sandals to her. "Let's get out of here," she said.

As they turned up their street, even the shade of the elms wasn't enough: she wanted the screening walls of her house, the darkness of her room.

When they came up the front walk of the house, Mother threw down her cigarette and ground it out with her heel like it was a bug. "So, you got an eyeful, huh?" she said.

Clio shrugged.

"DSDE was mean to those men," Petya said.

Mother slapped him in the face. It made a pink mark on his cheek, despite him being a foot taller than her. Petya stood stock-still, until gradually his face toppled into a grimace, Petya's silent way of crying.

"Don't you ever call DSDE mean," she said. Her left eye narrowed like it did when she meant business, and that would have been enough. You didn't go against that narrow eye. Until today, it had always been enough. But nothing seemed normal today.

Clio raised her voice: "It was my idea, I took him to the procession. You didn't have to hit him."

Mother turned that squeezed up gaze at her daughter. "Get in the house," she said.

She and Petya shuffled into the hallway, while Mother quietly shut the door. She turned to them, eyes full open *now, but cold, like a stranger's eyes. "Never say anything bad about DSDE outside this house." The bell in the hallway rang from the patient upstairs. Mother turned and went up, her shoes clacking on the old wood stairs. It was the first time Clio understood the way of secrets. If you tell them out of place, out of time, blows will fall.*

"I hate her," Petya said, rubbing his cheek.

"She should have hit me instead." Wishing she had. Clio reached up to him and hugged him around the chest, waiting for him to hug her back, waiting for something to be normal, wondering when things had stopped being so. Wondering why it had taken her so long to figure out that normal hadn't been around for a long time.

Finally he hugged her back. "A-OK?" he said.

Clio made an "o" with her thumb and index finger behind his back. "A-OK."

Presently the agent came back. As the window rolled down, he handed the colonel's ID card back through. "Suggest you travel with license-plate insignia in the future, Colonel. Avoids confusion."

"Confusion is the whole point, Kern. DSDE ought to know that better than anyone." The colonel tucked the card away. "And thank you for your courtesy," he said, waving the lieutenant to proceed. They pulled out of line, fast enough to throw Clio back. The window rolled up. "Moron," the colonel said.

Clio let herself breathe again. She looked closer at the colonel. Sandy brown hair, worn just long enough to push the edge of military standard. He turned slightly. An old-fashioned wave at the forehead, giving him a jaunty look. A trim, masculine profile, suitable for a coin, as in Roman times. Mouth held in an unself-conscious, arrogant, almost-smile. Not afraid of DSDE, this colonel. But maybe the Department of Social and Drug Enforcement was afraid of *him.*

The car sped into the Mercer Island tunnel, past graffiti reading, MOTHER EARTH ABHORS A TUNNEL, and YOUR CAR, YOUR COFFIN, and WHAT A FRIEND WE HAVE IN JESUS, where

"Jesus" was crossed out and "Texaco" painted in. Where I-90 merged with I-5, their limo stalled in congestion once more, until they slipped off toward what Clio saw was Boeing Field. Now, on the surface streets, they flew along, barely slowing for red lights. The gates of the airfield rolled open and they sped toward a Quonset hut in the distance, where they stopped. The colonel's aide hustled Clio out of the car, and hurried her toward the hut. Nearby raged machine gun fire and the smoke from burns. As the aide shuffled her down the hallway, Clio craned her head around to shout at the colonel, who was entering one of the first offices, "What about Rita and the baby?" But he was already gone.

The close roar of artillery startled her. "The fighting is half a kilometer away," the lieutenant said. "It's under control." Clio looked up into his round, black face. On his breast pocket she read RYERSON.

He led her to the end of the greenish-yellow corridor, and opened the door to a room smelling of Lysol and dust, with a low refrigerator and cot. Behind a cheap desk was the mandatory framed photo of President Gaylor in a prim red suit and cloche hat.

Ryerson nodded to another door in the far wall. "Lavatory," he said. He locked the door behind him, but Clio tried it anyway. Then she folded her blanket, set it on the end of the cot. Opened the refrigerator, found a Hostess pot pie and package of frozen vegetables. She ate the pot pie with her fingers and crunched down the vegetables until her throat was too cold to swallow. Laying the package aside, she went into the lavatory. A real toilet, with a warm seat. Started to wash her hands in the sink, made the mistake of looking in the mirror. A bald, hawkish, and white face, all eyes, mouth, and ears. Gods. Long face, very large hazel eyes, jutting cheekbones. Reddish five-o'clock shadow around her scalp instead of hair, with nicks as though dive-bombed by birds. Her eyes grew hot and a croaking noise emerged from her throat. She hung her head, bracing her hands on the sink, tears leaking into the basin.

After a long time she was able to shower.

When she emerged from the lavatory, naked, she saw a pile of clothes on the cot, but her folded blanket was gone. She looked around for the blanket. My damn blanket. Earned it, by God.

Pawed through the pile of clothes, finding army fatigues. Put them on, including army cap. Need that one, no mistake. She pulled it over her scalp. Strung the belt through the loops, cinched it in with a foot to spare. Put on shoes that just about fit. Always had big feet. When you're tall, gotta have long feet so you don't tip over, Mother always said.

Gunfire crackled between the bellowing of airplane landings and departures. Levelor blinds covered the room's sole window. She turned them open and peered through them to find that the glass was painted white. Yanking the blinds up, she pulled on the aluminum window lever. It didn't budge, but no surprise there. Still a prisoner, yes, *after what you've done*, a criminal by any standard. She rifled the desk for a paper clip, and was in the process of picking the lock when the door made a clicking sound and Ryerson was back.

He led her down the corridor. Gunfire again in the distance. She looked over at Ryerson. "NRA throwing a party out there, Lieutenant?"

He paused a moment before a door with opaque glass in the top half. "Food riots. This base is a supply depot."

As he opened the door, she saw a room not much larger than the one she'd just left, glowing greenish-yellow in the fluorescent light. The colonel sat behind a desk among papers and a half-finished meal. He waved at the tray and Ryerson retrieved it.

"Come, come, Clio," the colonel said, gesturing her to sit across the desk from him.

She sat. He regarded her, nodding. "You look better, that you do."

Meanwhile, a young corporal appeared in the doorway, carrying another food tray. A look of terror took over his face as the colonel sprang from his chair, gun drawn and pointing at the youngster's head all in one fell swoop.

"Who is this?" the colonel growled at Ryerson.

"Corporal Doran, sir," Ryerson said, frozen in place, holding the tray of the colonel's table scraps.

Corporal Doran backed up as the colonel advanced a few paces, still holding the gun at eye level. "No new people! I said no new people come near her!" He spoke to Ryerson, but never left off staring at Doran.

"He checks out, and replaces Okada, sir."

"Checks out, does he? How long you been in service, mister?"

The silverware on Doran's tray rattled against each other. "Eighteen months, sir," the youth said, looking at the pistol.

"Eighteen months," the colonel repeated. A glance at Ryerson was enough to convey, *not long enough*. "Put the tray down, soldier." Doran did so, placing it in front of Clio. "Now get out my sight." Corporal Doran fled. The colonel holstered the gun and turned to Ryerson. "Any more surprises?"

"Nosir."

The colonel smiled in mock gratitude. "Good. Call me the minute we're ready."

"Yessir."

Even as the door shut behind him, Clio's attention was all on the tray in front of her. Filet mignon, buttered broccoli, small red potatoes, real coffee. Clio looked up at the colonel. He nodded his permission.

She set upon it, hardly stopping to chew. Like a dog, Clio thought, eating like a dog, but can't help it. Now she noticed for the first time a small paper cup with two red pills in it.

"Take them," he said. "You're depleted. These will help."

She ate her broccoli instead, and he watched her eat for a while. "You don't know my name, of course," he began. "Jackson Tandy."

Clio concentrated on her plate.

"A name doesn't tell you much," he said. "I couldn't choose my name, unlike you Dive pilots. Clio Finn. There's a name that says something. Would you like to know what that name says to me?"

The steak was delicious beyond the normal bounds of food. It disappeared quickly.

"Clio reminds me of Cleopatra. The exotic Egyptian queen. But you've shortened it, made it a nickname. Therefore you don't think much of rank and regalia. But you still want to be superior, looked up to. Therefore Clio. And Finn. For Huckleberry Finn, of course. Probably your favorite childhood book. Adventure and the old ties of childhood. You hearken to the past while ranging out to your adventures. I like that, respect for the past." He watched her chew for a moment. "How'd I do, eh?"

"Missed," she said. The potatoes were buttered and had flakes of parsley and pepper.

Tandy pursued his lips. "Somehow I doubt that. But we'll see as we get to know each other better."

She glanced up at him as he leaned back in the cheap swivel chair, holding a pen between two hands, elbows on the chair arms. He held her gaze. A man of few nervous gestures, a patient man, watching her attentively.

Seconds ticked by. "You see me as the enemy," he said.

Clio shrugged.

"I represent the army. They tracked down your flight into the Amazon, eradicated your seeds, your planned Niang infestation. You believed they would save the Earth." He slowly shook his head. "That was a naive and dangerous mistake. I'm afraid the solution to our problems is far more complicated than your Niang fantasy." He stood up from the chair, tossing the pen onto the desk. He turned toward the unpainted window behind him. Evening came on amid spatters of rain, pressing against the glass of the lighted room like melting pearls. "For you, it was a great cause, I realize that. The rest of us were just the bad guys, afraid of change, eh?" He turned to see her reaction.

"What happened to Zee and Russo?" Clio asked. "You find them and execute them for treasonous agriculture?" She pushed the empty plate away.

"They're dead. Another case of overzealous prosecution. I'm sorry. Got too close to the defoliant spray. Heart failure. I'm . . ."

"Sorry. Yeah, I know." Dead, all dead, just as she thought. Even Zee, young, sweet Zee. To hear it straight out gave death recognition, released those small, festering hopes. OK, dead. Got it.

"To you—and them—any change was better than the demise of Earth. You'd seen the future—used Dive and traveled up twenty years—saw the Earth, it's biotic mantle gone, Earth, heading toward cinders. Niang represented the last hope: a nonmetallic future, and therefore without technology, but a future nonetheless." He leaned against the wall, arms folded. "What you didn't stop to consider is the downside of your alternative future. What was that downside?"

"Guess you're gonna tell me, right?"

He had a way of smiling for a millisecond, stabbing the conversation with a token smile. "It's a future I've seen myself, Clio. We take little Dive forays downstream, yes we do. I'll tell you what Niang means for Earth: the Dark Ages. The collapse of civilization. Of all technology, culture, law and order. Marauding hordes and bestiality beyond anything I'd want you to witness. The loss of all knowledge, all agricultural knowledge, medical knowledge, literary, architectural, electronic, philosophic."

"Which we're going to lose anyway, right?"

Tandy continued as though she hadn't spoken. "All lost in three generations as metal and plastic decay into compost."

"But the Earth could have survived. There would be green again."

"Yes, green. Means a lot to you, doesn't it? Even with the return of the Dark Ages. Ever read about the first Dark Ages?"

"They had the plague," Clio responded. "A rigid society controlled by a fanatical church. Burned people at the stake for acting strange. Yeah, I read about it."

Tandy brightened. "Not much different from today.

That's sharp, Clio. I enjoy that; someone who can engage in real conversation. But of course there *are* differences. Then, millions died. In the space of three hundred years, a quarter of the population of Europe, dead of the plague. Today, a tenth die, those that choose sexual and drug-based lifestyles. The difference between then and now? Science. And yes, quarries, as you call them, quarantine, is part of that. Not pretty, certainly. But necessary. The Niang future . . ."

A knock at the door. Tandy's aide. "We're ready, sir."

Tandy rose from his chair. "Later," he said to Clio. As she stood, he glanced down at the paper cup. "Take your meds." An order this time. She swallowed them with the last of the coffee.

From the coat tree in the corner he grabbed two army raincoats, handed one to Clio. He urged her out the door as she struggled to pull it on, trying to find the belt and failing.

Back down the hallway then, at a fast walk, with Ryerson holding the outside door open.

"What about Rita and the baby, Colonel? At the quarry," Clio asked as they emerged into the night rain.

"The dead man's wife? She's of no consequence, no consequence. Place your energy on your destiny, Clio. Not on hers."

A nasty east wind whipped her face. All Clio could see was the columnar beams of a car's headlights penetrating the drift of light rain. The smell of wet asphalt. She found herself helped into an open army jeep. Ryerson swung in after her. They sped off, past several massive hangars, and around to the vast tarmac of an airfield.

Ahead of them, a small commuter jet warmed up for takeoff. Ryerson leaned over to Tandy, pointing off to their right, where a dark van was speeding toward them. "Step on it, Lieutenant," Tandy ordered. The jeep sped forward and jerked to a stop at the end of the jet companionway as the van met them, and two doors swung open. Tandy jumped down from his seat, drew his service pistol and aimed it at the first person to emerge from the van: a slender, blond man in the black uniform of DSDE. Ryerson yanked Clio up two steps toward the open jet door, at the same time drawing his gun and, in a crouch, resting the barrel against the companionway railing.

The van's engine was still running, its headlights throwing the DSDE agent into silhouette as he stood before them. "Colonel Tandy," he said, "I understand from Captain Beecher that you are aiding a dangerous individual to break quarantine. The department has a problem with that, as you might imagine."

Without lowering the gun, Tandy responded, "I certainly can imagine that you have a problem with that, however, this individual is actually Clean, and therefore improperly placed under quarantine. Shocking, really. Fortunately, I was able to save DSDE the embarrassment of further infringements of this woman's civil rights."

The shadow noted the lieutenant's slow climb up the stairs, Clio in tow. "And stop right there, Lieutenant, unless you wish to be brought up on charges as well." Ryerson stopped. "I am placing this woman under arrest, as a federal officer of the Department of Social and Drug Enforcement."

Raising his hands, the agent moved forward until his features became visible in the airfield floodlights. The man was slim and fair, with delicate features as beautiful as any woman's. "This is a misunderstanding over jurisdiction, Colonel Tandy. I think we can settle this without violence." He nodded at the pistol. Tandy lowered the gun a fraction. "Clio Finn is a dangerous felon. Placed temporarily at the Issaquah Quarry until her trial date. You may have misunderstood the situation, Colonel. But you will hand her over to me at this time." He reached into his breast pocket, flashed an ID at Tandy. "Jared Licht, special agent, Department of Social and Drug Enforcement." He swung the ID around to Clio and the aide, though they were too far to read it, cocking his head and smiling in a provocatively cheerful manner.

The colonel, still with pistol, smiled back at Licht. "These jurisdictional disputes are always vexing, Agent Licht. On the one hand, we both want what's best for the entire situation. But on the other, we have our orders. I believe there is one way to resolve this quickly." Tandy drew a paper from his back pocket, reached out with it.

Licht stepped forward to look at it for several long moments. He smiled, a kind of "you win," generous, and lovely smile.

Tandy took the paper back. "Ultimately, we do all report to her. That's what brings all of the branches of government into one cooperative force. Chain of command. Frees us, lower down as we are and perhaps lacking the complete picture, from making ignorant mistakes."

Licht laughed, threw back his head and laughed, waving his associate back to the van. Then he spun on Clio. Pointed his finger straight at her face. "You. You, Clio Finn, are going to see me again. I look forward to that as much as you must dread it." The pointing finger became a raised hand of farewell. Again, the heartbreaking smile. He turned back to the van, then pivoted around to face Tandy once more. "Just one more thing. It *is* in my purview to search for contraband substances. She's a notorious drug user, Tandy, you realize."

"Your point?"

"Let's just be sure she's clean."

Tandy closed his eyes in apparent exasperation. "Lieutenant, get her on that plane."

"Oh dear, subverting my mission, now I can't be quite so cheerful about that one, Tandy."

Tandy's lip curled. "What do you want to do, strip her down?"

"Colonel. You shock me. A pat-down would do."

"She's clean, Licht."

"Well, we'll see."

In Tandy's silence, Licht walked to the foot of the stairs. Looked up at the lieutenant, who slowly took Clio by the arm and led her down to the tarmac. Licht pulled the raincoat off her shoulders and discarded it at her feet. Then, gently putting her hands on the railings, either side of the stairs, kicked her feet wide apart, frisked her, starting from the neck. Leaned in, whispered, "Murdering bitch. Here's a love bite, until I get you alone." He pinched her nipples, fiercely. Clio caught the grunt of pain before it left her throat, swallowed it back down. Don't give him the pleasure, by God. Licht continued the pat-down, not hurrying. Finally he stopped, leaving just the cold breeze fluttering against her skin beneath the uniform. Then she heard his car door slam. She stood up straight, watched the van rumble off the airfield.

They climbed up the stairs. From behind her, Clio heard, "Sorry about that." She spun around, looked down on Tandy a moment, despite the rain.

"Keep him away from me, Tandy," she said. "Just keep him the fuck away from me." Shaking, she climbed onboard.

He followed her, saying, "I'll do that, Clio, the best that I can. Sometimes, you have to understand, sometimes, you give a little with these people to get a lot."

"Give a little of *me*, you mean."

Ryerson was coming out of the head, wiping off with paper towels. "Pick a seat," he said. There were eighteen in this part of the cabin.

Tandy waved to the curtains down the aisle. "You'll be riding with me, Clio. This way." She noticed Ryerson's eyes glance quickly down at the floor as he found a seat. Poking through the curtain, Clio found the first-class cabin with five seats and a wet bar. Tandy hung up his raincoat in the stowage locker along with hers.

"You can get some sleep here," he said. He pulled back one of the seats until it lay nearly flat, then grabbed two blankets and a pillow from the overhead locker, tossing them on the makeshift bed. The plane's engines wound up to a frenzy. They buckled in for a moment, he on one side of the aisle, she on the other, as the plane sped down the runway and grabbed for the sky. Clio looked at the flattened passenger seat in front of her, saw how it was going to be. Just more of the same.

She turned to Tandy as the plane climbed steeply, and he met her gaze. Get it over with. She started to unbutton her shirt. Be glad to get the damn wet stuff off anyway. He looked at her with narrowed eyes as she started working the shirt buttons out of their soggy button holes. You get so that taking your clothes off is a weary thing, never mind who's watching. It comes to that, eventually.

The plane flattened out its climb and Tandy unbuckled, standing over her, looking down at her. He turned to the stowage bin above his seat, looking for something. Found it in the next one. Clean fatigues. He pressed them into her hands.

"That's not going to be our contract, Clio. May have been how you survived in quarantine, but that's not what you need to survive with me." He gestured at the head. "Go dry yourself off. Then come back here and get some sleep. I want you rested."

"Suits me," she said. She made her way into the head, managed to undress, dry off with paper towels and dress again in a space about twice the size of a coffin. Passed up looking in the mirror, passed up thinking about her body, the number of miles—rough, stop-and-go miles—she'd put on it. She washed her hands, mere skin over sticks. Opened the door, found the first-class seat made up like a bed, eased herself down.

Lying on her side, Clio could see the sleeping city below, as the plane banked and turned, a few squandered electric lights gleaming like campfires; then the mists closed in on the window and on her mind. Tired, by God.

"Where we going, Colonel?"

No answer, but she didn't expect one. "Jared Licht," Tandy said, after some time. "He's deceptive, got to watch that one. He's a lot like you, Clio." He noted the expression on her face. "Well, yes, think about it. He's an idealist, as you are."

"Not like me," she said again.

"A matter of degree, Clio. You have to know when you've gone too far."

Gone too far. Always go too far. The whine of the engines hugged the skin of the jet with the disturbing noise of air escaping from a balloon.

"Why does he hate me?"

"Hate you?"

"Yeah. Not drugs, is it? Because DSDE and Biotime both knew I was stashing drugs to keep me Diving. Harper Teeg told me they knew. But they needed me to Dive, so they looked the other way."

"You killed a DSDE agent, Clio. You were eighteen, an adult, and you killed a man."

"So, it's not about the drugs, then." Clio settled into her pillow, beginning to fade.

"DSDE isn't about drugs," Tandy said. "It's about control. They use people's paranoia about the Sickness and homosexuals and drugs, roll it all together. They're a tight-knit core, the department. You killed one of theirs. They raided your house, killed your mother, went after you and your brother. But you did kill one of theirs. Self-defense or not, they'll never forget that. Licht will never forget it." Tandy pursed his lips. "Well, never mind that now. We have a larger enemy to attend to."

She barely heard, as Tandy's voice joined the drone of the airplane. She dreamed, as so often, of home. This time of Mother giving her advice, arms crossed in front of her, cradling a cigarette, blowing out the smoke to punctuate her words. Even in her dream, Clio knew that the advice was a message from her own heart, so she tried to listen, and even as the words came out of her mother's mouth, they dispersed in smoke, lost.

She awoke with a start. Tandy handed her a can of Pepsi. "Wake up your mouth," he said. "We're getting ready to land." He watched her closely as she popped the top. "Bad dream?"

"Yeah. Dreamed I was captured by the U.S. Army."

"Or, you might say, saved, eh?"

Clio looked sideways at him. "Right, saved." Took a slug of Pepsi.

The jet noise changed in tone. Descent had begun.

Ten minutes later they deplaned onto another airfield, this one strangely vacant of terminals and activity. Except for a startling brilliance, in the distance. Gantries, launch scaffolding, it was. Clio drew in a gasp.

A space shuttle, by God.

A warm, dry breeze snatched the sweat from her face.

"We're going upstation, Clio," Tandy said.

Freeping obvious. Going upstation. The shuttle vehicle, primed and rumbling with prelaunch warm-up, nestled among the solid rocket boosters and towering external tanks, a four-pronged space truck aimed at the heavens. The thunder of the engines snatched her thoughts away, leaving only wave after wave of chills radiating out from her stomach to the ends of her limbs. Space shuttle, by God. An army jeep collected them, and Clio found herself raising her face at an ever sharper angle to view the towering mass. They stopped a short distance off and Tandy assisted Clio from the vehicle, across to the gantry elevator for the 120-meter ride up to the entry hatch, quaking all the way as the ground shook beneath the shuttle's roar. As they faced the main hatch of the shuttle vehicle, Tandy shouted something at her, lips moving, words lost, and then he grasped her arm, helping her through the one-meter-diameter circular hatch. Ryerson came through and closed the hatch, throwing the bolts home.

She turned to get her bearings. They were standing on the mid-deck wall, with everything standing on end as the shuttle poised upright for launch.

Here on mid-deck, ten empty seats lay on their backs. The lieutenant helped Clio into one. She jerked her arm away. Can damn well strap myself into a passenger seat. Can damn well fly this baby, too, come to that. She stumbled into a seat, yanked the harness around her.

Her steak and broccoli meal was in the process of deciding whether to stay or leave. On her right, the personal hygiene station, close to hand—might damn well need it. On her left, two bunks with privacy curtain stowed, revealing a taped-up photo of a teenage boy raising aloft a trophy, the kind unaccountably shaped like a vase with handles on either side. Directly in front of the passenger chairs, the external airlock for debarking in space.

The swishing of cabin vents closing. A crackle on intercom: "Mid-decks, this is Commander Onishi, we are initiating prestart procedure and are configured for liftoff.

Secure all passengers and baggage." A pause as the whooshing of liquid hydrogen built up in the external tank. After several minutes, the commander's voice filled the cabin again. "We are go for launch." Damn, too late to break and run. Clio leaned back, closed her eyes, trying to calm her stomach. Don't care about this stuff anymore, can't make me care. Just sick, that's all. Dinner churning around. About to churn real good, baby.

Then the thundering of the solid-rocket-booster auxiliary power units, and mid-decks trembling hard. Boy and trophy fell cockeyed to one side, then the roar of the first shuttle main engine, kicked up to deafening as second and third ignited, booming against the launchpad with nine hundred thousand pounds of thrust. Underneath, the deafening scream of the solid rocket boosters. Ignition. Clio felt her body turn to gel, spread over the chair, noise pounding on her. Liftoff.

After what seemed like a very long time, but which was actually seven seconds, the shuttle rolled over 120 degrees in proper ascent configuration, and she was head down as the ship built up fast to fifteen times the speed of sound.

Going upstation. Used to live for moments like this, in the days before. Now, baby, just going along for the ride.

FASTER THAN LIFE

CHAPTER 23

In a Vanda security cell, Clio slept for twelve hours. She was wakened by two army corporals who looked like they could bend steel with their bare hands. Behind them, a vastly smaller med tech stepped forward with a little paper cup and two red pills. She put them in her mouth, took a swallow of the offered water. The gorillas gave her two minutes to clean up, then herded her down the crew corridor of Vanda into the main causeway.

Clio squinted in the brilliance of lit corridors and polished metal. Magnificent Vanda, built in the days of space mania; no expense spared. The main gravity corridor was thirty meters wide, and long, designed to hide the curve with tricks of perspective. Swellings in the corridor signaled activity nodes with store frontages, and corridor seating with clusters of techs, crew, and, now, army. Trees and shrubs clustered around data-access VDTs. But for all Vanda's four-trillion-dollar price tag, they still skimped by on the sickly greenish fluorescent lights. Clio's head throbbed with the pounding of her escort's feet as they marched on. No time to gape at Vanda, and no need to.

Been here before, many times and long ago. Vandarthanan Station keeps on spinning, same as before. But not the same. Army, everywhere army. A presence onstation, to be sure, and watchful, they were, not as though waiting for assignment. Twice her guards showed ID as they crossed from one quadrant to the next, as defined by the massive fire and airlock doors stowed against corridor walls. The mood on Vanda had changed. No longer the collegial, self-contained scientific community, but an army base. Time was, Vanda had been the main base solely for Space Recon and the giant corporate enterprises feeding on it: Biotime, Timeco, Alpha One, those gallant companies of exploration, mining the galaxy for biota, bringing home the green.

Biotime and Timeco and the others—they brought home the green, all right. Some made it to Earth transition farms, where, Clio knew, they died. Earth went on rejecting the new DNA like a condor finding an eaglet in its nest, grabbing it by the scruff, and hurling it out. But Biotime, the rest of them, can't give that secret away.

People have enough to worry about these days besides the end of the world.

As her escort turned her down med corridor, it hit her where they were going. Heading to the lab for some tests, oh yes, could guess what tests. She yanked her arm free from the linebacker on her right and stomped to a halt.

They were on her in an instant. "Yeah, yeah," she said, as they used a little too much force. "Don't worry, I'm coming, just like to get there with my arms still in their sockets."

The corridor widened out to a seating area with med techs on break and a few Biotime staffers playing vid games. Almost got through, no one recognizing her, but there was Starfish Void. Her old Dive competitor was heading toward her. Inwardly, Clio groaned, stopped.

"Clio?" he asked. They were dead still, staring at each other. Starfish looked toward her army escort. Then he said again. "Clio?"

"So?" Clio said, managing a good smile.

"Jesus, Clio." He filled a long pause with a gaping stare. A foot shorter than Clio, he craned his neck up at her. "You gone army?"

Clio winced. "Maybe."

The linebacker tugged on her arm, while the other held open the door marked, DIVE SIM. Clio shrugged at Starfish, leaving him mouth open, like he'd just seen Elvis.

She walked through the door to face another old acquaintance: Dive Sim. Controls banked along one wall, and, opposite, the door to the heavy chamber where you slid in on the gurney and lay so close fitting, you felt like you were getting canned. The med tech kicked a stool into place so she could climb up to lie down.

She breathed a long, noisy sigh through her nose. Christ on a crutch. Should have known they would test her for Dive, should have known that's what Tandy wanted. But why did they need a crazy felon like her?

The techs secured the helmet leads, this time easy, without any hair to mangle the paste, and she lay there thinking, *Hope to God I'm over the hill, hope to God I got nothing left to give the bastards.*

And when she emerged from the chamber the tech made eye contact for the first time with a knowing smile that said, You squeaked by, one more time, you still got what it takes. She stared through him to see Tandy waiting there for her. From him, no phony smile, just a nod.

She staggered, feeling mildly vertiginous. Tandy grasped her arm and she managed to pull away without falling down. Sick to her stomach, which might be the test and might be another freeping A-plus on Dive, soldier, and don't need any help to walk, thank you.

Clio jerked the cap back on her head, walked through the door he held open, into the corridor where Starfish was waiting.

She looked over at Tandy. "Give me a minute? An old friend, hey." Tandy pursed his lips, a small shrug. Must mean yes. Clio hauled Void over to a side bench.

"Jesus, Clio," Void said, voice quavering in the unmistakable tremolo of burnout.

"No, I ain't Jesus. And stop your ogling, Starfish, you look like your jaw's unhinged."

"Jesus, Clio. We thought you were dead, lost in the *Starhawk* incident." He glanced over at Dive Sim. "How'd you do? Passed, I guess? You always pass, Clio."

"Yeah. Passed." She glanced away from his eyes, and those rueful irises, once brown, now cloudy at the edges like cooked eggs, sunny side up.

"Lucky. You were always lucky, Clio." He took a deep

breath, licking his lips. "We thought you died with the *Starhawk*."

"Sort of wish I had?"

"Clio! Nothing like that." He wiped his mouth with the back of a trembling hand. "But what happened?"

"I escaped. Just barely, got pretty chewed up. Lost some weight, and so here I am. How's tricks at Timeco? You still working?"

"Whole *Starhawk* crew lost, that right?" he continued. "Niang biota on the rampage, whole ship blew? That's what we heard." He was noting her shaved head beneath the rim of her cap.

"Head wound," Clio said.

Starfish nodded. "Tough break. You look good, though, Clio, for somebody who should be dead."

Clio smiled one of her old big ones. "Why thank you, Starfish."

"Sorry. Not the thing to say." Starfish's rheumy eyes swam in Tandy's direction again. "Who's the brass?"

"Colonel Tandy. Talking to me about a job. What about you? You don't look good, Starfish."

"No? No, I guess not. Not on active service now, Clio. I hit my limit."

Hit my limit. As though it were trout fishing and not spaceflight, Diveflight, life itself to a man like Void. He looked over at Dive Sim again. "Got a great package, though. Complete disability, lifetime Vanda status—as an advisor."

"I'll bet." Keep him on six months or so and then send him Earthside to some admin post. No pressure, no decisions. No fun. "So what's the news around here?" Clio asked. "Anything new? Besides army on-station?"

"Jesus, Clio, you mean you haven't heard about the *Galactique*?"

"Sure. Who hasn't?" But no clue.

"Jesus, Clio, the biggest damn ship in the universe, and word is they're going back to Niang. Biotime's got the contract." He nodded glumly. "So guess I know why you're here."

Clio shrugged.

He lowered his voice. "There's crazy stuff on Niang, Clio, real crazy. Heard they lost another crew there. And Jesus, bodies mutilated, and Harper Teeg gone so far out, there aren't any zip codes. You believe that, Clio? That Teeg could kill off a whole *platoon*?"

"He's crazy, for sure," she said.

"I knew him. He's not *that* crazy."

"So what's the word on-station?" Clio asked. "Who's the enemy on Niang?"

A crew member in an Alpha One uniform, blue, with a lavender turtleneck, walked by them, looked over at hearing the word *Niang*.

Starfish nodded at him, quickly looked away. Voice now a whisper. "Tell you, word is the planet's a death trap. Word is, the Nians will kill anybody in reach."

"Nians? What Nians? The place is all plants and lower mammals, nothing you'd call *Nians*."

"They're not human, Clio. Sometimes I'm glad I don't do the big Dive anymore."

"Humans can mutilate, can't they?"

Starfish shook his head. "Not like this. You been really out of it, Clio, if you haven't heard all this. How bad were you hurt, pretty bad?"

"Let's just say they had to sew some things back on."

"Jesus." Opened his mouth to say something.

"I don't like to talk about it."

"No, I suppose not."

"So what about these Nians? I been out of it, Starfish. So tell me."

He snorted. "I don't know shit. You ask questions around here, all you get is rumors. But you can ask around. . . ." Tandy was coming to retrieve her, and Starfish lowered his voice, moving closer. "Nobody believes this Harper Teeg shit."

Tandy took her arm.

As Starfish wiped his hands on his togs, the tremor of his fingers calmed for a moment. "Maybe we can get together sometime, shoot the shit."

"Gonna be pretty busy," she said.

As Clio and Tandy turned to leave, Starfish said, "Just don't forget your old friends, Clio."

I never forget, Starfish. Part of my personal hell. Never forget.

"Friend of yours?" Tandy asked.

"I guess so. All of a sudden."

"Helps to know who your friends are," he said.

As they crossed into C Quadrant, they were bound for the VIP suites. And then they stood in front of a door marked ELLISON BRISHER, CHIEF OF BIOTIME OPERATIONS. The door slid aside, and Clio entered the room.

Behind a square and massive mahogany desk sat the man himself. A smile punched its way into the folds of his heavy cheeks. God, Ellison Brisher. Clio hoped to hell he was in a good mood. He didn't have much reason to be mad. She had scrambled the Niang mission, abandoned two crew members, refused captain's orders, released contaminated biota shipboard, scuttled a three-hundred-billion-dollar starship, and conspired to destroy Earth's biological mantle. Still, she hoped he would be civil.

Ellison sat utterly still behind the desk, as though caught in his chair—which, in fact, he filled to overflowing. His eyes followed her without emotion as she walked across the deep carpet in a half dream: dreaming of sinking into a carpet of oblivion, dreaming of being shipboard with mechanical things, predictable things, dreaming of Dive, that ultimate dream.

His eyes flicked over her as she stood before him. He was going to play with her, like a grizzly with a hiker. Ellison wasn't hungry. He just wanted to play, she reckoned. For now.

He reached for a roll of chocolate fizzes, the only item on the expanse of desk. His wrist turned the candy in her direction. "Fizz?" She shook her head. Ellison peeled back the paper one fizz-length, popped a candy in his mouth. Munched thoughtfully.

Clio's body had become rigid, standing there, her arms frozen, jaw stuck, throat glued shut. Stop this. Don't take the silent approach with Brish, he won't like it, deprives him of fun. But he hadn't really begun yet, hadn't started the fun. This was preamble. Letting the mouse run for the pleasure of catching it again. All her disasters, all her moments of hell shipboard, planetside, stationside, and she had met her monsters head-on. But put Ellison Brisher behind a wide mahogany desk eating chocolate fizzes and smirking over her future, and she half died with panic.

"I must say you don't look well in that shade of green." Ellison wrinkled his nose. While still chewing, this had the effect of making him look like a rodent. "My God, Tandy, did you feed the woman? Skin and bones, a hag."

"She's eaten." Tandy took a chair. Clio ignored him for now, got enough to do, sparring with Brish.

Brisher's tiny eyes looked her up and down in the usual way. Anger stirred, in the old way. "Look Brisher," she said. "I'm not flying for Biotime. That what I'm here for, 'cause you want me to fly? Go pick yourself somebody else out of your stable, I'm done with that shit. Space Recon is a lie. The future is a lie. There isn't one. You know that, I know that. End of story."

Brisher sighed. Looked over at Tandy, then back at her. "That's a nice speech, Clio. Glad you got that off your chest." He made as though to shift in his chair, but his bulk wedged further into the seat than a mere bureaucrat's arms could dislodge. "I'm upset too, you realize," he said. "Your pranks, et cetera. Biotime is rather upset, not to mention the U.S. government and the United States Global Security Council. But we won't go into that right now. Except to say, it may be in your best interest not to jump to premature conclusions." He looked over at Tandy, perhaps for a clue on how to proceed. Tandy a blank, not helping.

Brisher continued. "Take a seat, Clio." He nodded at the chair opposite Tandy.

She sat slowly, warily, into its cool leather. Got to stay alert, something coming down, no question.

"When the special forces finally located you, they didn't intend to kill anyone. That happened by accident. They were instructed to bring you, vander Zee, and Captain Russo out alive. Then apply the defoliant." Brisher licked his teeth, probing for extra tidbits of chocolate. "They didn't quite carry off the assignment. They failed to retrieve you, for one thing. You went missing on us for what—three months? Once we did get ahold of you, we debriefed you under heavy serum—you weren't talking, you see—and you were able to fill in the blanks on what occurred on Niang, and then where you planted the seeds once back here, et cetera." He braced his fists on the chair arm and heaved himself to a standing position. Reached for the fizzes, popped one. He sat on the edge of the desk, as though he could move no further.

As his mouth still worked on the candy, he continued: "Told a good story, you did." A longish pause. "Told about the alien ship, in fact. You see, Clio, in all of this, the alien ship is the one piece whose significance you seem to have overlooked. You actually came across an abandoned alien ship in that Niang miasma. Never mentioned it to your superiors. Our first contact with an intelligent alien species. Rather big news. But I suppose you had other things on your mind, staying alive, saving the Earth, whatnot. Anyway, we sent a science team back to Niang to investigate. Eventually they found the ship and looked it over. Heading back to camp they were ambushed and massacred."

Now Clio started to listen. "Killed by Harper Teeg?"

Brisher ignored her question. "One man made it back to the lander. Before he died, he described an attack with automatic weapons. Unfortunately, he didn't have time to describe where the ship was, exactly. What he *did* describe were the star charts that survived the general decay on board. The charts showed several inaccessible parts of the galaxy. Places Dive can't get to. That ship likely had the capacity to travel pretty fast. Speed of light, even."

Clio's mind was racing. "Dive can go lots of places, anywhere in Earth's galactic path."

Brisher shrugged. "Well, the science team thought of that of course. And the message the man delivered is, this ship is faster than light. His opinion, anyway. Said it also had Dive capacity. What I'm saying, Clio, is that we may have found a civilization that's thousands, maybe millions, of years ahead of ours."

Clio barely breathed. FTL. The stars, within reach. Released from Dive limitations, the stars. To be part of *that*, by God, even with time-dilation effects, even to leave behind your own generation while they sped through their lives and yours stretched out and out. Never to come back to your own family and friends. But then, some—like her— had nothing to come back to.

"You talk about saving the Earth," Brisher continued. "Well maybe, with the stars at our disposal, we could do just that. Find cures, find decent DNA, share knowledge with advanced civilizations. Maybe we aren't doomed, then. Quite a few advantages, you see?" He stood, pivoting back into his chair with a sigh as he settled into the seat. "This may be a good moment for Colonel Tandy to pick up the story."

Tandy leaned forward. "We sent in a small armed force to take out the mutineers still hiding in the jungle and secure the alien ship. In the jungle, a whole platoon was picked off one by one. The bodies were found piled together and there was no sign of the ship. The remainder of the force gathered their dead and abandoned the mission."

He fixed Clio with an intense brown gaze. "A few of these soldiers weren't killed by gunfire. Two were killed by extreme trauma to the heart and cardiac arrest." He leaned forward, taking a folder from the desk. Opened it, produced photos. "These were the men." He handed Clio the photos.

Autopsy photos. Chest massively bruised. Face locked in a grimace. Clio handed them back. "Looks like they ran into a wall."

"We'd very much like to know what they ran into," Tandy said. "Because their chest cavities were penetrated, and the heart muscle ripped open. Apparently without external trauma." He handed her the next series of photos. She glanced at mangled chests, laid open by autopsy. "That's how they died. Trauma to the heart," Tandy said.

"How could that happen?"

Tandy nodded. "That's just what we'd like to know." He tucked the photos back into their folder, settled back to look at Clio. "Chances are, what we're dealing with here isn't human. Not Earth civilization. What you found, Clio, in that ship. Alien."

He rose and paced behind Ellison. "And it's not just a matter of Niang anymore. Last month, Joseph Ritters, chief Biotime engineer, was killed while on leave in Disney City in Phoenix. Killed in the same way."

Clio watched him spin this story, wondering how much to believe.

"Exactly the same manner of death." He turned to face her. "I'm going back to Niang, Clio. A joint army-Biotime venture, this time. A new ship, bigger than *Starhawk*, much bigger. I want you to come with me."

"Find somebody else."

"I need someone who can take us to the crash site. You're the only one left alive who knows where it is. I need you, Clio."

"I'm not going back." She rose, turning on Brisher. "You and your damn space adventures. What's this game? Get the common folk pumped up on faster-than-light? Promise them something else you can't deliver? Or scare the shit out of them with stories of invading aliens? Another ploy to take their minds off their problems? Think I care about your stars, your FTL? Tell you what I cared about, if you want to know. Earth. What I cared about. Lost everything else, and still kept going, lost my family and still kept going. Had a ship full of Niang seeds. Limping home, almost made it. Expected a rescue ship, got a warship instead." She turned to face Tandy. "Your army planned to blow us the hell out of the way, not even rescue the crew, just sanitize the whole event. I ended up with a pocket full of seeds. Even those you killed." Clio watched his face, calm as ever. "Now you want me to care about your next fucking adventure." She sneered at Tandy. "Should have left me in the barracks, Colonel, 'cause I just don't give a shit."

Brisher cleared his throat. She turned to face him, ready to mow him down.

"We have Petya, I'm afraid," he said. "We have your brother."

Now she would murder him. She wanted to fly at him, but the desk lay between them. "Liar!" she hissed.

"We can produce him, of course."

Clio heard a moan deep in her throat. She found the chair. And sat. Now fighting with herself whether she felt joy or bitterness. Petya. If they had him, then he was alive. If they didn't have him they couldn't use him against her, couldn't hurt him. Again, the question: Is life always the best thing? Is it best that Petya is alive? Or should he, like her, have died long time back?

"I want to see him."

"Right." Brisher rose, a match for the heft of the mahogany desk. "Yes, we thought you might want proof. Meanwhile, a recent picture." He fished in his pocket, brought out a photo, handed it to her.

Petya sat at a table with Tinkertoys spread out, hands folded, fingers locked in front of him. He wore a red plaid shirt and a baseball hat. He looked startled, as though seeing her looking at him. Probably the flash from a previous picture had surprised him.

"He doesn't like Tinkertoys. They're too easy," Clio said. Her face was hot as blisters. Whole room was damn hot. She took off her cap, rubbed her itchy scalp, stared at the picture some more. Little brother, yes. Alive.

"Who's the dumb shit that expects him to use Tinkertoys?" Clio said, without looking up. Hard to squeeze the words out. Throat sore, constricted.

Then Colonel Tandy was by her side. Gently took her by the arm, raised her to her feet.

Brisher piped up: "And you can start growing your hair back, for godsakes."

"That she will, Ellison," Tandy said. "Without your advice." Tandy walked her to the door. Turned, looked at Brisher a few beats. "She's mine now."

They walked in silence for a time, Tandy and Clio, toward the main station plaza. He guided Clio off toward A Quadrant, past the main green sward with its fifteen-meter trees, and past the cluster of shops dispensing coffee, sweets, and sushi. Passing VandaPet, Clio saw a small dog

inside, licking the window at her. A German shepherd puppy, ears too big for its face, reminding her of Rudy, beloved
old shepherd with the bad hip and penchant for ice cream.

"You like dogs, do you?" Tandy asked.

"I guess so."

"We'll come back, later."

He led her past the dispensary, where you don't want to
be seen, despite the meticulous screening for service on
Vanda. Past a jogger, dressed in baggy tunic. No clinging togs
allowed, no swaying buttocks, breasts. Bodies out of fashion.

And soldiers in the corridor. Strolling, shopping, loung-
ing. One in three a soldier, the army green subtly changing
old Vanda into a place she almost recognized but not quite,
like those dreams of home where there's Mother and Petya
and Rudy but those extra rooms and floors you never knew
existed, and when you go there you're lost.

So they have Petya, she thought. *Son of a bitch, I have
family after all.*

Tandy guided her off main corridor into D Quadrant,
and then Clio knew where they were headed: the docking
bays. Oh yes, show her the big ship.

As they peeled off at the spoke to the docking terminal,
Clio said, "I want some different clothes."

Tandy patted her on the back, two hard whacks. "Yes!
Clothes it shall be. Life worth living, after all, eh? The
woman will have clothes, by God. Biotime? Civvies? You
name it."

"Don't care."

Tandy grinned broadly.

"And I want to see Petya. When do I get to see Petya?"

"Soon."

Docking Bay Six loomed ahead. Broad emergency
doors stowed open, and they passed through to the observation platform high above the massive bay. On the left side,
the windows of loading operations—staffed with Vanda
techs hunched over terminals, lips moving, eyes flicking up
at Clio and Tandy, then back down to business. On the right
side, the cavernous bay. Occupied.

The *Galactique.*

CHAPTER 24

❦

The *Galactique* loomed sixty meters up from the loading bay, just below the observation platform and halfway to the 150-meter ceiling of Bay Six. Through the bridge deck viewports, Clio glimpsed the flight instrumentation and the bridge crew officers. Behind the forward section of the *Galactique*, the long span of mid-decks stretched out to, and beyond, the bay doors where the tail, with its ponderous jet drives, remained sealed outside station. Techs swarmed below, attending to the *Galactique*'s needs, accessing her belly with cable and hose, charging her up for the sort of voyage where the next service station is ten million years away.

The *Galactique* was taking on fuel for a run.

Clio felt like a fish being reeled in, let out, reeled in, set that hook, sink it hard. A crack made its slow way up her chest cavity, something rushed in. Hurt.

"A beauty, eh Clio?" Tandy watched her face instead of the ship.

Clio shrugged. "It's big all right." The thing lacked *Starhawk*'s grace—its mean, spare look—black and riveted and all business. Massive as a cargo transport and then some, but trimmed for a fight, with gun hatches and missile tubes. On the long back of mid-decks, two protuberances deprived the *Galactique* of any hope of a sleek profile. One, just aft of the bridge, Clio guessed for officers' quarters—and the other, unmistakably, the landing craft, nested in riding position.

"Thing can fly, huh?" Clio asked.

"Like to take it for a spin?"

The crack widened, blood below the surface. "Nah, looks like a tank. I like 'em fast."

"I heard that you do." He walked away a few paces, turned, cocked his head slightly in the direction of the loading catwalk at ship's bridge level. "Let's take a look."

She followed, feet obeying, heart scolding. Son of a bitch. An ugly son of a bitch. Too big to fly.

"Takes a crew of forty-six comfortably, seventy-two doubled up, as we are now, for the joint mission," Tandy said. At the catwalk, two guards, army, saluted Tandy and moved aside. Fully armed, she noted. Noted too how eyes flicked to her, then away. She pulled her cap further down onto her head, touching the shaving cuts on her neck tendons. The catwalk swayed, loose-chinked, as she and the colonel approached the bridge hatchway, door clamped open against the hull.

Following Tandy, Clio ducked onto the flight deck. She stood blinking in the glare of a large semicircular room, with instrumentation clustered around three sides, and overhead at the nose of the ship. Behind the pilots' chairs, pockets for navigator and captain.

Clio and Tandy emerged onto the rear of the flight deck without being seen. Then a Biotime officer leaned in to the ear of ship's captain, and he turned. Confusion flushed his face for a moment, quickly covered, as he smiled with grand white teeth. "Colonel Tandy," he said.

Tandy moved forward, shook hands. "This is Clio Finn, Captain." The two men gazed at her. "Clio, this is Captain Wendall Hocking, the *Galactique*'s commanding officer."

Clio's hand fluttered in an almost-salute. But no. Not Biotime anymore, by God. "Sir," Clio said.

Hocking's nose rumpled, and the smile vanished. He looked at Tandy. "Time for the tour then?"

Tandy spread his hands in an up-to-you gesture.

Seated at the helm, the pilot swiveled around and now managed to crane her neck past the captain. She smiled at Clio. Young-looking, dark eyes limpid underneath wall-to-wall eyebrows. A cheerful smile that Clio did not return.

Tandy nodded at Clio. "You'll be under the captain's charge for the tour, Clio. Enjoy." He fixed her with an amused look and walked off, ducking through the aft hatchway.

The flight deck embraced her with the pulse and surge of ship's life, the electrical, electronic, and hydraulic hum and sigh. Through the bright overhead lights, the flight panels sparkled with their own animation. Video screens revealed ship's thoughts, all bent on flight, flight.

Place smelled like a new car, a just-below-the-surface chemical stew that made you want to open a window. Like a whiff of the Toyota Tourister, when Mother got a good deal and finally turned in the old Dodge Caravan. Straight off the showroom floor it was, with seat belts that worked and a blank panel for a radio that they never filled despite many promises.

Clio was staring at Captain Hocking. He hadn't moved, nor had the two Biotime officers. Finally he cleared his throat. Frowned. Turned to the man beside him. "Commander Singh, navigator." The commander nodded at her, slowly. A friendly smile through a trim beard. Hocking nodded down at the pilot. "Lieutenant Voris, pilot." The pilot smiled again, wiggled her fingers at Clio in hello. Hocking pulled his flight jacket down more firmly around his waist. "Well, this is the flight deck," he began.

Clio smiled wanly. Right. The flight deck.

He waved at the consoles hugging ship's nose. "You'll be familiar with the flight panels. Takes the same mechanics to fly the *Galactique* as a smaller rig." He paused, looking back at her. "Most people are surprised about that. . . ." Waited for her reaction, gave up. "The only new thing we've added is the navigation post." Here he turned, waved at a workstation parallel to the captain's chair about six meters back from the pilots' chairs. "Reaction-control systems are dual on board, so maneuvers can be carried out from here or the mission deck. That's one improvement. . . ." He waved at Voris. "I'll let Lieutenant Voris take you through the boards in more detail. For now, let's take a look at mid-decks." Hocking droned on as though he'd conducted this tour a time or two before.

As Clio followed Hocking down the hatch in the flight-deck floor, she glimpsed Voris jumping up from her seat. Voris crouched down by the hatch, looking Clio in the eye. "*The* Clio Finn?" she asked in a low tone. "Honest to gosh?"

"Yeah," Clio managed to say as she continued down the ladder. "Cross my heart." Clio followed the captain several paces through a mid-deck corridor and through a hatchway to a cabin directly under the flight deck. "Science deck," Hocking announced. Crew stations pressed against the rounded hull, occupied by a dozen Biotime mission specialists. Several turned to acknowledge the captain, swept up Clio in the same movement; no welcome there. Commanding the huge cabin was a conference table strewn with gear and a plastic liter of RC Cola. Hocking raised an eyebrow at one of the techs. She bit her lip, made to remove the soda. Hocking spun on his heels, disappearing through the hatch, leaving them to dispose of the nonconforming drink.

In the corridor again, Hocking swung around to face Clio. His nose glistened with sweat, undermining an otherwise handsome face. "You will remove the cap, Finn," he said. Waited. "This is a ship where we follow the rules. That's one of them. You have ideas about carving out your own procedures, think again." He raised himself up a fraction, taking in a long breath. "I've heard all about you, and I don't like what I've heard. So far I don't like what I've seen, either."

Clio took off the cap.

Hocking glanced at her shaved scalp, its garish red nicks. They faced off for a moment.

"Well then, put it back on," he said. He spun on his heel and strode off. Singh came down the bridge ladder, double-time, caught up to them, whispered to the captain. Captain muttered back, disappeared up to flight deck. Singh, a slight man with black hair and small, pointed beard, gestured her to follow him, which she did, down the wide mid-decks corridor, past Biotime crew in the familiar bright green, and past army, not so familiar, in olive and tan.

The Biotime uniforms watched her, looked away. Army ignored her. Information was everything. What you knew told you how to act, and Biotime crew knew, by God. Knew about Clio Finn. Not dead after all. No, and getting a by God tour of the freeping *Galactique*.

Singh gestured, a delicate sweep of his hand toward a door marked OBSERVATION. "You will be waiting here for Captain Hocking," Singh ordered sweetly, and Clio nodded. Satisfied, Singh left her.

Clio entered the room.

It was twilight, created by the docking-bay light from a broad expanse of curved viewports on her left. Outside, a dozen Vanda techs ministered to ship's needs. Clio was in an amphitheater, the sort of place where you could gaze out on the far territories of space or hold a crew meeting. Clio fumbled down a narrow aisle, found a chair, and slumped into it. Remembering to breathe, she drew in a few deep ones. She felt sick, a pain up the middle of her rib cage. One step onto the bridge, and there was the old bank of flight controls, and she could feel the switches, computer keyboard, and flight-control stick under her hands. Felt the lights pulse down, the control panel lights surging up, felt her body meld into the pilot's seat. Even if it was the ponderous, overproduced *Galactique*. Could fly her the same as any, by God. She brought her hands up, covering her face.

After a time she looked up to see someone standing in front of the windows, a black silhouette cupped by the concave glass as though trapped in the merciless eye of a gigantic microscope. A large, bearish man with barrel chest and hair pulled into a short ponytail. His hands were clasped behind him in a contemplative pose as he appeared to watch the *Galactique*'s priming, but on closer observation Clio felt that he must have looked past the scene outside, with his face unmoving, his body planted solid. She didn't speak then, at a loss as to whether she spied upon him, or he upon her.

Without turning, he broke the silence. "This place is the only place on this ship where you can be in a room larger than a coffin and be alone." He scratched the back of his neck slowly, still gazing outward. "So I don't blame you, don't worry."

Clio found herself saying, "Blame me for what?"

He turned, his features totally eclipsed as the windows shone behind him. "For hiding, soldier."

"I'm not a soldier."

"Then you're a spy. I'd certainly have to report *that*." His deep voice filled the room, though he spoke softly. Clio squirmed in her chair, despite her innocence on this charge.

"Crew here like to rat on each other, do they?" Clio asked.

"We like to think of it as watching out for the common good, rather like Blockwatch. Carl the Crimedog says this community's not safe for criminals—that sort of thing."

"Like I said, you rat on each other."

"Now, that's cynical." The figure strolled down from the viewing platform. Stopped in front of Clio, took the seat next to her. "Mind if I sit?"

Clio shrugged. Brain starting to sort and sift, whether this was army, Biotime, DSDE. She was gauging which persona to adopt, but she usually worked it through faster, finding her mask.

With him seated next to her now, she saw a solidly built man of olive complexion, a round face and slightly hawkish nose, dark hair fighting for territory with grey. On his face, the creases of middle age traced a faint network of lines, dominated by a scar that pierced his left eyebrow, pointing to his temple like an arrow on a star chart. While she frankly stared at him, he also stared at her. For a while they let the ship's hydraulics and bangs from cable couplings outside fill the space in the theater. Didn't owe him a goddamn conversation.

She decided on the fuck-you persona, always the most dependable. Part of this one was to say little until provoked, then to lash out. She waited.

He turned away from her and slid down in his chair, stretching his legs out. "You want to be more careful, around here, in what you say. Doesn't do to be cynical about things—about security, especially—soldier." He clasped his hands behind his head. "On a cruise, this place, this observation cabin, is always in use. So you can kiss solitude goodbye once we're under way. Hope you like to live like a sardine. Ever been on a spaceship, soldier?"

Clio's back teeth clamped down on her response.

"Got no room for personalities, or not much," he said. "Too much personality, and you draw attention, make folks nervous. Best not to have a personality. Yours comes out in the first twenty seconds of conversation, which may annoy your superiors."

"Thanks for the advice." The man knew how to annoy.

He looked over at her. Brow creased a moment. "What's your job, soldier?"

"Got no job."

"Most grunts, they've got a job."

"Got no job." She let out the breath she'd been holding, let it out through her nose. "Used to be a pilot."

Quiet then, as he looked away, steepled his hands in front of him. Then, softly: "That's a fine calling, pilot."

"Used to be."

"Sometimes jobs get caught up in all kinds of crap," he said. "Politics. Public relations. Makes it hard to do your work."

The enormity of the understatement made Clio want to laugh. "Yeah, sometimes."

A beat. "You the Dive pilot we've been waiting for?"

"Somebody hopes I am."

"You're Clio Finn, then."

"Used to be."

He sat up straight, turned, smiled. The smile took over his face. "Guess it doesn't matter what you say, then. Can't be reported for treason, when you're Miss Treason herself." He watched her, his generous mouth still holding the smile.

Clio found herself liking that thought. "Guess that's right. The rest of you poor nulls can watch me in envy."

"So you're going to take us to Nasty Niang?" His smile faded.

"I doubt it."

"May not have much choice, I imagine."

"Who are you?" Clio asked.

"Timothy Ashe."

"Tells me a lot."

"Maybe I'm your friend. Maybe the only one you've got on this ship."

"Helps to know who your friends are."

His brows crowded down over his dark eyes, riveting Clio for a moment. "Watch out for people offering friendship, Clio."

"Such as you?"

"If you like. But nobody offers something for nothing. Friendship doesn't come cheap: it comes with some wicked tagalongs."

"What's yours?"

The cabin door opened. Lights up. Captain Hocking's glance took them in. "Ashe," he said, nodding. Then to Clio: "You. Follow me." He turned and left the doorway.

"Captain's doing me the honor of a tour," Clio said.

"The uniform. What's that all about?"

"Must've pulled the wrong ensemble off the rack this morning."

As she turned to leave she heard Ashe say, "Yes. That was the wrong one, all right. Unless you've gone army."

Clio turned her head back to him. Something in that tone of voice.

"Come by botany and see me, Clio," he said. "When you get tired of the bureaucrats. Most of the time I'm in botany."

Clio shrugged, following Hocking out for the rest of his tour.

The *Galactique* was second-generation Dive spacecraft. Second-generation, so already, at twenty-eight, she was an old spacer, having seen the first round where nothing was tested in the deep and things fell apart now and then. Here, as Captain Hocking squired her around, was the ship to leave all others in the dust. State-of-the-art fusion rockets—oh, not mere fission for mighty *Galactique*—with deuterium/helium-3 reaction and a thrust/mass ratio cranked up to do the job, and smartly. She glanced to the innocent-looking aft bulkhead on the botany deck, where, hulking behind six-inch plates, the massive controlled-fusion reactor presided over fully one-quarter of the ship's bulk.

First-generation Dive ships had been spare, with every ounce counting, as the engineers pared down mass as low as they dared. But now—now the number crunchers got Vandarthanan's formulas loosened up far enough to squeeze the *Galactique* through Dive with its forty-six crew cabins, comfortable officers' quarters and observation deck, and, at 160 meters in length, a sense of elbow room for spacers like her who'd ridden the early rigs and thought it good enough.

But for all its flash, *Galactique* was not much more than a big *Starhawk*. Three decks in the bulbous forward section: flight deck, mid-deck with a galley and observation theater, and lower deck. Stretching between rockets and galley, the two-deck span housing crew deck above and botany below. Simple. They could add flash, but couldn't improve on the old design. Took some comfort in that, she did, clinging to the old ways worse than any Biotime grunt twice her age. Loyalty, it must be. Stupid loyalty, to a ship blown to chunks somewhere between Earth and Mars, and so long ago made no difference anymore.

Captain Hocking was standing, waiting for her answer. A botany tech cocked his head, looked confused.

"Sorry," Clio said. "What did you say?"

Hocking pulled on his flight jacket, bringing it down over his belt. It rose again as he breathed. "I said, would you like to run the instrumentation pallet?" He nodded at the rotation switch.

Clio looked blankly at the pallet, then threw the switch. The pallet turned toward the bulkhead, humming mightily. Then it stopped. Clio hit the switch again. Gears ground.

The tech stepped in, threw the switch to Off, paused, then On again. More grinding.

Hocking wrinkled his nose. Waved at the pallet. "Fix that," he said.

As he and Clio climbed the ladder to mid-decks, she

could hear the pallet protesting. "That's never happened before," Hocking said.

Oh yes it has. Put a ship under pressure, lots of things grind to a halt. Things fall apart. Even in Space Recon, with its fantasy of precision. Hocking looked like a man for whom nothing had fallen apart. Believed in the illusion of mechanical perfection.

They arrived back on flight deck, walked aft to officers' quarters. Here were cabins for Captain Hocking, Commander Singh, and Tandy, along with officers' mess. Hocking stopped outside the last cabin on the deck.

"It's not that you can't work out here, you understand." The captain's nose had collected several large beads of sweat. Clio watched them, waiting for them to spill down. "You do your job, I do mine. Keep the channels open, but observe procedures, you understand?" He seemed to wait for her to answer.

"Yessir." Four years with Biotime, and knew when to say yessir.

"Good." Hocking jutted his chin up slightly, keeping the nose droplets from succumbing to gravity. He walked off, leaving her in front of Colonel Jackson Tandy's cabin door. By this, Clio deduced she was to enter. She knocked. Heard "Enter," from within, and opened the door.

She stood on the threshold looking into a large cabin, dimmed by the reddish glow of a carpet as a hard light flooded from the windows onto the floor. The curved viewports peered out directly upon the observation platform where she had stood gaping at the ship only an hour before, and where now Vanda techs swarmed to their tasks. Aft, a privacy wall for the sleeping nook. From the deep maroon carpet, matching upholstered furniture swelled, as though cast from a mold. A black lacquered credenza anchored one bulkhead. On its gleaming top a crystal decanter caught the loading bay's glare, turning it to a moment of glitter. A desk, in front of the viewports, faced the door, ready for business. Music filled the room, something classical. Tandy sat on one of the couches, eyes closed, right hand on the couch arm just touching his cheek as though it were a fleshy audio antenna.

She closed the door and waited for him to notice her. On the instant that the music finished he sprang from his seat, slapping his thigh. "Are you a fan of Bach, Clio?" He strode to the console in the black lacquered cabinet, snapped the power toggle. He turned back to Clio, head cocked. When she didn't answer, he said, "No, I suppose not. Too much to hope for. You'll like the modern music. Something with a beat."

"Yessir," she answered, wondering what kind of music she *did* like.

"I did too, at your age. Didn't know any better, did I?" He gestured her to a chair. "Sit down, Clio, sit down."

He sat opposite her, studying her face.

The room's smell settled around her. It was that slightly syrupy odor of new carpeting and fresh paint.

"How did you like the tour?"

"Beats the shit out of the quarry."

"Hocking's not exactly a riveting personality. A little stiff?"

"A pompous ass."

"Well, he's harmless. Give him predictability, Clio. He'll soon come around." He watched her again. If he was waiting for her to make small talk, he'd be waiting a long time. Now she stared back at him. The smooth wave of his hair at the temple was frozen in a snapshot of an ocean crest.

"Do you like to read, Clio?"

"Read, sir?"

"Yes. Books. Do you? Read?"

"I guess so, sure."

Tandy crumpled his mouth slightly, as though her answer wasn't quite satisfactory. "Never read any Milton, I suppose? Most people haven't. Those that have, if they've read *Paradise Lost*, they often find themselves rooting for the devil, rather than God. Here's this poor, ambitious, fallen archangel, picking himself up from the holy wars, so to speak. He's been crushed and routed, and his enemy,

God, has claimed the battlefield, heaven. But Satan's not beaten—that's the intriguing part. In some essential way, he's still proud, he's still got his principles. And eloquence. Great eloquence, as he rallies his fellow fallen angels to make hell a paradise of their own. By comparison, God comes off as a tyrant. It's a twist there, you see. Milton wanted to expose the devil's portrayal of himself as heroic, and God as the villain—he wanted to reveal the similar self-deceptions we all engage in, to justify ourselves. Quite masterful."

"I never read it. Was it in paperback?"

A brief, jabbing smile. Tandy absently ran his fingertips along a silver-framed picture on the end table. Within the frame, a woman with a tentative smile, pale blue turtleneck, and strand of pearls just dipping to the swell of her breast. "Paperback," Tandy said. "No, not in paperback. Milton lived in the sixteenth century. But nothing's been written since to compare with him. My opinion. Anyway, my point here is that you've lost the war, Clio. Like the fallen archangel in *Paradise Lost*, your principles had to give way to superior ones. But you still have much to live for, isn't that right?"

"Who's the woman? Your wife?"

He made as if to answer, stopped, leaned forward, fixing her with an earnest gaze. "Clio, if this is hell to you, make it a hell worth living in. We make our reality, Clio."

"Earth is dying. I didn't make that."

He shook his head. "You miss my point. You don't control the big things, but you can control your attitude toward what happens to you, you see?"

"Yeah. I can make excuses for myself, like Satan did. Convince myself that hell isn't so bad. Play classical music, fly the big ship, sleep like a baby."

Across the purple span of carpet, his face took on a florid cast, like anger. But he spoke calmly. "That's very good. You see Satan is an apologist, all compromise, no principles. That can be argued." Tandy stood up. "Can be argued. And yes," he said, glancing at the portrait, "my wife."

He walked to a low table in front of the viewports, returning with a large parcel wrapped in twine. He handed it to Clio.

She felt the soft, dense package, resting her hands on the twine. "My clothes, right?"

"Try them on." His eyes gestured toward his sleeping cell.

Clio rose, clutching the bundle. Without meeting his gaze, she walked past the privacy wall into his sleeping nook. A double bed, the first she'd ever seen on a ship, and she'd seen a good number. Lamps to either side, fixed onto the wall with real cloth shades, and at one side, a nightstand with several comm buttons, a miniature viewscreen, and a hardbound copy of *Donne's Sonnets*. Off to one side, the head, with plenty of room to walk right in and turn around, and with towels hanging, the same wine red of the carpet.

Clio sat on the edge of Tandy's bed, picked at the string of the parcel. A lethargy crept into her arms and back. Maybe she would lie down, shut her eyes here, in this cozy room with its comforting soft bed, lamps, and towels. Easy, of a sudden, to sleep. Instead, her fingers slipped the wrapper off the package, and it fell away revealing the green jumpsuit of Biotime, pilot's bars, black beret, socks, underwear. The underwear looked too small. Putting them on, they hugged against her ribs and buttocks. She looked down to where her belly should be. Its rounded slopes were now sunken, flat, like those of the models in magazines. Her legs protruded like stalks from the underpants, but her breasts refused to flatten out under the shirt. Hurriedly, she drew on the jumpsuit, plumping it up over the stretch belt. She tucked the pant legs into zippered boots, washed her face at the sink, dried off, and slapped the beret on without looking in the mirror. Then she rolled the army fatigues up, leaving them on his bed, a shed chrysalis.

She walked back out to see Tandy seated on his divan, arm resting along the top, waiting for her. "Excellent," he said, appraising her. "Not beaten. Not by a long shot. Just like the old days, eh Clio?"

"Yeah." This was the worst thing, to think that nothing had changed. "Just like the old days," she said. Her feet tingled in her boots as the deck beneath the carpet rumbled. "Ship's powering up, Colonel. Niang then?"

His smile slowly faded like a balloon losing air. "Yes, Niang. We're headed out, Clio. And we're waiting for you to make up your mind. Whether to Dive or die, so to speak."

"Why me, Colonel? Tell me why you'd put quarry meat like me in charge of a multibillion-dollar spaceship."

Tandy cocked his head. "Because you're the best. The best Dive pilot we've ever had. Think we want some greenhorn trying to steer the *Galactique* through Dive?"

"You let a greenhorn like Lieutenant Voris steer her through normal space."

"Lieutenant Voris?" He smiled a lopsided smile. "Watch her sometime. She's fast as a computer and could fly a troop freighter through the eye of a needle. But she's not a Dive pilot." Tandy watched Clio, his smile fading. "Why do you think you hold the record with sixty-two Dives, Clio?"

"Dumb luck?"

"There is no such thing as luck. You have the tolerances. You tolerate Dive and you tolerate the medications. You're the best there is, Clio."

She thought that over for a while. No one ever said a thing like that to her before. She felt a surge of pleasure. Then squelched it.

"Besides," he continued. "I like you. You've got spunk. Sometimes a person gives a hand up to a younger player. Call it mentoring, if you like."

"What happens to me after the mission? After you retrieve the ship? That FTL ship. Back to the quarry?"

Tandy sprang from his chair, clenched his fist in a victory gesture. "Yes! By God yes, Clio! That's the spirit. Life may be worth living, after all, eh?" He walked to the credenza, poured a drink from the crystalline decanter, then swirled the drink in his glass and sipped, savoring it. "We retrieve the FTL and what happens to Clio Finn? What happens?" He tossed the drink off, slapped the glass down on the credenza. "Whatever you want, Clio. *You* decide. I know how to show gratitude. And I like to keep the good players near me, if you want a place on my team. You're a player, Clio. DSDE can't touch people like you and me. They control the masses. Not the players." He raised his eyebrows at her, letting that sink in. "It's as I said, Clio, you make your destiny."

"Make heaven out of hell."

Tandy's eyes crinkled in the smallest of internal smiles. He nodded in slow motion.

Then she heard herself saying, "I want to see Petya."

"Yes. It's time, isn't it?" Tandy said. He walked to his desk console, pressed a switch. "Bring Petya to my quarters, Lieutenant," he said.

Clio went over to the viewport, stared unseeing through *Galactique*'s great starboard eye. Her hands left damp imprints on the silky synthetic of her uniform as she wiped them on her thighs. She pressed her hands against her temples, where too many things were stuffed. You had to press things down so they didn't explode, sometimes.

The night the DSDE agents came, Mother heard them first. She must have had a sixth sense, because all the sound she heard was footsteps on the porch, maybe a car door closing, but she was hurling some words at Clio and Petya, jabbing with her finger at the staircase. In slow motion, Clio glided up the stairs with Mother's voice behind her, "Go, go!" In memory, the staircase stretched forever, as Clio ran for her freedom, her life, and Mother guarded the hallway below, a tall, stalky woman with short black hair and a chin set hard enough to keep back creditors, spooky dreams, prying neighbors, and DSDE all those years. But not tonight. The night when the ceiling flew off, and all the protections escaped, and the promise broke of Mother living to see you on your way in life. That night was upon them. When Petya finally joined her at the secret window, Clio pulled the wall panel in place, taking care to slide it all the way shut. And they sidled out onto the roof and into the broad arms of the big blue spruce, just as they had practiced all those times, those other nights so different in kind from this one.

She and Petya ran and ran until they collapsed. Then, fatefully, and against all Mother's exhortations, they turned back. Like horses set free but no longer wild, they turned back to the house to lie in the tall grass and watch the lighted windows with Mother's words echoing in their heads: Run and never look back, hon. You both just run and Petya you help your sister keep up, you hear? The men inside were dark blotches against the shades, and Mother's screams roamed the house, leaking through every chink and crack and finally through the fabric of the plaster and siding, transformed by this passage into the woody bellow of the house itself.

Then when the man with the gun found them and forced Clio to her feet, Petya hit him with the shovel. Then he was lying dead, with his head gone, and the gun was in Clio's hand, so she knew she had killed him. Then they ran. And though she and Petya had been separated, she had been running ever since. And in all that time Clio pretended that Petya had escaped and was living somewhere, free in ways that she was not. Free enough for both of them. It was the kind of fantasy that became more real with the passage of days, as the fantasy became memory of the fantasy and then purely memory.

A knock on the door. Clio turned.

He stood in the doorway, her brother, with Lieutenant Ryerson behind him. Petya filled the doorway, dressed in blue overalls with yellow plaid shirt underneath. He took in the room with the swift, furtive gaze of those trained not to make eye contact, then stared at the carpet. He had seen her. Clio came forward, stood a few paces from him.

"Petya," she said. "It's me."

He looked at her quickly, then down at the carpet. "You get to wear a uniform?" he said. "They're green, because Space Recon is green. They collect plants?" Petya's fair hair was shaved close, like a convict's.

Clio took his hand, led him to the couch. She sat him down next to her, waiting for him to look her in the eyes, then let go of that intimacy for now. "I've really missed you, Petya," she said. Her voice was small and throttled, like a hand was clasped around her throat.

Petya opened the great paw of his left hand. A key on a slip ring. He turned the key along the ring until the ring fell off. "Oh, oh," he said. He put the key back on.

"What's the key, Petya?"

"I keep my tools and no one goes in except if they use a key." He looked up at her. "You have a locker, sis?"

Clio couldn't speak. She shook her head.

"I have a locker, and no one's supposed to go in there. Sometimes they go in there?" He looked up at Colonel Tandy, who sat opposite them, watching. Petya looked back down quickly. "Rudy's dead now. Dogs only live sixteen years. Mrs. Looby said, dogs only live sixteen years. He had a good life?" He looked at Clio.

"Sure. Dogs do, mostly."

"I rode on the space shuttle with bunk beds. People sleep there?"

"Some people do. Some people sleep on this ship too."

"Do you sleep here?"

"Yes." A whisper.

"Do you have a bunk bed?" he asked.

"I haven't seen my room yet, Petya. I'm a prisoner. They make me fly the ship. But I'd rather be back home with you."

"We don't talk about that. We're not supposed to ask?" He looked up at her, pale blue eyes finally making deep contact with hers. He looked at her pilot's bars. "You fly this ship?"

"Yes."

Now and again Petya stole a glance at Tandy.

"That's Colonel Tandy, the one in charge." Clio said.

Petya peered intently at his key ring. He was nine years older than when she had last seen him, but the years hadn't made their mark on his face. Tempting, for a moment, to imagine that the years hadn't happened, that she and Petya had never been separated, as it was always difficult to imagine other's lives when separate from yours; that people woke up, went through their days, slept and cared about the stack of events they were dealt—without you. Still, the years had slipped past them both, cheated years, that come not again. It would have been better, easier, if he'd aged, if the time apart had left footprints of lines. Something convincing. It hurt to breathe, now. Her throat had nearly swollen shut.

"Who is Mrs. Looby, Petya? Someone you stayed with?"

He nodded twice, up-down, in his deliberate way.

"Was she . . . good to you?"

He didn't respond.

"Because if she wasn't, I'll go punch her."

A smile started to break out on his face, then retreated.

"She's never been on a space shuttle?" Petya said.

"But you have."

"She wouldn't like the noise?"

"How come?"

"At the home, we don't make noise. Noise is bad?"

Tears came up, but Clio managed to send them down her throat instead of her cheeks. She swallowed hard. "Remember when Holland Lumm farted in church that time?"

Petya smiled broadly. "Pastor was really mad?"

"Yeah, but he got mad at *me*."

"Because you laughed?"

"I'm still laughing about that. Sometimes it's OK to make noise, Petya. Sometimes you've got to make noise, if something needs laughing at, or if something needs saying. Sometimes being quiet is bad."

The smile slid off Petya's face. He examined the maroon carpet as though searching for it there.

Tandy came forward, put a hand on Clio's shoulder. Petya jumped. Startled.

"You can see Petya later." He turned to her brother. "Time to go, Petya."

Petya put his key in his right breast pocket, buttoned the pocket, then rose. Clio rose too, and put her arms around him. Her nose came up to the key pocket.

Petya folded her up into his great, beefy arms, the kind of arms that could ward off a battalion. But his squeeze was light. Clio long ago taught him how to hug and not crush, and his body remembered this now.

"I'll see you later, OK?" Clio said. But the whisper was barely audible.

Petya shuffled out with the aide in that way of patients on meds.

Tandy came back and sat on the couch, opposite her, hands folded in his lap. He watched her, as always. Through her most intimate feelings, he was always watching.

"You bastards," Clio said. "Fucking bastards." An impossibly large swelling in her chest and throat now surged out of her mouth in words. "Keep us like farm animals, take our lives and keep us to serve you. Keep my brother—fill him with meds—and tell him what he can and can't ask about."

"Clio," Tandy began softly, "he was kept by DSDE, not army."

"Does he even know our mother is dead? Was he ever told I was alive? Did he ever have freedom to come and go?"

"He knew about your mother. He was told you were dead. DSDE, Clio. DSDE."

"No! Not DSDE! You're the same, can't you see? No difference between what you've done to me, what they've done to him, what you all do when you'll have your way and you have the power and we don't." Clio stood, approached Tandy as though she would strike him. He remained passive. "You've stolen his years, my years. You've murdered and stolen, and called it the public good, public welfare and safety." Now, despite her hatred, she was crying, not wanting to cry, feeling hatred, but crying instead. "I hate you, I'll always hate you. Don't talk Milton to me, confuse me with your stories. Let me keep it straight in my own mind at least. Let me at least know what I think!"

Tandy hadn't moved, though his face hardened around the edges. "We're heading out at sixteen hundred, Clio. I expect you to be ready."

"You want me to fly, then you got to give me assurance of Petya's safety."

"You have my word on that."

A pause for a sneer that overtook her mouth. "Not good enough, Tandy. I want him here. On the *Galactique*."

Tandy's mouth flattened for a moment. He started to say something, stopped. "You think he'll be happy on this ship, Clio?"

Happy. That he could use that simple, pure word, toss it off, use it against her, it made her tremble with rage. "Just . . . don't talk to me . . . about *happy*." She faced him for several long moments. "We're not going to talk *happy*, we're going to talk getting him off meds. You and your Nazi doctors can keep your damn pills away from my brother! You hear me? He doesn't need tranks, he's never been violent, and you're not going to null him out with pills! You tell them that!"

Tandy nodded his head, calmly, maddeningly.

"And Petya stays with me. From now on, he stays with me! He's coming along, or I don't fly. Is that clear?"

Finally Tandy said, "Yes, clear. He comes along." He rose. "You always like to protect people, don't you, Clio? Always rescuing. Folks in your barracks, that young woman and her baby. Your brother. Maybe someday you'll give up trying to fix other people and look to your own self-interest. You might find that some people, like Petya, are doing just fine without you. My guess is that will be a bleak day in your life, when you find that each of us is responsible for ourselves. When that day comes, look in the mirror. Ask Clio what she wants for *herself*."

He stepped to the door, opening it. Ryerson snapped to attention.

"Take her to her cabin," Tandy said.

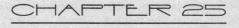

CHAPTER 25

A knock at the door. Clio snapped awake from a deep sleep. A spacer's habit, nap when you can, and wake up fast. Hadn't lost the knack.

"Come in," she said.

Door opened, revealing Tandy's aide.

"Get up, Finn," Ryerson said. "You've got A Shift." He didn't say *Lieutenant* Finn, just Finn. No Biotime rank even though a freeping Dive pilot, couldn't bring themselves to reactivate her commission. "I'll take you to the galley," he said.

She splashed water on her face, toweled off, stared at him. "Wait outside, then," she said. He left the room; then she used the head and zipped on her boots, pulled the cap as far down as it would go.

Out in the corridor, Clio faced her waiting escort. "Look, I know where the galley is. You tell Tandy I won't be needing baby-sitters on board." She stared him into uncertainty.

"You wait here," he said, walking to a wall comm unit. Punched at the keypad, lips moving. Looked over at Clio. "You're clear, then. On your own, Finn." As he strode past her he said, "Been a pleasure."

Clio watched him disappear down crew deck, boots tinny against the grated metal. She stood for some moments nearly alone in the corridor. Crew cabin doors on both sides, and names on plates: KYOO, HANSEN, TOBISON, LEE, MIJANO-VICH. She wondered where they had stashed Petya. Possible he was somewhere among these cabins, maybe confused, probably scared. She hoped he was OK, hoped to God she'd made the right choice. Thought about Tandy saying, *Maybe Petya does just fine without you,* thought about trying to save the people she loved, and how badly she'd always failed. Now here they were, dragging her brother along on a mission they might be lucky to survive, and she'd never asked him what *he* wanted to do.

She looked around her. To her left, the crew deck stretched sixty-some meters to the loading-bay hatchway. Halfway down was an open area with seating and what looked like vid terminals. No one sitting there now. Everyone with a task to do, and most in a hurry to do it.

To her right, a few cabins leading to medlab and, next, the hatchway down to mid-decks. *Can, by God, go where I please.*

She headed to mid-decks, drawing a stare from a botany tech. He glanced at her head, her scalp. Couldn't look good, for sure. She brought her hand up, petting the prickly stubble at the edges of her cap, and followed him down the ladder to mid-decks.

The aroma of coffee led her to the galley door. As she entered, a half-dozen heads turned, looked her up and down. No welcome there, except from Meg Voris, squirreled away in the corner with a table to herself, though the place was short of seats. Clio ignored Voris' wave, and went to the refrigeration hatch, where she pawed through the tubes, grabbed one that read STEAK AND EGGS, popped the top off, and squeezed a bite of breakfast into her mouth. Could have warmed it, but less time spent in present company the better, maybe. Leaned against the counter, watched as several of the crew finally gave up inspecting her and went back to their game of cards. Next to her, on the counter, a pile of leaflets. Rendered in full color, a drawing of a man and a woman each holding the hands of their children, facing into the sun, rising behind lush hills. Clio put the leaflet back on the pile, finished off the tube and flipped it into the recycler.

Voris was at her side, handing her a cup of steaming coffee. "I'm A Shift, too," she said. "How can you eat? I *never* can eat before a mission. I get sick to my stomach.

Tea is all I can tolerate." She held her cup up as evidence. "It's not that I'm nervous, just a nervous stomach. You know what you do when you're nervous? Just deep-breathe. It *really* helps." She looked eagerly at Clio.

Clio stared at the woman. *My God*.

"You can call me Meg. We'll get to know each other real well, so might as well be on first-name terms."

Clio's eyes narrowed at her. "Well, Voris, how soon till we undock?" The coffee was as black as jet fuel and tasted about the same. Delicious.

"Ninety minutes," Voris answered. "But don't worry, I've got this one, just ride it out, then we'll do a run-through."

"Not worried," Clio said through slurps of coffee.

"Of course you're not. I didn't mean to say that. Probably you could fly this thing with your eyes shut, right?" Voris' big dark eyes blinked once, slowly, beneath a broad curtain of bangs.

Intercom was toning them to a meeting in observation deck. Clio tossed back the last of the coffee and followed the group out to the meeting room just down the corridor, managing to lose Voris in the press of bodies. A few Bio-time crew clustered around observation's open door, and, seeing her approach, loosened up to make way for her, staring. She pushed into the crowded room, smelling of too many people. From behind the row of crew standing at the back, she saw Captain Hocking and Commander Singh conferring on the semicircular platform in front of the viewports. Clio pushed her way forward enough to see Hocking approach a lectern that was just now rising from the floor.

Somewhere between the time he stood with Commander Singh and got to the lectern, a spacer's worst nightmare broke loose.

As Hocking walked toward the lectern, his movements were framed by the viewports and the outside gantry from which a five-hundred-gallon drum hung suspended from steel cables. One moment the drum was a solid black cylinder like any other and the next moment it erupted in a roar and blast of fire, followed closely by its echoes or more explosions down the dock. The blast hit the viewport in a wave of fire, lighting up the room with a white flash, and freezing the crowd for a moment on Clio's retinas, though many rushed to flee the room. Clio felt herself thrown aside by the shove of bodies, felt her feet leave the deck, and her shoulders forced forward and down, as someone's hand slammed into her back. Now, with the wind knocked out of her, Clio fought to stand against the rush of crew to their posts. The air rang with emergency bells.

She felt a clamping grip on her upper arm jerking her forward, and, instinctively, she yanked back as shouts for order broke over the blare of the Klaxon. The hand jerked her again, and then she was face-to-face with Timothy Ashe, who pulled her toward the bulkhead.

"You . . ." Clio said, catching her breath. "You damn near pulled my arm off."

"You're welcome." Ashe crouched by her side, body almost relaxed-looking, but eyes intent on the viewports. His face wasn't handsome exactly, but life in the eyes, oh yes, a fire there. Clio rushed to distance herself.

"All stations!" someone was shouting nearby. "All stations!"

Now, through the thinning ranks, Clio could see the viewports and the scene outside in the loading bay. The gantry cables flapped wildly as debris shot through the bay toward what could only be the breached outside bulkhead doors. The bay was depressurizing by the moment. A uniform cartwheeled past the viewport, trailing red globules, followed by an empty spacesuit—headless, like the uniform.

Singh's face appeared in front of Clio. "Report immediately," he shouted, "immediately!" and hurried off. Now, through the nearly empty room, the bells rang deafeningly. Clio staggered to her feet, rubbing her shoulder.

"Report where?" she shouted after Singh.

"The bridge," Ashe said. "Maybe the captain wants to get the hell out of here." He rose to stand, somewhat taller than she. Then his eyes flicked their attention past her face to a point beyond the viewports.

Clio turned in time to see the gantry topple and lurch

down the dock like a gigantic insect in its death throes. As it slid out of sight, a cable flicked at the viewport. Its steel hook slid slowly off the plasiglass without leaving a scratch.

Then all was silent as the Klaxon ceased. Several people lay or sat on the deck nursing their hurts. Clio turned to the nearest, an older sergeant holding his ribs with both arms.

"Forget him," Ashe said. "Commander Singh wants you on the bridge."

"I don't need your advice, Ashe. I'm already in as much trouble as I can be."

"I don't think you are, Clio," he answered. "Not by a long shot."

Med techs were arriving with their kits. Clio turned and ran for the bridge, leaving Ashe frowning after her and the techs to minister to the fallen.

She jammed up the ladder to flight deck. There, Hocking, Singh, and Voris hunched frantic at stations, as the scramble of voices piped over comm, and the dock slid by the viewports in a slow crawl. The captain, on headphones, scowled in her direction, turned away, demanding clearance to undock, while ship was undeniably under way. Singh bobbed his head at her, eyes glancing toward the copilot's chair, where she threw herself, clamped in, and donned headphones to catch the pandemonium of Vanda Control. As Clio watched, Voris punched in prelaunch sequences in a blur, and ship's systems sang through the flight deck's electronic skin. Amid the commotion, Clio had time to notice that the kid was fast, real fast.

"Bay doors dilated ninety-one percent, Captain," she said, "we've got clearance, but it's close."

"Take her out, Lieutenant," he said, *"now."*

The ship backed out of the wreckage of the loading bay, leaving behind flailing hoses leaking fuel and the remains of the catwalk railings swinging within an arm's length of the ship. The deck beneath Clio's feet vibrated hard as docking rails carrying the massive ship struggled with their load. Clio felt the rumble travel up to her scalp, shaking her bones on the way.

"Get us *out* of here," Hocking said. Ship's systems rose to a whining pitch and keypads glowed warnings. The lights threw a florid cast over Voris' face, and crimson sweat ran down her hairline.

The bridge viewports cleared the station doors as Voris punched up the vernier engines and moved *Galactique* into space. Clio's pulse revved up along with *Galactique*'s engines. She skimmed the instrumentation quickly, ran her fingers over the boards, lightly, a caress. Nothing to do but watch Voris, and itch to take over. Back in the pilot's seat, by damn. Not that she cared, but back on flight deck and heading out, and heading out to *Niang*. She ran her fingers along the power-distribution switches.

"Finn," from behind her.

Swiveled the chair to see Jared Licht standing there.

Hocking pointed a finger at her. "Get him off the bridge, Finn."

Jared Licht. As her heart fell through her diaphragm, Clio tried out one of her old jaunty smiles. Punched it up, hoped it did the job.

He returned her smile, looking down at her, his form eclipsing the glittering lights of the deck consoles. Not as tall as she thought; standing, she would look directly into those violet eyes. His face, so lovely, you'd be a stone not to notice. But now, up close, she saw a tautness to his skin, stretched thin over his skull.

"You've set yourself up real well, Finn," he said. "Looks like the world is handing you just about everything you want. Your brother, your pilot's bars. Life is good, yes?"

"A beach."

He smiled delightedly. "A beach. Yes and it may just keep going your way. But you do have a way of screwing up, Finn. I sincerely hope that doesn't happen, and I'll be watching you to see that it doesn't."

"What the hell are you doing here, Licht?"

"You knew, of course?" He searched her face a moment. "You didn't! Your Colonel Tandy didn't tell you that I'm along on the mission?" Now his smile was genuine.

"Always happy to bring glad tidings. Yes, we're crewmates, Finn, shoulder to shoulder for six months, at least. Bit of a bumpy start. Looks like someone wanted to give us some farewell fireworks."

"Go fuck yourself, Licht," she said.

She watched him as his face darkened. For a moment it seemed to her that it was sadness she was seeing in those raptor's eyes, not anger.

He spoke in a low tone, out of the captain's hearing. "You always think you're immune, don't you . . . immune to all the rules. Someday you'll pay the price. Nobody's immune, Ms. Finn." He backed out of the cockpit area, stood at the hatch ladder. His face resumed a nonchalant malice. "Guess I'll go see if I can find somebody else to talk to. Maybe Petya wants to play tiddlywinks." He shrugged cheerfully. "Doesn't hurt to ask." And he disappeared down to mid-decks.

Clio gripped the armrest to keep from shaking.

Hocking turned to watch him leave, his nose glistening. He said nothing to the DSDE captain. Instead, he turned back to Clio, saying, "You will maintain flight-deck order and keep your visitors off the bridge, Finn, you understand?"

"Yessir. Sorry sir."

Through the starboard viewport a flash lit up Vanda's darkened loading bay, spraying bits of debris in their direction. The hull rang with the blows, but *Galactique* was bearing around to fire her engines, and did so, drowning out the collisions.

Clio's mind was on Colonel Tandy. No, he hadn't told her about Licht. Parceled out his information in small doses, did Tandy. Neglected to tell her that one of his little compromises was to allow DSDE on the mission, and a most particular DSDE: a man with a bead on her, waiting to take his shot.

"Configured for main engine burn, Captain," Voris said, and barely waiting for his answer, she fired the main thrusters, throttling up to a slow burn, and *Galactique* roared to life. Ship eased off the station and began its ponderous acceleration, that no emergency could rush, not even the urgency of Voris' flashing hands or the following explosions from Vanda's decimated bay.

Galactique was headed into clear, hard space. Over the earphones Clio heard, "Good job, Lieutenant Voris," from Hocking. "Stand by."

Voris turned to Clio, winked happily. "Count your fingers," she said, off mike. "I think we made it."

"Yeah, and I'll bet somebody wishes we didn't," Clio said.

Voris looked over at her, smile fleeing.

"Only thing I want to know," Clio said, "is whether they're back there on Vanda or along for the ride."

A NICHE IN TIME

❧

The creatures parlayed within easy reach of killing. He had to smother his mouth with his hand to keep from giggling, they were so vulnerable, at his disposal. Their studded boots caught an odd thread of light that the jungle crown allowed through, setting off a reddish twinkle of buttons, as though even their boots were magical. They were speaking now.

"Yi mastag, asark itha direcsh, bluspris," the shorter one said, perhaps a female, though no breasts obvious beneath the padded vest and shirt.

"Ewoll amet yi ta sheebass, an," the other said, raised his rifle, and set off, leaving her, leaving the target.

Harper Teeg covered his mouth, grinning. It was so easy to kill them, the Voo Doo men. He hesitated, though. This one was female, hair braided, with narrow, womanly features. Shame to kill a female, even if she was a Voo Doo, with killing hands.

A mole creature scuttled behind him and he jumped, scraping his rifle against the rock ledge.

She heard it. Crouched low, swung her rifle around, pointed it at his forehead, then swung away to his left.

The stupid bitch couldn't see him, none of them could see him, and he could do what he liked. Maybe he would let this one live. For now. Kill her partner, though, Teeg decided.

The troop of them were pursuing him through the jungle, combing the terrain methodically. The surface terrain. But from the network of tunnels he had easily eluded them, bided his time, and picked them off, and they died like anyone, like humans, like U.S. Army. Blasted apart by weapons fire. Voo Doo men had other ways of killing, though, nasty ways.

He lit his torch and scuttled down the tunnel, heard the crabbing of the moles, skittering out of his way, hating the light. He stabbed at one with the torch. Startled, it slammed into the rock wall. He advanced upon it, making rifle noises, kapow, kapow, as the six-legged creature pounded into the wall again and again. Then it lay stunned.

"Don't try to run from old Teeg," he said. "Can't have that." He slugged it with his boot. They'd have to learn to obey. The tunnels were his, the floor of the jungle was his, the Cave with its Treasure was his. Let come who may. These Voo Doos, U.S. Army, Biotime, DSDE, Clio Finn . . . Clio Finn, yes. Had tricked him, had poisoned him. But he had shown her a thing or two. So she didn't win in the end, didn't win. *Didn't win . . . didn't win,* he heard himself say out loud, sonorous and cozy in the stone throat of the earth. Not like those other voices in his head, the sharp cackles in the stone maze of his head.

He stopped at Big North Rock, clambored up to the peephole, scanned, and yes, there they were, a knot of six Voo Doos. One, a bit apart, and then he felt himself sight the rifle and pull the trigger, as though someone else were in his body. This Voo Doo had to die, and so he fell, but only to his knees, and he pulled the trigger again and once more. Teeg froze as the others pointed at his outcropping, figuring out the direction of fire, and pinched off a few rounds in his direction. He crouched low, sweating. *Stupid, stupid . . .* They were circling around to get the jump on him. He bolted down the tunnel, came to the High Ceiling Intersection, jammed into the smallest passage, one of five, killed the light and padded softly by memory. Down the long finger of the tunnel, then gentle curve to the left. At last the sweat skimmed off his face from a freshening current of air, as the blackness throttled up to grey. Then the Great Cave ballooned out in front of him. He ran to the cave entrance and knelt behind the tripod-mounted rifle, swiveling it back at the tunnel. Heart thudding like steam through cold pipes. Licked his flaking lips. Waited.

But they didn't come. Stupid.

He leaned against the thatchy reeds of his warren, relaxing. Then his mind snapped to, and he jumped up. Maybe they had come for his treasures already, stolen them while pretending to be searching above ground. He snatched up the torch and ignited it with his lighter, then bolted down the rock passage, lighting up the rock walls and a succession of chitinous screams as he plunged headlong toward the Great Cave. As he stumbled into the cavernous arena, an exhalation of frigid air issued from the Hell Crack. Teeg barked out a laugh. "Don't hyperventilate now! It's just old Teeg!" Circling wide, he scampered to the back wall where a ledge at eye level held his special things. Still there, counting them off: his pilot bars, a box with a last reserve of ammo, a wad of Voo Doo hair, a flaked wood bowl with some women's underthings he'd found in camp, and then the crystals. Lovely. Lovely how they pulsed with a lambent glow even in the cave recess. *Voo Doos want my treasures, don't they?* His fingers absently fondled the cloth in the wooden bowl, then fluttered to the bullets.

"OK, Voo Doos," he said. "Come and get them."

CHAPTER 27

Clio hauled herself down from *Galactique*'s flight deck, down the ladder to mid-decks, dog tired. Two consecutive eight-hour shifts running systems checks and combing for ship damage would about do it.

Incredibly, though Vanda's entire main loading bay lay in quiet ruins, *Galactique* was in good shape. Ship's hull took some dents, and minor repairs were under way, but main-line systems looked like they pulled through.

Her thoughts off and on the last sixteen hours had been on Petya, and now she made her way down the crew corridor to the end cabin, which was nothing more than a medical contamination cell with a pallet and sink, a hygiene station. Only sign of Petya was a shaving kit and three photos taped to the bulkhead. She peered closely at the photos. Unfamiliar faces smiled back at her, likely his new family, before DSDE tracked him down.

Back out in the corridor and only a few doors away was a handwritten nameplate: Licht. Damn anyway. Too close to Petya. Starting to worry hard now, Clio poked into the recreation area, where a dozen or so crew were watching *Gorillas in the Mist*, a sentimental old flat-movie about gorillas before their habitat perished.

Popped into the galley and observation deck, then jammed down the ladder to botany deck. Checked out two of the labs, empty now, and opened a third door. Petya was in the corner hunched over a dissected bit of electronics, so deep into doing that he didn't look up.

A large pair of feet were propped up on the center lab

table, and behind them, slung back in a chair, was Timothy Ashe, reading a paperback.

He looked up at her, said, voice booming, "Ah. The Red Queen. Welcome to study hall. Grab a book." He indicated a stack of paperbacks in the corner.

His easygoing air grated on her, after her ship search. "You could have let me know where he was."

His eyebrows raised, one going higher than the other, stopped as it was by the heavy scar. "Oh. Could have, I suppose. Captain doesn't like inconsequentials on the bridge, though. How'd you like being behind the wheel?"

"A thrill a minute."

"We going to make it to Niang? Ship come through the send-off party OK?"

"Looks like."

"Too bad."

Clio arched an eyebrow.

"Just means a damn boring trip, that's all. A trip like this could use a little excitement. Enemy space aliens threaten Earth spaceship on vital mission. That sort of thing."

"We've got DSDE on board. Enough alien threat for me."

Petya said, not looking up, "DSDE is on this spaceship."

Clio turned to him. "Yeah, I know. He been hassling you?"

"He came by my room to talk. I don't like to talk to him."

Clio looked over at Ashe, eyes darkening. He shrugged.

"He bother you?" she asked Petya.

Petya pressed the probe into the circuit board, watching the monitor, which displayed the circuit layout. "I can fix this, no problem."

Clio went over, drew a chair up next to Petya. "He bother you?"

"I don't like to talk to him." Petya looked up at her. "You shaved off all your hair?" He brought his hand up to touch a shaving scar on her scalp. "And you cut yourself?" His eyes were better now, clear of meds—or clearer.

"I was in a quarry, Petya."

Petya looked away, down to the probe in his other hand, unmoving. "I got lost on the road," he said, "and Mrs. Looby picked me up in her '83 Chevy Nova. I was lost. You were lost?"

"No. I waited for you by the water tower, waited a long time. I finally left, but I been waiting for you a long time, Petya. Then I've been flying these ships, but I never forgot you."

Petya still hadn't moved. "We were lost," he said.

"Yeah, I guess we were."

Clio rested her head on his shoulder a moment, wanting to be close, not wanting to push it.

"I've got to fix this," he said.

"I know." She drew back and smiled at him. "They shaved your hair, just like me. Looks like hell."

"*You* look like hell," he responded, in the old repartee.

"Oh yeah? Well if your hair was any shorter, we could play pool with your head."

A smile erupted on his face. "We look like hell," he said, going back to his circuit board.

Clio watched him for a time, face hot in that way of unwanted emotions, stuff that comes bubbling up from way below the mantle. She swung her chair around.

"So, this is where you hide out?" she said to Ashe.

He brought his feet down, leaned elbows on the counter, watching her. "How long's it been?"

"How long's what been?"

His eyes flicked over to Petya.

She shrugged. "Long time." She unraveled herself from the chair. "So you're ship's botanist, I hear."

"Yes. They think I'll come in handy when we find the crash site. ID the difference between plant growth and metal ship. Apparently there's some confusion about that."

Clio withheld an ironic smile. "Yeah. They get easily confused."

Ashe leaned back in the chair again. "And you, I hear you've decided to Dive."

"I guess so."

"And cozy up to Colonel Tandy." He smiled, making the comment rather more friendly than challenging.

"Not cozying up."

"Oh. My mistake." He stood, sauntered around the lab island, leaned against her side of it.

His dark features carried a smile in sharp relief, betraying an energy even when he was leaning, arms folded casually, against the counter. She felt something crouching in his shoulders, an impulse to run, a shout, some fullness about him.

"You got something against Tandy?" she asked.

He raised his hands in protest. "Got nothing against. Army's a fine profession. Tandy's a fine colonel. He may be a sly, subverted, posturing fool, but he's a fine man, I'm sure."

"So, he's army," Clio responded. "What's new?"

"It's new if you weigh in on his side."

"How many sides we got here?"

"More than one. More than one viewpoint."

Clio started to say something, stopped. Damned if she was going to speak up for Tandy. Damned if she was going to weigh in on any side when she didn't even know there *were* sides. "You don't think we should be going back to Niang, do you?"

He raised the good eyebrow. "Maybe I think we shouldn't go blasting our way through the jungle until we know what we're doing, what the stakes are. Maybe I think the colonel and his folks are quick to make a war out of any-thing they don't understand. Maybe I'm just an old pacifist, lost in a world I don't understand."

Couldn't miss the irony of that last. Clio found herself smiling, a real one. "Me too," she said. "Lost in a world I don't understand." Getting to like the man, by God. She started to push back her hair, the old sensuous gesture, encountered plucked-chicken scalp. Saw herself, skinny and bald, wanting to flirt with a man whose sexual energy could flatten her, wanting to get naked with the first man she'd felt friendly toward since Loren in the barracks, confusing, again, sex and comfort, confusing the basics once again. Jesus. Turned to go.

"You don't have to leave," he said. "Got plenty of paperbacks. Even some great war stories, right up your alley."

She turned at the door. Looked him in the eyes. "Hey thanks. For letting Petya work here."

She turned again, reached for the door.

"Clio," Ashe said. "You always keep such a tight rein?"

She stopped, didn't know what to say for once. Closed the door behind her, got into the corridor where she could breathe again.

Her stomach churning, and figuring it might be hunger, she headed for the galley on mid-deck. Found a tableful playing blackjack, crew mostly, but three army. Heads turned, and back to the game, ignoring her. In a voyage of more than a few weeks, tensions could build in the cheek-by-jowl crowding of a mission like this one. It helped that a third of the crew were on sleep shift at any one time, but crew pressed in on each other nonetheless. They respected each other's silence, the only privacy most of them had. This might have been the reason the crew ignored Clio, respecting her privacy. Might have been. But hell, had to be dead or deaf or both not to have heard that Clio Finn ran rampant on the old *Starhawk*, brought down the ship and all its crew. How they reconciled that rumor with her co-piloting *Galactique* was anyone's guess.

Clio made herself a meatloaf sandwich, squeezing a brown, ketchupy-smelling paste from the tube, flipped open a minicarton of protein gelatin, and settled in to her meal, leaning against the counter, watching the game. Dealer at her end of the table, army, had two eights, easy to beat, and sure enough lost the hand; paid off. Turned real slow to stare at Clio, and she obliged him by moving off to a side table, minding her own business.

"Getting sensitive, hey Lewis?" one of them asked the dealer.

"Try to blame her," another one said, "but you a null-ass player, Lewis."

"Just don't like no quarry meat staring down my back," Lewis responded.

Clio kept on chewing. Wished she had some water to wash the sandwich down with. Not going to get up now.

"Yeah, I heard she spent her vacation in a quarry after she had a little accident with a spaceship."

"You in or out, Burks?" Lewis dealt another hand.

Money slid onto the table.

Clio ate her sandwich and thought of Timothy Ashe. Something disconcerting about him, couldn't figure what. A man who might be flirting with her, but not coming on directly. A man who was taking Petya under wing . . . and why was that? A man who seemed to know things about her, like time spent with Colonel Tandy, and with a bone to pick against army. Irritated her, lecturing her about army. Holed up as he was in his botany lab and spouting pacifism, never having seen the army up close. Never having taken the army on. And lost. And lost all that she had lost. Damn intellectual fool.

Behind her, the hand played out, and Lewis lost the deal. "Hey, Finn," he said. "I thought *army* barbers were bad. How much you pay for that haircut?"

Clio answered, not turning around. "Plenty." Then she heard herself saying, "How much you paid so far to stay in that game, soldier?"

One of his buddies hooted. She heard a chair scrape back. Jesus Christ, here we go.

Lewis came around, grabbed a chair, and sat on it backward, leaning on its back. Long face, hatchet-thin. "Heard they got you set up for one more Dive, then they gonna use you for science experiments, Finn." He got a better idea. "You and your retard brother."

"Guess I'm just shit out of luck then, boy. Same as you."

He swung out of the chair and pushed her, a warm-up slap to her shoulder. "You just don't know when to shut up, do you, Finn?"

Clio carefully placed the sandwich back on the paper plate. Managed to swallow what she was chewing. Kept her eyes on the sandwich. Just let everybody cool down.

Somebody said, "Stow it, Lewis."

He punched her shoulder again. "Heard you're a good fighter, that right baldy?" Pushed her harder this time, sent the chair skidding back. Army buddies jumped up and grabbed Lewis, pinned his arms.

"Leave her the fuck alone," one of them said. Lewis stopped struggling.

"Yeah." Shook his head. "Guess I lost it." Some tension eased. Clio picked her plate up from the table. Army started back to the gaming table. As Clio passed Lewis, he elbowed her in the stomach, and swiped his foot behind her, toppling her; the sandwich went flying. She scrambled into a crouch and dove for his knees, driving him back against the bulkhead, where his head slammed hard enough to bring down the fire extinguisher in a glancing blow off the side of his face. She was straddling him as Commander Singh appeared in the doorway, and crew fell to attention, the fire alarm wailing like an avenging ghost.

Clio slowly climbed off Lewis.

"See to this corporal who is bleeding," Singh ordered, shouting above the fire tone. One of them went over to help Lewis. "This alarm is unnecessary?" Singh asked.

"The extinguisher fell off the wall, sir," Clio said.

"You will be seeing to that," Singh ordered.

Clio deactivated the alarm at the wall hookup.

"What is the cause of this?" Singh demanded.

The senior Biotime technician spoke up. "Lewis attacked her, sir. She insulted his card playing."

Singh looked at her as though he were personally hurt. *God, the man wants me to do well,* Clio thought. *Poor son of a bitch.* She rubbed her midriff, which felt dented from Lewis' elbow.

Singh scanned the group. "This galley will no longer be in disarray within a very few minutes." Finally one of the crew figured that for an order, and responded, "Yessir." Then Singh turned to Clio, nodded her out the door.

"He bashed me in the stomach, sir," Clio said, following him to the God-loving bridge.

"This will be a story for Colonel Tandy, Miss Finn." He did her the courtesy of climbing the bridge ladder first, not treating her like she was in custody. She followed him. So, Tandy will handle this. Didn't know who she'd rather face, Tandy or Hocking. Tandy'd maybe be another one who'd be disappointed in her, and maybe it was easier to face somebody who despised her than somebody who liked her, and why *that* should be the way of the world was freeping well beyond her.

But she didn't give a shit in any case; why should she?

She waited outside Tandy's cabin while Singh went inside. Lieutenant Ryerson stood his post outside, saying nothing, eyes saying everything. Then Singh was waving her in, and she entered, met by Tandy's lilting classical music. Tandy was at his desk in front of the viewports. While he left her standing there, she could hear his pen scratching, a fountain pen, in fact. Finally he looked up.

"Corporal Lewis slugged me, sir," she said, "without provocation. Or not much, anyway."

A fleeting smile, gone before it bloomed. "Clio, Clio."

"I had to protect myself."

He thumbed a switch, silencing the music. "You didn't kill him, did you?"

"Nosir."

"Then we will trust the medics will give their full attention to Corporal Lewis, and we will go on with more important matters."

He raised a hand to fend off further discussion. "Corporal Lewis is of no consequence. Corporal Lewis is a moron who delights in baiting people, especially the less powerful. I think he sadly misjudged whom he had taken on." He rose from his chair and beckoned her to the viewport. Before them the stars flecked the blackness in a sweeping vista of the far terrain.

He swung a hand out, encompassing the view. "What do you think of when you look at the stars, Clio?" They stood side by side, like the two explorers they were, viewing as though from a promontory the harsh and thrilling territory beckoning them.

"Guess I don't think, sir." In the silence that followed she added, "Maybe it's more something I feel."

"Awe, respect, things like that?" he asked.

"Not exactly. Maybe longing. Don't know why."

"Longing, yes. I can see why you would. For myself, I look at these stars and I think of the future. The stars are the future. The Earth has had its day, its allotment of days, but the stars, the stars are an inexhaustible source of days." He looked momentarily at her. "I don't know if you understand what I'm saying. It's as though the stars are *time*, time that represents the currency of our human lives, so that if we are to live we must have the stars—spend them wisely, of course—but we must reach out and grasp our days." He turned to look at her, his face lit wanly by the ancient light piercing the viewports. "Do you see?"

Clio knew that he wished to be understood, so she said, "I think so, sir."

"We deserve the stars, Clio. We aren't ignorant shepherds herding our goats and marveling at the starry night sky. We are a great civilization on the brink of claiming the stars for our own, and all the planets they warm. Exploration and wealth and knowledge unlimited. Unlimited, Clio. But we are thwarted, confined by the minor technology of Dive, denied the freedom to roam the galaxy—and beyond—at will. It's as though a magnificent stallion were tethered to a tree, and could only range in a limited circle. But cut that tether, and then you will feel the wind in your mane, by God, and the Earth crumbling beneath your hooves!" His eyes narrowed as he seemed to see, not the panorama of the Milky Way, but his vision of the liberated stallion thundering across the plains.

They were silent a long time then. Finally he said, in a lower tone. "I bore you with my musings." He smiled at some private thought. Then: "I can talk myself into a sweat, Suzanne always said. My wife was a great listener. She put up with me, you see. Knew I had these high callings, to do and achieve great things, or be a part of them." He smiled again. "So she listened. Not that she didn't have a thing or two to say for herself. She was brilliant, more brilliant than I, and light-years beyond me in reading and culture. She was a published poet, and . . . well, a great lady, as they used to use the term. A great lady."

"Your wife is dead then, sir?"

Tandy looked over at Clio and his expression changed from reverie to briskness once more. "Yes. She's gone. Five years now. Long enough not to dwell on it, I suppose." He turned from the window, moving to the sideboard, where he poured himself a drink. "Can't offer you one, I'm afraid. You're on duty soon." He brought his drink over to the sofa, gestured her to the seat opposite.

"What I started to say to you, and never quite got to, is that our mission is of the most enormous consequence." He sipped his drink, savoring it. "Faster than light, Clio, faster than light. This may be the prize awaiting us on Niang. There can be no more momentous undertaking, has not been, since the dawn of human civilization. And *we're* a part of it." His eyes glowed with the intensity of his thought. "*You're* a part of it, Clio. Can you imagine what that means?" He regarded her for a moment. "You do remind me at times of my Suzanne. Yes, at times. You're a good listener. Intelligent, as she was." He smiled a stabbing, brief smile. "Don't worry, Ms. Finn. I will not court you. I meant that as an observation, merely. And it is a very high compliment. But not a courting gesture, no, you'll not find that from me. And I'm sure you're not looking for it, either."

"No, sir. Thank you, sir." Had that one right. Didn't go well to sleep with the brass. Made things crazy on a small ship a million years from home.

Tandy finished off the rest of his drink, put the glass down next to the framed photo. "Do you ever think about your place in history, Clio?" He wasn't looking at her now, and continued: "Most people have no sense of that. It's nearly impossible to pull back, see the broader field where you struggle, see it in relation to the progression of human events. Yet here we are, embarked on what may someday be called the Niang Turning Point. Your name, for example, may be famous among explorers, much as Christopher Columbus, Coronado, de Gama." He glanced at her. "Something to think about, isn't it? 'Clio Finn, searching for Earth's biological salvation, stumbles upon the first alien artifact and ushers in a new age of galactic exploration.' "

"That telling leaves out a lot," Clio said.

"Of course! History seeks a thread out of the maze of events. Therefore simplification, simplification."

"How about this," she said. " 'Clio Finn's corporate sponsors reject Niang's offer of biological renewal, and opt instead for one more piece of technology.' "

"I won't argue the biology aspects with you, Clio. You know where I stand on that one. But history may well mock that idea, as it does the Spanish search for gold and the fountain of youth in the New World. Neither were found, nor did the Spanish ever understand that the wealth they had discovered was the land itself. That's the myopia of our day-to-day lives. We miss the point." Tandy leaned forward, resting his forearms on his knees, hands clasped in front of him. "History may also note that Clio Finn's discovery of an alien spaceship ushered in not exploration, but conflict. The first interspecies hostilities."

"So that despite the peaceful beginnings of Space Recon," Clio said, "humanity managed to convert the enterprise to their favorite pastime, war. A languishing military finds its niche."

"Melodramatic, Clio. You think that I welcome armed conflict, no doubt. Not true. However, it may be forced upon me—and somehow, given what has transpired, I do in fact expect it." He leaned back, arms along the back of the couch. "I do in fact."

"Why have they attacked us?" Clio asked.

"The Nians?"

"They aren't Nians. There are no Nians."

"No. Probably true. But it helps to pin a name on them, and Nians may do until we learn more. In any case, I think its clear that they're keeping us from the ship. They mean to prevent our discovery of the ship's technology. Of faster-than-light technology."

"Why don't they just destroy the ship?"

"Perhaps they are marooned, possibly they are the crew of the crashed ship itself, and they may not have the firepower."

"They could do a pretty good job of dismantling the ship and hiding parts of it."

"Perhaps. Good questions, Clio. I don't know the answers."

They sat in silence for a few moments. Then he began to talk of the stars again—rambling on at times, looking over her head at some point of clarity visible only to him, searching for answers, and at other times gathering her into the conversation with his eyes. But then the conversation went on without her, while she struggled to have something to say, until she realized that what he needed was someone to listen and maybe understand him. At times she thought she did, at least the part about the stars. The stars being our future.

As his voice hummed in the room, Clio swung her legs onto the footstool and leaned her head into the soft leather chair, closing her eyes. "All my life, been looking," she said.

"Looking?"

"At the stars. Ever notice how they always look 'bout the same distance away? No matter how far you go, always 'bout the same distance away . . ."

He made no answer and she sank toward sleep, lowering into dreams as though by the thin strands of Tandy's classical music. As she sank, she was seeing the *Galactique* cutting its ponderous trail out from Vandarthanan Station, out from Earth's vicinity, heading for Dive point. Space was silent—but here, the surge of a far-off symphony, and underneath, deep beneath, was the barely heard whirr of electronics, the sigh of hydraulics and clicks of vent openings and closings, together with the underlayment of seventy men and women striding the decks, rattling the ladders . . . and moaning in their sleep like her. . . .

Later, she might have felt a blanket draped over her,

might have heard, "Niang is a new destiny, you see? Leave the past behind you, Clio, as I must . . ."

leave the past . . .

leave the past . . .

Clio hesitated just outside medlab, hand about to clench down on the door latch. Here were more pills to take. People always shoving pills at her. And no doubt which ones this time, with the *Galactique* headed into Dive point, and the Dive pilot needing medicating, and needing it bad. She unlatched the door and pushed.

"Finn reporting."

A sandy-haired youngster in a white lab coat turned to check her out. But not alone. With a start she saw Jared Licht sitting on the gurney, swinging his legs. But of course he would be here. Here were drugs. Not exactly recreational drugs, but a drug . . . and thus of interest to DSDE.

"Guess we'll have to boost your attention span, Finn," he said. "Can't have you falling asleep when the ship needs someone at least marginally conscious. The Department understands."

"The Department can go fuck itself."

Licht smiled brightly. "Yes! Talk dirty to me, baby."

The medic was holding a small plastic cup with pills in it. Nearly dropped the cup at her profanity. More red vitamin pills plus the familiar blue tabs, dexichloromine, the old contraband she'd used—now regulation issue.

Clio swallowed the tabs, turned for the door.

"Wait." This from the medic. "I'll have to observe you for a few minutes until they take effect." He looked apologetic as Clio turned to stare him down.

"I don't need observing."

Licht sprang from the gurney, sauntering close to wash her with those violet eyes. "Of course you do. Doctor," he said to the medic, "you can leave her in my care for the moment." The medic's brow crumpled. Licht gazed at him with his pale smile. The medic fled.

"It's a shame to get you back on your old addiction,

Finn. I must say I don't approve. But national security calls."

She walked to the other side of the pallet, putting it between them.

"Starting to feel the old kick yet?" he asked. The black of his shirt set off his face and hair like a pale fire. "Don't feel like talking, do you?" His face parodied a hurt reaction. "Sometimes people don't like me, Finn. When people don't like me I figure they've got something to hide. So then I keep a real close watch. From that perspective, you might as well be friendly, you see?"

"What do you want from me, Licht?"

"Oh, I want your body, and when I'm done with that I want your mind. Sex will be intriguing with you, Finn. You can't imagine how much I'm looking forward to that, planning for it. Plans flicker into my mind at unpredictable moments—like now, in fact. You do add delight to this otherwise hellish bus ride to nowhere, you'll never guess how much." He was around the gurney before Clio snapped into action herself, and felt her arm grasped. "Did I answer your question? Or did you want more details?"

"You answered it."

Up close his face was hard; she could almost see the chisel marks.

"If you touch me," she said, "I'll break your fingers." She called up a demur smile, hoped it didn't wobble.

He dropped her arm, hands thrown up in an innocent, palm-out gesture. "*Touch* you, right here in medlab? My goodness, Clio, you have an active sexual imagination yourself. But I don't think you quite understand my devotion to protocol. What will happen is, you will complete your work for Tandy, and that means, let's see . . . two Dives, I believe, and after you've completed your tour of duty, after they release you, you will come under my jurisdiction to face charges for recent offenses. And old ones. You do remember the old ones? Murder charges stay on the books, Clio. Forever. When I have custody, it will be for quite a long while. Until then . . ."

The door opened and Timothy Ashe walked into the

room. He looked at Clio, then Licht. "Am I interrupting an official conversation?" he asked.

"Yes. You're interrupting," Licht said.

"Sorry," Ashe said, walking to the bulkhead supply drawers. "Only take a moment." He started opening and closing drawers. "Where do they hide the aspirin?" he said to himself.

Licht drew a long breath, watching Ashe with close attention.

Clio felt a sudden relief, not to be the object of Licht's gaze. Like a gazelle on the plains when the leopard changes targets.

Ashe looked back at them. Repeated, "Anyone know where they keep the aspirin?" He shrugged. "Headache."

"You can't issue yourself aspirin," Licht said. "Medics do that."

Ashe slammed the last hatch door shut. "Well that's bloody stupid."

"Not at all. Ship's rules. As I'm sure you know, Mr. Ashe."

Ashe leaned back against the counter, eyes fixed on Licht. "Doesn't mean it isn't bloody stupid." His expression took on a surprised innocence. "Oh. Not something one says to DSDE, though, is it? Department of Social and Drug Enforcement might write me up for bad attitude."

"Depends on the game you're playing," Licht responded.

"Let's see . . . game." Ashe's forehead wrinkled in concentration. "Blind Man's Bluff? King of the Hill?"

Clio interjected. "Pissing contest?"

Licht swung to face her. "You'd lose that one."

"Losing anyway, mister."

"Well." Ashe pushed off from the counter, walked toward them, taking Clio by the elbow. "This has been fun. Next time we'll try to stay longer. Beer and chips? Oops, more contraband. Maybe it's just not going to work out between us. Can't say I didn't try." Ashe steered Clio to the door.

From behind, Licht said, "Not at all. I'm sure we'll meet again. Small ship, you know."

Ashe shut the door behind them.

"Thanks," she said.

"My pleasure." They started to walk down the corridor toward the mid-decks hatchway. "Figure you didn't need Jared Licht just before the big Dive."

"Got that right."

"So how you feel?"

"Feel? Let's see. Like my body's on loan from the morgue. Like my last meal is alive inside my stomach."

A large smile cut a path across his face. As Clio started down the hatchway she added, "The usual."

Clio climbed the ladder to the bridge, where Hocking acknowledged her, barely, raising his chin a couple centimeters. Singh nodded his head at her. The deck greeted her with the gleam of its close-packed instrumentation, like the teeth of the beast they pretended to control, here in the mouth of *Galactique*.

"Sir," she said, sliding into her chair.

Voris, in the copilot's seat, smiled at her as though they shared a fun secret. But nothing was fun about Dive. They were heading into it, and coming up close.

"Lieutenant Voris," Hocking said. "You will arm the engines and bring us to sixty-five-percent burn. Then you will turn the helm over to Finn." Hocking took his place, strapped in. "Finn, you will execute the Dive maneuver at the Dive point coming up."

"Yessir."

Clio wiped her hands on her pants leg. *Damn blue pills give you the shakes, and where is the heat on this deck, anyway?*

Voris patched into Clio's channel. "I just want you to know, Clio, that I have complete confidence in you. I know you can do it."

"That's a big help, Voris."

"Meg. Call me Meg." She executed the burn, a long one, with a sure hand. The *Galactique* pushed forward out of its comfortable cruise toward a full gallop. With *Galac-*

tique's mass, entering Dive point was a tricky affair. In the days of the diminutive *Starhawk*, a ship could slip in knife-clean, and a petit mal would seize near-space for just a moment. But now, the mighty *Galactique* pressed the envelope, as the engineers said, taking Vandarthanan's theory a couple more steps.

Clio heard ship's engines strain.

Beside her, Voris said, "I guess this is really it. This is my fourth Dive, so it's not that I don't know what it's like." She looked over to see if Clio was paying attention, continued anyway. "The other times were for practice, though. Now, my first real mission, and we're headed to *Niang*, and nearly blown apart before we even started. We were lucky to escape."

"Yeah, just a damn string of luck."

"You mean it wasn't so lucky? But look on the bright side, like the captain says, it's really a venture we can all be proud of."

Clio busied herself with running systems checks. "Immortal words, all right."

"At times like this," Voris' words crept in again, "I know I have my congregation standing behind me. It dissolves the fear of space and Dive and death, Clio. It does."

"Good for you, Voris. Now could you leave me alone and in quiet to be scared shitless?" Clio felt the ship strain, lights blinked irritatingly, ship kicked up toward Dive velocity. Not like the old days when *Starhawk* responded with power to spare, chomping at the bit.

"You say that to shock people, Clio, but I know how brave you really are. What I don't know is where you get it from, with your soul in the state it's in."

Captain Hocking: "Helm to Finn, Lieutenant Voris. And cut the chatter."

"Yessir."

Clio's board signaled helm control, and they reached for Dive velocity. *State my soul is in.* Had to be a sorry state, no doubt on that one, if soul was what your stomach told you about how you fit into the world. Had to be a sorry state.

"Blessings, Clio."

"Christ almighty, Voris, stow it before I cut your channel."

"That hurts."

"Dive point coming up, could we have a professional crew, here, and pay attention?" Hocking asked, voice not exactly whining. "Dive point coming up, on my mark."

Clio readied her hand over the switch guard on the Dive button, ready to engage the coils at maximum velocity.

"Good luck, Clio," Voris said, a slow drip from a faucet.

I will kill her, Clio thought.

Then: "Dive," Hocking ordered.

"Yessir." Clio hit the button, switching them over to Dive, switching them to the tunnel track through the space-time continuum, and backward, getting *direction* right, backward in time. Ship's coils hummed, vision thickened, humming rose to a drilling whine. And ceased.

Vision cleared, console blinking red, an alarm blaring. Normal space, the *Galactique* had put a toe in the cold water's edge and retreated, fast.

"Finn," Hocking shouted, "you miss the switch? Or what's your call?"

Console showed they were losing velocity. Voris, on scan, called out the coordinates. They had missed.

"Couldn't say, sir," Clio responded. "For starters, coils are hot as hades and thermal-control systems are on over-load." A battery of lights flared up and cabin pressurization wobbled a split second, an instant too long for Clio. "Call to stand for code-one alert, sir, I'd recommend."

Klaxon subsided, leaving Hocking hollering for no reason, "I'll make that determination, Finn." Then, at lower decibels, "Don't overreact, now. Ship is coming back to normal."

From Singh: "Computer is signaling for code-one alert, sir. Shall I instigate?"

"No. I said no. Is anyone hearing me say no?"

"As you say, sir." Singh's head bobbed back down to navigation boards.

Voris' eyes were wide; she was sitting quiet, letting things settle, but watching the boards close.

Silence hovered among the four of them. Then, from Hocking: "Finn, you will ease us into our burn, and slowly."

"Take two," Voris said, Clio's channel.

Clio looked at her, wondered if that was humor. Voris wasn't looking at anyone, now that Hocking was peeved; Voris knew how to keep her head down.

And they revved up to Dive point again, gathering speed at such a pace as *Galactique* could muster, coils a little warm for Clio's judgment, but what the hell, blow the carbon out, see what the ship could do. And as they gathered speed, Clio knew in her gut they had made the *Galactique* too damn big, that this behemoth was never meant to Dive, should have been a freighter, a *troop carrier*, by God, which is what she was, come to think of it.

And they hit Dive point and lumbered through this time; crew blacked out, and Clio was alone.

Bulkhead receded, but pressed in, belying their metal-framed certainty, and the weight of time filled the cabin, pressing against her face. The familiar heat in her stomach, slightly nauseating but swelling upward to her throat, and the chronometer clicking away, and she wanting to go to sleep with the rest of them.

Clip gripped the chair arms and blinked liquid from her eyes, trying to center her attention. Pilot. Yes, *Galactique*, and get a damn grip. Done this before, a time or two. She swiveled her chair, checking on crew, all out and skin translucent like shallow water in moonlight. Then glancing up to viewports, the time-elapse trails of the migrating stars coursed across the viewports, and the chronometer screen scrolled and scrolled, a thousand years and now eleven hundred. Going to be sick. Threw up once a long time ago, but never again, most Dive pilots made *that* mistake only once, with every event in hypercolor and sensual display.

Ran a systems check. OK, feeling better, deal with the ship. Your job. Watch the boards and pilot when called upon, evasive maneuvers as needed, as, say, any galactic matter larger than a basketball.

Perspiration rolled down her face and torso, med reaction, maybe, but also nervous, by God. Ship faltered into Dive, too much mass, and mass narrows the Dive point, crimps the perimeters. So the ship squeaked through—but arrogant bastards, to cut it this close, scrape the paint off but no dents. Too damn close. On a science mission, don't need forty-six cabins, don't need a crew lounge, an observation deck, spacious officers' quarters. Trying hard not to, then giving in to the thought: an astral *Titanic*, where the everyday power of the universe can flick a wrist and send your glittering ship to the bottom of the cold, deep sea.

But, steady, old girl. Clio patted the boards like the old Dodge Caravan that refused to die, thanks to Petya's jurryrigging, patted the $280 billion *Galactique* on the nose, and said out loud, "We'll make it, old girl."

And then, called up visual on the heat-exchanger system, checked it out, and then checked it again. So Clio worked the boards, displaying ship's systems, and crosschecking coordinates, and feeling the old exhilaration, the wind in her hair, the sun on her back, like a bike ride down the longest hill in the universe. And how long ago was it she had lain in the Issaquah Quarry barracks and thought she would never fly again? Seven days, or eight, counting as the bird flies, thirty-four thousand years as the ship flies, and now she was back here in the pilot's chair, as though this were the only real life, and all the rest mere side trips.

Ran systems checks again, and, with seventy-two sleeping crew and passengers, kept the eerie bridge company until the chronometer came to a standstill. And as the bridge crew stirred, the Niang system's young, hot star hove into view dead ahead: a diadem pulsing with what might have been turquoise as Clio lost consciousness.

Dreaming of Earth. Lovely green rolling hills, all mowed and smooth. Real oaks here and there shading white headstones. Clio walked through the lovely green, with tiger lilies in her hand, and stood before Mother's grave. Mother sat at her desk piled high with papers and bills, smoking a cigarette, while one still lay smoldering in the ashtray. Clio set the flowers in the vase on the desk. Mother looked up and said gently, "I told you not to bury me." Clio tried to say, *I couldn't be there, I'm sorry, I'm sorry,* but the words were zeros on the breeze. Mother looked at the flowers. "Plastic," she said. Clio saw that they were. *There aren't tiger lilies anymore. The flowers were the first to go, Mom.* Her lips moved, but no voice. Mother handed her a Kleenex. "Blow," she said, and went back to her bills.

Someone offered her a drink of water. Took a sip, but no, can't drink yet. Pushed it away, flopped back down onto her bunk. Head pounding like it wanted to go nova, and room rippling around. "Jesus Godalmighty, can you kill the damn light?"

Somebody dimmed the room, sat back down on the bunk.

Best not to talk when every word hurt like passing kidney stones. This is the worst part, post-Dive, soon be over. Clio groaned and turned toward the bulkhead, wrapping her arms around her stomach, trying to keep it from taking a walk.

She slept again.

Woke up to the smell of coffee. Tried moving a leg. Then, by degrees, up on an elbow. Someone sitting in the chair next to her bed. "Why's it so damn dark in here?" Clio asked.

Lights went up. Ashe standing next to the bed. Must be Ashe. Black eyes, scar up his eyebrow, large-framed. Ashe.

"Guess you'll live," he said.

"Maybe rather not."

"I hope you don't expect me to assist at a suicide."

"Gonna die without any help. Head gonna fall off."

"Can I get you something?"

Clio moaned. He sat down on the edge of the bunk. "Lie back down," he said. "On your side."

Wasn't used to taking orders from the crew, but maybe lying down was a good idea. Felt his hands massaging her shoulders. "This will help your headache," he said, "it's something my father taught me, get the blood down from your head into your shoulders."

Not sure about this. But *did* feel good, and, Jesus, how long had it been since anybody had massaged her shoulders?

"You've been sleeping for thirteen hours." He worked on a knot under her left collarbone. "The old crate made it through Dive, and if that weren't miracle enough, looks like you made it too. Petya's been fine, spent most of the last day down in botany getting my old PC to work and then beating me at vid checkers."

Clio gave herself up to the massage. Turned to lie face-down on the bed, thinking of taking her shirt off, but can't do that, might be misunderstood. A signal all right, don't have to be Einstein to get that one.

Like the times before, when she and Keith would drive down to the potholes in his antique '79 T-Bird, 351 V8 with the mag wheels, and they would leave the radio blaring with the doors open and the Schlitz malt liquor in easy reach. And Keith might ask her if she wanted a backrub, and she'd lie down in the spiky grass, turning away from him to unbutton her blouse. Spreading it out, she'd lie on the earth and feel his hands take over her back, and pulling her jeans down, massage her everywhere. And she could remember wishing he'd just keep on working her back, so hunched up it felt like she was storing marbles under her skin, but then he'd turn her over, and pull off her 501s, and look at her while he undressed himself, knees straddled over her thighs, and at that point, the massage was more or less over. She sometimes thought how things you said were signals for things you didn't want to say, like, "Want to go down to the potholes and pop some lids?" or, "Like a backrub?" or, "I should get back," when he was finished, instead of lying there with her, maybe holding her and watching for shooting stars or satellites or space junk.

And once, a flashlight in their faces, as they sat in the T-Bird drinking beer, and what was DSDE doing out in their hideaway? And the man asked for driver's licenses and health cards and left them sitting a long time and then came back and asked what they planned to do with the beer, since it was a crime to litter, and a crime to have it in the open car, and they said they'd put it in the trunk. DSDE looked at Keith like maybe that was the wrong answer, and Keith kept saying, "sir," embarrassing Clio with his deference, but then she saw that he was shaking a little bit, and once again thought about how the beer wasn't what they were dealing with. It was about being scared, and giving DSDE the respect, the power they liked to get. And they drove off, while the black van followed them home. And when they got to her house, Keith said, in that way that didn't ask for a response, "I'll call you."

"Just relax," Timothy was saying.

"Trying to."

His large, deft hands pressed and molded her aching muscles. Found a knot, started to work on it. "You anxious about revisiting Niang?"

"No," she responded automatically.

"Can't be a pleasant memory," Ashe said.

"No. Not pleasant, but maybe beautiful." Niang, the world forest. Green, as Earth had been.

"You lost friends, I guess. That's always real hard." The knot was starting to soften up. "Sometimes, though, going back, it gives you another chance to say goodbye."

"I've said enough goodbyes."

"You going to say goodbye to Niang this time?"

She closed her eyes against these thoughts. Niang held the promise of life renewed, a new Earth. How do you say goodbye to that?

Ashe pressed on. "Must have been hard, that trip home. Did you feel betrayed by Niang then, as the ship rotted away?"

"Not how I felt. Not betrayed by Niang. Betrayed by Earth, by army, Biotime. Niang was like a wild animal on that ship, that shouldn't have been caged in the first place."

He was quiet then, and her thoughts turned to *Star-*

hawk, the science deck giving way, blowing apart, as equipment slammed toward the gaping hole to space . . .

She pulled away from him, sat up, full now of unwanted emotions, resenting him and his damn probing.

"How's your headache?" He sat quietly on the edge of the bunk, his big frame graceful, at rest, no tension anywhere.

"Headache's gone," she said. "Thanks." But what she felt was annoyance, a ripple in her stomach, asking, why does he meddle with me?

He nodded, still sitting quietly, letting the time be quiet.

Or maybe it wasn't annoyance she felt, as the ripple moved down into her groin. She wanted to touch the arrow scar above his eyebrow, and rake her hand through his thick black hair, pulled back as always into a ponytail. Small wiry white hairs escaped from the smooth rounded crown of his head. Still he watched her, a little too personal.

She put her hand on his thigh, rested it there.

His eyes narrowed, but he covered her hand with his own.

"Coffee," she said, her gaze sliding over to the cup. He reached for it, handed it to her.

She sipped at it, cold now, but it tasted good, cleared her mouth. Handed it back to him. She sat up and reached for his hair, pressing her hand against it, down to the nape of his neck, feeling its wiry profusion.

He put his hand to her head, running his warm hand over the stubble. "You have a beautiful scalp, Clio," he said.

"That's a great opener. Original." She smiled.

He pulled his hand back, set it in his lap. And somehow, in that gesture, she knew the moment had passed when he could pull her toward him. Yes, the moment had passed. He had passed on her.

She pulled back. "Hey. That's all right," she said. "Catch you some other time, maybe."

"Clio . . ." he began.

"Look, Ashe," she said. "How many missions you been

on? You got to know how bedding down works on a ship like this. Don't take it too seriously, just take your pleasure real easy, and nobody makes a big deal out of it." She swung her legs off the bunk.

"*You're* making a big deal out of it," he said quietly.

Clio stared at him.

"Yes, you are. You're hurt, and trying to toss it off. At least be straight with me."

"Well, son of a bitch. You be straight with *me*. You like me or not?"

"Sure I like you. Doesn't mean I have to use sex to prove it."

"OK, fine." Clio called up a gentle smile, one that wouldn't look too obvious. "I got it. You don't have to prove anything. OK, fine." She sprang up, headed for the sink. Ran the cold spigot and washed the sleep and frustration off her face.

Water running, she heard Ashe say, "Talking with you is like a tennis match, Clio. Why don't you say what you goddamn mean?"

That one set her off. She grabbed a towel, furiously drying her face. "You know, Ashe, you been reading too much pop psychology. You want to practice psychology, try asking yourself why sex is a number-one huge production for you. Ask yourself why you got some unnatural curiosity about my personal feelings, my past, my brother, things I don't tell *anybody*, much less some guy who doesn't tell me null about himself and who holes up in a botany lab all day reading paperbacks and playing vids and criticizing who my friends are. Ask yourself why you come in here while I'm sleeping and wait on me hand and foot, and rub my back, and then when I try to say thank you, back off double time."

"That's your way of thanking me?"

He was sitting there looking very serious, even a little sad, if that was possible under the circumstances. But with Ashe, any reaction seemed possible.

"Ashe," she said. "Just get the hell out of my quarters."

"You know," he said, standing up, "so far you seem to

have two emotions, Clio. Wary and hostile. If you have trouble getting men into your bed, you might try on a different mood."

"Get the bloody hell out of here."

But he was already on his way.

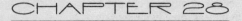

CHAPTER 28

It was eleven days out in shiptime when the *Galactique* began to stink.

Army used barracks jokes to cover their nervousness, but the crew didn't laugh. In truth, bad smells were no laughing matter aboard a spacecraft. It meant that the lithium hydroxide canisters in the air-circulation system were failing to filter not only bad smells, but carbon dioxide. Thus, while army told their potty jokes, edgy Biotime crew checked each canister, pulling up floor sections on the crew and mid-decks, and replacing each unit with a fresh canister.

Still, something wasn't working.

This shift the captain sent Clio to assist with air-circulation checks, his way of underscoring his authority and her dubious status: a pilot, but no rank. Dive pilot, by God, but no *Lieutenant* Finn. She took time to fetch Petya from botany lab and then reported to Susan Imanishi, chief engineer, in front of the access hatch to lower deck. She nodded to Imanishi. "OK. Let's go."

Imanishi looked dubiously up at Petya.

At that moment the hatch opened and Corporal Lewis of the galley wars climbed through from lower deck. Behind him, maintenance crew handing up a foot-wide electronics panel for servicing. Imanishi made way for them.

Lewis wore a head bandage.

"Nice hat," Clio said. Took Petya by the hand and shouldered past Lewis.

"You dirtbag bitch," he said, behind her.

"He called you a bad name," Petya said as they clambered through the hatch.

"Yeah, guess he doesn't like me very much."

"That's OK. He doesn't like me either."

God. Clio stopped, halfway through the hatch. "He been bothering you?"

Petya looked sideways. "Not really."

Lower deck embraced them with its snaking pipes and muttering of ship systems. Here, in ship's bowels, all pretense of human quarters dropped away and you knew for sure you were just in a metal tube with a bit of air and heat, while outside lay space, inimical space.

Imanishi's voice came in a rain-barrel fullness from further into lower deck: "Make sure he doesn't bang anything with his head."

Petya had to crouch slightly, to avoid the pipes coiling along the ceiling. He touched one of the sweaty tubes, and a slipstream of water slinked down his arm. He pulled back, shaking his hand.

"Don't touch anything," Imanishi said.

"This isn't a china shop, ease up," Clio said to her.

The hiss and sigh of hydraulics surrounded them, along with the acrid smell of oil and metal. A faint, almost imperceptible glow underlaid the dim fluorescent light peeking out from the mass of coated wires and threading pipes.

Imanishi made her way to the back floor panels, and knelt to pull them up.

"There are slug trails down here," Petya said, running his hands along the stowage panels on the outside bulkhead. He crouched down, leaning into the exposed stowage locker, throwing a shadow into Imanishi's way. She glared at him. She pressed a finger against his shoulder, pushing him away with the least possible contact. Petya sat back on his haunches while she pulled out the lithium hydroxide canisters.

The lights pulsed down and then back up. All three of them looked up from the canisters toward the ceiling where the wire-covered bulbs burned. Pulses like that weren't good, meant a power surge, and that shouldn't be happening. During the half-second of gloom, Clio saw an orangish phosphorescence streaking over the panels around her. Afterimage on her retina? Then, with the lights back up, she saw the canister indicator light blinking red, flashing against the wet pipes and the sheen on their faces.

"These are the major CO_2 filters. They shouldn't be anywhere near depleted," Imanishi said.

"CO_2 filters are broken?" Petya asked.

"What's it goddamn look like?" Imanishi said. She opened the readout panel on the first canister and pushed Reset, with no result.

"Reset button doesn't work?"

Imanishi looked up at Petya with a snarl in her eyes.

"Broken?" he pressed on.

Imanishi switched her glare to Clio.

Clio smiled a whatcha-gonna-do smile.

"Help me haul these things upstairs," the engineer said. "We're going to open these babies up and see what's the trouble."

Petya nodded, and hoisted both canisters on his shoulders.

"I can help fix these?" Petya asked.

"And pigs can fly?" Imanishi responded in cruel imitation.

As Petya grabbed for a ladder rung, the lights dipped again. On the canister closest to Clio, a lambent orange fingerprint winked at her briefly before the lights surged back.

Petya helped Imanishi get the canisters down to science deck, then rejoined Clio outside the galley. Here the regular crew played poker, Lewis dealing again, poor bastard. Petya wandered in to watch, while Clio headed up to crew deck, taking the ladder two at a time. She sauntered down crew deck toward Lewis' cabin, waiting for a moment when it might be clear of people. The moment came. She slipped into his cabin, slapping the cabin lights off, and stood there a moment. Blackness and nothingness. Nothing but the amoebas on her retinas. No strange glow, no orange filaments left their marks here. She moved carefully toward the cabin drawers, opened one at a time, stirred up the contents slightly, finding nothing but the dark room with its darker shadows. In a bottom drawer under some clothes, a few magazines: girlie stuff, she imagined. She slipped back out, with the hallway full of crew, and no one seeming to notice her coming out of the wrong cabin. Lewis was just a hunch. Wrong hunch, it seemed.

Meg Voris was waiting outside Clio's cabin. "What took you so long, Clio?"

"Captain wanted me to swab out the latrine."

Voris cocked her head, followed Clio into her cabin.

Clio disappeared into the hygiene station, taking the last pee she'd get until the lander run-through was executed. Ran the cold water and splashed her face and head, now with a two-week growth of hair. Looked better bald, by God. But cheeks filling in a bit, maybe not so cadaverous, as she force-fed herself on the tuby glue that Biotime called food.

From the main cabin, she heard Voris say, "Just saw Licht bullying Petya down in the galley, Clio."

Clio appeared in the doorway of the head. "Son of a bitch," she said.

Voris winced.

Clio strode to the door.

"Where you going?"

"To rescue Petya. Think you can handle that?"

"Why don't you stay here, Clio. Maybe *I* can talk to Licht. Sometimes all it takes is a third party—a dispassionate outsider."

Clio's eyes were flat. "Thanks, but then I wouldn't get the satisfaction of wiping his ass with his ears."

Voris let out a sigh. "Clio, you're not that bad." She looked at Clio as though part of her hoped Clio *was* that bad, so she'd have someone to work on.

"Or how about this," Clio said. "You go tell Licht he's wanted in officer's mess."

Voris' thick eyebrows closed together. "That'd be a lie."

"No, I'm *telling* you, Licht is wanted for a senior staff meeting in officer's mess, ASAP."

Voris flicked her eyes left, calculating.

"Think how Petya's suffering at the hands of evil, Voris."

Evil. That was a word she perked up for.

"OK." Voris shuffled to the door. Turned. "Licht will just end up mad."

"Well, nothing's perfect."

Five minutes later Clio led Petya through the hatchway into launch bay, with Voris behind, protesting.

Clio spun on her. "Look, he's coming along on maneuvers."

Voris shook her head. "Captain won't like that. Petya's not authorized."

"This is the launch bay," Petya said. "Landing pod launches from here?" He put his hand over his mouth as his voice boomed back to him in the vacant, metallic bay.

"Look, Voris. I'm stretching orders a bit. I'm making a point to Hocking, to Tandy and the rest. Licht's terrorizing a passenger on this ship. That's wrong, and nobody seems to give a damn. What's more important here, justice or the rules?"

Voris chewed on that a moment. "The rules," she answered. "On a starship, it's the rules."

"OK, right. Important rules are more important than minor injustices. But this isn't an important rule." Clio took Petya by the arm, headed for the lander hatchway.

Voris keyed in the hatch release, and the lander door slowly clanked open. "I don't know," she was saying.

Clio urged Petya through the hatch. "Come on, Petya. We're going for a ride."

He examined a hatch bolt closely, sliding it in and out. "A ride?"

"Right," Clio said. A gentle nudge to his back, and he climbed through. "Is that OK?"

"A-OK," he said, head swiveling to take in the lander interior. He ambled over to the navigation panel, which surged now with electronic life.

"I don't know about this," Voris muttered.

"Voris, you ever gonna put your ass on the line for anything? You ever gonna deal with real people and their problems or you always gonna bore people shitless with your Church philosophy and waste trees by leaving those damn pamphlets everywhere?"

Voris strapped in, mouth clamped thin.

Clio helped Petya buckle up, then found her own chair. She toggled the mike. "This is *Sun Spot*, powering up and prepping for undock, you copy?" Lights popped up amber on the autopilot board, as Clio activated the flight controls.

"Hey." Voris swept Clio's hands off the board. "You're supposed to watch."

"Copy, *Sun Spot*," came over comm, "you are cleared for undock. Disengage when ready."

Voris separated the lander from the *Galactique* and moved them off in a slow burn of the small lander engines. She swung *Sun Spot*'s main thrusters away from the mother ship and throttled up slowly, kicking them safely out of the *Galactique*'s environs. Out the starboard viewport Clio could see Niang, a small green dot the size of a dime glowing bravely against the starry galactic backdrop.

She spun her chair around to smile at Petya. He was watching Voris raptly. Then she opened a channel to the main navigation station. "Commander Singh, this is Finn, over."

"Yes, Ms. Finn."

"Can you patch me through to Colonel Tandy? A favor."

A pause. "I can do this," he said.

Then: "Colonel Tandy here."

"This is Finn, Tandy. I got a good mind to call our deal off."

"Where are you?"

"I'm in the lander on maneuvers with Lieutenant Voris. I just rescued Petya from our favorite sadist. Thought you said you were going to take care of that."

"I thought I had. I don't directly control Licht. You know that. I'm not pleased to hear he's been up to his old tricks."

"Yeah, he's just a tricky fellow, all right."

A longish pause. "What do you want me to do?"

"Whatever it takes, Tandy. You have power. Use it. May cost you something; but whatever it takes, do it."

"All right, Clio, I'm going to spend some chits on this one. Just remember, we don't always control the things we'd like to control."

"Bullshit."

He broke contact.

"That's not the kind of language we use," she heard Petya saying softly, behind her from the passenger seat.

"We're going to execute a slow one-eighty," Voris said, turning back to business.

Clio sat back fuming, watching Voris go through her lessons. *We don't control things*. Goddamn but Tandy had his little sayings that sometimes had the ring of truth. Brought Petya on board to protect him, ended up putting him in DSDE's path, ended up giving DSDE a hostage so they could jerk her around at will. Ended up blowing it. Again. She put her hand to her forehead, trying to massage out the spike planted dead center.

Two hours later, when Voris considered Clio checked out on the lander craft, they redocked. Clio took Petya in tow and headed for Tandy's quarters.

"Hey, Clio," Voris said as they secured the hatch to loading bay. "You did good."

"Gee, thanks."

Voris beamed.

In front of Tandy's door, Lieutenant Ryerson stood guard, and opened it for Clio and Petya as they approached. "Madam," he said. A gentle mocking. Let it pass.

Tandy was standing at the windows, hands clasped behind his back. "I'm glad you brought Petya," he said.

"You promised to do something about Licht."

"Petya," Tandy said, "do you play checkers?"

"I play checkers."

"Good!" Tandy slapped his hands together, strode to the computer. Called up the checkers program. "Go ahead." He swiveled the chair for Petya to sit.

Petya hesitated by the door. Clio nodded to him, which got him moving, but slowly. At last in front of the computer, he towered over Tandy. Sat down.

"I can do level two?" Petya said.

"Fine." Tandy punched in the change, then took another chair to sit nearby.

"You're not going to ignore this, Tandy."

He waved her into silence. Watched Petya make his opening moves. Tandy turned to face Clio. "You're off duty. Care for a drink?"

"Yes."

Tandy made them each a stiff drink of scotch. "Not regulation aboard a ship, but rank has its privileges."

"Its vices."

"Perhaps. Petya," Tandy said, turning back to the game, "how do you like being on the *Galactique* so far?"

"This is a nice ship?"

"I think that it is. How do you like being on board?"

Petya was silent a long time, just playing checkers. "I like it," he said, finally.

Tandy looked over at Clio, raised an eyebrow. "How is everybody treating you?"

"When you're an officer, people have to mind you?"

Tandy scratched his chin. "You could say that."

Petya hit the keys, moving ahead of the computer, moving toward a win. "Do I have to mind the officers?"

"Like who?"

"Like Licht?"

"He's not an officer."

"Not an officer?" Petya watched without emotion as the computer took three of his checker pieces.

"No."

"I don't have to mind people if they're not officers?"

"You don't have to mind Licht."

Petya's face flickered with the silvery light of the screen. "Niang," he said, "has blue trees? Chlorophyll works different there?"

"You won't be going down to the planet, Petya."

"I have to stay here?"

"You need to help take care of *Galactique* while some of the army troops are gone."

"I get to stay here."

"Any problems with that?"

Petya punched up another game. "A-OK," he said.

Tandy left Petya to his game and walked over to seat himself across from Clio.

"Nothing like leading questions, Tandy," she said.

"Then *you* ask him, Clio." He waited a beat. "You are assuming that Petya is in trouble. Not true. It is true that he's being harassed. But not true that it's an untenable situation for him." He took a long sip on his drink, regarding her. "You're rescuing again."

Clio slapped her glass down and jumped to her feet. "Goddamn it, Tandy, who are you to say what bothers him and what doesn't, you in your cushy officer's quarters?"

"Ask him."

Clio looked over at Petya, deep into his game. "He's not a stone."

"I didn't say he was a stone. I'm saying you're over-reacting. Just what Licht wants you to do."

The air went out of Clio's next comment. She sank back down on the sofa. "Son of a bitch." Then: "Why does he hate me so much?"

"Licht?" Tandy fixed her with his gaze. "I had him checked out. Jared Licht has a score to settle with you."

Clio nodded. "I killed a DSDE gangster eleven years ago during a raid on my family. It's old news."

"The man you killed that night was his father."

Clio stared at him. Jesus. Always did know how to make enemies. "A man like Licht actually had a father, huh?"

"Yes. And he'd still have one if it wasn't for you."

"Guess the event must have twisted the poor guy. Used to teach watercoloring to nuns. Now he's a raging sadist?"

Tandy smiled and shook his head, slowly. "You can be tough, Clio."

"Guess I'm just twisted. Like him."

"Worthy adversaries, perhaps."

Clio shrugged. A rivulet of sweat coursed down her left side, under her arm.

"Nothing you can't handle, I'm sure." Tandy emptied the last of his drink. "Ignore Licht's forays against Petya, and pretty soon he'll just come directly after you." He smiled a small, ironic smile. "Just what you'd prefer, I imagine."

"You're just trying to weasel out of our deal."

His hands went up, facing out. "I said I'd keep Petya happy. I have." Tandy got up, poured himself another drink, leaning against the credenza. "Or is it *me* you want to fight with?"

"Jesus Christ. Why is everybody always trying to psychoanalyze me?"

Tandy smiled, completely relaxed now, damn him. "Maybe because you make such a fascinating study."

Clio watched Petya as he tapped at the keyboard. All those things she thought she would never feel again, never *wanted* to feel again, all of them clamored up her throat as she watched her brother playing checkers. Rage, sadness, love, fear. All that stuff that could snare you, blow your cover, give people a handle to jack you around. Licht had that handle. Been waiting to use it these eleven years.

She draped her arm on the side table, looked down at the picture of Tandy's wife, as the cabin lights blinked out, then on. She met his eyes, and he shrugged.

She looked down at the framed photo again and he noted her gaze. "I used to be like you, Clio. Looking for a fight." His voice was as soft as a fog in the room. "She taught me there were other things to do with my life, other ways to feel. Never did figure out why she took me on. I was bright and scrappy and brittle as an iced-over puddle. And she loved me. I don't think it was pity, although, God knows, it could have been. She was in her life in a certain way that's hard to describe . . . like she was living it a little deeper than most people. Maybe she knew she had to experience things fully the first few times, because there wouldn't be many times for her. Do you think people know these things? Anyway, I began to live that way, not like her, not that—exquisitely—but a fuller way. Still picked my fights in the world, but fights worth winning." He focused back on Clio.

"How did she die?"

"Badly. It was an assassination attempt on me. Old Greens, making some statement about army, the government, some pointless cause. The car blew up. But it was Suzanne in it, not me."

Clio stared at the floor. "I'm sorry."

Petya had turned from the computer and was listening to this story. Said: "You could fix the car?"

Tandy looked over at him. "No. Couldn't fix the car."

"It was broken?"

"Yes."

"But the car didn't matter?"

Tandy's lips started to move, stopped. After a moment he got up from the couch and made himself another drink. Brought it to the observation windows, watching the starry far horizons. Niang's sister planet commanded the upper left quadrant of Tandy's sweeping view. A bauble of ice, glistening with the reflected vibrancy of the system's hot blue star.

Clio sat for a time, thinking about Tandy's story, her own troubles forgotten. Then: "We'll be going, Colonel." She stood up, hesitating when he took no notice of her. "Thanks for telling me." She moved to the door.

"Come back sometime, Clio," he said.

She turned back. "I will."

Tandy tossed off the last of his scotch and poured himself another as Clio and Petya quietly shut the door.

Niang turned beneath them, filling the crew lounge viewports. The planet's single great continent moved underneath them in serene parade, a long, unbroken world forest of blue-green, interrupted by an island-spattered ocean, and then jungle again.

Several crew were gathered at the lounge viewport, gaping at the immense continent Gaia with its botanic cloak, the cloak now known to be inimical to metal and therefore to human civilization. Clio stood with them, rubbing her upper arm, tattooed with enough antiviral shots to keep a rhino healthy in a quarry.

"You been there, huh?" one of the techs said to Clio.

Clio swiveled to stare at the young man a moment. Thinking he meany *quarry*. Then she noted his gaze out the viewport. "Yeah," she answered.

"What's it like? Down in that jungle?"

An image came to her of the deep forest, with brush strokes of turquoise watercolor steeped across the canvas in ever-darkening shades, of the tall, leaning, frondy trees and the smells of candied resins. . . . Clio opened her mouth to say something, ended up saying, "Too many goddamn trees. If you're not on the ground mission, just be glad."

The tech nodded. "Something awful about that much wilderness. Like it would crush you."

"It would eat up the *Galactique* as a snack," Clio said, "Spit *you* out though."

The tech laughed, with the others.

Clio smiled. "Spit us *all* out. Just eats metal." Clio found a couch near the viewport and propped her feet on the table, on top of a pile of Voris' pamphlets. Then, reflected in the viewport glass, she saw Timothy Ashe stroll into the lounge. When he sat next to her she made a stab at ignoring him. Two and a half months on board the same spaceship had not made her easy with the man yet. She maintained her gaze out the viewport.

"The planet of the nasty Nians," Ashe said. Placed his feet on the table next to hers. "You getting your courage up to hit the battlefield running?" He spoke low enough to keep their conversation confidential, as other crew played vids, or read magazines.

Clio ran her hand through her hair.

"Nice hair, but I liked you bald. Something sexy about it."

"Thanks. I think." Droll as she knew how.

"Welcome." He kicked her foot gently with his own. "The colonel working himself into a lather about the Niang war games?"

"I wouldn't know."

"Sure you would. Spend a bit of time up there with him, ought to know if he's in a lather or not."

"You jealous where I spend my time?"

"Maybe. Maybe I'm finally ready to take you up on your overture."

A twist in her gut, even though she knew he was needling her. "Get fucked, Ashe."

He raised his good eyebrow. "Always lead with your chin?"

Clio took a deep, secret breath. The man wasn't worth it. She looked back out the viewport, watching the top of a thunderstorm crawl over the great sea. What was it crew started calling Niang, first time they saw it up close, the first time? Eden. The fecund and unblemished verdancy of Earth, an innocent Earth, before the Fall. But how long had it taken the crew to throw aside human conventions of morality and charity? How long before the men were strutting with their hunting weapons and the women were vying for the sexual attentions of the leader? Three weeks, maybe four. Whatever innocence the Niang forest had, it ended when *Starhawk*'s crew set foot in it.

"Ever read any hostage stories?" Ashe asked.

Clio gave up on trying to get some private time.

"You know, stories of people, of women, who are kidnapped and held for a length of time?"

Clio shrugged.

"It's a psychological tendency."

"What is?"

"For women to fall in love with their captors."

"Yeah. We just love to be abused. Lock us in our bedrooms, beat the shit out of us. A turn-on."

"Why is that, do you suppose?"

"It's just the perennial woman's struggle to keep a man in performance mode. Throw in a little equality, a little affection, they go limp."

Ashe was smiling hugely. Something about that damn smile, like he couldn't keep himself from laughing about things, even if he was trying to be irritating and even if she was being snotty as hell. His presence next to her made the tips of her fingers zing as though tiny amounts of electricity were escaping from her body. She wiped her hands on the thighs of her flight suit.

"You find yourself attracted to Tandy," he said. "But you can't admit it to yourself. Because he's army, and you have those old grudges."

"It just eats at you doesn't it?"

Ashe turned, looked at her. Black eyes deep as the grudges he knew she held. Then a big smile moved across his face. "Sure I'm jealous. If I thought all it took to get you in bed was slapping you around a bit, I wouldn't have to get into these excruciating talks with you. Most men'd walk a mile to avoid a conversation like this." He was quiet a moment. Then: "So do you love him?"

"Don't be stupid."

"Tandy *is* using you, you know. And he *is* enjoying having power over you. His assignment was to bring you back from death, from the quarry, and make you want to fly again. Now that you're here, you don't owe him. You don't owe him gratitude, you don't owe him friendship or sex or love. Because the moment you agreed to Dive, he got what he wanted. Anything else is extra, and you decide what and how much to give. With eyes wide open, Clio." He took her chin in his hand and turned her face around to look at him. "Wide open."

Clio started to fling some remark back at him. Found that her lips parted only slightly and no words.

She sat for a moment, fuming, then sprang up and went to the nearest vid, threw in a game disk, Dormitory Raid, and concentrated on racking up hits. Just as she approached the record score, a Klaxon screamed to life, toning out a general alarm. Clio pushed the chair back, jammed into the corridor where the thudding of crew racing for stations joined the din of the Klaxons. She turned to run for the bridge, her emergency station, and ran flat into Jared Licht, blocking her way.

"Get out of my damn way."

Alarm subsided, but no all-clear, and Licht was still standing there.

"Allow me to be the first to ask, Miss Finn, how you've been getting along with Jackson Tandy lately." He grasped her upper arm. It hurt.

"None of your business."

"Soon will be. There's been a murder on board."

Clio's heart threw in an extra beat. "Murder? Who?"

He smiled. "Hoping it's not someone you're feuding with? So do I, Clio. Could tend to make you look bad."

"You're not saying Tandy's been murdered?"

"No, not Tandy. His aide, Ryerson. But likely an attempt on the colonel's life, and foiled by Lieutenant Ryerson." He watched her face, enjoying the expressions that must have flitted over it. "So where've you been, last six hours, Finn?"

Licht gazed over her shoulder, face brightening.

She turned around: Ashe was just moving out of the crew lounge.

"Well," Licht said, "that could be a convenient alibi, if you two were keeping each other warm during last sleep period. That right, Ashe?"

Ashe shrugged. "You want information on my sex life, Licht, you'll have to use your usual means. Peepholes, isn't it?"

"That's one of my *means*, Ashe. Others involve two parties, Q and A, back and forth. An interactive means." Licht turned back to Clio. "I love people who give me a run for my money. Most people are so timid around me."

Clio yanked her arm away. Backed off from him. "I'm due on bridge, though I would love to chat." She bolted down the corridor. Hit the ladder running, slid down to the mid-decks holding the outer poles of the ladder, and scrambled up to the bridge, just in time to see two army grunts waiting for her to emerge from the hatch so they could descend, chair-carrying a sheeted body, and here and there spatters of blood. No mistake.

Clio emerged onto the bridge where the other flight officers, except Hocking, were already at stations.

Singh looked up at her, very serious he was. Voris in pilot's chair, looking pumped up enough to peddle a couple times around Niang.

Clio sat, waiting for Voris to launch into it.

"You don't want to look down the corridor," Voris said. Then, silently formed with her mouth, the word *blood*, and shivered. "Somebody got to him with a knife." She drew her hand across her throat. "Must have been somebody he knew, because no way to sneak up on anybody in that corridor, and Ryerson was on guard outside Tandy's quarters, that's what I figure." She looked at Clio, her eyes glistening and dark. "He had *three* children. Can you imagine how his wife is going to feel, and now she won't even get to bury him. Haven't you noticed at funerals, when there isn't a body—say somebody's lost on a mission—and then planetside you attend the funeral? How sad that is?"

"Yeah, I noticed that. Have they got any suspects?"

"I don't know. Hocking's down there with security, and Jared's involved in the investigation. I was on duty."

"Who found him?"

"Colonel Tandy." Voris fished in her pocket, pulled out the remains of a package of Tums, peeled back the wrapper, and popped one in her mouth. As she sucked on the mint she patted her stomach. "It just makes me sick to think of it." She leaned in toward Clio. "And what's worse, we've got a murderer on board this ship. Somebody we know, very likely somebody we know, Clio." Her eyes, big as a child's at a horror movie.

"Yeah. Maybe *you*, Voris."

"Clio! Don't say things like that. We can't start distrusting each other."

"We can't? Somebody just got their throat cut. Not in an army brawl, but in a lonely corridor during third sleep period. And maybe could have been two murders, if Ryerson wasn't the target. So me, I'm going to watch my backside."

"You mean they were after the colonel?"

"If Ryerson was standing guard at his door, what do you think?"

Voris peeled off another Tums. "How do you think of these things, Clio?"

"How do you not think of them?"

"I just don't automatically think the worst of people."

"Yeah. Give our murderer the benefit of the doubt. Just a lonely son of a bitch roaming the corridors looking for somebody to knife. Jesus, Voris."

"You shouldn't say 'Jesus.' "

"Are you sure you weren't hit by a truck when you were little?"

"You can be mean, Clio."

"Just think me of as an addled Dive pilot who had a few too many trips, one too many starships blow up with her aboard, few too many little blue tabs." The sight of Voris' incredulous face inspired her to add: "Forced into indentured service aboard the *Galactique*, with brother as hostage should she jump for freedom."

Voris broke the gaze between them. "You'll never forgive, will you, Clio?"

"I can forgive. But the bastards keep doing it. You're not asking for forgiveness, you're asking for galactic stupidity." Voris started to say something, but Clio grabbed her sleeve, forcing her to look at her. "You want to believe the world is a nice place where evil is a little weed that can be kept in check. Open your eyes, kid. Space Recon is corrupt down to its toes, and DSDE is the twenty-first century's Third Reich. You refuse to see this shit, then you're helping keep it alive, and your goody-two-shoes act is as full of crap as I am." Clio pushed Voris away and remembered to breathe. Shit. Really out of control, girl. She shut her eyes, trying to push back the surge in her belly.

"Turzilla to bridge, over." On headphones.

"Go ahead." From Singh.

"Crew decks in order and at stations, sir." The deck officers were reporting status.

"You will stand by."

"Yessir, acknowledge."

Voris stared ahead, sucking on her mint. "You don't think much of me," she said, off mike.

Then, on mike: "Lee reporting." The science officer confirming status on science deck. "All present and accounted for, commander."

"Acknowledged. Stand by, Lieutenant."

Voris' face darkened by the moment.

Clio took some pity on those big brown eyes. "Look, Voris. You got a soft spot: this religion of yours. It's a target on a ship full of bored, jittery crew. You chose it. If it's so goddamn important to be liked and fit in, find a football team to go nuts over. Easier for crew to understand and easier to take the knocks. Otherwise, toughen up and get on with things." Clio looked at her unmoving face. "You get what I'm saying?" Trying to say it nice.

Hocking was standing there, hadn't seen him.

"Finn. You're wanted in officers' mess."

Clio swung her chair to face him. Hocking's nose was loaded up with sweat, glistening like a frozen waterfall.

"Yessir." She followed him down corridor to the mess. Just beyond, army forensics scavenging for clues around Tandy's cabin door.

In the officers' mess Tandy and Licht broke off what they were saying as she and Hocking walked in. Tandy was seated at a table in the center of the cabin. To one side, a couch with table and magazines. Behind him, the mess counters and a large refrigeration hatch. He nodded curtly, and gestured her to sit opposite him and the captain, who now took his place next to Tandy. Behind him was Jared Licht, leaning against the mess counter, arms scissored together in front of him. Jesus. Looked like it was an investigation for sure, and guess they were starting with her.

"So where were you last few hours, Finn?" Licht asked without preamble. As he leaned forward to hurl his question, Clio could see that a band of sweat limned his brow, making his face unnaturally bright under the close mess lights.

Hocking shifted in his seat, interrupting. "No one's accusing you, Finn, you understand that? We're only trying to gather as much information as we can." Licht settled back against the counter, in a pose hardly less threatening for being relaxed. Hocking continued, "You know the gist of what happened?"

"Lieutenant Voris told me that Lieutenant Ryerson was murdered, sir."

The captain scowled. "Yes, a knife to his throat. That much every crew member on this ship has heard by now. Anything else you know that sheds light on the murder?"

"Nosir."

"Anyone you know with a grudge against Lieutenant Ryerson or Colonel Tandy?"

Timothy Ashe briefly flitted into her mind. *Definitely doesn't like Tandy, but murder?* "Nosir," she said.

Hocking drummed his fingers on the table, still scowling. He looked over at Tandy, who had been inspecting his coffee cup, and now swirled the last of it, watching the contents.

Licht asked, as easily as a warm knife through butter, "You've got no love of army. They came after the *Starhawk*, came after you and your crewmates in the Amazon. That right?"

For a split second Clio considered denying it, denying everything. Then heard herself saying, "Maybe." Had nothing to hide. Maybe try honesty for a change.

Licht cocked his head. "Care to elaborate?"

"All you bastards are in on this. Think I'd pick you off one by one? If I was going to do *that*, I'd have started with you, Licht."

"Now see here," Hocking said.

"Yes, start with me, baby," Licht said. A crumpled smile inhabited his face.

"See here," Hocking repeated, louder. "Let me ask you directly, Finn. Did you kill Lieutenant Ryerson?"

"Nosir."

"Or know of anyone who did?"

"Nosir."

"Can you account for your whereabouts last sleep period?"

Jesus. *Was* she a suspect? "Class-E science vessel, *Galactique*. Sir."

Tandy's eyes flicked up. Scolding her.

She added, "My quarters, reading magazines, then crew lounge for a couple hours. With Timothy Ashe, ship botanist, for part of the time."

"Not a very convincing alibi if you two are . . . sweethearts, or whatever," Licht said.

The captain dabbed at the bridge of his nose with a handkerchief, where instantly sweat reappeared. He was powerless over DSDE. Perhaps not technically, since he was ship's captain, but looking to his long-range interests, Wendall Hocking would not be one to offend DSDE.

Licht threw in, "What about your retard brother? He's got an unfortunate tendency to shoot people in the face when he gets mad, doesn't he? Or was that you, Clio, killed that agent, back on Mama's farm?"

He watched her, unblinking, unmoving. Neither of them breathed. Finally a twitch appeared on Clio's face instead of the smile that she had planned. "Keep your claws out of my brother, Licht," she said. "Wanna know who I think killed Lieutenant Ryerson out in that corridor? Probably was you, Licht. Only so many times you can read the Uniform Drug and Social Enforcement Code on a six-month tour of duty where no one will talk to you before you go space-crazy."

Licht shrugged. "*You're* the experienced murderer, Clio. You and your brother. This investigation will have a hard time forgetting that."

You'll never forget, you bastard, she thought.

Then Tandy rose, fixing Licht with a dark gaze. "If we're done accusing each other, perhaps we can have a serious discussion about our situation," he said. Hocking, who by now had run out of stock phrases and was helplessly watching Clio and Licht trade insults, looked hopefully to Tandy.

"Sorry, sir," Clio said.

Tandy walked to the coffee spigot, filled his cup, turned around to face them. "I wanted Clio brought here, not to accuse her, but to include her in our discussion." Tandy eyed Captain Hocking, then Licht, in turn. "Clio's got to know what we're up against. In Dive she's got to be fully prepared, since she's the only one awake. Or is she?"

Clio's eyebrow went up on that one.

He sipped at his coffee for a moment. "I propose to set aside for the moment *who* killed Lieutenant Ryerson and ask ourselves instead *what* killed him."

Clio watched him in startled silence as did everyone else.

"Let's ask ourselves what possible motive exists in this murder." A stab of a smile jabbed at his mouth, and disappeared. "Let's postulate that Ryerson was killed in order to access my quarters, where it is my custom to sleep during third sleep period. This much we've already surmised. But why would someone want to kill me? Personal vendetta?" Here he looked at Clio, and shook his head. "I don't think so. Let's look at what is really at stake here: a mission to retrieve the most important technology since nuclear weapons. FTL. Someone wanted me dead in order to weaken our military mission. Someone or *something* wanted me dead. Gentlemen, we have a Nianist spy on board."

"Nonsense," Hocking said. "We're all human, surely. You're not trying to say we have an alien life-form aboard the *Galactique*?"

"I'm saying it's possible, yes, If not a Nian, someone in their pay." Tandy looked at Hocking until Hocking broke the gaze.

Hocking scowled at the table. "Nonsense."

Licht pushed himself up to a seated position on the counter top, dangling his legs. "From what I've heard, they don't need knives to take out their prey."

Tandy pointed his finger at Licht. "Right you are! Then why—if it *is* a Nian—why would they have killed Ryerson with a knife?"

"Cover," Clio said. "They didn't want to blow their cover."

"And right again," Tandy said, eyes gleaming. "We've already had two assaults against this mission. One in the landing bay at Vanda. The other when Chief Engineer Ritters was murdered, Earthside. As his replacement, Susan

Imanishi might be worth checking into. However, that would be too obvious. And if we consider the possibility of sabotage with the air-circulation failures, it's clear the mission is under attack."

Hocking said, "Perhaps from . . . one of our people . . . in the pay of the Nians?"

"Yes," Tandy acknowledged. "Perhaps someone in their pay. If any of us can imagine being in the pay of an alien threat to Earth and this vessel."

"If it *is* a Nian, who's to say they even look human?" Clio asked.

"They might very well," Licht said. "We already know their morphology is humanlike." He noted her confusion. "Their ship, from the configuration of living quarters and seats, is built for humanoid creatures. No little green men or what have you."

Tandy nodded. "Exactly. I believe it's very possible that our Nianist—or traitor—will strike again on this ship, or will infiltrate into our ranks for the ground mission. He—or it—may target me and the other officers, or, in league with cohorts on Niang, undermine our mission from within. But it will strike again, and against our most vulnerable and key operations. And it will do so secretly, for as long as it can. Bear in mind that there may be more than one."

Licht had perked up. "Who's to say we aren't riddled with these aliens?"

A trickle of sweat left Captain Hocking's nose and dripped into his lap.

"Not practical," Tandy said. "Think of the difficulty of penetrating this crew list. Crew and army contingent did not volunteer. They are an extremely select group, known to their officers or Biotime for years. To position yourself for selection to the *Galactique* would take years, and even then is a matter of chance. Same for my select infantry unit. No raw recruits here. All personally known by me or my officers. If someone has managed to infiltrate us, they've taken years to set up."

Licht said: "With Dive, they might have planted themselves in Biotime or army a decade ago, worked their way into position slowly. Could have quite a lot of them, hoping that one of them would succeed in making the team."

Tandy looked at Licht with new interest. "Yes . . . a determined, patient foe."

"We must warn the crew," Hocking said.

"Ah, sir . . ." Clio said.

Hocking looked up at her.

"Sir, begging your pardon, but you tell a bunch of stressed-out spacers in this rabbit warren of a rig that we got an alien looking to cut up his next human and you're gonna set off a panic. Not pretty on a ship two million years out from port."

Tandy raised an eyebrow at the captain.

"That may be a point," Hocking said.

"Alert the officers, captain," Tandy said. "Tell them everything we surmise and tell them to be watchful over everyone. Meanwhile we will continue our preparations for the ground mission."

They dismissed Clio. Back on the bridge, her thoughts in a stew, she tuned out Voris' chatter, trying to lose herself in routines of systems checks. Meanwhile, one by one, the crew from first and second shift traipsed up from mid-decks to the officers' mess for questioning.

When she was nearly punchy from lack of sleep, Singh excused her, and she went to check on Petya before hitting her bunk.

Day after tomorrow was ground mission. Not ready, by God. Mission was under sabotage, rotten from within. Crazy to go ahead, but Tandy would never turn back, that much was clear. Mission was going sour, just like the last time. Niang will make you nuts . . . Jesus, girl, got to get some sleep.

But first, she ducked into botany—no sign of Ashe— and sat with Petya while as he took apart the mechanism on a power-distribution switch.

His patient, methodical probing with the computer lead calmed her nerves and she began to breathe again, relaxing. Though they hadn't said a word to each other, she felt this time together with a sweetness from the old days, when she would watch Petya in fascination as he reassembled a dead alarm clock, in all its mechanical mysteries, there at the kitchen table—with the smallest screws lost in the maze of squiggles in the gold-flecked formica. Somehow to Petya, they were never lost. He reached with his big fingers and plucked each one from the table, and Clio would rest her chin in her hands and lose herself in the quiet certainty of mechanical things.

As she stood to return to her cabin, the lights surged down and back again. For a full—seemed like a years-long—second, she saw the room filled with streaks and smudges of yellow-orange phosphorescence, glowing strongest on the stack of paperbacks Timothy Ashe had been thumbing for the last seventy-five days of their voyage.

"Timothy makes smudges?" Petya remarked, turning back to the distribution switch mechanism. "They glow, when the lights go off," he said, tightening the switch plate screw with a microdriver.

SO SHALL YOU REAP

The landing-pod hatches clanged shut and the sound of locking bolts reverberated through the hull as *Sun Spot* prepared to disengage from the ship, now orbiting 320 kilometers above the planet.

"Acknowledge, *Galactique*," Voris said, and rested her hand just above the onboard computer's firing key. She looked over at Clio. "Ready?" Like they were heading down a hill on a toboggan.

"Yeah, hit it," Clio said.

Voris engaged the thrusters to move out from the *Galactique*. Immediately behind Clio and Voris sat Colonel Tandy; his second-in-command, Captain Pequot; and six Biotime crew, including Timothy Ashe. Behind them, forty-two army special unit fighting men and women huddled in the transport section, clutching their duffels and assorted weapons.

"Somebody forgot my parachute," one of them said.

Then another, "Yeah, and the sandwiches your mother packed."

"Too bad she couldn't smuggle them out of the state pen, Reiner."

Voris hit the main engines and *Sun Spot* dropped away from the ship in a fast deorbit burn toward Niang's atmosphere.

"Whooee!" someone said from the back. "My stomach feel like it flew up to the ceiling. And stuck, you know?"

"Man, you so full of antibiotics and orals you don't *got* a stomach no more."

"That why I been shitting bricks?"

Ship rumbled like a hundred skate boards clattered over the hull.

"We are in communications blackout," Voris said. They were in entry interface, with heat building up outside to 1500 degrees centigrade and ionization blocking all communications for a few minutes. The acrid smell of passengers crowded in too tight and scared despite their jokes, came to Clio's nostrils. *Pushing it*, she thought. The mission is pushing it, too damn many passengers. Maybe not so many on the return trip. The thought made her stomach clench up worse than it already was, watching Voris— merely a kid by Biotime standards—pilot the lander. Thinking of Timothy Ashe sitting among them: possibly ship's saboteur, and possibly something else as well, something too ugly to think about, maybe too ugly to believe. The sheer unbelievability of it must have been what kept her from alerting Tandy that Ashe's skin left a strange residue that traced him to the hold of the ship where he had no business, no *loyal* business, being.

Voris switched to aerocontrols and executed banking maneuvers to control the descent, and they were headed in for landing in Niang's central plateau region. The heads-up display over the viewport projected *Sun Spot*'s speed and altitude, and Voris piloted by instrumentation and sight, moving down across the blue forest in a steep glidepath, finally zeroing in on the old *Babyhawk* clearing, until now invisible in the jungle mass. Finally positioning *Sun Spot* for the landing burn, she executed a flawless touchdown with a soft bump of the landing struts.

"Contact," Voris said.

As they lined up for debarking through the plastic quarantine airlock, Clio found herself standing next to Ashe. He began to crouch down to exit through the outer hatch, when he noticed her looking at him. He stopped in midcrouch. Looked at her as people do when you fix them with an overlit stare, and a small frown of curiosity flicked across his face—which he would have pursued had it not been his turn to cycle through. By the time Clio came out and held the flap for Lieutenant Imanishi behind her, the moment had gone and he sauntered off toward the circle of crew gathered around Colonel Tandy.

Tandy had decided to occupy the old *Starhawk* camp. The clearing was the only one near enough to the alien ship, and big enough. Therefore, as Clio and the ground-mission crew emerged from the airlock they were greeted with the cast-off remains of the *Starhawk* mission, as well as the press of Niang's atmosphere, like the sweaty hand of a mother pushing a fevered child back into bed on a hot summer day.

Despite the 1.1 g and the tropical heat, the most pervasive impression Niang made was the overpowering sugary aroma that hit your nostrils like a cotton-candy tent at a county fair, and settled on your skin in a microscopic layer of stickiness. Clio was instantly drenched in sweat, her upper arms clinging to her breasts and pulling away with a slight gluey rip as she moved.

Forty kilometers away on all sides of their position, the soaring trees of Niang huddled together, leaning into the clearing as though straining to hear Tandy's words as he issued orders. Behind the front line of trees, the noise of the jungle ruptured the air with the billion screaming creatures of the woods, each with a voice, and each caught, it seemed, in midsentence by the gross entrance of *Sun Spot* and its stalky, two-legged occupants.

A buzz crackled in the air as the advance unit tested the new perimeter wire, strung up along the old perimeter posts, and now re-forming the nervewire first defense against the hostile Nians and unlucky flying insects that seemed attracted to their doom.

Clio surveyed the ruins of the old mission. Mess tent, hygiene stall, med tent, and botany tent partially collapsed, semibiotized struts jutting out like broken bones, and the thready remains of yellow nylon tenting, fluttering in the mild Niang wind like November leaves.

The cleanup army team struck the old tents, piling usable items in the compound's center: those things not stolen or broken by the Niang monkeys or Teeg, if he still lived.

Ashe crossed the compound to stand beside Clio. "Daydreaming?" he asked.

Clio sidled a fraction of an inch farther away from him. "No."

"Must be a tough time for you."

Clio looked into his face. The scar bisecting his right eyebrow pointed to his cranium as though trying to tell her something, lead her to something.

"Where'd you get the scar?"

Ashe looked carefully at her, puzzled, maybe. "Hit with one of my brothers' skis when I was twelve."

Clio looked away from the dark eyes, wondering how she could have found him appealing.

"Something wrong, Clio?"

She punched up a smile. "Just trying to keep my mind off some bad memories."

Across the yard, Captain Pequot emerged from the newly erected command tent and gestured at them.

"We're wanted," Clio said. Ashe's eyes had flattened suddenly, taking on a serious cast. He followed her across the compound, just behind her. Outside Tandy's tent, Ashe said in a low voice, "I need to talk to you, Clio."

They entered the command tent where Tandy's officers waited around a small table with a light suspended above it, creating a pool of illumination, where now Tandy was leaning forward searching a map stretched out before them.

He looked up as they entered. "Ah, Clio. Ashe." He stood upright, surveying the group, and beckoning Clio and Ashe forward. "Since we're all here, then." He took in the others in a slow sweep of his gaze. There was Pequot, second in command, and a Lieutenant Ginny McCrae. On Biotime's side, Voris, Imanishi, and the assistant engineer Randy Ellis, and Robert Richardson on astronomy. Finally, Ashe on botany and Clio.

"We set out as soon as it's full light tomorrow," Tandy began. "Finn, you've located, in as near a guess as you can, the probable location of the ship." He pointed to the topo map, and a red X. Ashe moved closer to the table, elbowing in slightly to see where Tandy pointed, then withdrew to the relative shadow surrounding the map. Clio noticed that he touched nothing.

Tandy went on: "We will penetrate the jungle directly opposite the new med tent and stay together as one unit, with half the escort in front and half in back of the science team. In case of attack, the fighting unit will surround the civilians and assume a defensive posture of three hundred sixty degrees. No matter which direction the initial assault originates from." He looked to his officers.

McCrae nodded and leaned forward, hand on table, other hand pointing. "This is reportedly thick vegetation, sir. If we hit it with scatter shell first, we could deprive them of cover from the outset."

Tandy shook his head. "No. Deprive *us* of cover as well. Furthermore, and more importantly, we do not have the exact location of the ship and there is danger of damage."

"I agree," Imanishi said, stepping close to the flood of light. "We don't know how delicate this mechanism is that we'll have to deengineer."

Pequot fixed her with a hard stare. "This is a military mission, Lieutenant. You'll have nothing to decode if they rip out our throats before we find the ship."

"That was my point, Captain," Imanishi said.

Tandy held up his hands, calling for quiet. "We each have our job to do. Let's each do what we do best. Imanishi, we'll be counting on you more than anyone to determine what mechanism and programs to retrieve from the alien ship. Richardson, you'll ID those star charts, especially if they're too fragile to remove from the ship." He looked up at Pequot. "Your job is to see that she and Ellis get there in one piece. That's priority one. Priority two is getting the FTL out of there and safely back to the compound." Turning to Ashe, he said, "Your job, Ashe, is to help Imanishi. This ship has been sitting in the jungle a long time. Finn tells us its metal parts are decaying rapidly. You'll help the engineering staff in systems ID, separating biologicals from mechanicals."

Clio spoke up: "It's not decay, sir. It's more of a replacement. A botanical replacement of metal."

Tandy glanced at her. "Yes. Metal to leaf and vine. Exactly. Hell of an ID problem. Which are ship's systems, which are Niang overgrowths. It's all coming to the same thing in this jungle. That's why you're along, Ashe."

From the deep shadows, a deeper voice responded, "Yessir."

"Voris," Tandy added, "you're in camp. Stay alert for the need for emergency evacuation."

Voris nodded bleakly.

Tandy turned to Clio. "Finn, your job is to lead us to the ship. Retrace your steps. For this reason, you'll be in radio contact with Lieutenant McCrae on point. You'll travel in mid ranks with the crew."

Clio nodded. She looked at the topo map and thought how clean and orderly maps always were, how unlike where they'd be, how utterly unlike.

The meeting broke up, and Clio started to follow the group out the tent flap, then at the last moment turned back to Tandy, who still stood looking down at the map.

"Colonel. Could I speak with you a moment?"

He looked up, nodded. Tandy was leaning forward, both hands pressed on the table, his shoulders tilted slightly forward, allowing the light to catch his colonel's bars. Clio squinted against the slicing light.

Tandy was waiting. "Yes, Clio?"

Clio stumbled past her preplanned opening. "About the Nian, sir, among us."

Tandy's eyes snapped alert.

"He could pick us off on the trail."

"If he's among our retrieval team, you mean?"

"Yessir."

"Do you think he *is* among our team?"

Clio heard herself say, "Nosir."

"But you're *afraid* he is? Or she?"

"Yessir."

Tandy stood up, out of the light, rubbing his eyes. "Is that something that you or I have control of, Clio?"

Clio shook her head, slowly, feeling sick.

"Then we will do our best to react swiftly and skillfully should that prove to be the case." A brief smile. "Won't we." He went back to his perusal of the map.

"Yessir." Clio's voice came small and weak from the part of her throat that was not swollen shut. "Thank you, sir."

When she made no move to leave, Tandy looked up again, this time, with a piercing gaze. The exhaustion of the last twenty-four hours showed in the circles under his eyes, accentuated by the glare of the overhead light. "What is it, Clio?" he asked.

"If the Nians oppose this mission," she said, "wouldn't their best ploy have been to kill the Dive pilot? To try to kill me, not you? The mission can't get home without a Dive pilot."

Tandy walked around to her side of the table, leaned against it. Spoke softly: "I've been wondering the same thing, Clio."

Something about the way he said that. Clio tried to clear her thoughts, tried to figure out what to do, to say. Tried to figure out what the hell was going on. Then a slow crawl of nausea up the front of her body, like a slimy creature reaching for her throat. Jesus God. Tandy suspected *her*. She opened her mouth to protest, shut it, realizing that the guilty always protest their innocence.

Tandy broke the silence. "Why do you suppose we traveled secretly, leaving the quarry? We expected attempts on your life." He pushed away from the table, came up to her, searching her eyes with his own. "But not a one, Clio. Not a one."

"Why sir?"

"I don't know. It appears that you are of value to them in some way."

"Value?"

"Can you think why that might be?"

Clio swallowed, but no saliva left. Mouth like glue. "Nosir."

Tandy shrugged, moved back to the map, then glanced

around at her. "I think you can rest easy now, Clio," he said. "If they were going to threaten your life, they would have by now. But don't let your guard down. And neither will I."

"Yessir," she said. Nodded to him with a head too full of thoughts, like a water balloon, all wobbly and ready to crash to the floor.

She left him standing there in the tent, staggered into the hot blue light of midafternoon Niang.

At the compound's edge, armed infantry patrolled along the perimeter wires, their attention as watchful inside the camp as outside. At intervals the special-unit forces had set up cells where small artillery emplacements were prepared for a concerted attack from the jungle.

Ashe, who had been watching for her outside the mess tent, met Clio halfway across the camp.

"You don't look well, Clio," he said, all his attention focused on her.

Clio made her way to the hygiene tent, where she might have an excuse to be alone. She stopped for a moment outside the privy. "Tell me something, Ashe."

He watched her, waiting.

"Is this whole mission as crazy to you as it is to me?"

"It always has been crazy to me, Clio." Very serious he was, black eyes drawing her in.

"Does it figure that the enemy, whoever they are, would kill off the two previous missions, keeping folks away from this stupid ship, like some galactic game of King of the Hill? If they don't want us to find their FTL drive, why don't they just destroy it?"

"If it was me, it's what I'd do," he said, expressionless.

"If it was you."

"Yeah, I would."

She looked him square in the face. "I don't owe you anything, Ashe."

His eyebrows closed in on a frown. "No, I never thought you did. But you think you owe *army*? What'd you ever get from army but murder, death, and loss?"

"What's this mission headed for out there, Ashe?" She nodded at the leaning forest. "Murder, death, loss? Isn't that right? What I end up with, either way." She backed away from him. "Keep this in mind, Ashe: I'm gonna be watching you. I don't like your attitude. You got a real bad attitude. Colonel might like to know about that."

"Colonel's watching you, too, Clio. Just be careful."

"He needs me to get home. I don't worry about army."

"Worry. You worry, Clio. Tandy doesn't need you to get home."

That got her attention.

"Think about it, Clio. They can head that big slop bucket into Dive and coast home, hoping like hell they don't run into anything. Maybe nine chances in ten they'll be lucky. Pretty good odds. Odds they'd rather not take, maybe. But don't assume Tandy needs you. He's a ruthless pragmatist. A side you've never seen, maybe, or have you had glimpses, now and then?"

She pushed past him. "Get out of my way."

He stepped back, and she entered the privy, where the familiar stench held some comfort against the candied press of Niang air and the sudden confusion and reversals of the three-month ride from Earth, where she'd been just as miserable as now but at least certain of who was who.

She braced her elbows on her knees and held her head, trying to find peace in the darkness of the palms of her hands.

The mission team wound into the jungle. Through the cloud cover, bluish light leaked into the undergrowth, a slow sedimentation, barely reaching their boots. Slick trunks of the trees emitted the sticky-sweetness that clung to their nostrils and fatigues. As wet as they were from humidity and sweat, they barely took notice when a slight drizzle began, cascading from layer to layer of the canopy above them, splattering on the undergrowth silently, drowned out by the depths of chittering, screaming jungle voices.

When possible, they walked double to shorten their exposed flanks, but usually it was not possible, with the undergrowth pressing on both sides of the path they beat before themselves.

In three positions along their line, they carried the pulse guns, shoulder-launching artillery that could lay down a quick burn on either side of its main discharge. The remainder of the unit wore visors on infrared with peripheral enhancers, and carried their weapons slung at half ready on shoulder straps. The science team was unarmed, to Clio's chagrin. Leave the fighting to army, Tandy said.

He walked a few paces behind of her, speaking, by his head movements, to Captain Pequot, but silently, over headphones. Her own channel crackled. "We'll bear to the left here, Clio, is that your sense?"

"Yessir. In this vicinity." In truth, the terrain was all the same, and the plants in their endless variety had a sameness too, with their strange fleshiness and tubular shoots probing the mission team's flanks, perhaps drawn to their warmth.

Tandy turned to acknowledge her. A turquoise glint off his visor substituted for eye contact.

They had been trekking for nearly an hour when, down the line, one of the soldiers swiveled and drew down on a swaying vine. The hairy ropes hung from the canopy in masses, like the long roots of lily pads where, above, their flowers might unfold in the true light. The soldier moved on, twitching now and then at his too-keen peripheral vision.

Another crackle on the headphones. "A Niang monkey on the right. No, three, several, stacked on a vine." It was Ashe. "They've seen us now, and I think they've frozen. Yes. Harmless." No need to point them out. Two pulse guns were trained on the hairy, spiderlike herbivores, finally panned away. The line continued its march. In the center clump of mission specialists, Clio was followed by Imanishi and her assistant, then the astronomer Richardson, with Ashe tending toward the rear, his big frame easy to pick out though everyone wore camouflage fatigues and visor helmets. She looked back from time to time, and he seemed often to be watching her, perhaps even as Tandy watched her, and as the soldiers seemed to watch them all, hands upon their rifles.

Clio loosened her shirt, tied it halter-style around her midriff, inviting a breeze. A deeper rattling on the canopy announced heavy rain. It washed over them in a blur of light and water, forcing Clio to tuck in her shirt again, and sending chilling trickles down her pants.

"Damn rain," Imanishi said, off mike. "Can you see anything?"

"We won't see anything," Clio said. "If they come, we'll just hear them."

"I can't hear a damn thing," Imanishi said. "Not a damn thing."

"They can probably hear *you* just fine," Clio said.

Imanishi looked over at her, lifting her chin to peer at Clio from under her visor.

"Directional sound amplifiers," Clio said. "If *we've* got them, I'm sure *they* do."

"Shut up back there," over the earphones.

Clio's right boot was leaking, filling her sock with the warm recycled water of her tread. Wished to goddamn hell the other one leaked too, even them up, as they slogged on and on through endless forest.

Off to the side, on a bush with a full head of tubular stalks, a small creature with a face like a plate balanced on the end of one of the stalks, which teetered up and down as the rain struck. The creature cocked its head at her, looking surprised. As she passed, she noted that it was being devoured from behind by the open, sucking ends of a tube leaf.

A rifle shot thudded and the line ahead fell into a crouch.

"Down!" somebody yelled

Clio scrambled to get her body low, slipped on a woody tendril, regained her footing, as other shots sluiced through the wetness. "Our fire, our fire," Pequot yelled. "Hold your fire until you sight a target."

Several moments passed and nothing, then, "A goddamn bandanna," someone said on mike.

The lead grunt with the pulse rifle waved a red kerchief from the barrel of the gun, where it flopped soggily like a piece of raw liver. "It's a bandanna, ripped to shreds, but its one of ours," Lieutenant McCrae said, on mike.

"A warning?" This from Pequot.

A garbled pulse of static from the front of the line.

"Say again, McCrae?"

The static squawked and faded, squawked again. Clio heard, ". . . on a bush. Can't say for sure."

"Front and rear guard, pull skkkkkkskkk," managed to emerge from the earphones before they exploded with noise. Clio couldn't tell if it was the earphones or the drumming of rain on her visor hat, but sounds flooded together in a common deluge of noise, momentarily camouflaging the gunfire that now erupted unmistakably in the rear of the column, joined by screams.

Somehow Clio found herself splayed out on her stomach with a mouthful of mud, as someone behind her shoved into her and pushed her chin along the muddy side of a small torrent running next to the path.

"Oh my God," Clio heard, thinking it was her own voice until she saw Richardson next to her, huddled into the small of her back. "Oh my God." A ball of light rolled before their eyes as a pulse weapon lobbed a molten missile off to their right. Amid the roaring of the vegetation, burning and hissing in the rain, she heard Pequot cry, "Cease fire! Sir, I think they've fallen back." And Tandy responding, "Close ranks!"

Tandy was dragging her by her elbow up from the ditch. "Are you all right?" Clio was covered in mud, almost the color of blood.

"Yessir, fine."

Pequot shouted, "Radios are out, sir. We've lost contact with the rear of the line. Front ranks are closed in and we took some hits." Sheets of rain swept over them, blurring the world.

Tandy released Clio's arm, turned toward the captain. "They'll be repositioning now that they've drawn out our fire. Establish a perimeter around that tree," he ordered.

Pointed to a massive tube tree fifteen meters out from their position.

Tandy helped her up and they ran for the tree, as a tight unit of three soldiers laid down cover fire. When they were halfway across the small clearing, the main attack hit.

One moment Clio was running in sync with Tandy; the next, she was falling backward and, impossibly, upward in a strangely quiet explosion. Then she was falling, a long fall down, landing on her shoulders and back of her head, deaf and paralyzed. For a few moments she could smell burnt sugar, as when long ago she'd left the fudge pan on the hot stove all night. She opened her eyes to see a peach-colored smoke slide across her face, then gagged and passed out.

When she opened her eyes, a face was pressed close to hers. "Clio. Can you hear?"

She could, barely, through the torrential rain. But couldn't tell where the respective parts of her body were. As she moved those respective parts she guessed that she was lying on a hill, head pointing down.

"Can you move your feet?" It was Ashe. He was whispering to her.

"Yeah."

"Let's see."

Clio moved them.

"Try again."

Moved them again, she figured.

"OK, I'm going to move you a little. Don't cry out, they're nearby."

She bit on the insides of her cheeks. Around her, gunfire in regular doses, and the awful smoke scraping at her chest.

"We're going to make our way to that rock outcropping. Lean on me." An explosion threw them to the ground again, and her ears faded out. The jungle lit up with a fluorescent glare, showing a split-second image of a dozen soldiers moving in a wave some twenty meters from them. Tight caps on their heads and vests studded with light. The dimness returned. The jungle roared. Thunder, she realized, as the braying of the storm repeated itself, then receded into the forest depths.

He helped Clio to stand and she swayed against him, struggling to clear her head.

"It's just over here," Ashe said.

"Over where?"

Clio held her hand in front of her as though to part the curtain of water now lashing down on them.

"I can't see."

"Hold on to my arm."

She gripped him tightly and struggled to find footing, then found herself roughly pulled to the ground. Ashe put his hand over her mouth, whispering, "Hush." Then she saw the boots and legs of someone creeping by in the fog. Clio stifled a cough, freezing against Ashe's side. As the boots disappeared into the murk she noticed they were regulation army. "One of ours," she whispered, then knew it for a damn stupid comment, doubting now that Ashe ever saw U.S. Army as one of *his*.

Then they were leaning, panting, against sharp rock. Again, the jungle brightened and reverberated to an eruption of thunder. Clio hid her face in her arms against the rock, burying her body from the sheer noise of this storm, which seemed to be trapped within the jungle canopy itself. As the thunder rolled away, gunfire continued, off down the hill. She could see nothing except Ashe's arm, pulled tight around her shoulders.

"Let's move behind the rock," Ashe said. He guided her up a slope and behind the outcropping. The smoke thinned. Wisps slid by like miniature cirrus clouds. They leaned against the stone face where the rain eased its pummeling. A flood of water swirled past their boots and on down the hillside. They crouched down, backs against the rock. Clio closed her stinging eyes.

When she opened them she saw an apparition. The figure stood some ten paces away, fading in and out behind the smoky curtain, torn by the rain. Armed and bearded. The apparition had seen them. Was, in fact, aiming its weapon directly at them.

"Oh God," Clio moaned. Then, bitterly, to Ashe: "One of your friends?"

"One of *yours*?" he responded.

The figure moved toward them, coming into focus. The grimy fatigues, headband, and tattered vest gave him the look of a street bum. Except he was armed with a rifle.

Clio looked into his blue stare, and down the length of the rifle, and knew him. "Harper Teeg," she said.

He cocked the rifle. "Welcome home, baby."

CHAPTER 30

❧

Torchlight flickered off the passageway walls as Teeg herded them into the sudden silence and darkness of the underground cave. From above, a muffled turbulence reached them. Clio's wet fatigues now clung to her like a lifeless, cold second skin. She shivered. The breath of decay on the tunnel's breezes wafted to meet them.

"OK, stop," commanded Teeg. He circled around them, holding both rifle and torch, making him maybe a good target, but Clio passed on it. Size him up first. He thrust the torch close to Clio's face. Peered closely. "It's you all right!" He spun around once in front of them. "Damn, if it isn't you!" His voice surrounded them, as though disembodied. The smile left his face as he shoved the torch now into Ashe's face. "And who's this son of a bitch?" He surged closer. "Eh?"

"He's a crew member. Got lost with me in the battle. Name's Ashe."

"Ashe-trash. 'Bout right for a name, Ashe. Ashes to ashes and dust to dust!" He shoved the torch back at Clio. "Don't try to distract me!" He jerked her arm, pushing her ahead of him down the corridor. Something chittered at them from the ceiling. Teeg purred a fair imitation back at the thing. "Left!" he commanded when the passage bisected, and they felt the floor slope down, and saw in the strobing firelight the passage widen and widen again until they entered a space where the firelight fell away to blackness.

"Know why I knew you'd come back?" Teeg started to giggle. "Know why?" He shoved at her with the odd-looking rifle.

"No, tell me why you knew I'd come back, Teeg." The cavern was warmer than the corridor had been, and Clio's teeth stopped chipping away at each other.

Ashe leaned in. "He's crazy. I'll find a way to overpower him."

"No talking!" Teeg swung the torch in an arc at them. Bits of flame and smoke flew away to the upper reaches of the cave. "What was I saying?" His foot came up and hammered Clio in the stomach, sending her flying backward to land on her back, hard. "Don't try to confuse me!" he screamed. "I'm too smart for you, for you and your tricks!" He advanced on her, then pivoted in an instant as Ashe lunged from the side. A shot rang out from the rifle and its echoes filled the space into a thousand recesses. Ashe stood frozen, like a cave bear, swaying from side to side. Then he staggered back, holding his left arm.

"Bull's-eye!" shrieked Teeg. "Got ya!" He danced in front of Ashe, waving the rifle.

Ashe fell to his knees, lowering his head as though he would topple. Blood soaked his sleeve in a dark, expanding blotch.

"Ashe . . ." Clio began.

"Ashe-trash-crash!" Teeg intoned.

Clio moved toward Ashe.

"Leave him! Nobody move, or I'll take out the trash!" Teeg was moving into raging hysteria, jumping and swaying before them.

"You got him, Teeg," Clio said. "That's enough."

"*I'll* decide what's enough, woman."

"Right. You decide, Teeg."

He stood in front of them, glancing from Ashe to Clio and back again. Then he pointed the rifle into the dark. "Move," he said.

Ashe slowly rose, cradling his limp arm. He moved to Clio's side and they trudged forward into the darkness. Ashe was quiet and Clio made no move to help him, unsure whether she wanted to help him, or could.

"Can't get the jump on old Teeg, no," Teeg was muttering. "No, and those that tries, dies."

Clio moved to steer him off that course of thought. "You were saying how you knew I'd come back . . . how'd you know that?"

"Keep moving," he said. "Because you never left, that's why."

"I never left?"

"I see you in the cave, oh you've been around. I got eyes don't I?"

"Tell me about it, Teeg."

"Later!" The rifle in the back, and they hurried their pace, now making their way down a reeking corridor that lightened perceptibly, turning to grayish murk.

Clio felt something run over her foot. "Rats," she said.

"Rats?" He giggled from deep in his belly. "You'd *wish* they were rats, if you had to sleep with them, like I do. All in good time, all in good time."

The stench of sewage rose up to meet them. Teeg's own wastes, no doubt—perhaps beyond smelling from his standpoint. Clio stole a look at Ashe as the corridor lightened further and a freshening breeze announced the cave entrance. Ashe's face was set in a deep scowl of pain. The shirtsleeve looked wetter and redder than before, although it might have been the brightening light around them as they now approached the burning entrance to the cave. She squinted hard against the white hot sun, which was rapidly drying the sandy ledge before the great cave.

"Teeg," Clio said. "I'm real cold. You got any clothes?"

Teeg doused the torch in the soil of the cave floor. Rummaged in a pile, watching them off and on. Found a man's fatigue jacket, brought it over to her, and helped her on with it, one arm at a time. "Button it up to the top," he said, "or you'll catch cold." He sat down on a ledge near the cave wall. "You don't want to catch cold. No. That's what happened to Liu, caught a cold, and ffffft, gone."

Half of Teeg's face was lit by the light from the entrance. On the half that she could see, rain or spittle hung from his beard, and his eye trembled in its socket like a trapped critter. Here was the formerly handsome Harper Teeg, once the copilot of the pride of Biotime, the *Starhawk*.

"You been hiding out a long time, Teeg," Clio said. "You must be pretty lonely here, all by yourself."

"All by myself! Hah!" He rocked back and forth on his ledge, drawing his knees up to his chest with the rifle cradled next to him. "Got my critters, don't I? Got my Voo Doo men. Got you."

"You almost came home with me, that time. You could have come home with the crew," Clio said.

Clio and Ashe sat in the center of the cave anteroom. The noon sun now parted the storm clouds and sliced off the blackness of the cave at the entrance. "You could still come home," she said.

"This is home. Land that I love, God bless New Merica, my home sweet home. Could have been your home sweet home, the plans I had. Now going to be different." He tugged on his beard. "Way different." He sprang up. "You," gesturing at Ashe, "get over there." Ashe followed his pointing, into the corner.

Teeg ordered Clio into the opposite side of the cave and made her lie face down. He tied her right foot with a rope attached to the wall.

He patted her foot. "Payback time, Clio. Payback time." He settled back onto his ledge.

"Can't you see, Teeg, it's *you* that turned against us. Not me. You said this was Paradise, and we should all stay. But most had families, and wanted to go home."

"Home sweet home." He swung the rifle toward Ashe. "I see you over there. Trying to hide. I know you're planning to escape, so I think I'll just kill you now."

"Teeg!" Clio said. "Don't punish him for what I did. He's just a man like you, working for Biotime, just like you used to. Hasn't figured out all the things you've figured out. But you can teach him."

He kept the rifle aimed at Ashe. "So who are you, Ashe-trash?"

"I'm a man like you." Ashe was resting his back

against the wall, and facing the cave entrance, his face merely a blur in the faint haze of light.

"You in love with Clio Finn, here?" Teeg cocked his head. "Don't lie to me!"

A pause from the back wall. "Yes."

Clio's heart sank. Wrong answer. Competition for Teeg. "Teeg . . ." she began.

"Shut up! She lead you on like she did me?"

"She confused me. Maybe that was my fault."

"You're a pussy." Teeg scrambled to his feet. "Meowww." He advanced on Ashe with the rifle. "You don't have what it takes to live in New Merica." He stood over Ashe, pointing the rifle. "Lie on your face, so I can tie you up."

"Teeg, I'm cold," Clio said. "Starting to shake."

He ignored her. "Lie on your face."

Ashe slowly did so. Teeg raised the butt of the rifle and brought it down on Ashe's head. "Till I decide what to do," Teeg said. Placed a solid kick into Ashe's side. He lay unmoving.

Teeg unlooped a coil of thin-gauge rope hooked to his belt and tied Ashe up. "If they come," he said, "I'll be ready. Got plenty of ammo, especially because I'm a hot shot. Hot shot. You remember, Clio?"

"I remember."

He unhooked her rope from the wall and tugged on it. "Come on, we're going for a little walk." He tugged on it again. "Here, doggy, doggy." He lit the torch with a match. Shook the matches in her face. "All the comforts of home, see?" He held the torch in one hand, rifle in the other, and pushed her into the cave recess, with the ankle rope trailing behind her.

"If they come for my treasure, they'll have to get past old hot shot."

"You call this cave a treasure, Teeg? I call it dark and cold."

"You cold? Wait here." He turned back, poked through his pile. Brought her a reeking blanket. She draped it over her shoulders, gripping it in readiness to douse his torch.

"There are secrets in this cave, Clio. Secrets the Voo Doos are after, and now the army comes looking." He giggled. "I outsmarted them. They won't find it, no sir, won't find it."

"Who's the Voo Doos, Teeg?"

"The ones you been fighting out there. The ones that want the same thing you do. The ones that kill with their hands." He prodded her with the rifle butt, and she stumbled on. "They all want their Faster Than Light."

Clio kept moving, barely breathing.

"Same as you, you all want your Faster Than Light."

"Yeah, we all want it, I guess." The light from the cave entrance leaked away as they moved deeper. Now the passage walls wavered with torchlight.

"Me, I don't care," he continued. "You know why I like it? I like it 'cause it's pretty." He giggled. "Ain't that a kick? All the powers of the universe come looking, and it's my freeping objet d'art!" That sent him into a long streak of giggling, coming up from his chest.

They were in the big cavern again.

"Over here," Teeg said. His voice came to her as though from a great distance, from someone else. He tugged on the rope and Clio staggered to follow. Somewhere a moan of wind, and then a shattering cold airstream sluiced over her legs. Teeg dragged her toward a dreadful sighing of what surely must be a wraith roaming in the deepest cave domains. Finally, as an exhalation of ice slapped into Clio's face, Teeg ordered, "Stop here. Kneel," he said.

Clio went down onto her knees.

Teeg had laid down the torch, which now flickered wildly in the moaning breeze. She felt him press a fist-sized rock into her hand.

"Toss it," he commanded.

"Where?"

"Into the crack!" he said, grabbing her hand and swinging it forward. The rock sailed out toward a line of shadow darker than the rest, blacker than the mere black of the great cave.

Then nothing.

After a few moments, Teeg said. "Hear that?"

"No."

"No! Of course you don't, you cow! Know what this is? The deepest crack in the world, that's what! Goes down so far, all the way to hell! Throw a torch down, it burns to a crisp before it hits bottom, that's what! Critters know better than to come near here, Teeg knows better!" He yanked on her rope, and they backed away. "I call that the Hell Crack. Don't ever be coming in here without me, Clio." Teeg's voice sounded almost tender.

"I won't." *Unless it's to push you in, you slime.*

They shuffled through the blackness with the sputtering torch illuminating only their faces. Clio's feet resisted walking on a ground she couldn't see, with crevasses nearby. But she moved on, prodded by Teeg, just behind her.

The torch burned lower now, its pungent smoke catching the firelight in a hazy nimbus around them.

"Here," Teeg said. He fixed the torch in the cave wall. In the dimness Clio saw a thin stream of intense white light. Then another.

Before her on a ledge lay a short array of sparkling lights, ignited from the coals of the torch. At first it seemed to Clio that she looked on a book with a jewel-studded cover; some treasure of buried knowledge, bedecked with the embellishments of a secret priesthood. As her eyes adjusted in the cooling light, she saw that it was more common and more strange than this. It was a circuit board. A computer circuit board, flat as a wafer, and, at intervals, clustered with clear fragments of glass, crystal, or diamond.

"My treasure," Teeg said. He ran his fingers over the board in a light stroke. "Treasure," he repeated, turning back to Clio, half his face glowing from the torch. "Look! Go ahead and look!" he shouted.

"I see it, Teeg."

"Yes, yes," he giggled, "now you're in on it, sin on it, been on it."

"So it's pretty. You want to tell me what it is?"

His voice dropped the giggle, became eerily normal. "Weren't you listening, Clio?"

"Trying to listen."

"Good for you. This is the treasure, the FTL treasure you all are busting your asses to find, that you won't find, 'cause it's buried, see?"

Clio took a breath, let it out real slow. "This circuit board is the FTL hardware from the ship?"

"Bingo."

"You sure?"

Teeg slapped her so hard she reeled backward. He lunged for her, pulled her by her jacket close to his face, and releasing, with his words, a fetid miasma. "Don't contradict me, woman." He pulled her to her feet. Clio measured the strength of his grip, weighing her chances. "I won't be hitting you unless you make me mad. Toe the line, Clio. You got to learn to toe the line." Clio rubbed the hot welt on her cheek.

"I'll tell you, but not because you asked. I was going to tell you anyway, now that we're together again. How I know about the FTL? I caught me a Voo Doo man, first time they came around my caves. They looked for him, snooped everywhere, but they never found him. I buried his body way back in, because I didn't want him rising up again. Sometimes he does anyway, glowing. . . ." Teeg swiveled to look off to the side. Took another torch from the wall and lit it from the embers of the first one.

In the explosion of light, Clio saw the unmistakable planes of crystal embedded in the circuit board.

"I had to hurt him real bad, and for a long time, but he finally told me they were looking for their crashed ship, which I knew where it was, see? And I took him there, secret, and when he showed me the FTL hardware, I pulled it. Took his rifle, too, the kind Niana doesn't eat. I shouldn't have killed him after everything he went through and the promises I made. But he wasn't human. He didn't count.

"That's enough for now," Teeg said. He spun her around and herded her back through the cavern. "I didn't really want to leave Ashe-trash alone out there, but you had to see the treasure. Now that you've seen it, you can't ever leave. This was your initiation, Clio. Now you're New

Merican, like me." He giggled, joined by ricocheting voices, giggling too. "Bet you wish you hadn't seen it, don't you?"

Something pulled at her rope, a critter scampering after the trailing cord.

"Oh, it's you again!" Teeg feinted toward the creature, stomping on Clio's rope in the process. She stumbled. "I didn't give you permission to hassle her yet. You need permission." He spun around, screaming at the ether. "You need—you all need, permission!"

As Teeg turned to address his creatures, Clio pulled again on the knot around her ankle, as she had done repeatedly. It was loosening.

Ashe was sitting up when they returned to the first cave. Clio bent down next to him. "How are you doing?"

"Well enough," Ashe answered. But his face was as pale as Teeg's.

Teeg fastened the torch and returned to stand in front of them. "This guy's a pussy," he said. He was frowning and nodding.

Clio sidled closer to Ashe.

"Move away from him, Clio."

"No." She huddled close to Ashe, bringing her hand down to her ankle, ready to slip the rope off.

"Oh, you're going to get punished for this. You don't go against old Teeg. You'll learn that. I just got to remember to hold my temper. Now move away, Clio."

"No."

Teeg lunged for her leg rope, yanking it away, and as it slipped free of her ankle, he fell back, sprawling.

Clio was on him in an instant, straddling him and striking his rifle arm. The gun fell to the floor. She scrambled toward the weapon, but he threw her away from it with a thrust of his hips. From a prone position he grabbed the weapon and raised it to point at her chest while scrambling to his feet. Clio froze. Teeg swung the rifle to the left, covering Ashe in a slight sweep. But Ashe was gone. Teeg turned to sweep behind him. Ashe was standing there, already reaching down for Teeg's neck. Ashe's fingers pierced flesh, sinking deep, and then Teeg made a small thrust upward with the rifle, followed by a murderous chopping movement, pounding the rifle butt into Ashe's solar plexus.

As Ashe doubled over, Clio dove for the weapon, knocked it out of Teeg's hands, and grabbed it as it clattered to the cave floor. Teeg was backing frantically out of the cave, waving her off, as Clio aimed straight for his chest.

"You don't get to use guns!" Teeg shrieked at her. "You don't get to!"

"Stop right where you are, Teeg," she said.

Teeg was backing swiftly toward the edge of the cave lip and the river chasm below.

"Stop, Teeg!" Clio ran into the glaring sun, not realizing that Teeg took that for a hostile move.

He stepped into the thunderous air, and fell.

As Clio watched, still yelling "Stop," Ashe grabbed her from behind, pressing his arm under her chin. She dropped the rifle. He forced her to her knees while he picked up the weapon. "So that was Harper Teeg," Ashe said. "The legendary Harper Teeg."

Clio stood up, bones and flesh aching. She looked into Ashe's face, smeared with dirt, wisps of hair falling around his face. "The scar," she said, "It's not from getting hit with a ski, is it?"

"No."

A battle wound then, she thought. *Ashe has seen a few battles. Not a botanist, of course. Knew that much, goddamn it, knew that two days ago and held my tongue. Why? Stupid fool bitch.*

She walked slowly to the edge of the river canyon. Teeg was lost in the boiling white soup. She turned to face Ashe. "Now what?" she asked.

"We're abandoning this mission, Clio," he said.

"I figured that much."

She shed the heavy jacket Teeg had given her. Here in the brilliant sun, the tropical heat removed even the memory of the cave's frigid air. "We'll cross the river just upstream."

"Where are we going?"

"My camp."

"Your camp."

"It's our main tactical camp. I guess you'd call it Nian headquarters."

"What would *you* call it?"

"My camp."

"I take it you're not asking me if I want to come?"

"No." He nodded toward the cave entrance. "First we search the cave."

He motioned her forward, and they entered the dark arch of Teeg's labyrinth once more. As Ashe poked through Teeg's personal belongings, he kept a firm grip on Clio's arm; a grip like a robotic industrial vise. She knew what he searched for, and knew where it was, and kept her silence.

Ashe looked down toward the deeper black of the passageway. Then he seemed to reconsider the hopelessness of one man searching the immense reaches beyond.

After a moment of indecision, he guided her out of the cave.

Clio nodded at the rifle. "Is that to make sure I don't run?"

"No." He checked the chamber for shells. "This is for army, if they pursue us."

"Am I on the honor system, then?"

Ashe compressed his lips, struggling to say, or not to say, something. Then he put his large hand on the back of her neck and guided her—firmly, no mistake—onto the shelf of rock at the cave entrance, and then off to the right where a gradual slope of blistering rock dove from sun to shadow and into the jungle brush.

Clio scrambled over the roots and woody vines that formed the rumpled floor of the jungle. Behind her, Ashe silently urged her onward, following, to one side, the roaring path of the river. His eyes found hers glancingly, enough to point her onward, but then slid away as though he were reluctant to look at her—even, perhaps, ashamed to look at her. The rifle was slung over his bulky shoulder. He no longer threatened her with *that*, at least, but still, he had forced her into the deep shroud of the forest as his prisoner, had shown himself at last, revealed his identity as spy, enemy, liar, alien. He was all those things, all those months shipboard, yet he pretended to care for her, for Petya, and never was ashamed, never let his eyes slide away from hers in that hooded way. But now. Now that she knew him for what he was, his disguise missing, a shame of nakedness came over him. Clio snorted. A miserable thing it was, to be such a liar and only feel shame when discovered. And shook her head at these musings. Why did it matter any longer what qualities Ashe had or lacked? She was his prisoner, as she had been Teeg's a moment before. He saw her as Teeg had seen her—someone to use. Teeg's purpose was clear, but what was Ashe's purpose in this forced march? As the *Galactique*'s Dive pilot, she was worth something. So, ransom, then.

As though mimicking her sudden clarity, the forest floor now revealed a narrow path crossing theirs. They followed this new direction, down a well-trampled line of mud to the brink of the river where a giant fallen tree trunk formed a crossing. The river surged through the ravine of jungle, lashing at times against the underbelly of the tenuous bridge before them. Following the command in Ashe's quick look, Clio scrambled up onto the tree trunk. The top surface had been scraped flat to a width of nearly a meter, revealing thready turquoise fibers which now caught the overhead sun in a sparkling, hairy glow like the hide of a dew-drenched animal.

She picked her way over the river's crash and flow, feeling Ashe at her back, even as the spray whipped her fatigue pants and sent a boiling mist into her face. The crossing was the boundary of safety. Now she was in enemy country.

Ashe's voice pushed against the river's own. "Do you want to rest?"

In answer, Clio turned to the clear trail disappearing into the tangle at the end of the tree bridge and strode into the dark thicket.

An hour's silent march from the river, a nearby shout stopped Clio in midstride. Ashe moved up behind her and spoke the password, apparently, since they moved on then without further challenge until Clio could just see, through the forest web, the tops of tents camouflaged the very color of Niang.

Here at the camp perimeter they were halted again by a Nianist soldier. A trickle of light from the canopy glinted off the metal studs of his vest, which seemed, on closer inspection, to be the tips of crystals protruding. From under the snug leather cap, wisps of red hair crawled onto a pale brow. Now Clio could see that the sentry was a woman with a heavy dusting of freckles over her nose and cheeks. The woman squinted at Clio, bringing the freckles closer together, exchanging words with Ashe, odd, lilting words now and then punctuated with a word that might be English. She recognized "Clio Finn," at least. The sentry waved them through and they emerged into the harsh expanse of light filling the Nianist compound.

Within sight were close to three dozen soldiers, some carrying others, wounded, on stretchers. A tall Nian with black skin and white hair pulled back into a single braid strode up to Ashe, engaging him in a fierce, quick conversation, barely noticing Ashe's wound. His eyes darted at Clio now and then, taking her in with those forays as though she were some animal curiosity. They all stared—those that could spare a moment—gazing up from their tasks, which seemed both familiar and wrong. Some sat on the ground outside tents, holding short rifles and massaging them or probing them with bare fingers as though searching for something. Clio dropped her gaze. A human in Nian country.

They walked toward the middle of the camp, past a dense cluster of troop tents ranged around a large pavilion, flaps drawn aside to reveal a brightly lit interior. Quiet inside. But figures moving, some bent over tables. Unmistakably, a surgery.

"Stay here," he told her. He left her and disappeared inside.

Clio allowed her legs to give way beneath her, sitting heavily on the ground. Around her ranged some hundred tall, dome-shaped tents. All were bluish in tint like the one she sat near, and all shone with a rubbery wetness much like a membrane. Even in this large encampment, the jungle songs overran, as though the myriad tents housed Niang monkeys and insects. At that moment Clio would not have been much surprised if they did; her thoughts were that chaotic, the camp so filled with otherness.

In the distance, at what must have been the far edge of the compound, rose a high turquoise wall of a plateau crowned by nests of large-gauge artillery. On the right flank of the encampment, just visible, coursed a river—surely the same river, or a tributary, of the one they had crossed near the great cave.

Ashe emerged after a very long while. He now wore the Nianist military garb of studded vest over combat suit. He urged her on with his wounded arm. From its range of movement, it looked fully healed. A noise she had been ignoring for a few seconds now exploded into a major din as a small aircraft darted directly over a clearing next to the surgery tent. In an instant the craft dropped to the ground, roaring. Two crew were poised in the open hatchway and sprang out, pulling stretchers occupied by the wounded, assisted by others who raced from the surgery. The ship then jumped skyward without helicopter blades or noticeable thrusters, seemingly propelled by sheer noise.

Crewmates rushed the casualties to the med tent, except for one soldier who spasmed, arching his back and jerking. A woman in a white jumpsuit hurried to his side, knelt by him, sliding her hand into his chest up to her wrist. Clio slowed her pace, gaping at this spectacle, forgetting to walk, feeling her own chest constrict at the sight, but Ashe took her arm, firmly pulling her from the scene.

Before long they stood at the base of the great plateau, where Ashe led her to a well-worn path that curved sharply up the side of the central rock formation. At the top, the view swept out before her, away and away to the hazy rim of the world. A sweet wind flowed across her, cooling her skin and sweat-drenched hair. After the hugging forest and the press of ship's bulkheads, Clio felt a shock of exposure on this aerie, where, it seemed, Niang eagles should nest, not the fat batteries of artillery, hunkered down in rock. Her step must have faltered, since Ashe now had her elbow firmly cupped in his hand and pulled her to near the edge of the plateau.

She dug her feet in as they neared the edge.

"A starship pilot, and afraid of heights?" he asked, stealing a quick look at her.

Damn right, afraid of heights, never having been higher than the top of the shuttle gantry without being firmly enclosed in something.

"There's a shelf just down here," he said, leading her down a small culvert to a ledge, broad enough for reassurance, and covered in a spongy material that looked like it could offer some cushion.

Ashe sat and threw open his satchel, taking out slices of dried meat and fruit.

"You hungry?" he asked.

She sat down, watching him make a sandwich of dried meat and slices of a yellow gourd that might be a vegetable. He handed it to her.

As they ate, two more medical crafts flew in with wounded, piercing the camp with their landing noise, muffling the uproar of the jungle.

In the bronze light of Niang's sun, Ashe's skin took on a tawny cast, like an outdoor creature, not the lab-ensconced botanist he had pretended to be. He watched the jungle top as though seeing individual things, his eyes probing and present to the canopy which to her was all of one piece, the turquoise of endless trees, steaming in the hot sun. She shoved aside these gentle thoughts of Ashe; he was the enemy. She thought of the pictures Tandy had shown her, the carnage of rib cage and heart. The breeze chilled.

Ashe had finished his sandwich. While she worked to regain her appetite, he pulled from the satchel a small medallion on a thong. Etched into what might have been bone, a spreading tree covered the pendant. "My father gave me this," he said, rubbing his thumb over the polished surface. "I don't take it with me to your world, since it could raise questions, but I don't like being without it." He looked over at Clio, handing her the medallion, his good eyebrow raised.

Clio took it, examined the familiar-looking tree captured within the ring of bone.

"My grandfather remembered his grandfather who remembered his grandfather who knew the true stories of the Days of Change," Ashe said. "He lived to be one hundred and forty-four, one of the oldest among my people, so when he taught the stories to my father, and my father to me, we remembered truly. I remember truly. I haven't been home for many years. But my father is old. Soon his Telling will pass to me. If I'd never left, my vocation would be a Teller of the Old Trees. Instead, I'm a fighter."

Clio rubbed the bone with her thumb, bringing out the etching with the oil of her skin. From long ago came the image of flickering lightning on the plains in earliest spring and seeing in the distance, as she and Petya trudged from the school bus near Medicine Creek, the exposed bones of the mammoth ash tree in Walter Reesley's back forty. "It's the ash tree," she said. "You have ash trees."

He didn't acknowledge the comment, but continued his story as though she hadn't spoken. "During the Days of Change people had to group together in fortified cities. They learned to be self-sufficient within the city walls. Outside were the Nomatics, the gangs, holding on to the remnants of the Days of Metal. After the last of the automobiles, the Nomatics roamed and marauded with horses. Within two generations the Nomatics lost reading. They adopted war as a vocation. They forgot their humanness and where they had come from. Within the cities we forgot nothing. We had books, and what we didn't have we wrote down from memory, everyone telling what they knew. As the climate changed, it was hard to preserve books and notebooks made from paper, and recordings biotized. That's how we became Tellers."

"And how did you become murderers? Tell that story, Ashe."

He blew out a long breath through his nostrils, an angry, controlled breath. "We will fight and kill to protect ourselves, how not? Did you think your people have a patent on war?"

They were both silent for a time, then. Finally, Ashe resumed his story.

"After the Change was complete, people began the slow climb back to technology. A technology without metal. The Nomatics faded into obscurity, became agrarian, and they remembered nothing except tales of warrior glory.

"We found ourselves changing physically. Slowly, yet within a lifetime, some people saw that their bodies were changing in small ways. So we were becoming more like Niang. But we had our Telling tradition. So we decided not to forget who we had been, what the planet had been. Because after a while the children didn't know what raspberries were, or potatoes. Or a pine tree. And this grieved the parents who remembered. And then each family vowed to Tell one piece, and many chose the trees because they missed these most of all."

Clio took the offered canteen, confused by this talk of pine trees and raspberries and Days of Change. She remembered to swallow. Niang water was cool and citrusy.

"After a thousand years we had caught up and surpassed the knowledge of the Days of Metal, far surpassed. Our science grew from chemistry and biology and bioengineering, out of necessity. Nothing else was compatible with Niang flora. But we still Tell of the Old Trees."

Clio laid the amulet on the moss between them. "Is there so little beauty, then, in your changed world, that you need to remember the . . . old things this way?" She thought of the omnipresent turquoise, the tubular themes in branch and leaf, the soaking sweet resins.

He looked at her in some surprise. Then looked out over the forest canopy. "No beauty? No, Clio, Niang *is* our standard of beauty. We Tell the old stories to protect the . . . Niang beauty."

"As a warning?"

"A warning. I guess you could say that."

"So Niang used to be like Earth," Clio said, venturing her best guess.

He took the medallion and placed it around his neck, under his shirt. "No."

Clio looked at him in confusion as he stood up and gazed off to the horizon where steaming jungle and low clouds broiled under the peaking sun.

"Earth used to be like Earth," he said. "Now it's like Niang. That's where I live, Clio, on that Earth. That future Earth."

Clio forced herself to breathe. She watched his solid back, wrapped in the studded leather of his true people. Her own body seemed suspended and paralyzed, rapt by the Telling.

He turned to look at her. Said, very gently, "The seeds grew, Clio. The seeds you brought back from the first Niang mission. That you planted on the Amazon coast, that you released into the ocean. They floated and seeded the world, Clio. You succeeded. You brought home the Green." His eyes filled with the light of his Telling. "The Earth survived."

She sat frozen, watching his face, trying to comprehend the three words he had just spoken. She looked past him into the living wall of the jungle. The surround of trees held in the moment, keeping it from flying to pieces. "Survived," she heard herself whisper.

He kneeled down beside her. He looked at her with great tenderness. "Yes. Because of you."

"Liar," she said, still holding at bay that great wave of hope that threatened to engulf her. It hovered there, before her, in the air, in Ashe's fathomless eyes. "Liar."

Tears built up on her eyelids. She flicked them off with her hand.

"It's the truth, Clio."

She looked out past the gun emplacements to the war camp below, and fairly sneered with cynicism. "And so you've come back to murder us—to keep us from Niang—

or what?" Did he think she was stupid, to fall for this little tale of hope?

"I've come back to steal your fire." He settled into a seated position in front of her. Clio let him continue, let him rant on. "We've come to retrieve the FTL technology, Clio. To prevent Tandy's people from taking it. Or die trying."

"Why?" she blurted out, despite her resolve to let him dig himself deeper into his absurd story.

"It empowers Tandy and his people. When the universe splits, his will be the stronger arm of reality. My universe will die. Maybe not right away, but eventually, it will die." He paused, waiting for her objections, but he encountered a cold stare. He continued: "During this time, right now"—here he spread his hands wide to encompass the plateau, the vista before them—"the universe is splitting into two Cousin Realities, two future ways of dealing with faster-than-light travel. One is peaceful, one is not."

He noted the expression on her face. "Ever hear of doppelgängers? Parallel universes? Not a new idea, but until recently in my time, not proven. It explains a lot, in physics and theories of space-time. Vandarthanan laid the theoretical groundwork with equations that proved that parallel universes could exist. That is, two parallel universes can exist. Two Cousin Realities. Not often. But once in a great while. In my time we proved it experimentally. To our great chagrin." With his finger he drew a figure in a bald patch amid the moss, a figure of a forked stick. "Think of it as a tuning fork—you've seen a tuning fork?" Clio nodded, the barest movement possible. "Mine is the left-hand tine of the tuning fork, let's say, and the one we fear is the right-hand tine. One day, the left side will atrophy and die. Cousin Realities compete for the energy of existence. Only one can endure."

"So you're not just from the future. You're from a different universe, and also from the future. That right?" Clio found herself getting angrier and angrier as his story spun out.

"That's right," he continued, oblivious. "Right now,

we're here," he said, pointing to the handle of the tuning fork, a short way down from the crotch of the fork. "If I can prevent Tandy's mission from acquiring the FTL circuit, this time of probabilistic uncertainty will resolve itself in a new way, and my reality will then be the stronger Cousin. His will wither. Not soon. But eventually."

Clio pushed herself to her feet, looking down on him. "Great. In other words, a galactic pissing contest."

Ashe didn't stir. A breeze caught Clio's hair, cooling her head, if not her brain. She turned from Ashe and gazed out to the turquoise enigma of Niang.

"Which universe am I in, then?" she asked. "The good one or the evil one?"

Ashe paused. "You're in both ... or will be, when the split happens."

She swung around, exasperated, and he noted the look in her eyes. Patiently, he continued his Telling: "No one knows how these things can be, just that they *are*. Two Realities will emerge out of this cloud of probabilities ... they will be peopled with the same people, but they will be different Realities. One Reality—mine—is the one in which the seeds survived and changed the Earth. In the other Reality ... the seeds die, Clio. The Earth becomes a wasteland."

"That's the future that Hillis and I discovered. Why didn't we find the green, changed Earth?"

He shook his head slowly. "I don't know, Clio. But I do know this: Tandy and his kind will find other worlds to inhabit and ruin. They will argue that worlds can be harvested as humanity grows and moves on. Once they have FTL, nothing can stop them. With this technology and their aggressive spirit, their reality will seize the thrust of evolution. My reality, I'm afraid, doesn't stand a chance."

Clio breathed a deep, slow breath. "How can I be in both Realities?"

"I don't know, Clio. You think I have all these answers. I don't."

She looked at his face, seeing what appeared to be a simple, open man, telling something he seemed to believe.

"It's just a lot to absorb," she said. "You're telling me that everything I know is dead wrong and a bunch of stranger-than-hell stuff is true instead."

"Sit down, Clio." She stared at him, not liking orders. Then she sat down, facing him. "There's more," he said.

"Oh, wonderful."

"You might as well hear the whole story," he said.

"And you might as well know that I think this whole thing is crock of shit, Ashe. I'm sorry, but it's got as many holes as a ventilator grate." She pointed to Tandy's side of the tuning fork, etched in the dirt. "If you've seen the Cousin way downstream where you live, then you already know what's going to happen, right? So why bother to change the past? You got yourself two universes, Cousin Realities, or whatever. One is strong, one is going to fizzle, and which is which is already decided. End of story, right?"

"No. We can change it," he answered. "At great cost and great danger, but we can change it if we're lucky."

"Then what the hell did you see when you traveled to your Cousin Universe? Strong or weak Cousin?"

Ashe was already holding up his hand, palm out to her, trying to stop her flood of questions. "When we looked before, we saw a strong Cousin, with FTL. When we look after this successful mission—if it *is* successful—we'll see a weak Cousin." He nodded, noting her creased brow. "That's because . . ."

Clio interrupted. "You mean your travels to the future and to the Cousin Reality haven't told you whether you pull off this mission? Don't future history books talk about it?"

"If you'll just shut up long enough to learn something maybe you'll learn something," Ashe replied mildly. Then, resuming his Telling, he said, "You are talking about the paradoxes that can occur in time travel. You sense that they can't logically happen, and you're right."

Mollified somewhat, Clio waited as he continued.

"Yes, future history books in the Cousin Reality talk about how Tandy brought the FTL home. But after we prevent him, there will be different history books, telling a different story." He paused, looking directly at her. "Because when we succeed, and change the outcome of this time of probabilistic uncertainty, Tandy's future will wink out of existence, and will be replaced by a new future. Still pretty ugly—they'll still have Dive—but at least they won't have FTL. And most importantly, they lose the power, the thrust of existence."

"But your people, from your reality. In *their* minds, they remember seeing a strong Cousin, don't they?"

Ashe shook his head. "No."

Clio just stared at him.

He continued. "Our reality winks out too. And is re-created to conform to the new events."

Clio's eyes narrowed. "Your world is destroyed?"

". . . and is replaced by something I hope is somewhat close to the one I left. We don't know what we'll come back to. Nobody does, it's never been done before." Ashe drew another tuning fork almost exactly over the old one, but slightly to one side. "This is the new configuration of the Cousin Realities. The tuning fork shifts."

Clio gazed a long time down on the forked drawing between them. It was crazy. But it *was* coherent. Crazily coherent. She was softening toward this tale, this man. Maybe *she* was crazy. "How do you know all this," she asked.

"Vandarthanan's theories, extended a bit. We're in an era when the time stream is unstable; highly unstable. Because of FTL, and what it means for the future of our galaxy. Vandarthanan's equations suggested that an insta-bility like this was possible. It's described in the Non-Paradox Laws."

"Paradox Laws," she repeated. Decided to let that one lie for a moment. She got up again, trying to clear her head. "Why do I even for a moment believe all this?"

"Because it's the truth, Clio. I've got no reason to lie to you. In a way, it doesn't matter what you believe."

"Then why are you telling me?"

"Because it matters to me . . . what you think matters to me."

She turned to gaze unseeing at Niang's smeared

horizon. "So my humanity, my reality," she said, "is depraved and deserves to die. . . ."

"You knew this, Clio, all along you knew this," he said. "Why else did you bring home the seeds, knowing what they would do to your world and its metal technology."

"It was a last chance for Earth. I never said my people were evil."

"Your people! Your people killed your mother, locked up Petya, treated him like a subhuman, hounded you through all your years of hiding. Your people created quarries. Rounded up the unfit, those choosing the wrong life partners, the wrong politics. Your people withheld the vaccine for the Sickness . . ."

"The vaccine!"

"Of course. They found one, kept it for the chosen few, used the fear of death and epidemic to rein in those who wouldn't conform. Oh, Clio," he took her hands in his, facing her squarely. "Clio, you knew all this, somewhere inside. What your people have come to . . . this dark dominion. You've run from it all your life. If your reality someday dries up—someday far from now—isn't it for the better?"

Clio sank down again, put her head on her knees, shutting her eyes, trying to track, to comprehend it: the universe splitting, the Cousin Realities, the universe destroyed and reborn. She brought her thoughts back to the part she *could* comprehend. She looked at Ashe. "The Earth survives," she said. "At least in one universe, the Earth survives."

He nodded slowly.

When he slid next to her she allowed him to put his arm around her, and she rested against his side. They sat a long time then, gazing out over the camp to the blue-green world beyond, as a small place within her chest, which had been all bone or rock, began to soften and open. She knew it was hope that would flood in if she let it. For a while she leaned against Timothy Ashe, and let it.

CHAPTER 31

In the compound was a tent given over to washing and showering. Inside, towels and jumpsuits hung from stiff wall extrusions. Glowing patches in the tent ceiling and walls lit the shower compartment and dressing area, but the interior still remained half-murky, as though Clio were inside a jellyfish. When she put on the Nian jumpsuit, it lay on her skin like a thin, rubbery silk.

She met Ashe just outside the tent. She looked at him, struggling against her natural cynicism. Tried to smile. Failed.

His mouth flattened ruefully. "It's hard, isn't it?"

"Yeah, it's hard."

He waited, watching her. As though battle skirmishes weren't being fought just a few miles away, as though the world didn't hang in the balance. As though they had all the time in the world.

"I guess I'd like to know what you want from me," she said, finally articulating the foremost thought in her mind.

"Still think I'm after something, huh?"

"Aren't you?"

"No."

"You don't want me to do something, refuse to Dive the ship—take Tandy home?"

"No. You can Dive or not Dive. As I told you before, they can get home without you. You're free to go back with them."

Clio was about to say, *And if I don't want to?* But she stopped herself, afraid, suddenly, of the answer.

Ashe took her by the arm, and walked with her to the edge of the camp.

"Where are we going?" The noises of camp were now entirely submerged beneath the fathoms of jungle song.

Without answering, Ashe led her into the deep forest canopy where, after several minutes' walk, they came upon an outcropping of rock jutting into the sun. At ground level a panel was set into the rock, a bone-white sheet of no material she could name. She scratched her fingernail down it. Smooth as glass, cool as ice.

"I'll take you downstream, Clio, to see." He gestured to the slab before them, apparently a door.

"Your future?"

"No. Theirs."

She drew back. "The event ripple . . ."

"Not a problem, Clio . . . we've overcome that. Trust me."

It was ludicrous. *Trust me.*

Trust this man in the Nianist combat suit. In the unearthly jewel-studded vest. Trust his story of the future at war with the past. The future fighting against Clio's present, fighting against what would become a parallel future, the Metal Future. A ravaging and insatiable humanity, stealing the thrust of existence with their aggressive spirit.

Yet she stepped forward with him as the door slid sideways into the rock.

Clio paused in front of the dim recess before her. "What will we be in this future? Will we be visible to others?"

"No, not visible," Ashe said.

"Then like ghosts?"

He raised the good eyebrow. "We are between dimensions, therefore not visible. Nothing to be afraid of."

"I'm not afraid. Just curious."

The door slid closed behind them. They were in a small, domed room, where a gentle light blossomed to dispel the shadows. On Ashe's side, a hump grew—it seemed right to say *grew*—from near the panel door. His right hand rested upon the bulge a moment; then the tips of his fingers slipped through the surface a moment to a depth of about six centimeters. As Clio watched, the skin puckered up a moment on her neck, as though something dreadful had touched her. Ashe stood with his fingers dipping into the bulge for several minutes, while the air in the compartment surged and ebbed, accompanied by a low hum almost out of hearing range.

Finally Ashe removed his hand—clean, she noted—and stepped to the panel, which opened.

The first thing Clio noticed was the smell. Something had died. Clio covered her nose, as Ashe put his hand on her back, guiding her outside.

As they stepped through they were surrounded by a veil of fog. An acrid, pulpy smell assaulted Clio's nostrils. Before them, a ghastly landscape poked now and then from drifts of smoke. Something was burning. Through the brackish air she saw stumps of trees spotting a denuded terrain, split by rivulets of stream water brown with silt or chemical stew. Clio coughed, expelling the gases from her lungs. Ashe removed a small, gelatinous face mask from his pocket, put it on. He looked like he had a centimeter of vaseline covering his face. He handed her another one.

"It will filter the air," he said. "Don't fight it."

Clio took the gluey membrane, pressed it to her face. The mask thinned around her eyes, nose, and mouth, allowing her to see and breathe.

It was coming on toward dusk. The sun strained against the gaseous fabric of the horizon. She and Ashe stood higher above the surrounding land than before, as erosion had cut away and exposed more of the rock. They made their steep descent to the plain, clambering down over jutting rock, yet in an effortless way, as though in partial g. When they began to walk on the soggy ground, they left no footprints, but in every other way the world and their presence in it seemed to be ordinary. As though they had corporeal form.

On the stumps of trees Clio saw lichens crusted with a turquoise pallor like an outbreak of a Niang eczema. But the forest was gone. Gone in every direction, its passing marked only with stumps and a few fallen trunks collapsed inward in the hollow way of Niang trees.

Clio bent down to examine the blue-green lichens. "What's happened here? A forest fire?"

He looked at her, frowning. "The killing of a world. What else?"

She crouched down to touch a fallen tree. Her hand went through the collapsed surface, not as through thin air, but as through a sticky liquid. She looked up at Ashe, who looked solid, not like a ghost. But their presence here was ephemeral.

Around her the silences rested fathoms deep. "Who did this, Ashe?"

"The Metal Future. Eventually, they will be capable of this. It's only a matter of time."

Somewhere in the distance, the rumble of fire could be heard. But nowhere, the sound of a living creature, other than the sound of their own voices.

"You could call me Timothy, you know."

An exhaust of smoke moved across the landscape, confining their vision to just in front of their faces. "Let's get out of here, Timothy," she said. "I've seen enough."

They turned back, stepping over the oiled body of a feathered creature that might or might not once have flown.

"How long?" she asked. "How long does Niang have?"

"One hundred seventy-five years—give or take."

"How can you kill a world in two hundred years?"

"Clio. They *tried* to kill it. Those in the Metal Future were afraid of Niang biota. They had abandoned Earth, and found a few other worlds to inhabit. But they were afraid of Niang, afraid of terrorist attacks like yours. So they experimented with eradication techniques. Eventually they found a kind of anti-DNA phagocyte to do the job. Whatever was left, they set on fire."

Sickened, Clio turned away. He took her hand, leading her up the first steep slope of the outcropping.

Clio found her footing, climbing ahead. She turned and offered him a hand.

Startled at first, he took it, hosting himself up.

The smog tore, revealing a deeper landscape, but no different, as the sun, setting now behind a mound of hills, infused the air with a dying glow. In the distance, she looked out on the snaking path of the river as it burned with a moving line of fire.

They sat on the rock outcropping, back in Clio's time, back in the vibrant, sweet-smelling forest. An insect the size of a hawk swooped in front of their faces, hovering, its mica wings a blur, then flitted away. Clio inhaled the sweet air of the forest, her face mask in her lap. This had been her second glimpse of the future. Both times it was a preview of destruction. And this man sitting next to her represented life and hope. Somehow, despite his incredible story, he seemed true. And his Telling, all true. She looked at his profile as he watched the forest, and her heart told her: *Yes*.

He noticed her watching him, and turned to look at her. "More questions?" he asked.

What happens to me? she wanted to ask. Instead she asked a safer one: "Why didn't you just go back in your own history and *not* send the ship—the one that crashed? It would be simpler."

Ashe nodded. "Yes and no. Simpler if it worked. If it didn't—if for any reason we failed to stop the ship being sent—we wouldn't get any other chances to set the past right."

"Just one chance?"

"It depends on when you arrive. Once you travel to your past, everything prior to your arrival becomes fixed. If you arrive on the fourth of July, 1990, then next time you can't go back and change anything on the third of July, 1990. July third and all previous time is immune to tampering. It's fixed." He noted her confused expression. "We've never tested it, but it's true according to the Past Intervention Law—one of the Non-Paradox Laws. I told you before, the universe abhors a paradox. Therefore it also abhors travel to your own history. It does just about everything to prevent it."

Clio scrunched up her mouth in concentration. "So you

traveled back in time—to the beginning of the problem—so that if you failed, you'd have other chances downstream?"

The insect was back again, treading air about a meter in front of Clio's face.

"It's attracted to the glutens in your face mask. Put it in your pocket," Ashe said.

Clio slipped the mask into the breast pocket of her jumpsuit. After a time, the creature gave up and flew away.

"OK, so we got all these paradox laws," Clio said. "But why didn't you just Dive back and steal the FTL from Teeg? In Dive, you could have traveled back a hundred times, each trip a minute or an hour *after* the previous trip, and kept looking for him until you found him."

"Well, first of all, we have *tried* to find him. He has a labyrinth of caves that he knows like the back of his hand, and he's paranoid as hell."

"*Was* paranoid," Clio corrected.

"Was. Tenses get a little mixed up in the Telling of this one. The more important reason we never found Teeg is uncertainty. The Vandarthanan Uncertainty Principle."

"Another law?"

"Yes, another Non-Paradox Law. Sort of a 'You can't have it all' rule. The universe allows Dive to be accurate about either time or space but not both at the same time."

"We deal with that one in Dive all the time."

"Right. The bottom line is that you can't travel very accurately to the past. It hasn't mattered to your Biotime missions, because great accuracy was never an issue. You got in the general vicinity of the planet through Dive, and traveled the rest of the way in real space, and it didn't matter whether it was a million years ago or a million and ten years."

"But it matters for your mission."

"Yes. It matters. We knew we had to get to Niang—the place had to be precisely accurate—so we couldn't be sure *when* we'd arrive. Give or take a few years, we'd hit it near enough. But not close enough to send a lot of missions back time after time. If we'd been unlucky, we would in fact have arrived *after* Tandy escaped with the FTL, making his actions immune to our tampering."

"Because of the Past Intervention Law." Clio looked to him for confirmation.

"Right. The past would close up behind us."

"A hell of a maneuverability problem."

"About as easy as shooting the rapids in Hell's Canyon in an inner tube."

"And yet you made it," she said.

"The Niang team made it, yes. Arrived here two months early, nearly perfect. Mine was a simultaneous mission to Earth . . ."

". . . to sabotage the *Galactique*."

"Yes. I arrived nine years before the first Biotime mission to Niang . . . and I've been stuck in your lovely little world ever since."

Clio stood up, brushing the dust from her jumpsuit. She turned to look at Timothy Ashe, and in that moment the larger things, the world, the universe, were too big to hold. Things that Ashe, like Hillis, could hold in his mind and sacrifice for, were to her simply too big. She wanted to know about Clio.

"When does the universe split?" she asked.

"I don't know," he said. He stood to look at her directly. "Soon, we think. When Tandy takes the FTL home, we're guessing. Or when we prevent him."

A silence lay between them. He waited, as always, for her questions.

"And what happens to me?" she asked.

He watched her carefully. "What do you want to happen?"

Clio smiled a thin smile. "I don't want to be a prisoner anymore. Never again."

"I don't want you to be a prisoner, either." He was looking at her darkly, from eyes gone flat black. "You might come back to my world, Clio. Might be able to. There's great danger. It's only a theory, and if we fail, you could die."

"Tell me."

He hesitated, then said, "Sometime soon this cloud of uncertainty will clear, and two realities will emerge. We think there will be a few moments during which I might be able to take you home. Everything will be in flux, and dimensional rules may suspend for an instant. Whether this is a harmless blink of an eye or the biggest event ripple you can imagine, nobody knows. But when it's over, I must return to my own time and you . . . must remain in yours."

"I can't come with you."

"It will be a time of flux, dimensional uncertainty. We don't know what might be possible. Some of us think there's a chance."

"What happens if I don't make it?"

"At best, you would remain incorporeal and we could return you to your time."

"At worst?"

"At worst, it won't be a good time to be in Dive. Anything could happen. It could kill you. Even worse, for a few moments we may enter our Cousin Reality and have to cross over to my own—it's an extended function of Dive, so it would still be highly dangerous. And there would be two strikes against you." He paused, running his hand over the top of his head as though sorting through the tangles of his thoughts. "I don't know which Clio I would be with. If it's the Clio in my Cousin Reality, I don't think you would survive both the traverse to my own reality and the jump to the future. In both cases you—normally—cannot be in corporeal form." He turned away. "It's bizarre and dangerous. Dangerous for everyone on my expedition, but most of all for you, Clio."

He turned back to her, and a look of confusion filled his face. "You're smiling."

"I thought you were going to tell me I couldn't go."

"I almost have," he said, gently.

"No. You said it would be damn dangerous. It's not the same."

He searched her face, starting to say something more. She put her finger to his lips. "Don't push it, Ashe. I always do what I put my mind to."

He smiled. "We'll see." Then he led her back to the encampment.

In that short journey back, Clio felt buoyant, suffused with a lightness, as though, having heard too much, juggled too many facts and feelings, she had retreated for a time to sheer body. However dog-tired, her legs and arms ran with energy, and her chest, like the bellows of her heart, filled with deep breaths.

She let herself follow Ashe to the places he was determined to show her, let herself meet his friends, some of whom spoke her English. Ashe introduced her to the black man with the braid whom they encountered at the rim of the camp and who was the ground expedition leader and Ashe's good friend.

"Russell Oaklan," Ashe said to her as the man turned from a clutch of officers to greet them.

"Clio Finn," Clio said, now finding his eyes willing to meet hers.

"Be welcome here, Clio Finn," he said. His smile crossed his face like a brief laser. "This one tells our true . . . remembrance, that you of heart remem now?" He shrugged, smiling again full into her eyes. "The words of this lose with slack Telling."

"It's OK," Clio said. "I think I got the gist." She felt her own real smile, that stranger, answer his. "I think he tells OK."

Russell Oaklan nodded. As Oaklan turned back to his officers, Ashe pointed off toward the clearing where a large, segmented landing craft came for them, settling on the ground with a brief explosive noise. And then Clio let Ashe take her to the mother ship itself, the Nian ship in orbit, because he asked her, and she wanted to believe, to move beyond logic and hope.

The smaller craft grappled onto the sleek white pod ship, diminutive compared with the *Galactique*, and cylindrical, like the oldest of the science-fiction moving pictures. Clio stepped through the rounded airsac into the throat of the ship, where the floor met the bulkheads in close approximation of right angles.

The passageway surged to brightness as they boarded. At once the unmistakable fragrance of Niang came to Clio's nostrils, a musky underlayment where oil and hot decking should have been.

It was, as Ashe told her, a trained construct, both grown and engineered, the created entity of a decade's interaction of crystal self-assembly—much like shells or bones—and discreet DNA engineering to build in deep-space tolerances. And it was a Transition ship, faster than the speed of light, a time-Diving pod, and fighting ship. And it lived. At the cellular level, much of this ship was alive, breathing, exchanging fluid, responding to environment and creating environment, including an energy-absorbing and stealth-like profile.

At points the passageway widened to workstations. Clio glanced at two crew members seated at a workbench. Filaments sprouted from the fingertips of their right hands, and were probing the console where a pinprick of light responded now and then. A small, compact woman had threads of some sort inserted into her temples. Clio stopped just past the workstation, leaned against the bulkhead, closed her eyes.

Her stomach wrinkled up in wave after wave. She noticed now a bench underneath her that she hadn't seen before. Ashe pressed her gently onto it.

"I don't feel so hot." She rested her forearms on her thighs.

"Those tendrils patch crew into the deep biological systems so that they can exchange information with the ship."

That didn't help. The wave threatened to climb up her breast. Clio breathed deeply. The corridor was very warm and humid.

"I felt that way, Clio," Ashe said. "When I first saw a lumber mill. You kill to build and create. We guide and prune." He sat next to her, putting his arm around her. He smelled slightly of sweat, and musky humanness. Despite her nausea, she felt a different, more keen and piercing sensation slide into her belly.

"It's a gentle way, Clio," he said.

She rose and pressed down her jumpsuit against her midriff.

One of the crew at the workstation had detached her leads and had come to the opening to gaze at Clio. Ashe challenged her with a snap of his black eyes, and the woman returned to her console.

"Why do they watch me," Clio said as they made their way deeper into the ship.

"You're Clio Finn. They all know who you are. From legend."

"Legend. Great." Clio glanced back at the technician. "Do I measure up?"

Ashe grinned. "Probably not."

They entered the bridge extrusion. The control console nestled into the rounded nose of the ship, alight with a sharp glow of crystalline instrumentation surrounded by the melded interstices of ship's body, also radiating a pale, translucent fire. In this surrounding luminescence, Clio saw two crew members chatting closely. They parted. The one in authority came forward to meet them. Ashe spoke to her, then turned to Clio. "This is Captain Hickory." The captain nodded to her, eyes narrowing in a careful scrutiny. Her white hair was short and wiry, face nearly seamless, except when she smiled, which she did now. She stepped aside, allowing Clio and Ashe to approach the extended console.

The console was oddly flat, here and there pitted with depressions for fingerholds except where a growth protruded, as in conventional toggles. A flickering from many membranous screens, but no glossy reflections off portals, for the room was devoid of windows, accentuating a womb-like feeling—not altogether pleasant. She let the instrumentation display itself before her as she listened to her own breathing in the metal-free quiet.

It was both a ship and a life-form, both familiar and alien. The combination made her irritable and wary, as though such ambiguity were so much worse than outright *difference*. And no metal. No solid, cold absoluteness of metal.

She watched as a crew member inserted his fingertips into the panel. A section pulsed with a deeper glow.

Ashe noted her reaction. "It's biochemical, Clio. We interact through touch. The ship responds at the molecular level."

"It's really alive then . . . almost humanlike. . . ."

"It's not conscious, not in a human way. Still, we treat it with respect. It has life, life that we share on a molecular and cellular level. If cut, it feels a kind of pain. We don't cut it."

"But you control it, engineer it. It's not a creature. Not free."

"No, not free, not equal in the sense you mean. This isn't paradise, Clio, please be clear on that. Humans still dominate my world. If there's some—metaphysical unity or something—that we're supposed to achieve, my people certainly haven't found it. If there are levels of knowing, we've got at least to the level of Respect. Maybe that's just the first rung on the ladder, I don't know."

Clio watched as the crew member pulled a section up from the plane of the console. It emerged as a wedge. In its deeper layers lay white sheets like flattened bone. Here were the deeper circuits, like the circuit Teeg had stolen. The bones of FTL.

"This is an FTL ship?" she asked.

He nodded. "The pod uses simple fusion for short transits. For long voyages, an interface with the fabric of spacetime. Not a matter of propulsion." Ashe nodded toward the instrumentation, with its bank of screens like a film of soap stretched taut. "It's laid into the programs, into the fabric of the pod itself and especially into one circuit plate."

"How much could my people learn from one circuit board, from a technology so advanced, so basically alien?"

"They could take the program, deengineer it, figure out the whole approach. Given enough time, it could be done."

They stood for a minute in the eerie hush of the place. Whatever the pod's secret ways, they were as silent as the blood rushing through her own veins.

He led her off the flight deck. The corridor branched

into a narrow passageway and a door parted before them, sliding aside like a nictitating membrane.

They were in a small room with a bed platform and two chairs, where above them in the ceiling was set a portal to the wavering stars. Ashe saw the direction of her look. "It's a projection screen, a relay of the actual local stars. We're working on deep-space translucency. Windows."

Clio sank into a chair. "Why bother with me, Ashe? Don't you have a war to fight?"

"We want you to understand. And to side with us, if possible. You have a right to know. Because this is how it all grew to be, Clio. Those seeds you planted. This is how it grew."

She closed her eyes, seeing the bridge, with its waxy flat surfaces, its secret controls, accessed by biologically knowing hands. Her seeds had grown beyond her comprehension. Her civilization had become unrecognizable. "I could never hope to fly this ship," she said.

"No."

She remembered sitting at the controls of the crashed ship on Niang, the living surface of its instrumentation. "Ashe," she said, "what was that crashed ship doing on Niang—the one that Teeg stole the FTL from?"

"It was a science expedition to Niang to research the native biota . . . as it was fifteen hundred years ago. Paleobotany. Biology is our fascination. Almost a fatal fascination in this case. Anyway, we lost the ship in a crash; everyone on board died. We sent another expedition back in time to dismantle the FTL circuitry. But when we found the ship, it had been ransacked. Key pieces missing. When Teeg took that circuit, he set in motion the twinning . . . the time of probabilistic uncertainty . . . the Cousin."

"And you'd do anything to get that circuit back . . . even destroy your own universe. But once on board the *Galactique*, couldn't you have sabotaged the ship in some way?"

"After the bombing of Vanda loading bay, I never really tried." Ashe answered her unspoken question. "I met you."

Now, that was about as near a declaration of love as Clio could imagine. And all of a sudden she could imagine herself in love with this man as well. Yet she probed: "Was I worth letting down your people?"

"Question I asked myself a lot. Guess I answered yes."

"But you killed Ryerson."

Ashe looked at her, steady on. "Ryerson got in my way. I wanted to eliminate Tandy as a factor in the ground mission. He's a powerful man. I meant to kill him."

Clio put her head on the back of the chair, resting. When she opened her eyes, Ashe was standing next to the chair, his hand resting along the back, close to her head.

"You're tired," he said. He touched her left temple with his fingertips. "I brought you here so you could sleep." As he spoke he stroked the side of her head in that slight indentation between her eyebrow and hairline.

It was a gentle pressure, his fingers on her skin, but she felt it deep in her abdomen.

"Does that feel good because you're doing something biotic with your fingertips?"

"Yes. I'm massaging your temples."

Clio breathed as shallow as she knew how, keeping that touch on her face, sensing that he would retreat if she spoke. Mucking up the legend, he might say. She found that she had brought her hand up to touch his wrist. "Just as long as it's nothing more."

"It's nothing more if that's what you want."

"I might want ordinary physical company."

He knelt down at the side of the chair, slid his hand behind her head. He watched her for a long while. "You're so tired. You look so tired," he said. "I hope I'm wrong."

"That's right." Clio cupped his face with her hands. "You're wrong." He moved toward her as she pulled him to her, and she touched his lips with hers, felt his ordinary warmth and tasted his ordinary taste, as the shock of contact hummed through and through her. He pulled back for a moment, moved to rest his face in her hair. The sweetness of the moment peeled back like a ripe fruit, the innocence of it, so unlike the fast clash of desire with shipboard lovers, quick to move to the main point, all fretting hands and workmanlike skill. Ashe spoke her name, way back in his throat, murmured sweet names in her ear, some that she recognized. And kissed her again. She stood up, came around to where he was kneeling, and pulled the zipper at her neck. She stepped out of her boots as he unzipped them. He stood up far enough to sit on the edge of the chair, pulling her toward him by the waist, into the sheltering enclosure of his thighs. He waited until she had pulled the zipper all the way down to her belly, and unfastened her belt before he pulled the flight suit away from her, tossing them aside along with undershirt, pants, dog tag.

"You are unearthly beautiful, Clio," he said. He held her at arms' length, looking at her with eyes grown deep as the forest. She couldn't remember anyone looking at her like that, though she'd seen the harsh mask of hunger many times. This was tenderness and joy, all cloaked in a velvety desire. He slipped out of his vest. She helped him undo his fastenings and things fell to the floor. Then he took her hand and led her to the bed platform, lying down and pulling her on top of him. His palm held her breast to his lips, as he kissed her again and again and she felt him thrust hard against her belly. Then he grasped her around the waist and pushed her lower and she heard him call her name as he entered her, felt his hand on the small of her back, pressing their bodies together, and she said, "My God, Ashe, you're wonderful, oh you are wonderful," and his face was flooded with his smile, and he said, "Call me Timothy."

Afterward, Clio lay in the crook of his arm while overhead, the stars pursued their courses across the screen-wide section of sky.

"What do you think of when you look at the stars?" Clio asked.

"Just then I was thinking of home. Looking up at a starry night at home."

"Do you want to go home?"

"Not at the moment." He reached for her face, drew her close and kissed her. "I love you, Clio."

"I want you to love me."

"You got it."

"Did they tell you to love me, to seduce me?"

"Yes. They assigned me to befriend you, any way that I could. To win your trust, win you to our side."

"So much for mucking with the legend." Clio drew back.

He brought her close again, hand guiding her shoulders to face him. "But I couldn't do it. I pushed you away, baited you, scolded you. Refused you. Because from the very moment I saw you I loved you, loved you more than anyone, anything else. Between you and the struggle, I chose you. I'm a lousy warrior."

"Love at first sight?"

He smiled. "Yes."

"You believe in that?"

"Yes."

"Is it so easy to believe?"

"It is when it happens to you."

"So when you told Teeg that you loved me, you meant it, even then?"

"It was the truth. Is it so hard to believe?"

She looked full into his face. The scar splitting his eyebrow flared on his temple as though remembering the old wound. She traced it with her finger. "Tell me again," she said.

He pulled her down next to him. "I love you, Clio."

She lay on her back, watching the square of local space in the ceiling. "You know what I think of when I look at the stars? I just think how fragile they are."

"I never thought of stars as fragile."

"Yes, you did. Isn't that why you're a warrior?"

He pondered that. "Maybe so."

Clio slid toward the edge of the bed, swung her feet over. Saw her pile of clothes mixed with his. She jumped up, shook out her fatigues, and stood holding them against her body. "Get dressed, Timothy," she said.

He reached for her. "I'm not done with you yet."

She dropped her clothes, strode toward the bed, crouching beside it. "I'm not done with you, either." She touched his forearm, gripped it hard. "But there's something I've got to do."

"It can wait."

"Not anymore." She grabbed her clothes again, jamming her leg into her suit. "Waited too damn long already. I'm going to drop it to hell, throw it down the deepest crack on the planet." She zipped up her suit to her neck, tucked her dog tag in. "Timothy," she said. "I know where the FTL is. I know where it is. And I know how to bury it."

"What are you talking about?" he asked as he grabbed his clothes.

"The Hell Crack," she said.

STRANGER IN PARADOX

CHAPTER 32

❧

Clio and Ashe crouched just below the Great Cave. Through a web of vines, they kept watch on the cave entrance and the sprawling ledge before it. In the swath of azure sky exposed by the hunkering rock, insects swirled in humming masses, netting the air and darkening it. Clio's sweat-laden fatigues released their rank odors as the morning heat built.

Hidden behind Clio and Ashe in the cover of the forest was the largest force Ashe's people could muster, along with armaments positioned and aimed at the cave entrance should it prove necessary.

Ashe moved forward, scrambling up to the cave's stretched lip with Clio close behind. They plunged into the sudden dusk of Teeg's New Merica headquarters. Ashe yanked a torch from the wall and lit it.

The cave air settled on their faces with instant clamminess. Clio brought her kerchief over her nose, to ward off the reek of the passageway, following the remembered route, the subtle landmarks of stone in the wavering light.

At branches in the passageway Ashe marked their route with his belt knife, with a sound like a claw on a cage. Clio squinted her eyes to help remember, then plunged on, following at last a slipstream of cold air as much as memory. Before her loomed, at times, the image of Jackson Tandy, the man whose dreams she would defy and destroy. Sometimes she saw him standing before the viewports of the *Galactique* longing for the stars, for the next stage of human adventure. But mostly the image was the two of them sitting against the cold barracks wall, the warmth of his arms, the time beyond time, as he waited with her for life to seep back in. He was always for going on, leaving the past behind. Look at hell around you and call it heaven, it's the best you've got. Make it yours. *No, Tandy. Don't you see? We're not ready to reap the stars, look at what we've done with the one we've got. She saw his eyebrow wrinkle, the slow shake of his head. Clio, Clio. You long for the stars, same as me, lost your family, same as me. . . .* Liquid on her face turned icy in the draft. She rubbed it away.

"*Not* the same as you!"

"What did you say?" Ashe's voice.

"Nothing."

"Quiet then," he whispered. "Is this the cavern?"

The walls were gone. The torchlight fled into the darkness, surrounding them with an ineffectual nimbus, serving only to expose them to anyone hiding here. At this point they should go forward thirty or forty paces, then directly left to the cave wall, skirting the chasm without a bottom. If memory served. Ashe took her hand as she moved ahead. Held on tight, he did, as though he could pull her back from the abyss. As though he could sense the loosening of her belly as she pictured the fall of the FTL circuit into the bowels of Niang and her own long plunge over the edge. They shuffled forward. Here, the air stilled and the torch flames quieted, leaving only the huff of Clio's breathing. Each step was a decision. Her resolve flickered with the smoking torch as she pushed forward, nearly blind now. Nearby the chittering of Teeg's rats joined the sputtering of the torch.

"This way," Clio whispered. She turned to the left. Not far now would be the cave wall, with its nook cradling the crystal-lit treasure. They trudged for a few paces, still seeing nothing. Clio stopped, pulling on Ashe's hand, listening to the warning of her body.

"Douse the light."

Ashe knelt down, extinguishing the remains of the flame.

Eyeless, they watched. She crouched down next to him.

Far to the right, a dull pulse of light appeared. She waited until Ashe saw it too.

"You see?" he whispered.

"But it's in the wrong place."

With his insistence, she moved forward some paces, then dropped to her hands and knees, touching the ground before putting weight down. Something skittered across the back of her lower legs and in the next instant her right hand dropped into sheer space and her stomach spasmed. A frigid draft of air ballooned up from below. She heard herself cry out between clenched teeth, and Ashe was yanking her arm, pulling her backward, and she lay on the hard ground, side by side with the great chasm, the Hell Crack, her arm dangling over. She jerked it back. Next to her she heard the cocking of a gun. A light struck up and Corporal Lewis' face floated into view.

"Well looky here. It's Clio Finn," he said.

Then Ashe's voice. "Is that you, Lewis?"

"Who else is with you?" Lewis hissed.

"Clio."

"Who else?"

"Nobody," Ashe answered. "We're alone. God, we've been lost in this maze." Their agreed-upon alibi.

Clio tried to get up. Right hand floundering into nothingness. "Get me the hell away from this," she said. "Help me." The cave floor tilted, trying to roll her into its throat.

Ashe's hand pulled her along the ground. She huddled against him.

Someone else moved into the light. A woman.

"You're alive, then." It was Imanishi.

"Barely," Ashe said. "We ran into Harper Teeg. He captured us during the firefight. Son of a bitch had plans for Clio after he got rid of me. Do you know how to get out of here?"

"Yes." A voice just out of the light.

Clio knew that voice.

Jackson Tandy stepped forward. His hand glowed halfway to his elbow. As he loomed closer, Clio saw the glowing pink coals of his hand. The glowing embers of his prize. Push him now, she thought. Push him over the edge of the chasm. One chance to do it right.

She could push him now.

He knelt down next to Clio. "Are you hurt?"

"Get me away from this goddamn crevasse."

Tandy pulled her toward him, away from Ashe and the crevasse. She had him in her hands, clutched his arm.

"Sounds like the old Clio," Tandy said. "He didn't hurt you, then."

Clio scrambled away from the looming crack.

"Are you all right?" he asked.

She pulled back from his hands. "He slapped me around a little. Crazy. He was crazy."

"Did he tell you about this?" Tandy held up the circuit board. The board and his hand pulsed with the same luminescence.

"No. What is it?"

"Didn't brag about this little item, eh?"

"He bragged about how we were going to be happy ever after in this stinking hole. So what is it?"

He advanced on Ashe. Imanishi shone the flashlight in Ashe's face. "I give you credit," Tandy said, "for keeping Clio safe. He could have killed her."

"I guess so. How many survived the ambush?"

"Three, so I thought. Now, looks like five. Lewis and Imanishi and I escaped and managed to press on to the ship. We found it. Also found someone else still alive . . . Harper Teeg."

Clio turned her face away from Imanishi's flashlight. *Holy God. Teeg.*

"Jesus," Ashe said.

"Even better than Jesus," Tandy said. "He told us where to find this." He held up the small, chitinous plate. "Told us to look in this cave. That's why the Nians left the ship lying there. No point in destroying it. The essential piece was missing, you see. Harper Teeg stashed it away here."

Lewis snorted. "Didn't mean null to him. But he hid it

like a goddamn trophy." He murmured, low: "We persuaded him to tell us what he knew."

"Now what?" Imanishi asked.

"Now we get out of here," Tandy said.

Clio's mind was still on Teeg. "Where's Teeg now?"

"He's dead," Lewis said. "Spilled his story, and died. Like he was just waiting for us. Waiting to tell somebody."

"He also raved about you and Ashe," Tandy said. "We thought you were dead, that maybe Teeg had killed you."

"Let's get out of here," Imanishi said.

"We'll go out the back door," Tandy said.

A pause before Clio asked, "Back door?"

"Yes. Closer proximity to camp than the other."

"How do you know there *is* a back door?"

"Lewis went back to reconnoiter. Whole cave system is riddled with entrances. We can take our pick." Tandy turned to Ashe. "Are you hurt?"

"No."

"Then take the flashlight, in the lead." Tandy gestured into the deep of the cave.

"Your army grunt might do better. He's been over the ground before."

"No, I think you'll do."

Imanishi handed over the flashlight.

"Watch your step," Lewis said. "Can't afford to lose the flashlight."

Clio's eyes had adjusted to the twilight brown thrown by the broad-beam flashlight. The chasm was just to the left. She could push him now. Her arms crackled with tension. Push him now.

The group moved off, following Ashe. In the rear of the line, Tandy fell in step with Clio, clapped her on the shoulder. "Luck starting to turn, Clio," he said. "Luck starting to turn."

She was on the inside, next to the crack. A pebble bounced off her shoe and took flight into the spacey depths.

"Yessir," she said, her heart plunging with the stone. "Luck starting to turn."

· · ·

They slogged through the web of undergrowth, fore-arms in front of their faces to fend off the slapping tendrils and branches. Dusk was coming on. So while they could still see their way, and despite the crashing noise of their passing, Tandy urged them onward to camp. The enemy could hear them if they lurked nearby. Tandy was betting that they weren't.

And, as Clio knew, Tandy was right. While the colonel fled with his prize, Ashe's forces were massed in front of the Great Cave, several kilometers back toward the river.

They bored on through the hovering mat of the jungle until they popped out, suddenly, into a clearing where the last shreds of day hung from the canopy. Fantastic shadows and highlights shaped the jungle floor with tricks of light, but enough daylight remained to show the scatter of bodies across the field. The dead lay where they fell, Nian, army, and Biotime sharing the same repose. As Clio picked her way into the scene, she saw a man lying draped in dried blood where Niang ants swarmed like a coat of fur, and next to him, a soldier reclining simply as though too tired to go on.

Then, farther, lay Richardson, right arm still in its sleeve but lying akimbo across his ankles, and there Pequot, on his back and staring in ugly surprise at the tropical sky. Clio and the others moved through the clearing in slow motion, Tandy and Lewis watching the trees, and she, Ashe, and Imanishi watching the dead. Here lay a Nian woman, whom Ashe looked at with eyes giving nothing away though her long hair lay in a striking image of frazzled and burned filaments so delicate that they collapsed into dust as the ants tried to use them for a bridge to her face.

"Keep moving," Tandy said, "there's nothing to be done here."

It was no place to stop for water and rest, with its stench of open bodies, but Clio's legs begged for surcease. And the decent thing to do was check for survivors. Even in this carnage someone might yet hang on.

"Nothing to be done here," Tandy repeated as Clio

knelt beside an army private, body intact, peacefully dead. Tandy waited while she stood up.

"Someone may still be alive here, sir," she said.

"They're all dead. Nothing even you can do for anybody here, Clio."

Clio flipped him a look for his sarcasm, but moved on, as Corporal Lewis hung back behind her, waiting for her to obey Tandy's orders, and they all plunged into the thicket on the other side of the clearing. Light was slipping fast from the jungle, and Tandy urged them faster, though their boots slipped on the ragged braid of the floor, and they staggered at times from exhaustion. The sweat of their bodies lay congealed on them as the jungle cooled.

Imanishi fell in beside her. "I heard a groan," she said. "Somebody groaned, back there."

Clio looked at her in stupefied silence.

"It could have been my imagination," Imanishi said, defensive.

Clio caught up with Tandy. "Imanishi said she heard a groan, sir, back at the ambush. We may have a survivor."

"We may *all* die, if we're stuck in this maze at dark. We are all in very great danger still, Clio, do you understand that?"

Clio looked into his face, but the growing dusk threw a gauze over her sight. She could barely make out his eyes. He turned away, and she followed his back, stumbling on into the mounting dark.

After what seemed like hours they heard a sentry challenge them as they pushed free of the forest and emerged one by one into the clearing before base camp. A white-hot light swept over them from floodlights at the perimeter wire.

"Who's there!" came the challenge.

"This is Colonel Tandy and Operation Zeal!"

"Proceed forward, sir!"

"Extinguish lights and lay down a cover fire; we may be followed!" Tandy cried, and amidst the staccato rifle fire, the four of them raced across the thirty meters toward the perimeter wire.

The moment Clio lunged into a sprint, Niang erupted

with all the noises of hell. The thudding of pulse rifles and tearing cracks of hundreds of rifle rounds combined with the shouts of the camp and screams of orders from officers as their ragtag group crossed the clearing. When they reached the perimeter of camp, Tandy hurled orders to lay out canisters and evacuate, while a dozen people jumped to obey. Ashe kneeled down to help Imanishi, who had collapsed just inside the wire, endurance broken now that she had crossed over. Voris and two guards rushed by, each holding a white, cylindrical canister, cradled like a baby. Clio stared hard, trying to figure out what they were for, here in the midst of a hell-bent retreat, but there was no time for wondering as Tandy hastily pulled Clio onward to the lander.

The translucent airbag serving for a quarantine airlock wrapped partway around the ladder to *Sun Spot* like a giant blister. Clio, Tandy, Imanishi, and Ashe removed their fatigues and boots, and stepped through the flexible hatchway, resealing it behind them, as the airlock shuddered, expelling air and refilling with a frigid, noxious mist. Flakes of grey, sublimated gas fluttered off Clio's eyelashes as she scrambled up into the lander, eyes feeling like smooth ovals of ice. Once inside, they pulled on white paper togs. Clio managed to look at Ashe as a new volley of gunfire erupted outside. Ashe shook his head, bleakly, once. Not his people out there. Tandy was firing at shadows.

Clio strapped into the pilot's seat, a chair she most definitely did not want to be in. The rest of the mission crew scrambled aboard along with Voris, looking sick to her stomach, black hair flecked with icy particles. Clio threw the prelaunch system switches. On a signal from Tandy, *Sun Spot* thundered to life.

CHAPTER 33

"Main engine burn," Meg Voris said. She flipped the main toggles to fire *Galactique*'s primary engines, sending a shudder through the hull and releasing a distant aft roar of ignition and firing, enough to push eleven million kg's out of comfortable geosynchronous orbit. Ship balked, easing off orbit with immense reluctance.

"Bring her up smartly," Hocking said, in the headphones.

Clio watched Voris take the ship to full thrust. Jesus, in a hurry they were. Barely time to strap in and secure landing bay before *Galactique* came around, pointing home. Or that general direction.

Clio adjusted the headphones on her ears, scratching her head, caked with mud and decontamination chemicals. No time to clean up. No time to rest, though Tandy had driven them three hours through the jungle, his eyes unnaturally bright, his energy inexhaustible. And no time to rest in camp, as they rushed for the lander, as the crew hurried to set out the canisters: canisters Clio now realized were poison gas with their clouds of golden vapor that spilled onto the verge, sliding into the jungle like a killer's hands through his victim's long hair. And everyone, enemy or mission straggler, was soon dead in that cold flaxen cloud.

Though the flight deck was cool, her hands left a trace of sweat on the keyboard, marking her every move. Clio wiped her hands on her togs, breathing deeply to keep the shakes away.

"You had it pretty bad out there," Voris said on channel. "Worse than any of us."

"Yeah, pretty bad."

"But you succeeded. That's the main thing."

Clio closed her eyes as she felt the bell of the flight deck push down around her, the bulkheads moving in, she was sure they were closing in, in one of those monstrous flights of imagination that, once begun, tend to play out. The flight console crowding down on her body, the control stick aiming toward her chest, and the ceiling controls lowering. She closed her eyes hard, thinking of the jungle, of the close but limitless jungle. No time now for claustrophobia. Six years in space and never felt it. Liked, in fact, the reassuring close spaces, guarding her flanks and sheltering her.

"Are you all right, Clio?"

Clio looked over at Voris. Felt the sweat on her face, rivulets cutting through the grit. Face hot just under the surface and cold as hard space on the outside.

"You don't look so good."

"Feel fine."

Ship was roaring with the main burn, filling her ears, trembling under her feet. All the grey metal on the deck gleamed back at her, glossy, unseeing, purposeful and cold. What was she doing here on the bridge of this infernal ship, all odds against her, the prize stowed away and under tight guard, surrounded by fellow-crew—every last one of whom would die to prevent her from doing what she was going to do?

Voris turned back to Clio. "Remember when we left Vanda and I said it was going to be a piece of cake?"

Clio snorted. "Yeah."

"I guess I didn't have a clue," She looked over at Clio. "What we were up against. Not a clue."

"Maybe nobody did." The roaring of engines sounded like the screams of banshees riding the hull.

"I never killed anyone before," Voris said.

Clio glanced over at Voris, who worked the console, whipping the *Galactique* into motion like a big girl and yet whimpering over a few bodies.

"People die."

"But we killed them. The gas. Some of our wounded

were maybe still out there. We defended the lander, and we opened the canisters on Tandy's order. I set one out. We were in a hurry, everyone shouting, the whole camp shouting. I set one out, and the stuff traveled like fire." She looked up at Clio. "I can't forget it."

"It's war. People die."

Her brown eyes still looked at Clio, hungry-like. "You're tough, Clio."

"Try to be."

"But you don't look so good, either."

"Tell you the truth, feel like my stomach's about to take a walk."

"Why did we need the gas, Clio?"

"Cut the chatter," came Hocking's order, a tinny voice in the earpiece. Behind Clio and Voris, Hocking and Singh scanned the readouts for pursuers, and punched up ship's guns, now fully armed.

Voris' eyebrows came together in a thick brown line. "What about taking a stand, then?"

"Take on U.S. Army?"

Voris hesitated. "If it was right."

"Being right can get you in a bunch of trouble."

Voris went back to the flight console, on systems check. "Just the same, it made me sick."

Hocking's voice interrupted: "Finn, you report to medlab, on the double."

"Medlab, sir?"

"You taking orders?"

"Yessir, but . . ."

"On the double, Finn."

She turned her chair slowly around, making eye contact, and took off the headset.

"Can I ask why?"

"We're heading into Dive. As soon as you're ready."

"This is too close range, sir. Way too close. We've got a planet below, way too close."

"Close range, and we're going to risk it, Finn. Niang is expendable. Our cargo isn't. And it's orders."

"Whose orders?"

Hocking sprang from his chair, drew his gun. They were all armed, all the officers, armed from the hour Tandy's aide was killed. Even Voris carried a small pistol strapped to her belt. He pointed his gun, irrationally, at the ceiling. He clamped his teeth together and tilted his head back slightly, creating a close approximation of authority. "Are you questioning my direct orders?" Looking down at her, down the slick length of his nose, he waited for her answer.

"Yessir."

Voris cringed into the back of her chair. She whispered harshly, "Clio!"

Clio swung on her. "Dive'll kick the atmosphere to hell and gone. It's against all regs, this close to a living world. You want to be responsible for blasting Niang to dust, you willing to take responsibility?" She turned back to Hocking.

"That is not your call," he said. "Nothing is your call. This is time of war, and you will follow my commands." Still, the gun pointed at the ceiling, prompting Clio to push just a little harder.

"I want to talk to Tandy."

Hocking worked his jaw forward and back, dislodging his words with effort. "Colonel Tandy is the source of this order, if you want to know. Colonel Tandy wants us out of here immediately."

Tandy appeared in the hatchway from officers' quarters. Singh nodded quickly to him, but Tandy was fixed on Clio.

"Is there a problem here?" Tandy said.

Hocking looked at his pistol, then slowly holstered it. "She refuses to Dive, Colonel."

Tandy was cleaned up, with shaved face and new uniform, and, for all his reputed hurry, he took time now to gaze at her calmly, and in an even voice said, "Is that right, Clio?"

"Nosir. Not that I refuse. Just questioning the timing."

He nodded. Not agreeing, clearly not agreeing, but just maybe understanding. Just maybe sizing up the strength of her opposition.

"Clio, I'll see you in my quarters." He turned without waiting for her, disappeared down the corridor.

Clio threw herself out of the chair. Down the corridor, she caught up with him just in front of his cabin door. "What the hell is going on here, Tandy?"

Tandy ushered her in to the cabin, closing the door without haste. He strode to the desk console, dousing a thunderous crescendo of violins, and turned to face her. "That theory of Vandarthanan has never been tested."

"Tested? Of course it's never been tested. Jesus Christ, who's going to *test* a cataclysmic storm? You willing to *test* it on Niang?"

"We must hurry, Clio."

Clio marched into the center of the room, spun around. "You're in a hurry. I'm not."

He sat down on the couch, arm along the top, watching her.

"What's a few more hours in this space?" she demanded. "You think the Nians won't follow us through Dive? You think Diving early is some tactical advantage?"

"It might be."

"Might be! But you don't know."

He watched her in silence a few more moments. "Still in love with Niang, aren't you?" When she didn't answer, he continued. "You still believe Niang is the Great Answer. The happy ending to all our troubles. The great regreening, worth any price."

"You make my ideas sound so childish."

He pursed his lips. "Not childish. Idealistic and wrong. I never said you were childish."

"I won't Dive this soon. I won't do it, Tandy."

"No, I can see that."

"Don't try to talk me into it."

"No. You have your principles." His voice conveyed a noncommittal tone, verging on irony. He glanced up at her. "And you have bargaining position, after all. You're the Dive pilot, right?"

Clio grew wary, waiting for the trump card.

"I'll give it twenty-four hours. Would that suit you?"

Clio thought fast. Twenty-four hours, might be enough, had heard of ships Diving within thirty-six, had heard of ship captains cutting it that close.

His eyebrow arched, waiting for her, while she calculated how far she could push him, now that he had the FTL aboard and was fleeing for his life, in time of war.

"Twenty-four hours, then."

He patted the couch top. "Done."

"That easy?"

"A man in my position, Clio, learns how to find solutions. Learns how to listen to his officers, his advisors. How to give up a little, to keep much."

"What are you keeping?"

"You. Your loyalty. You learn how not to push people past their closely held principles. You push someone past that and you're dealing with a dangerous man. Or woman. A man who'll do anything. An unpredictable man. The worst kind."

"You've nothing but contempt for my principles."

"Not true, Clio. Not true. Your principles are very important to me. I do fundamentally disagree with your positions, but I know what they are. You seldom surprise me. I can count on you. Do you know how valuable that is to a man like me? To count on someone?"

"Nosir."

"Sure you do." He got up, smoothing his uniform. "Think about it. You'll find me surprisingly consistent as well, Clio. And that might be important to *you*, someday." He crossed the room to the credenza. Opening a bottom drawer, he withdrew a large-caliber pistol and placed it on the desktop. "You know how to use one of these?"

Clio's throat was so dry she had to struggle to keep her voice natural. "Of course."

He nodded. "Good. I keep it here in the bottom drawer." He replaced it, and returned to stand next to her by the couch. "I want you to spend Dive—when we finally Dive—I want you to spend Dive in my cabin. And I want you to kill anybody who comes through that door. No matter who it is. If it's Captain Hocking himself. Anybody who's awake in Dive other than you is the enemy, and you will kill him."

"I'm supposed to be on the bridge during Dive, sir."

"Yes. And that's where an enemy will count on you being. But you won't be. Do you understand?"

"Yessir."

He smiled. "No arguments? No principles compromised?"

Clio managed to look in his eyes. "Nosir."

"Good. Then I can count on you?"

She nodded, words stuck away down her throat, in a knot of bile and self-disgust.

A drop of water plunked onto Clio's forehead. She jumped. Looked up, saw the hot-water return pipe laden with sweat as it carried ship's excess heat to dump into space. Here in the deep hold, pipes coiled along bulkheads, fluids sluiced along metal systems, jointed and riveted like any plumbing anywhere. They sweated and knocked and banged, filling the deck with creaking mechanical workings, as though she were in a tenement basement and not lower deck on the freeping scientific marvel of the world.

Damn, where was Ashe, anyway?

Underneath the creaking of ship's hydraulics, the great hum of *Galactique*'s engines sang through lower deck, asserting the primacy of thrust and movement that gave the ship its purpose. That marked the ship as slower than light, a rocket-driven metal canister daring the distances encompassed by Dive, dwarfed by the immensity of their voyage; a voyage whose terrain was a mere gulf stream in the great ocean galaxy.

Beneath the throb of ship's bulkheads, the ladder to mid-decks rattled. Someone was coming. Clio backed into a small space next to a stowage locker, tripping the handle of the main compartment. It swung open, its metal panel slapping against her elbow. Shit. Clio pushed it back, clicking it into place. Listened.

Footsteps moving in. Then a whisper: "Clio? It's Timothy."

She stepped out. "Jesus, what took you so long?"

"Had to wait until the corridor was clear." He moved to her, pulling her into his arms.

Clio pushed away. "We have to hurry. I'm on duty any minute."

He pulled her back. "I know that we have to hurry. Just don't pull away from me like that."

She took a deep breath and expelled it into his big shoulder. "Jesus, I'm shaky."

"It's good to breathe. Do it some more." He wrapped her closer to him until she eased off and leaned into him.

"I'm real shaky, Timothy."

"I know. So am I."

She pulled back again. "This is a damn mess. Everything's gone wrong."

"Not everything. They still don't know who we are. Who you are."

"We could've just pitched it into the damn Hell Crack and been done with it." A vent in the bulkhead released a gasp of oily air, ruffling Clio's pants legs. Unconsciously, she backed away slightly. "Now what are we going to do," she said. "Storm the bridge?"

A clank from behind jolted her body.

"The CO_2 exchanger. It clanks," she said, but whether for his benefit or hers, she wasn't sure. She raised an eyebrow at him. "So what's the plan?"

"The plan is easy, Clio. Our best shot is Dive. As soon as crew is out, we comb through Tandy's quarters . . ."

"*We?*" She wrinkled her forehead, remembering. "You can ride out Dive, eyes open, that right?"

"Yes." He waited for her, watching carefully.

"It's just pretty strange, that's all."

"Not strange, Clio. Just different. We've DNA-engineered Dive tolerance. What's strange is your whole damn starship crew, except one, out cold for two whole hours."

"OK, so we go through Tandy's quarters and find the circuit board, right?"

"Yes. Then we signal my ship to stand off a few kilometers. We drag Petya to loading bay and make our escape in the lander."

"OK. Fine." In the silence that followed, she looked up into Ashe's steady gaze. "I said fine."

"I know what you said. I also know you're not fine." He paused, voice lowering. "I have no right to try to take you with me, Clio. It's too dangerous—for you and Petya."

"Look. We're going. You said we had a chance. I'm going to take that chance."

"It's Tandy, isn't it?" he said. He stared at her, hard.

"Yes, it's Tandy," she threw back. "What if I can't find it and have to wait for him to wake up? He'll be real happy just to hand it over."

"Not my job to make him happy. Not *your* job, OK?"

"I said OK!" She looked around as her too-loud voice resonated through the ship's bowels.

"He trusts you, Clio. Get close to him."

Clio turned away, banged her fist against the stowage door. It came unhooked, slapped against her hip. She slammed it shut. "I'm not going to seduce him, if that's what you mean."

"OK, you're not going to seduce him."

"Well, that's what you want, isn't it? For me to disarm him in bed?"

"I'm not saying go that far." He paused. "*Have* you been to bed with him?"

"No! That's not what our relationship is like."

"Your relationship. So you have a relationship."

"No. Yes. I know him, in a way. He doesn't know me. I guess that's not a relationship."

"Right. It's not." Ashe pulled her close to him, lowering his voice. "Clio. I don't ask what you can't do. But this is war, it's not pleasant, it means doing some hard things. It means the end of your friendship with Tandy. You've chosen. If you're having second thoughts, I need to know." He searched her face.

Clio met his eyes. "We'll steal it during Dive. He'll be out cold, you can help me search."

Clio looked down the corridor, thought she saw the

phosphorescence marking his passage. "You touch metal, and leave an imprint. Your skin has some secretion. Be careful of that."

"Can't wear gloves around here, can I?"

"I have to go." Clio moved past him into the center of the corridor. "We've got twenty-four hours until Dive. Meet me on the bridge as soon as we hit Dive point." She turned, but he pulled her back.

"Clio, I hate this. He has some power over you, Tandy does."

"Jesus Christ, Timothy, leave it alone!"

"No, *you* leave it alone! The moment you think you've got a relationship with Jackson Tandy, you're lost. He's poison, Clio, a damn army colonel who'd flick you aside in an instant if you got in his way. You don't mean null to him, Clio. I hope you don't think otherwise. See the man for what he is and let him go."

"I have let him go! And it makes it goddamn harder when you keep bringing him up."

Ashe stood there, his shoulders hunched and massing their energy for a fight, for some physical feat, whereas all he was asked to do was let it be. He glowered. "I hate this," he said.

"I know, Timothy." She left him, moving quickly toward the mid-decks ladder, following the snaking course of the corridor, in a hurry all of a sudden to flee the dim recesses of this deep place. At the hatch ladder she stopped, turned around. "I love you," she said, words spoken to the cool shadows, words too soft to penetrate. She clattered up the rungs.

"You OK, sis?" Petya looked down on Clio as she clutched her sides, trying to keep from shaking. The little white paper cup sat next to her on the gurney, empty of the blue tabs and the red vitamin pills.

"I'm fine. Sometimes, before Dive, I shake a little."

"Before Dive, you get scared?"

"Sometimes."

"The pills keep you awake?"

"Yeah, they help."

"You're the Dive pilot. You're supposed to stay awake. If I took pills, I could stay awake?"

"No. Only works on a few people. Are you curious, Petya? About Dive?"

He fiddled with the metal stirrups at the end of the gurney. "I'd like to be awake when everyone else is asleep."

"Why?"

"It's like a ghost? You walk around and no one can see you?" He moved to the computers, hit a few keys. Hit them again, though the computer was off. "You think Mom can see us?" he asked, not looking at her.

Clio felt a cold wave ripple up from her stomach.

"Mrs. Looby said if Mom is in heaven she can see everything we do. But if she's a ghost, that means she's not in heaven?"

"I don't know, Petya. I never figured that stuff out. Mom thought that when you die, it's over."

"Mom knew it was over?" He had moved to the X-ray machine, probing the lanky extension, jointed, like the long legs of a preying mantis.

Clio sank into memory. The drills at home, the ones that Mother made them practice up until the last time, the time it was no longer a drill. The night it was all over. The drills weren't like anti-Green drills or fire drills at school, the kind of stupid exercise they made you do for no good reason, and where everyone laughed and never thought the least bit about bombs or fires. The house drills were a different sort. Mom never said "when they come for us," but underneath her matter-of-fact practice session, underneath the boring race up the stairs to the hidden closet, was the certainty that they would come, someday the race to the closet would be real. They would come onto the porch, hammer at the door. There would be only seconds.

Mom never ran up the stairs for drill. Clio never asked why, and suddenly she felt immensely sad. Not that Mom hadn't escaped that final night, but that Clio never asked her why. Why she didn't drill with them. That Clio never asked her mother much of anything, but day after day soared in the exquisite center of her adolescent self, never asking, never wondering.

"Mom knew?" Petya asked again.

Clio looked up. Looked into his eyes a long while.

"Yes. I guess she did." Clio felt her mother's presence in the room, leaning against the counter over there, smoking a cigarette in that hurried, nervous way. Eyes darting, seeing everything. *So, you going to do it? You going to steal this FTL thing?* Clio waited for the cautions, the advice. Mom took a few short puffs, looking keenly at her daughter. She stubbed the cigarette out in the little black ashtray, barely finding room amid the butts. *I know you can do it, hon. You're smart. Just keep your wits, is all. Nobody can keep you from what you put your mind to. I can bear seventeen years witness to that, gad knows.*

She never could bring herself to say *God*, even casually, even swearing. Well, then, if she didn't know about God and heaven, she knew no less than Clio. Just knew her daughter. Knew DSDE. Some things are given us to know. Other things, no point wondering.

It was then that the medlab cabin door opened. As it did, it seemed to usher in a cold stream of heavy air. The vision of Mother withered as Ashe came through the door, his face a brittle mask, except for his eyes, which said, *I'm sorry. I'm sorry, Clio.* Behind him, Jared Licht with a gun. Licht closed the door behind them.

"I'm afraid I've got rather bad news," Licht said to Clio. "Your friend here appears to be in a bit of trouble." He pushed Ashe toward Clio, so he could cover both of them at once.

"What's going on, Licht?" Clio said. "You finally had your nervous breakdown?" All the while the air seemed to leave her lungs, her body, as though she were full of holes, holes everywhere.

Licht's violet eyes burned bright. "Well. What's going on, as you put it, is that I got ahold of this flashlight." He drew a flashlight out of his flightsuit pocket. He turned it in his hand for their benefit. "I won't bother to show you what

it looks like with the lights out, but suffice it to say that it
. . . well, it *glows*, actually. Seems this was the flashlight
that Ashe used to lead you out of the big cave down there."
He cocked his head, waiting for a reaction. "Isn't that a tad
strange? I looked about, and found that the whole ship has
traces of this—this neon *ooze*. Turns out, it comes from *him*.
I'm afraid that just can't be explained very easily. Or you
tell me, Ms. Finn, he's *your* friend. Has he always *oozed*
this way?"

"I wouldn't know."

"Hm. You wouldn't know. Well, we'll see. Eventually,
it will all come out."

Clio avoided looking into Ashe's eyes, couldn't look at
him without giving herself away. Here she was, sitting on
the gurney, her every move watched by Jared Licht and
his gun. While her body leaked all her courage. So many
holes . . .

"What are you trying to say, Licht? Why don't you just
say it instead of dragging out this little drama."

"Isn't it obvious? I think I've caught myself an alien.
Genuine Nian. Right here in our timid little botanist. A
space alien." He made a face. "Rather lurid, but there you
have it."

"You've really gone off the deep end this time, Jared,"
Clio said. She took that moment to casually slide off the
gurney.

"Wait right there," Licht said. "I'm toying with the idea
that you're involved in all this. As close as you are to him."

"Close? Not close at all."

"Well my, my. The ship springs a leak and how the rats
do flee." He glanced at Petya in the corner. Petya was
showing obvious stress, blinking hard at Licht and his gun.
"And maybe your brother's involved. Aiding and abetting.
Well. We'll come up with something." Licht rummaged
through a few drawers, finally finding what he was looking for.

"You are such a career prick, Jared," Clio said.

Licht turned around, with a syringe in his hand.

Moving up close behind Ashe, he thrust the needle into the exposed part of Ashe's neck. "A little sedative, to keep our spaceman under control." Ashe rubbed his neck, then stood swaying a moment before finding a chair and sinking slowly into it.

Petya took a step toward Ashe. "It's not true?"

Ashe looked up at him. "I'm not a monster, Petya." His words came slowly, carefully. "I'm just different from you. Whatever they try to tell you . . . make you believe. Just remember. That I am human like you."

"Doesn't even bother to deny it," Licht said. "He's just going to roll over for us. No run for the money."

"I'm sure you were looking forward to practicing your arts, Licht," Clio said.

He pulled a chair out, sat opposite Ashe. "Why don't you tell us about it then, Ashe? Since you're talking freely."

Ashe rubbed at his neck where the shot went in. He raised his eyes, speaking to Petya. "My world, Petya. It's a land of vast forest. A beautiful place of . . . many trees, where people honor the trees and . . . do no harm to them, live with them. There is no Sickness. No DSDE. Families stay together. Not afraid."

Licht sighed, waving the gun. "Get to the point."

"The planet . . . is a living thing," Ashe continued. "We live without metal, Petya, and the machines of a metal sort . . . we live without them. Our cities, our technology—biological. Can you understand that, Petya? We work with the forest . . . and it grows to our needs. We are much like you. Human, Petya. Some years ago a ship—one of ours—crashed on Niang. Held a precious secret. Secret of how to travel to the stars . . . without Dive. I tried—tried to keep your army from finding that secret, to keep DSDE from that secret . . . Once they have it they can conquer worlds. They can conquer my people. Your world is dying, Petya. I don't want the same thing to happen to mine. I hope you can still be friends with me. If not, it's OK, just don't believe them that I'm a monster . . ." His voice was badly slurred now, and he stopped in confusion.

Petya turned to Licht. His face was tightly stitched up in a frown. "I don't think you should point a gun at Timothy."

Licht stood up in alarm as Petya took a step toward him. Clio jumped in front of Petya, putting her hand on his chest to stop him. She turned to Licht. "He's just concerned about the gun."

Licht waved the gun at them. "Tell him to sit down."

"I don't want to sit down," Petya said, frowning mightily.

"Petya!" Clio hissed.

"You shouldn't point guns at people?" Petya said.

Licht drew himself up, growing calm. "I'll warn him one more time. I have a dangerous criminal in my custody. If your brother threatens me in any way, I'll shoot him."

Petya shoved Clio aside. "I don't like you," he said to Licht.

Licht aimed down the length of the barrel, cocked the gun. Clio flew in front of Petya once more. "Licht! Don't shoot! If you kill me you're in deep shit. You can't get back without me."

"Stand aside," Licht commanded.

Ashe rose, wobbling. "I'm your prisoner. Why don't you just turn me in and get it over with?"

Licht's face turned slightly toward Ashe, gun still pointed at Clio. He shook his head, smiling. "You're crazy, Clio Finn," he said. "I almost killed you." He looked at Ashe, nodded at the door. "Let's go."

As Ashe reached the door, Licht stopped. "That brother of yours, Clio. He's a menace. He should be put down. Keep him in line or someday I *will* put him down." He nodded to Ashe, who turned to open the medlab door.

"For now," Licht said, "I think it's Ashe who'll be put down. Like a dog."

They left the room. Just as the door swung shut, Petya bolted past Clio, and burst into the corridor after them. Clio was a long second behind him, but soon enough to see Petya stumbling into the corridor crying "No, no!" and a startled

Licht sweeping his booted foot out. In the next moment—a moment too short to measure, but embedded ever after as a whole scene in Clio's mind—Licht turned to watch Petya crash to his knees, and then Clio saw Licht's black-shirted arm bring the gun to the back of Petya's head, which was tilted slightly toward the floor, as though for execution. As Clio threw herself forward too late to stop him, an explosive report filled her ears, and she heard herself screaming, screaming as her eyes soaked in the color red from all directions.

At the same moment Clio saw in her peripheral vision that someone else was standing there, a woman, and then Jared Licht fell forward and a spray of blood appeared on the bulkhead. Licht collapsed on the deck, unmoving, while Petya removed his hands from his ears and peered over at Licht's body.

Voris stood there, gun pointing now toward the floor. "Is he dead?" she asked.

The side of Licht's head was gone. No one answered.

She wiped at a few spatters of blood on her sleeve, smearing them. Her whole flight suit was pockmarked with Licht's blood. "He was going to shoot Petya," she said. "Right here in the corridor, in the head, like an execution." She looked over at Clio. "That can't happen here."

Crew came running, stopped when they saw the body, and Voris with her gun. "I had to kill him, didn't I?" She looked at the crew members. A trickle of blood coursed down her cheek like a tear. "Petya was on his knees and he was going to shoot him in the head. Just kill this innocent boy, shoot him in the head. Do we let people do that, and just stand by, and do nothing? Stand by and do nothing?"

Clio stepped across Licht's body and kneeled beside Petya, folding her arms around him. She looked past his trembling shoulder to the gathering crew. "Call the captain," she said. Then she looked up at Voris, who stood holding the gun loosely by her side as though her arm were dead.

"You stopped him, Meg," Clio said. "You did right."

Ashe swayed against the bulkhead and toppled, senseless, to the floor.

"What's with him?" asked one of the crew.

Clio looked down at Ashe, fallen like a giant tree. "Can't stand the sight of blood," Clio said. "Take him to his cabin."

CHAPTER 34

They were all asleep on the bridge. Outside the viewport at Clio's left, the stars left snowy tracks in their rush to the future. The ship was in Dive. The killing of a DSDE agent, with a ship's officer involved, was no small matter, but nothing would keep Tandy from this Dive.

Clio, seated in the copilot's chair, scanned the bridge crew's faces—Voris, Hocking, Singh—all asleep. Singh's eyelids fluttered as though behind those heavy lids he frolicked, swept away by some dreamtime Bacchus. Hocking's head had fallen back against his headrest. A blatting snore rose to a crescendo, then subsided amid flutish moans. Voris slept like a child, her arms cradling her torso. She was under ship arrest pending an investigation, but meanwhile she sat her post.

This would be the last time Clio would see Meg Voris. The thought was not without some relief. Voris of the simple beliefs and crowd of words, always leading with her chin. Clio had treated her no better than the rest of the crew had, by turns derisive and distant. But here was the only person on the bridge who drew the line against the bastards—publicly, her life and career on the line. Maybe at the hearing, she would do OK, if things hadn't gone so far that DSDE could put a gun to the back of a young man's head for losing his composure. Maybe, she would keep her bars, her freedom. Earned them, by damn. It occurred to Clio then that Voris was—against all likelihood—her friend.

She turned away from the crew's sleeping forms. *Jesus, girl, get a grip.* The cabin wavered, as the Dive distortions rippled simple vision, reflecting the overemotional frame of her own mind deep in Dive. Get a grip. Chronometer racing forward, Dive fleeing by, leaving the past in a headlong rush from Niang.

Clio unclipped the seat restraints and stood. Time to get this show on the road. So little time, got to hurry. No time for looking at faces. She stood, pulled the zipper of her flight togs down far enough to grasp the chain around her neck and pull out her dog tag. The tag was flesh-warm, almost hot. It read: *Clio Finn, 6747NRP, Biotime Corp USA, 11-7-92, Vandarthanan Station, Central Administration.* Just so. No hometown, no next-of-kin, just Central Administration. In the event of her death, this is where they would send her personal effects, her files and final paycheck. The tag might have read, *Clio Finn, Dive Pilot, daughter of Evelyn, sister of Petya, 11-7-92, Upham, North Dakota. In case of death or alternative future, contact Meg Voris, Vanda Station.* And, as epitaph, *"Don't Tread on Me."* Then, remembering the Issaquah Quarry, perhaps *"Queen of Hell"* might do. Or, passing on Mother's home-spun advice, *"No one can keep you from what you put your mind to."* Maybe that last one, then. Clio hung the chain around Voris' neck, and tucked it into her flight suit. *Give 'em hell, Meg.*

She scanned the console one last time, the chronometer surging past three thousand years, time a-wasting. Time to burn, all that time. She shook her head to clear it, and headed off flight deck for officers' quarters.

Tandy's room was overwarm, releasing the tincture of scotch from a half-full glass on the sideboard. Clio leaned against his cabin door, taking her bearings.

The sitting area was empty. Tandy would be in his sleeping nook behind the screen to her right. Ahead of her, the wall of viewports beckoned with their staggering prospect of a billion stars. Ashe was not, of course, waiting for her, still out cold as he was on his bunk belowdecks. Licht must have pumped him full enough to bring down a bear. Clio planned to find the FTL circuit as soon as she could, then wait by Ashe's side until he roused. If still in Dive they might escape in good order. If not . . . they must somehow fight their way to the landing bay to escape in *Sun Spot*. With a hostage they might get away clean.

The near stars streamed past the viewport, in hypervelocity, but framed between the sideboard and the wardrobe like a surrealistic window on another reality. Which indeed it was, the macroreality, the surrounding sea of stars, vast and everlasting. She snapped her attention back to the task at hand. The circuit board.

Clio began at Tandy's desk, pulling open the center drawer. A personal thing, a man's desk. Feels like voyeurism, feels like what it is, thievery. The contents of the drawer displayed themselves in immaculate order. She palmed stacks of papers, envelopes, tissue packets, files, his maroon Waterman fountain pen, ink fillers, a packet of Lifesavers. Ran her hands under drawers, lifted the desk pad, comm unit.

Similarly, the sideboard with its stock of crystal glasses, scotch, brandy, and two bottles of fine Chardonnay. Those last might be saved for a special occasion. But whom would he share them with? She pushed away the thought that it would be her. Probably he had a crony or two. Perhaps an off-shift glass with Singh now and then—or even Hocking, might not be all that bad for an hour's company. And even as she thought it, her deeper mind said, False, false. Singh and Hocking never once sat over a drink to talk with Tandy, they never shared more than a formal and awkward officers' mess, after which each rushed back to his separate duties and the comfort of his own opinions, like soft, round stones cradled in the hand and worn smooth by frequent handling. None of them had the slightest interest in the others. Perhaps, too, Tandy had not the slightest interest in *her*. What did he know of her, really? Claimed to know her, yes, claimed to count on her, gave her his gun, but didn't know her. . . .

She patted the sofa pillows, threw them on the floor, feeling in the creases. Replacing the pillows, she moved to the side table. There, the beguiling face of Suzanne Tandy, pretty in a delicate sort of way, too fragile for the imposing silver frame. Suzanne looked on with disapproval as Clio opened the table drawer, thrust her hand into its empty confines.

Now she turned and surveyed what was left. The bedroom. Looked at her watch. Still over an hour. Plenty of time.

Just behind the sleeping partition in the dimness, Clio could make out the shadowy bed and Tandy's sleeping form. She turned up the lights. He lay passively, at ease, though in a military way, while she rummaged through each drawer, under the mattress and bedclothes, then the bathroom. Nothing.

Looking into the cubicle one last time she noted the bed's reading light fixed to the wall with a gold-colored metal base. She drew closer, pulled on the lamp. It swung away from the bulkhead, revealing a small safe with keypad. Clio stared at this for a long while. Not that there was any question of attempting to break the heavy safe with ordinary tools. But the presence itself of the safe meant her search was over. And her hopes, also, hopes of making a clean break during Dive, the fantasy of the safe escape, and Tandy never the wiser until they came to him, saying, *Clio Finn's gone, sir. Apparently in the lander.*

Clio gave the main cabin a cursory second search. In the sideboard, bottom drawer, the .45 still lay. She checked the chambers. Fully loaded. She could take it, but if Tandy awoke and looked for it, he would have early warning of her intentions. Where was Ashe when she needed him? Lying there out cold and useless, when he should be here helping her search. Ashe should be waiting in the sleeping cell for Tandy to awake, then force him to hand over the circuit board. Clio should be on the bridge as ship came out of Dive. That's how it should have been. Now she could wait with loaded gun pointed at Tandy's head . . . but not knowing if Ashe was awake or not, then what would she do? How could she contact Ashe's ship? It was a mess.

She shut the drawer with its gun, glanced a last time at the privacy wall in front of Tandy's sleeping cell, then left his cabin and made her way down to crew deck, and down to Ashe's cabin.

He lay on the bunk, unconscious like the rest of crew, but with a difference: she didn't have any idea when he would wake up.

"Timothy!" Clio shook him. His shoulder barely registered her rocking.

"Timothy," she called again, close to his ear.

His eyes opened to slits, fell shut again. "Timothy. Goddamn it, Timothy, wake up or I'll slug you!" No good. He slept peacefully while she paced the tiny cabin, measuring out the moments, precious moments of Dive time. Their best chance to steal the circuit board and the lander was ticking away, and he slept on like there was no tomorrow. Then, reminding herself there were drugs to modify effects of drugs, she yanked open the cabin door and ran down the corridor to medlab. Here, the dreadful scene of Licht and Petya and Meg: Licht standing, arm stiff and gun thrust against Petya's temple, cocking the gun, the explosion, the imprint of blood on the bulkhead. She pushed open the medlab door, strode to the nearest drawers, yanking them open, searching for something, anything to pull Ashe from his slumber. She slammed the drawers shut one after the other, until she thought to look into the portable first-aid kit. There, a dozen capsules of mazicon. She grabbed two and flew back down crew deck to find Ashe as she'd left him.

She rushed to the bed, and knelt by his side. Drops of sweat from her forehead darkened the collar of his Biotime greens. "Goddamn it, Timothy! Just wake up, will you?" She broke a capsule under his nose, then another. His brow furrowed, pulling the forehead scar inward like a needle registering her voice, and slept on. "Timothy," she cried, "what am I supposed to do? This ship is flying itself, no pilot on the bridge. I haven't found the circuit board. Everybody's gonna wake up any minute. What am I supposed to do?" She slapped his face. "Just come back, baby. Just come back. . . ." Her stomach was in tatters. She rummaged in Ashe's desk for food, found a box of Milk Duds, ate them one by one, wishing it were hemlock, sitting on a chair and staring at Ashe's lumpen form. "Goddamn it, Timothy," she said, her mouth full of chocolate. "Goddamn it."

"Like a trooper. Swear like a trooper," Ashe interrupted. His lids were half open, revealing cloudy eyes.

"Timothy!" Clio ran to his side, hugged him, then batted at him. "We have to hurry!"

"OK. Hurry. Sounds good." He sat up, then slumped against her.

"Shit! Goddamn shit to hell!"

"Anyone ever rinse your soapy mouth?" he said into her shoulder.

"Rinse my mouth out with soap? Yes. Lots of times, it really works." He flopped back down. "We are doomed," she said at him.

"Attagirl. A for attitude."

"Don't you get it?" Clio quit tugging on him. She jumped up. "Don't you know what's going on here?" Clio's voice was already an octave high and rising. "We're coming out of Dive any goddamn second. We haven't got the circuit board and we haven't got your ship lined up to get us the hell out of here. While you've been sleeping it off, I've gone through every square inch of Tandy's quarters and come away with nothing. Zip, null, and zero. I don't have it, Timothy. We're screwed."

"I figured," he slurred at her. "Water." He reached toward the washbasin.

Clio sloshed a glass full and brought it to him. "What did you figure?"

He gulped the liquid down. "Figured we wouldn't find it. In a safe, right?"

"Yes, its in a safe, damn it! So you figured I wouldn't find it!"

"Figured. But Tandy . . . can find it. Hands it over, we hit the bridge, take a hostage and escape in the lander. More water."

Clio fetched it, fighting the urge to douse him with it. "How can you be so damn smug! This is exactly fifty times as dangerous as our first plan, and you don't even care!"

He swung his feet onto the floor, sitting now in a

wobbly upright position. He took a moment to get his bearings. When he looked up at her his eyes locked on hers. "I care. I care a lot. I just figured it would go this way. I was prepared, Clio. You weren't."

"You let me believe a fantasy."

Ashe's face darkened. "Oh no, Clio, you built that fantasy all by yourself, no help needed. You were terrified of confronting Tandy, so you let yourself believe he hid it under his pillow, and you'd find it while he was out cold. Well, you gave your plan a try. Now it's time for mine." He rose, carefully. "How much time we got?"

"Twenty minutes, I figure. No more."

Ashe nodded. "You ready?"

Clio nodded. She grabbed his elbow, steadying him, and propelled him toward the door.

"I'll secure the bridge," he said. "Signal my ship. Wait there for you. When you get the circuit, meet me there." He pulled away from her arm. "You go ahead. I can walk."

"We're going up together." She watched him sway in place. Any moment he would crash to the deck. She turned to open the cabin door. Stopped.

"He saved my life, you know."

"Yeah. I've heard this before, Clio."

She resisted the tug on her arm as Ashe moved to open the door. Memory replayed. It released an anesthetic glue, rooting her feet to the floor. She saw herself sitting on the barracks floor, the cold, thin wood as cold as her heart, and Tandy's arm around her shoulder, and she, climbing back from the cave of death, and only his arm to lean on in all the wide realm of despair.

Ashe moved closer, and put his hand on her shoulders. "I know."

"He saved my life." Feet still glued down, Ashe still pulling on her arm, pushing her toward the door.

"Maybe he did. He's still poison."

"No."

"Yes! He's used and betrayed everybody who's come in his path. You, your brother, even his own wife for godsakes."

Clio turned around, eyes snapped wide. "What do you mean? That wasn't his fault. He grieves for her, he worships her. . . ."

A beat. Ashe was looking at her. "Jesus, Clio. Is that what he told you, that he worships her?"

Something about that look in Ashe's eyes. Clio stared back.

"Is that what he told you?"

"He told me that there was an assassination attempt on his life—the Old Greens, or someone." Still, Ashe was gazing at her with that cold, dark silence.

Clio stammered on: "Only she was in the car, not him."

"That's bullshit. Suzanne Tandy wasn't killed by a car bomb. I thought you knew what he did to her."

Clio stepped back from him, but Ashe closed the gap. "You're going to listen to this, by God. You listen: She had a nephew, secretly gay, he was getting by with it. He contracted the Sickness, and Suzanne somehow got him to the underground rather than see him shipped to a quarry. She found a contact in the underground and the nephew made it. Suzanne didn't." Ashe looked at her beneath his dark brows. "Your Colonel Tandy found out and flew into a rage. He beat the truth out of her. Then he personally drove her to a quarry and interred her there for betraying him. Afterward, he expunged every last trace of her possessions and personal history from private and public record."

"You can't know that! How could you possible know that?"

"Clio. We have a dossier on most of your VIPs. Like I said, it's war." He moved in close, gripped her upper arm, told out slowly: "She was a fragile woman. She died within six months."

Clio pulled her arm away, backing against the cabin door. "I don't believe you. He adores her."

He snorted. "Talk about a fantasy. He murdered her. She went renegade on him. It nearly cost him his career. He was finally cleared of charges stemming from the nephew's quarry-dodging. But he never saw her again."

Clio closed her eyes, trying to absorb it. "He flew into a rage . . ."

"And beat her into a confession."

"He put her in a quarry . . ."

"Took her straight to the Issaquah Quarry, not even a smaller, more humane facility. Took her to the camp of death you know so well."

"She died there . . ." Clio squeezed the words out, looking at them, hanging in front of her.

"Like a bird in an oil spill. A nasty, dirty death. Do you want the details?"

"No."

Clio stared past Ashe to the bulkhead behind him. The rivets marched along the panels in lockstep, holding the cabin in place, stitching the ship together like Ashe's words stitched together his telling. It was the plain truth. Tandy's story was a fantasy. No, a plain lie. Just your average, daily, evil lie.

"He lied to me," she said. "All lies, all of it." She closed her eyes, trying to cool them, trying to stop them from leaking. To be made such an utter fool of, to be such a pathetic, foolish thing. "God, what an utter fool."

"He's a master, Clio. Don't kick yourself."

"He never loved her," Clio said, opening her eyes to gaze at the ship bulkhead, that simple, predictable, physical thing.

"Why does it matter so much, Clio?"

Clio turned to look at Ashe, into his eyes. "It doesn't. Anymore."

She could feel emotion draining from her body through a hole in her side, like a boil subsiding from a lancing. She felt the warmth trickle out.

"Are you OK?"

"We don't have time for this, Timothy."

"No. But are you OK?"

"Yeah." She turned toward the door, but he spun her around to face him.

"Can you go through with this?"

She took in a cleansing breath. Remarkably, her lungs

held it, despite the tatters of her insides. "Yeah," she said. "I can do it."

Ashe raised an eyebrow.

"I can do it. I've put my mind to it. OK?"

Ashe nodded. "OK. Then let's hurry."

Clio looked at her watch. Ten minutes. Still time. They pushed out the door and into the corridor, headed for the bridge, in slow motion, as in a dream of doomed escape. Ashe leaned heavily on Clio's arm, stomping his feet to find the deck plates, while Clio steered him down the long, long crew deck, stretching like taffy to the tiny hatch to mid-decks.

In the rush into Dive, no one had cleaned up the remains of Licht's bloodstains on the bulkhead. Now Clio and Ashe stumbled toward this blotch outside medlab like sacrificial heroine and hero to the labyrinth of the minotaur. Licht rose up to prevent them, tissue-thin in the way of ghosts, warning them of the futility of their venture. *Doomed,* he said. *Doomed, Clio. Like me, like me.* He reached for them as they clattered past, but Clio set her jaw. "Out of my fucking way, you Nazi," she said, bursting through his insubstantial form, and his prophecy, all at once.

"He's dead, Clio," Ashe said, noting her glance at the bloodstains.

"No, he'll never be dead. He's eternal, like Tandy. They endure, they reincarnate." She helped him to negotiate the hatch ladder. Ashe's feet fumbled to find the rungs. "Hurry," she prompted, clambering down after him.

They plunged down mid-decks, down past the galley, then up, up the ladder to flight deck and officers' quarters. Clio went first, then reached down, giving Ashe a hand.

The Klaxon screamed through the dead silence.

Clio's scalp rippled under the searing blare. Coming out of Dive, oh holy shit. "God, Timothy," she said. "We're not going to make it."

"Yes we are!" He struggled up, hauling himself to his feet. "Run for it, Clio!"

She raced down the short corridor to Tandy's cabin,

then stopped short and softly opened the door, closing it as softly, and moved to the sideboard.

From behind her, she heard: "So it's you, Clio."

She turned, and Tandy was there, his form dark but recognizable, the trim build, the quiet rootedness of him, even in the dim lens of her eye and the darkness of the room. Clio's tongue clogged her throat, barring her answer.

"I'm glad it is," he said. "How did we do?" He turned up the lights and went back to the sleeping nook. Clio heard water running. She darted to the sideboard, opened the smooth, black drawer, and withdrew the gun, stuffing it in her pocket. Tandy came out again, hair neatly combed.

"If you mean who tried to break in," she managed to say, "I saw no one."

Tandy gazed a moment at her, head cocked a fraction to the side. "Good," he said. "That's good. Then we've ditched our Nianist spy in the jungle, eh?"

"Yes. Home free, looks like." She locked her knees to keep them from trembling.

Tandy crossed the room, passing her, and poured himself a drink at the sideboard. "I don't for a minute think we're home free," he said, "not for a minute." He tossed off the drink, then turned and leaned against the sideboard, empty glass held in his hand, carefully, as though still savoring the bouquet. "You won't let down your guard, Clio." A statement.

"Nosir."

"They will be relentless."

"They'll follow us. You expect a fight."

"Yes. One of them may even be on board this very minute. I trust no one."

But you trust me seemed to hang in the air between them. The gun bulged in Clio's pocket, surely visible, weighing down her flight jacket. She kept her eyes firmly on Tandy, her lips tilted in what she hoped was a relaxed half smile.

He seemed to pick up her thought. "Not entirely true, eh? I gave *you* a gun, didn't I? And, in fact, *you* could be the

Nian." He emitted a silent laugh. "Clio! That was a joke. A poor one. I apologize."

Her taped-on smile must have fallen off her face. Now she waited for him to turn his back to her, to give her a chance to pull the gun out of her pocket without catching it on the fabric of her flight suit.

"The Nians are alien, Clio. They look like us, but they are not like us. They are composed of an unnatural biology—as is their ship."

"Their ship?" Clio said, stalling.

"Yes. The ship is theirs. The crashed ship. Harper Teeg told me that it wasn't being invaded by jungle, Clio. It was composed of the jungle in the first place. It was a Niang creation. Wherever the Nians come from, they are the most dangerous of alien races. They pass for human, but they are not human and they can destroy us." He walked to the great curved viewports, gazing out. "I saw one of them kill Captain Pequot, Clio. It sickened me."

He was quiet a moment. He turned to face her. His eyes darted to the gun in her hand.

The look on his face. Wincing, as though warding off a blow. "Oh Clio," he said. "Not you. Not you."

"Feel betrayed, do you?"

He started to speak, stopped. Shook his head slowly. "Oh Clio," he said again. "How did they get to you? What did they have to offer?" He closed his eyes for a moment. When he opened them, his voice was steady. "You always loved Niang. I should have known."

His face had fallen into a deeper tracery of lines, making the forehead wave of his hair seem a mimicry of youth. "Where are your accomplices, Clio? Your vested, crystal-studded Nians with the killing hands? Where are they, Clio? Or are you alone on this ship?"

When she breathed, air entered the cold of her breast. All cold inside. "I'm not alone," she said. "I have plenty of help. Just now I have a job to do and I'm in a hurry."

"What did they offer you, Clio?"

She shook her head pityingly. "My freedom, for starters."

"Where can you possibly be free among them? Freedom is a state of mind, Clio. Which of us is free to do exactly what we please?"

"You are."

"Clio. I'm a colonel in the U.S. Army. Who is less free than a link in the chain of command?"

"You are free to be in the army or not. To travel where you will. To openly oppose your enemies. I've had none of those things. See the difference?"

"Clio, I . . ."

She stopped him. "Problem is, you don't use words to say anything. You use them to be sure nothing is said. I'm tired of your words."

Softly, he said, "What did they offer you that I couldn't?"

"You don't listen, Tandy. Listen now: Freedom. My freedom. And the truth."

"The truth?" he said.

Clio stepped backward to the table by the couch, snatched the silver-framed portrait and tossed it carelessly to Tandy, who caught it. "The truth about your wife who you murdered."

He peered at her out of narrow eyes.

"Why did you let me Dive this ship, Tandy? Why did you rescue me from the quarry? Was it your way of making amends? Put one in, take one out? Only it doesn't work that way, you can't even things up like that. The one who died there, your wife, she *mattered*. And Rita and her baby mattered, who you shoved aside like they were nothing in your grand scheme of things."

Very quiet now, his voice barely a murmur above the muffled hum of the ship: "She mattered to me. More than you'll ever know. I loved her. I love her still. You don't understand how it was, I don't know what they told you . . ."

"The truth."

"The truth! Their version."

"I'm not interested in *versions*. I'm not interested in

your spin on this, Tandy. You murdered her, betrayed your
own wife, then kept her picture on display for sympathy.
You disgust me."

"Not true, not true. I keep her picture to remember how
she was, before she threw me away for Robert—her
nephew. They told you it was her nephew? He was dying,
Clio, you see? He was beyond help, yet she threw me away
for him. She searched my private papers, my private files
for information on the underground, then took him there.
All behind my back, without the least trust that I would have
helped her . . ."

"Helped her!"

"Helped her, yes. Helped her to see the larger good."

"Your good . . ."

"No, the *larger good*. It's what I've tried to help you
see, Clio. To see beyond the individual, beyond personal
loss. We all have losses—you think I haven't had losses?—
but to rise above them, that's our duty, Clio. Don't you
see?" He was beseeching her now, but his words slipped
from her icy brow. Ice, all ice now.

"I thought you saw," he finished in a whisper.

"You know what I see? I see a petty tyrant, spouting
'the end justifies the means.' 'The stars are the future!' For
the *stars* you were willing to exploit a down-on-her-luck
Dive pilot. For the *stars* you yanked my brother from whatever peace he'd found and held him hostage against me. For
the *stars* you left Rita and her child to the revenge of the
quarry guards. Where are they now, Tandy? Ever do a
follow-up call?"

"The stars are your calling too, Clio."

Clio nodded. "Maybe they are. But Earth matters,
Tandy. That's the part you don't get. Earth matters. You
can't pick and choose. What's here is what matters,
you can't talk your way out of what's here, what's in front
of you, what's in your care. She was in your care. I was in
your care. You used us." She couldn't stop the torrent of
words. His betrayals were many, she had to list them all.
"And the antidote to the Sickness . . ."

His eyes flicked up to meet hers.

"Yes, I know about that too, how you all give out the cure to your favorites, and keep it from the rest. Guess I was a favorite for a while, huh? Those little red 'vitamin' pills that you had me take. Because I'm infected, aren't I? From the quarry, I'm infected."

"Clio, we'll save you. It's not too late. The pills . . ."

She interrupted. "I don't care about your freeping pills, Tandy. Keep your antidote."

He remained silent for a long few seconds, a small, dismissive smile poking the side of his face. Then he said: "I was wrong about your name, wasn't I, Clio? You never saw greatness in yourself, like the Egyptian queen. I had you all wrong."

"Yeah, you had me all wrong."

A wistful nod. "Not like Cleopatra, then."

"Cleopatra to your Anthony?" She had seen the old flat-movie too. "No, not like her. And not a fallen angel, either."

"I'm not often wrong about people." A beat. "Why *did* you choose 'Clio Finn'?"

"I liked the sound."

Somewhere belowdecks the gentle thud of a cabin door closing, vents clicking, the rattle of a loose deck plate as a boot tread on the way to some ship routine. On the bridge, Ashe was waiting. She gestured the gun toward the sleeping cubicle. "Get the circuit board," she said, her voice a hard crackle.

Tandy sighed deeply. "It's not in the safe," he said.

"Let's open it anyway." She followed him into the darkly shrouded sleeping nook, gun cocked. "Turn on the light," she ordered, keeping well back.

Tandy flipped the light on, and pulled on the lamp arm. It swung open to reveal the keypad, which he poked his code into. The safe opened. She moved closer for a better look.

It was empty.

"You bastard," she snorted. "You never trusted me."

His eyebrow flew up. "Apparently with good reason."

"I would have done nearly anything for you," she said. "I trusted you."

"So who's been betrayed? Tell me that, Clio?"

The words cut, shifted the ice. "Where is it?" she growled. Too much time, she had taken too much time already. How long had it been? And she was no closer to her goal.

"It's in the next cabin. Officers' mess."

That might be true. Likely it wasn't here, in this cabin.

"Go." She gestured him out.

In the corridor, Clio craned her neck to look onto the bridge, but saw only Singh's knee as he sat his navigation post.

They entered the officers' mess. A half-eaten Pop-Tart lay on a plate, crowned with a slab of congealed butter.

"Get it," Clio ordered, freezing her heart against assaults of forgiveness, gratitude, and the habit of loving swine.

"Clio." Tandy spread his palms. "I can see that I've failed you. I didn't want to fail you. In fact, I wanted to help you, but I can see you can never forgive what I've done. But please . . . please, Clio, don't use your hatred of me to give away the human race."

Now that was ludicrous, if he only knew. *Human race.* A poor choice of words, Tandy, reminding me of the very reason I'm here. "Get it before I shoot you in the leg."

Tandy opened the refrigeration hatch, taking out a brown paper bag. He put it on the table between them.

"Clio," he said. "Don't I *matter*? Is it your turn to say who matters and who doesn't? Your turn to call judgment?"

The ice slipped again. She looked at him, seeing his face as it used to be, before the betrayals. "You matter. Even now, you matter to me. Never doubt that. Now remove it from the sack."

He pulled out the long, wafer-thin, chitinous plate, with its crystals sparkling in a controlled fire. He pushed it to the middle of the table. Then, as she stared a split second, mesmerized by the treasure, Tandy pulled put a pistol from the same bag.

"Don't touch the board, Clio, don't even make one move." A smile creased one corner of his mouth, and fled. "You didn't think it was going to be that easy, did you?"

"It was never going to be easy."

"Clio, put down your gun, very slowly. You're going to put down your gun and I'm going to reach over and take it."

"You don't have to decide anything. I'm going to decide for you, because you're too tired. . . ." Rita moaned behind her. *The sun hit his colonel's bars, and a glint blinded her . . .*

"Put down the gun, Clio."

Tandy was standing snug against the table, while Clio had at least three meters between herself and the table. Maybe just enough room.

"You're not going to kill me in cold blood, Clio."

She lowered her gun to her side.

Tandy nodded slowly.

Then she dove, dove under the table, sliding underneath on her stomach while Tandy backed up to get his aim. But Clio was a fraction of a second ahead of him as she raised her gun arm just high enough to shoot point-blank at his chest. In the next instant, Tandy's shot rang hopelessly wide, as he fell, staggering one step backward and crashing against the refrigeration hatch and sliding to the floor. From his seated position he slowly raised his gun to Clio's head as she tried to rise from her belly-flop position on the floor.

His hand trembled as the light faded from his eyes. He squeezed the trigger halfway and then, looking at a point beyond her face, he lowered the gun to the floor.

Clio scrambled into a crouch, but he lay utterly still, his gun still in his hand, and a small hole in his breast pocket slowly unfolding into a full, red blossom. Kneeling beside him, she waited as his pupils dilated to fill his irises, two dark holes to the depths of his mind, where the Metal Dominion had incubated, and now lay cooling in death.

She spoke softly: *"Clio* was the muse of history,

Colonel. The Greek muse. I thought you'd guess that. There were several muses, but Clio was the one that was best for Dive, the one that knew about history, about going back. I never told anyone before."

His eyelids fluttered, once. Then he was gone.

CHAPTER 35

Clio latched the mess-room door behind her, darting a glance down the corridor to the bridge. Singh's knee just visible, as before. She clutched her pistol close, and crept forward. At the hatchway she ducked through onto the bridge.

Voris, Hocking, and Singh were bound and gagged. She nodded at Ashe and held up the sack. The room flickered mutely, perhaps shocked into silence, like the brain seeing the fatal cells' first encroachment. On the pilot's console, the main release switch controlling launch-bay systems pulsed hot.

Ashe looked at her a long moment, then turned to Hocking. "Do it," he said. Ashe reached over Hocking, toggled the comm, all decks, and removed the captain's gag.

A line of sweat on Hocking's nose glowed from the reflected console lights. He leaned into the mike. "This is the captain. All crew will stand down and retire to science deck. Petya will report immediately to the bridge." He looked up at Ashe.

"Repeat it."

"This is Captain Hocking. This is an emergency. Petya will report to the bridge. Crew and all army personnel will abandon stations and retire to science deck." The echo of his voice from all decks rippled back to the bridge in exaggerated booming, like the Wizard in Oz, behind his curtain. Hocking looked over at Clio as though he might heave himself out of his chair at her.

Ashe toggled the switch off. Above her gag, Voris'

eyes were round and wide, kept in bounds only by the thatched line of eyebrows pressing down.

Clio met those eyes. But no time for talking, no time to say, *My act of courage, this time, Meg. My act of courage.* Clio looked away, found Commander Singh's stricken face. He stared down at the navigation console.

Ashe broke the silence. "Now listen," he said. "Clio, Petya, and I are leaving. If we are impeded in any way, people will get hurt." He turned to Singh. "We're taking the captain with us. We'll leave him in the lander when my ship meets us. Fire on us, he dies too."

The slap of heel on metal announced Petya on the ladder from mid-decks. His head appeared in the hatchway. Though his face was placid as ever, he froze in place. Clio crouched down next to him. "We're leaving this ship, Petya. We have to leave. Don't be afraid." Ashe gestured her down, then turned to loosen Hocking's bonds. Clio started down the hatch ladder as Petya retreated.

At the bottom, Petya said, "Leaving the ship?"

"We're going home with Timothy, would you like that?"

He nodded.

"Good. Because we have to leave, Petya. I'm a prisoner here. They've kept us prisoner all these years, Petya, you and me. It's time to leave."

Hocking clattered slowly down the ladder, still gagged but unbound, followed by Ashe. Above them, a vent released a sigh of warm air, full of the oily fragrance of ship's body.

"Let's go," Ashe said. He looked into Clio's eyes. "Is Tandy dead?"

"Dead. Yes, he's dead."

Ashe nodded, searching her face.

"I shot him," she said.

He motioned to Petya. "You first," he said, indicating the ladder to crew deck, and Petya lumbered up the rungs. Ashe nodded for Clio to follow.

She stopped a moment. "What if the universe splits now? We've stolen the fire. It could split now, Timothy."

"We haven't stolen the fire yet, Clio." His face was all business, as he turned her around, urging her up the ladder. "Hurry."

Directing Hocking up first, they scrambled up the hatchway ladder, emerging on the long tube of the crew deck. Ashe hurried them along, guiding Hocking with a palm in his back, pushing him to keep pace. Hocking's eyes watched the doors, hoping, perhaps, that this once his commands weren't obeyed, that Tandy's crack force, or what was left of it, would burst through to bar the way to the launch bay.

Clio linked arms with Petya, who, like Hocking, dragged his feet. With her other hand, Clio clutched the paper bag against her side. Then back down the corridor, retracing their path, this time with the treasure in hand, the return from the cave and the monster slain.

Clio and Petya reached the loading-bay hatch first, and Petya stepped forward to crank the hatch, swinging it open. Then he stepped back.

"I can stay here?" Petya asked.

"No," Clio said. "No, Petya, we have to hurry." She pressed on his shoulder to turn him toward the hatchway.

He retreated a step.

"This isn't a game, Petya. Let's go."

He stared back, setting his lower lip.

Clio looked to Ashe.

Ashe said softly, "What's the matter, Petya?"

"I can stay here?" he repeated.

"Don't you want to come with Timothy and me?" Clio said.

In answer, Petya turned from them and walked down the corridor to the second-to-last cabin door, his quarters.

Clio bolted after him. "Petya! We don't have time to fetch anything! Please." She pulled on his arm. Like coaxing a stump from the ground.

He turned around, looked down from his six-foot-two height, to a point on her collarbone.

God. He was going to clam up. Clio pulled her hand through her hair, fingers tracing a shaking path.

"Petya," she said. "We're in great danger. Remember when we ran from DSDE, across the field, the night they came for us, and we had to run so hard? We have to run one last time, Petya." She tugged on the rooted stump again.

"No toasters," he said.

Clio's voice flew upward. "Toasters?"

He looked down into her eyes. "Toasters. Car radios, computers. Things that break. Plants don't break?"

"Sure they break! Everything breaks, Petya." Clio looked around to find Ashe approaching them, Hocking in tow.

"You'll miss your machines?" Ashe asked.

Petya nodded.

"But we have to hurry, Petya," Clio said, trying to push past all this with words.

Ashe's eyes were forest dark. "You want to stay here, Petya? Is that it?"

Clio turned on Ashe. "Shut up! Just shut the fuck up! Don't try to tell him what he wants!"

"But *you* can tell him what he wants?"

Clio began to hurl back a response, stuffed it. She turned back to her brother. "Petya. Do you want to be apart again? We could be together."

Ashe laid a hand on her arm. "Clio. Don't."

Petya looked now at Ashe. "You could stay here?"

Ashe shook his head back and forth in a narrow arc describing the range of choice.

Petya faced Clio. "I could stay here?"

Clio could barely see him now, as he stood there, all blurry. "Do you want this, Petya? Because it's forever. Later, you can't change your mind."

"I can decide?" He looked at her for permission. Would live with what she said. Would obey.

"Yes," she whispered. "You can decide."

The ship waited in drafty silence as though holding its breath.

"I'll miss you?" Petya said.

Clio moaned. Heard herself saying, "No, no . . ." And then Ashe was behind her. A gentle pull on her shoulder.

Clio stepped up to embrace Petya. She spanned his torso with her arms, pressed her flesh against his, flesh of her family, of her span of days, of her span of heart. She pushed away at last, looking up at him. Said: "Yeah, I'll miss you too." Ashe was pulling her away, everything was pulling away, flying off from the center. "Miss you more," she said, still backing up.

"Will not!"

"Will too." She felt the hatch jutting against her back, and Petya stood by his door, the yellow plaid of his shirt all collapsed into formless buttery grey.

Ashe helped her through the hatch. Halfway through she turned and looked at Petya, still there by his cabin door, and he said, "Will not," smiling.

She smiled back. "I love you," she said. She felt a hand on her shoulder, pushing her through the hatchway, while part of her struggled to stay in the safe old place, while everything conspired to squeeze her out, whispering, move on, move on. . . .

Hocking clambered through the narrow door, and then Ashe. He slammed the hatch door shut, and as he threw home the bolts with his right hand, for a moment Clio saw *through* his hand, or thought she did. But the next moment, as she looked in alarm at Ashe, he was solid as ever. Then she felt Ashe's arm around her shoulder, turning her to the waiting, open hatchway of *Sun Spot*.

The lander hummed as Clio braced herself with the handholds, then swung her legs through the main access hatch. All this way. She had come all this way, to the depths of the solar system, to the depths of time, to recover herself, her family. *Petya stays with me, from now on he stays with me. He's coming along or I don't fly, is that clear?* And now she had lost him too.

She slumped into the pilot's seat. Stared at the panels.

From behind her, Ashe placed his hand on her shoulder. "His choice, Clio."

She pawed her eyes clear. "His choice," she repeated, "Goddamn it all to hell."

"His happiness, Clio."

She swiveled around to face him. "Think I don't know that? Think it helps?"

Ashe turned to Hocking, grabbing him and pushing him into the copilot's seat. "Tell Singh that my ship is coming alongside. We have no reason to fire on *Galactique*. They're coming to take Clio and me on board. But if Singh fires on my ship, I'll kill you." He opened a channel.

Hocking paused, swallowing. Then he spoke: "This is Captain Hocking. Do not fire on the Nian ship coming in. They intend to take Timothy Ashe and Clio Finn on board. *Galactique* is in no danger."

No response to this.

"Do you hear me, Commander Singh? Do not fire."

Then, over the comm: "There is no Nian ship, Captain."

"It'll be here," Ashe growled.

They waited. Clio punched up visual on *Sun Spot*'s boards and searched the screens. Nothing. And then the screen jumped back a little, away from her, in a visual distortion as though she were looking at the screen through a camera lens. Clio stared at this scene for a moment, then slowly turned her chair to check out the rest of the cabin, all the while thinking, *knowing*: The universe is elastic, and you're seeing it stretch, sister. Not wanting to look, but looking anyway, she saw *Sun Spot*'s interior gone dim, and then looking at Ashe she saw that he was drained of color, his face and clothes a black-and-white image in the wrong universe. Looking down on her Biotime flight suit, she saw it was bright, even luminous, green.

It had started.

Ashe, apparently oblivious, strode to the bulkhead stowage bins and pulled out a spacesuit. "Put this on," he said to Hocking. "When my ship undocks from the lander, you may lose cabin pressure."

Until this moment Clio had shoved from her mind the real terror of what lay ahead: the splitting in two of all things and her fate. It hit her now, that terror. She had faced death before, time and again; and once, almost chose death, asking, Is life always the best thing? Death was no stranger,

had held no power over her. Until now. Looking at Timothy
Ashe, her Teller of Trees, her warrior, her true lover . . .
death held power. It mattered.

Her futures were full of death. The universe would
split. In each universe, she was quarry-bound. In one, her
seeds would not sprout, Tandy would retrieve the FTL technology, Ashe would escape without achieving his goal, and
she—she would remain in the lander with Hocking. In the
other universe, the seeds would eventually bear fruit, and
meanwhile Ashe would steal the FTL circuit from Tandy,
and Clio's fate, no different than her twin. She would
remain on the lander. Again, quarry-bound. The Cousin
Realities might exchange dominant/subservient roles. But
Clio's role was ever the same. Quarry meat.

Unless . . . unless . . .

Clio turned back to the screens. They were still oddly
distant, but suddenly she could see a small blip, dead center,
materializing as though it had come from behind a curtain.
"The ship!" Clio said. *Your ship. It's coming for you.* Her
heart felt like a hot stone.

As Hocking struggled into the suit, Singh's voice came
back: "We have them on screen, Captain. We will hold fire
as long as they do the same."

A transmission came in from the pod, in Ashe's language. He leaned in to the mike to respond, speaking
rapidly . . . his *lips* moving rapidly. Clio heard nothing. His
voice had become invisible.

Clio grasped Ashe's hand, still solid, and warm, and
they waited, silently, as the pod ship moved in, slowly
growing to fill the screen.

Ashe looked at Clio. His eyes flicked over her, as his
brows lowered.

"Yes," Clio said. "I know, Timothy. It's time." His
face, flickering now between color and sepia tones, filled
with anguish, telling her that he must have seen in that
instant all that she had seen, and what it meant.

Then, through the viewport, Clio saw the tapered and
translucent pod nudging up to *Sun Spot* like a whale investi-

gating a diving bell. The sounds of grappling began outside the lander emergency hatchway.

She heard Ashe say, "Clio. I don't think . . ." and then his words were ghosts, but his body blocked the way to the hatch, and he was shaking his head. She knew what he meant to say.

"Don't tell me I'm not coming, Timothy! One way or another, I'm coming. Don't you see? It's death for me either way, death as the world splits, death in a quarry. I want to choose. Now open the damn hatch."

Ashe waited long moments looking at her, then slowly took the brown package from Clio's hands. *It goes with him,* she thought. He threw the hatchway bolts, yanking back the door, and the sweet, fecund air of Niang filled Clio's nostrils. Ashe gave her a boost up and through the hatch, scrambling after her. And they were in a translucent airlock, a narrow sac through which they crawled no more than five meters to the pod's hatchway entrance. The biotic door split down the middle and parted.

They entered the ship. Ashe held her firmly around the waist with one arm and began to run for the bridge, yelling something in his language, the words, whatever they were, loud and real. "Dive," he said to Clio, "we have to Dive. Now."

A crew member emerged from somewhere, pointing at Clio and yelling back. As they argued, the corridor, the crew member, and Ashe faded to shades of grey. Reaching for Ashe, Clio's hand went entirely through him. At that moment a high-pitched noise sliced into the corridor, like the sound of deep ice cracking on a vast, frozen lake, a zinging needle of noise that pierced Clio's head, drowning out her shouts of, "No, no, not yet. . . ." The noise screamed to fill the ship, driving Clio to her knees in terror.

And then Ashe was beside her, trying to embrace her, but it was like mist surrounding a statue. He could not hold her. She heard herself saying, "Goodbye. Goodbye. I love you . . . remember me . . ." but her words froze and broke in front of her.

From deep in the glacial ice, cracking apart forever, she

heard Ashe's voice escape in an echoing funnel of sound: "Say yes, Clio, say yes, say you're coming with me . . . say it!"

The ship was disintegrating before her eyes. The stars poked through the tattered fabric of the bulkheads, and Clio cried out, "I'm coming with you! I belong with you!" And as the screams of the parting worlds drowned out her words, she knelt there whispering to herself, to the universe, "Yes . . . yes . . . yes."

Ashe was gone. She crawled along the floor of the ship, as a cold, heavy fog built up around her, blotting out vision, anesthetizing her muscles. She struggled to keep moving. Everyone was gone, replaced by this grey miasma that sucked up all sight, all sound, as the cold cleaving of space-time reached to take her down to some awful sleep.

And then she saw someone. Emerging out of the fog, a woman appeared, crouching as Clio was, not three meters away. They looked at each other. The woman had short white hair, and dark skin, and wore a light grey flight suit. She appeared as a photo negative.

And then Clio knew. Recognized the curly hair, the eyes, the eyes that recognized *her*. This was Clio Finn. From the Cousin Reality just at this moment created. A breeze stirred the other Clio's hair. Clio opened her mouth to say, *Why did you come here, you were supposed to stay on the lander* . . . but her mouth was blocked with ice. She heard instead, saw instead, the other Clio's mouth move, saying, *No quarry. Not ever again.* Then a thin smile, wobbly and brave. Trying to smile.

Now Clio felt the mist hitting her cheek, as a cold breeze blew toward the right, tearing the fog into streamers. With an ugly moan, it built to a roaring wind, forcing both of them sideways, as the Clio image reached out for her with a wavering arm, with a face now strained with fear. *We are dying,* she said, not in words that Clio could hear but in words that she *knew,* knew without doubt. Clio reached out her own arm, but the gale took her, forcing her sideways, and she skidded on all fours until she hit the corridor edge, where the wind flattened her against the bulkhead. The grey fog was funneling down and soundlessly disappearing next to her. She could just make out a hole the size of a quarter through which the air in the ship was barreling in a frenzied rush.

She saw her double pulled to the bulkhead, where the hole was churning everything away, saw her brace her arms against the bulkhead, fighting the pull, saw her turn her head to look at Clio for a brief moment, her eyes two black vortices. Clio reached out her arms, struggling against the smash of wind, reached for this fading image of her own self, but then the shadow image simply lifted her hands lightly from the bulkhead and, in a long, slow surrender, closed her eyes. At the same instant she faded to match the insubstantial fog, and collapsed into a thread of smoke, vanishing through the hole. The thinning mist followed her, dissipating as the last smoky tendrils sped through. Then the hole squeezed shut in an instant.

Clio's eyes watered fiercely from the cold wind. She rubbed at her face with brittle fingers, then stopped when the absolute silence was broken by a shuffling sound. She turned.

Several meters away, a man was staggering to his feet, facing away from her.

"Timothy!" Clio whispered.

He turned and saw her. He was dressed in Biotime green. As she was. He began walking toward her, all the while his form never wavering, and he kneeled down, surrounding her in a massive embrace, while she held him too, solid as worldly flesh.

When they parted for a moment, Captain Hickory stood before them.

"Where are we?" Ashe asked.

"Home," she answered. "We're home."

Clio reached to touch Ashe's face, at the point where his scar cleaved his eyebrow in two. Her finger touched and rested firmly on his skin.

"Timothy," she said, "I saw her . . . I saw *me*. We both tried to reach you. We were on the pod, and there were stars and ice and fog. And only one of us was going to go home, with you, only one of us survive."

He held her face between his hands. "Clio, Clio . . ."

"She died, Timothy. She's gone."

He brought her back into his arms. "I'm sorry, Clio. I tried to find you, I fought for you. I couldn't find you."

Clio looked beyond his shoulder at a certain point on the ship's bulkhead, where there was a small dark spot, like a bruise. "It's OK, Timothy," she said softly. "She wouldn't go to the quarry. Not ever again."

They helped each other to stand. In the dim corridor, the lights surged with a new brightness as the pod ship stabilized. Underneath the smooth, chitinous white of the ship's bulkheads, a pale turquoise light cast its glow.

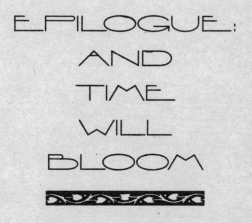

EPILOGUE:
AND
TIME
WILL
BLOOM

EPILOGUE

A bronze light fell across the pillows, inching its way up to Clio's face, which was passive in sleep until struck by the warm cane of sun. Her eyelids rippled, then opened.

Her arm flopped down to locate Ashe, found instead the main shaft of light from the eastern windows. She sat up and stared at the timepass. Seven o'sun, and late to be lying in, despite the excuse of last night's midsummer festival with its deep night-sky painting, still floating on her retinas in pink, chartreuse, gold, and white.

Ashe was in the field long since, and Hildy would be expecting her. Clio threw the covers off and stretched to the low ceiling, allowing the arm of sun to press on her buttocks and the small of her back for a moment. Then she grabbed a robe and rushed to the bathhouse.

Only one other woman remained on the women's side. Mina lolled in the great bath, hair tied in a tufted ponytail on the top of her head. She opened one eye.

"How's the baby," Clio asked, in the new tongue.

The woman glanced at her abdomen, where a cup of tea on its saucer perched like a frog on a water lily. "A-OK," she answered, in the old tongue, Clio's first tongue.

Clio smiled each time she heard the term. Learning went both ways. In this circle at least, most friends were a part of the Finn Telling Path, or Ancient History 101, as Clio sometimes called it.

The shower coursed over her, peeling off the web of sleep. She scraped the shower droplets from her arms, legs, and breasts, then dove into the bath, sending a shock wave coursing toward Mina.

"Sorry!" Clio said, realizing her mistake.

"For nothing," Mina said. She snatched the capsized cup from the bath. "It was too bitter, anycase."

"I'll make you some different cup," Clio offered, already drying off and stepping half wet into a loose chemise split high on both sides.

Mina, lost in the unrippled waiting of her ninth month, smiled and waved her soon back.

Clio flung herself on the best-looking cycle from the rack and pushed off into the path for a head start from home circle toward the base.

Her cropped hair fluttered in the warm breeze, drying instantly, as she sped down the hill. To her right, the rising sun lit the frondy forest tops in glittering turquoise and pumped the dew skyward, blurring the far horizon. Beneath the nectarine fragrance of Earth, the July harvest of simoetha added its local musk. Clio waved at the fields near the jungle edge, squinting to find Ashe. A man stood, shading his eyes with his arm, and waved back. Eyes in the back of his head, had that man. Or watching for her descent at seven o'sun, yes, likely watching for her.

The rest of the simoetha harvest would soon be brought in by organicals, but the first phase needed human dexterity, and only from the mature men of the village whose hormonal balance calmed the fruited vines. Worst luck for Ashe to draw fieldwork in July, though he claimed it kept him fit. Clio had drawn December, with most food laid in and only a few adventurous weeds to coax into dormancy.

People said their lots suited them, solar opposites in so much else. Burly and slender, dark and fair, biological and mechanical, the calm and the flood. Sisters said their energies had to arc high to meet, drawing down good sexual power. The men shrugged and said opposites attract. Now and for four joyous years they drew down that power and spent it between them without slacking, whether through body or heart.

Clio pumped hard on the flat road, feeling the stretch and good pull of leg, ankle, and pedal. Past the series of domes marking the edge of growlabs, past the tented center pavilion and the water reclamation vinery, skirting the village center where market would impede her passage.

Hildy waited for her outside the simulation domes, tapping the timespan at her waist as Clio slid to a halt in front of her.

"Did you stop to bring Timothy his lunch?" Hildy asked. The smile at one side of her mouth revealed how likely she thought that excuse.

Clio grinned. "Let's get started."

Hildy was due soon in hospice to preside over a regen on a dancer's toe. She turned her broad shoulder toward the lab, walking in short quick paces to match Clio's leggy strides.

In the cockpit of the pilot sim they sat in matched chairs, with a box under Hildy's feet to brace her up.

"Ease her out," Hildy said.

In response, Clio found her fingerholds and sank deep, opening the channels to ignition and taxiing. The screen showed the runway speeding beneath.

"And breathe," Hildy said, smiling now almost as broadly as Clio, smiling as Clio repeated her past ten performances in the pilot's seat. *Made the connections. Broke through to psychochemical exchange. Connected.*

"Oh God," Clio said. Every day she thought she might sit here and sink her fingers in inert tissue. Only it would be *she* who was inert. But today, again, contact. "I have it Hildy, I can feel it. I flow with it." She glanced over at Hildy long enough to veer off the flight path and nose into the ditch.

"Well, you flowed with it for a moment there," Hildy said. She slid her own finger into the console to reset the sim.

Clio rested her forehead in her hands. "It feels like the old days, Hildy."

"A few rungs below a starship, this solar plane, eh?"

"Not the point." Clio raised her eyes to smile out of all bounds at her friend. "It's a start. It's a hope."

"When are you going to tell Timothy?"

"Tonight. If you're sure I'm connecting, if you're still sure?"

"Clio. We've done all the tests. You're changing, your body is changing. It will be a long time before you can fly, even so. It might be years." She always told smoothly out, withholding nothing.

"Even so," Clio said.

"And likely never a spacecraft, Clio. There are limits."

Clio sunk her fingers into the warm, tingling membrane of the flight console. She felt a smile burst out in answer to Hildy's Limits.

"Let's do it again," she said. Beneath her fingertips, the plane surged forward to flight speed.

APPENDIX

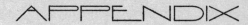

TIME DIVING: VANDARTHANAN'S THEORIES AND COROLLARIES

—Excerpt from *Codex Universalis*, ed. 13, 3563

Vandarthanan, Sri Sarvepalli, described the theoretical mechanics of time travel in a set of complicated equations. Subsequent analysis of these equations by his followers and critics elucidated more of the practical and technical aspects of what has come to be called **Time Diving**. While Time Diving is now commonly used, it is widely recognized that only the most rudimentary understanding of the implications of Vandarthanan's equations has been achieved, even today. The mathematical elegance of his equations belies their stubborn reluctance to give up their secrets. In his public comments on the development of Time Diving, Vandarthanan expressed his own deep concerns that the dangers of the Time Dive were not fully identified or understood. He became a vocal advocate for strict limits on human exploitation of Time Dive, and was instrumental in promulgating scrupulously conservative procedures for Time Diving; procedures necessary to reduce the risks inherent in time travel. These protocols comprise the longest continuously observed worldwide agreement in human history (see Time Management Conventions, below).

The Danger of Paradox[1]

The singularly most dangerous aspect of the Time Dive is the potential for creation of paradox. Though he was

---

[1]In popular understanding, the most common example of a paradox is called the Grandfather Paradox: Suppose one were to go back in time and meet one's own grandfather, accidentally killing him. This would negate one's own birth. Who then, has killed the grandfather? Vandarthanan argued strongly, and his equations warned, that we not find out.

never able to provide empirical proof, Vandarthanan believed that the occurrence of a significant paradox—perhaps, indeed, any paradox—could have cataclysmic consequences. As he said many times in his writings and speeches, "The universe abhors a paradox." Though Vandarthanan's equations are still not completely developed or well understood, an analysis of them suggests that an unavoidable time paradox might generate the time-based equivalent of matter-antimatter annihilation, with profoundly destructive local effects.

The Protocols of the **Time Management Conventions of 2014** dictate that **Time Insertions** may only be made at a distance from human presence or activity, reducing the probability of paradox and unintended interference in human proceedings, recent or remote. In addition, in the twenty-first-century Time Dive technology still had not overcome the Time Dive effect of the **Event Ripple**, a local space-time disturbance whose destructive magnitude depends on the "time and distance depth" of the Time Dive. Historical remoteness and physical distance from Earth are both Protocol requirements for Time Diving.

Earth-based Time Diving is prohibited under the Protocols to avoid paradox and interference in the local **Time Stream**. Such a Dive would significantly increase the probability of paradox, such as the Time Diver meeting himself or herself, or changing something—however small—whose multiplicative effect would be significant and inconsistent with the future-time of the Diver. If the Time Dive on Earth is very deep—that is, goes far back in time—any changes, no matter how trivial, become amplified over time in a geometric progression, creating more likelihood of paradox. However, there is less risk for a shallow Time Dive of only a few days, particularly if the Dive destination is remote from human population and activity.

Although Earth-based Time Diving is forbidden by the Protocols, one historical instance occurred in 2019. This now-famous incident, relating to the destruction of the **Space Recon** vehicle *Starhawk* and the two-day near-space

Time Dive of **Lieutenant Clio Finn**, led to the planting of **Niang** seed on Earth.

The Direction of Dive

During the existence of the twenty-first-century Space Reconnaissance program known as Space Recon, Time Diving was used for exploration and biotic mining of Earthlike planets in the galaxy. Before the discovery of **faster-than-light travel technology**, Time Diving allowed humanity to overcome the impossibly vast distances from Earth to star systems outside our own.

Vandarthanan's equations describe how Dive brings the traveler outside the normal space-time continuum. While the ship is in Dive, it could be said that the galaxy rotates independently "under" (figuratively speaking) the ship and its occupants, such that upon reentering the time stream the Dive ship will have jumped distances unachievable by any other practical means. To return to "now" and home, the Dive mechanism is reversed and travel is directed forward to the approximate place of the Dive Insertion. This moment in time is called the **Future Ceiling**. Upon returning, the Dive ship may then be farther away from the point of Dive Insertion than when it left because of the inherent unpredictability of the movement of the galaxy. The ship then travels in real space the distance to reach home, since the craft is a spaceship as well as a Time Dive device.

Though a Dive ship theoretically travels "forward" in time to return from the past, the mathematics of the process is more akin to a return to a previous state of time, a very different mathematical and practical proposition than traveling forward in time beyond the Future Ceiling.[2]

The Time Dive used by Space Recon was always a time shift to the past. In traveling to the future—beyond the Future Ceiling—it is not possible to take physical action of

---

[2]The Future Ceiling was so called because of a scientific mistake. At one time it was believed that travel to the future was not possible. It was believed one could not travel past the current date where a Dive began. Subsequently, the technology became possible. However, the convention of calling the "current date" the Future Ceiling has remained.

any kind or to have any physical interaction with people or events beyond the Future Ceiling. Travelers to the future remain observers. It is not true, as is widely thought, that Vandarthanan believed humans would be seen as "ghosts" by people living in the future. Such travelers remain entirely incorporeal, and as such are not visible or perceivable in any way by inhabitants of the future, nor can they affect events, people, or things in the future.

The Probabilistic Future

An important corollary to the laws derived from Vandarthanan's equations is that of the **probabilistic future**. This is the concept that the future can be mathematically described as an array of identifiable **temporal probabilities** whose relative magnitudes depend on what happens now. The future is an ever-changing array of vectors describing possible futures. The farther into the future one travels, the more possible **future vectors** there are and the less likely that any one such vector has a high probability of coming into existence. The idea that the future already exists as a set of mathematically described probabilities—from the perspective of the Time Diver—is an extraordinarily complicated subject in mathematics and difficult to explain in words to a lay readership, adding to the suspicion and mistrust of Vandarthanan's work among the general public. In addition, the popular and persistent idea of traveling to the future to "find out what happens" is not scientifically possible, since the future—probabilistic and **multi-vectored time**—is inherently indeterminate.

The Time Diver cannot select his or her favorite future vector, visiting over and over again. Such selection is theoretically and practically impossible. Vandarthanan's equations conclusively demonstrate that for any Dive to the future, the future vector upon which one "lands" is a virtually random occurrence.

The Cousin Reality

An extremely rare and nonrandom phenomenon of future Time Diving, however, was first suggested by Vandarthanan's work. This phenomenon is the potential for the existence of an ultimately temporary but no less potentially catastrophic **Cousin Reality**. The Cousin Reality is a high-probability time vector that could exist, under certain circumstances, parallel to our own.

A Cousin Reality is quite different from the "future vector" concept discussed earlier. A Cousin Reality occurs when time branches in two, carrying forward two parallel versions of reality in current time. It is a reality in which each individual has a **"doppelgänger"** in a parallel time vector. Cousin Realities are implacable competitors for existence since only one such reality can endure in the long run. Cousin Realities result in a state of **reality-time dissonance** that the mechanics of the universe strive to resolve. In this profound state of disharmony, one reality will gather strength at the expense of the other. Even though Cousin Realities may exist simultaneously for thousands of years, ultimately one reality diminishes in power, finally to the point of extinction. Thus, one reality is called the **Dominant Cousin**, and the other the **Servient Cousin**.

Vandarthanan and his students speculated that this hypothesis could not be tested by visiting a Cousin Reality in current time, which he maintained was theoretically impossible. Rather, a Cousin Reality would be discovered by future Time Diving and finding that over repeated visits, the random nature of that travel was suspended. His equations predicted that a Cousin Reality would serve as a **temporal attractor**—future Time Dives from either Cousin would be attracted to the other.

Although a highly improbable occurrence, the Cousin Reality concept fascinated—some would say obsessed—Vandarthanan as he grew old. As the father and chief proponent of **spatiotemporal mechanics**, Vandarthanan became increasingly isolated from mainstream mathematics and physics, and during his lifetime his Cousin Reality ideas were widely disputed. (Although, of course, the existence of a current Cousin Reality was borne out by subsequent events.) In the final years of his life, Vandarthanan was widely quoted in the popular press, becoming politically active in human-rights and ecological issues, which contributed to his isolation from institutional scientists and his harassment by conservative government factions. Ironically, when Vandarthanan died, at the age of seventy-eight, his scientific reputation was at its lowest ebb but his popularity as a folk hero was soaring. Sri Sarvepalli Vandarthanan is considered by some to be the greatest visionary of the twenty-first century, and yet he would have—as he said many times—preferred to remain an anonymous mathematician.

The Non-Paradox Laws

The Non-Paradox Laws describe three principal constraints on maneuverability in Time Diving. Vandarthanan enunciated these laws as a series of speculations in his last published work, "Probabilistic Dimensions of Reality Intervention." Although most of his fellow scientists believed that Vandarthanan had failed to prove his major point—the potential existence of Cousin Realities—the Non-Paradox Laws first described in that paper gradually made their way into mainstream science. Vandarthanan's Uncertainty Principle was confirmed experimentally in the years after his death. The Past Intervention Law was widely accepted on a theoretical basis. The Law of Probabilistic Resolution—although tested once in human history—remains Vandarthanan's most famous, and infamous, unproved theory. While formulated in the esoteric symbolic language of spatiotemporal mechanics, the function and effect of each of the laws is relatively clear.

Vandarthanan's **Uncertainty Principle** states that it is not possible to Dive both to another identifiable place in the universe and to another time with accuracy. If the exact depth of the Dive is specified, then the resulting location cannot be predicted with accuracy.[3] Conversely, if the

---

[3]The technical explanation for this uncertainty resides in the attempt at a simultaneous solution to Equation #15a for both time and location. The solution results in eigenvalues of zero on both sides of the equation.

placeis defined with precision, the time of arrival is uncertain. The uncertainties of Time Dive have been confirmed by experiment and actual Dive experience. In the early twenty-first century, because of Space Recon's broad tolerances in defining both place and time of arrival, the limitations imposed by Vandarthanan's Uncertainty Principle were not an insurmountable deterrent to space and time travel.

The **Past Intervention Law** holds that in travel to the historical past everything in local space prior to the traveler's arrival time becomes temporally fixed—from the standpoint of intervention. Travel into the past beyond the point of an earlier **temporal fixation** is possible, but is subject to the same limits of nonintervention as are encountered in travel to the future—the traveler cannot intervene in or interact with the past to affect events, people, or things.[4] In Vandarthanan's terms, the traveler's opportunity for intervention in the time stream is limited. The active past, as it were, closes up behind the traveler.

The **Law of Probabilistic Resolution** states that to alter the course of history by interfering in the flow of the time stream during a certain period of unstable temporal probability will both destroy and re-create the time stream in a new form. This law applies to actions and interventions during what Vandarthanan referred to as a time of monumental **probabilistic uncertainty**; in other words, an era when the time stream is highly unstable and conditions are present that could lead to creation of a Cousin Reality.

Vandarthanan and those who followed in his footsteps were especially interested in the development and dynamics of this law, because it implied that past intervention could be used to modify the future in some predictable way. The speculation was that Time Dive could be used to manipulate a key **historico-temporal element** (an "independent variable") that was crucial to the strength of a Dominant Cousin

---

[4]In this case, several highly complex real-number values asymptotically approach unity as a point of temporal fixation is reached.

Reality. Changing any such element, much less a major one, would inevitably result in paradox, which Vandarthanan theorized would have profound but predictable consequences—both the existing Dominant and Servient Realities would "blink out" of existence, succumbing to the "collapse of probability."

In their places would be generated two new Cousin Realities, presumptively identical in form, but reflecting the new probabilities created by the manipulation of the time stream. One reality would be the once-Dominant Cousin divested of its probabilistic supremacy and ultimately destined to wither. The other would be the former Servient Cousin—now Dominant—which would have acquired the main thrust and probabilistic strength of temporal evolution. The time vector of the "present" to which the traveler would return from the Dive to the "past" would be slightly or profoundly different depending on the nature of change to the historico-temporal element.

In summary, if one determined that humanity had a Cousin Reality, it would be known that only one such reality could survive into the future. In addition, if it was determined that the other reality is a Dominant Cousin, it might be reasonably argued that one should intervene to prevent the development of the Cousin Reality's supremacy. To embark on this course of action, it would be necessary to find the critical historico-temporal element that determined this supremacy and manipulate or eliminate it through a past intervention.

Just prior to the time of this seminal event, the time stream theoretically would be on the verge of splitting, drastically limiting the time available to take action. The traveler cannot repeat the Time Dive several times until the mission succeeds, because of the Past Intervention Law. Furthermore, the Time Dive will have no guarantee of arrival at the right time to take effective action, because of the Uncertainty Principle. The traveler will be aiming for a narrow window of time and place prior to the branching of reality. Last, and most troublesome, the future—the time vector from which the traveler came, and presumably would strive to return to—will be forever changed by operation of the Law of Probabilistic Resolution.

—D. K. Wheaten, rev. 3560

ABOUT THE AUTHOR

KAY KENYON has worked as a radio and TV actor and copywriter, and in a Cousin Reality as a bureaucrat. She was raised in Duluth, Minnesota, and now shares a vintage old house near Puget Sound with her husband, who is also an avid reader of science fiction. Between them they have four sons and a very large cat. This is her first novel.

And be sure not to miss

LEAP POINT

The Next Exciting Novel By

KAY KENYON

Coming in Spring 1998

Its name is Nir, and it's the latest craze in VR technology: the ultimate retina game that promises a pay-off of total ecstasy. But what it actually delivers may be far more final—and far more frightening.

The year is 2014. And in the small town of Medicine Falls, no one is expecting anything unusual to happen. Certainly they are not expecting to become the proving ground for a very sinister invasion indeed. But linked in with Nir and a strange cult figure named Zachariah Smith is a deadly truth. And an antiques dealer named Abbey McCrae is about to discover what the rest of the galaxy collects. . . .

They chose Medicine Falls for the Leap Point because it was average and unremarkable in every way—except for being just a little desperate. At the same time, the town was isolated, twenty-five kilometers from the closest node of civilization.

Gazing up at the starry night sky, a typical citizen might remark how the stars were like diamonds sprinkled on velvet, or how bright the Milky Way was, far from city lights, or a few odd ones might wonder if the sun was atwinkle in someone else's night sky at that moment. As of course it was. A signal fire. What some might call a lighthouse beacon.

But Medicine Falls didn't look up very often. Folks were preoccupied with alfalfa to be baled and shopping to be done. And at night most people gave themselves up to vids and the Net, never looking up.

Except for Rachel.

At the moment, she was gazing up into the recesses of the station's ceiling far above, where a flaw in the roof metered out a slow plunk, plunk of melting snow.

Zachariah Smith followed her gaze upward, seeing more, immeasurably more, than the cracked and abandoned roof of the Lowell Street Train Station. In his mind's eye he saw a bustling tide of shoppers and travelers under the brilliant station lights. The glory days of Medicine Falls revisited. The glory days of Zachariah Smith—lightning rod to the city's new life.

It wasn't the kind of new life that most folks probably had in mind, but they were about to get it anyway.

"Can't you tell me what it is?" Rachel asked for the

dozenth time. Her voice reverberated in the empty mall hall, with its row of dead view-screen store fronts.

"It's a secret. Like I said." He kept his voice low, but the echo swooped out like a long, velvety tongue to snap up the remains of Rachel's question. The only other sound was the slap of their boots through the oily, tie-dyed water.

A spray of light bulged into human shape in front of them. "Say, neighbor," the promo holo said, nearly causing Rachel to climb up Zachariah's arm. "Make your mo a real show." The female image was wearing a short gel-fit, with tiny fish swimming through its transparent depths. She turned her forearm to display the glittering band of light nodes from her high-fashion cuff computer.

As the holo disintegrated, Rachel pushed at her hair, trying to force it back under her woolen cap. "My hair is crashed," she said, pressing for some compliment perhaps. Poor dummy, to worry about her hair at a time like this, trying to compete with a holo, to trivialize what was about to happen. They passed the sagging remains of a food-o-mat, with its boxes full of desiccated pie and long-dead mildew. It wasn't *the* smell, but it was bad enough. He hurried her along.

Leaving the retail corridor, they entered the central rotunda. Here, the great domed ceiling loomed over them, with a few meter-long icicles marking the roof's slow leaks.

Rachel looked up at them dubiously, as though one might pick this very moment to come stabbing down.

Like most folks, she didn't know much of anything. But then, he had to admit, there was plenty he didn't understand either. Like what they *did* with his donations. He succeeded in keeping that curiosity at bay, tucking it away in a little box, to open later, if need be.

When, for instance, it was time to come back here.

Behind them in the mall hall, another promo holo strobed in and out of life. For a fleeting moment it festooned their shadows in front of them, moving across the glistening pond and up the far wall. Ghosts, Zachariah thought, the station is filled with ghosts, ghosts of other Rachels, ghosts of past glory, the bustle of commerce, the piercing whistles of

·trains coming, trains going: Minneapolis, Duluth, Madison, Great Falls, Jackson Hole, Sioux City, and points beyond.

"Zachy . . ." Her voice wheedled at him.

He sighed and turned to face her. "Rachel, if you want to go home, just say so." He threw a snappish edge into his best creamy-deep voice.

Her eyes turned flinty. "This place stinks," she said. "What if there's Freakers here? What's so damn important, anyway?"

"Well, you won't find out unless you come look, will you?"

Another glance up at the toothy dome. "How far is it?"

Rolling his eyes, Zachariah took her by the arm, sloshing ahead. "The longer we stand under those things, the better chance there is of becoming a kabob."

"Zachy!" she giggled, in feigned delicacy.

If she called him that again, he'd slap her silly. Unwillingly, the image bobbed into his mind of shutting up that high-pitched shred of a voice . . . an image he quickly filed out of sight. Violence was not his way. He was a healer, a Server. In truth, it wasn't Rachel that set him on edge. It was the smell.

And here it was again.

They entered a corridor leading out to the eastbound train platforms. In this darker and more confining space, he felt Rachel stiffen slightly as he kept his hand on her upper arm. With a quicker step now, he pulled her along, their boots clicking on the tiles as they left behind the orange pond in the rotunda.

"What's that smell?" Rachel asked, stopping and planting her feet solidly.

"Could be a cat died or something." In fact, the smell was so thick he could *taste* it, as though he'd licked something foul. But Rachel was the sort who looked to others for validation of her own senses. "Guess you never smelled a dead cat before, eh, Rachel?" he said, and she started on again.

Halfway down the concourse he stopped at a door, a door like all the others. "This is it. We'll just stay a second."

She placed her hand on the doorknob and looked back at Zachariah irritably. "Are you coming?"

Well, no. Not that he was afraid. Ordinary people feared new things. That was the difference between them and him, between Rachel and him. He was pretty sure she'd throw a fit—probably fry her motherboard—in that room. No spirit of adventure at all.

Rachel looked at him, and he nodded his encouragement.

She opened the door.

In that instant he shoved his hand into her back, just hard enough that she staggered forward into the room. Quickly, he slammed the door shut behind her, holding the doorknob firmly as Rachel banged on it from the other side.

"Zacheeee!" she wailed. Then: "Please, Zachy," her voice soft and close, through the crack next to the door frame. "It *stinks* in here."

Her uncannily normal voice sent a little shiver up over his scalp as he gripped the door handle, now twisting slowly first in one direction, then the other. For a few seconds he heard the sound of shuffling and the soft scrape of her clothing against the door. Then:

"Oh . . ." Her voice broke into a surprised crack and began ratcheting up in pitch. "Oh. Oh. Ohhh . . ."

He would have plugged his ears but the door needed holding shut, so he squeezed his eyes closed, but still he heard several rhythmic gulps of air, which might have been Rachel, filling her lungs to accuse him . . . and then a thumping sound, and a brief, soft buzzing, like an insect incinerated in fire.

After a few moments the room grew quiet and he opened his eyes.

Head pressed against the door, he was forced to pull that hot stench into his lungs while fighting to distill some oxygen. He pried his fingers loose from the molten door handle and waited for a semblance of calm. Then he slowly pried the door open and looked into the room.

A glint of light from the hallway struck the shattered faces of built-in computer wall displays. He stepped into the room, leaving white tracings in the fine dusting of ash as he walked. On the ceiling, a scorch the size of a tire surrounded the cracked globe of the overhead light.

Rachel was gone.

In the center of the floor lay a heap of oblong packets coated with long, waving filaments that snapped as he touched them. He fumbled the packets into his knapsack. Then, looking up, he saw it, lying in a pile of glass near the wall: Rachel's wool cap, with a thread of steam rising from it. . . . Zachariah crammed the last few packets into the sack and stood swaying in place, eyes riveted on the hat.

"I'm sorry, Rachel," he said finally. Then the stench really did get to him, and he stumbled backward from the room, slamming the door and sprinting down the hall. At the main doors he sidled through the hole he'd cut, staggering out onto the old train platform, inhaling great gulps of searingly cold, sweet air.

Abbey McCrae cradled the World War I Fokker triplane in her hands. Its balsa wood frame was in nearly mint condition after seventy years, a relic from the days when kids played with real things instead of the electronic bits. She carefully placed it back on the shelf next to a plastic-encased pamphlet entitled "You and the Atomic Bomb," and amidst a thousand other twentieth-century acquisitions here in the storeroom of Abbey's Anteeks. She set her morning cup of tea on the typewriter stand next to the faux leopard multi-lounger, electronically dead but otherwise still damn comfortable, and breathed in the aroma of decades of dust, rusting metal and the attar of sachet bags. Wonderful.

Among the golden era favorites, inventory from the mid-twenty-first century dotted the shelves like poor cousins among royalty. The more sophisticated, the more electronic people got, the less they were rooted to life in real, honest-to-gosh stuff: behemoth pink ashtrays flecked with gold, Avon automobile cologne bottles, and framed posters of Martin, Bobby, and John.

She held up a twenty-year-old velvet painting of Lennon, Cobain, and Garcia. Not bad. And where was that avocado bread box with the rooster decal on the roller door?

Renalda clambered down the stairs from the upstairs apartment, followed closely by their dog, Harley, his huge neck graced by a chain collar that Renalda had recently chromed for his sixth birthday.

"Hola!" A sharp spike of perfume hit Abbey's nostrils like spilled pop on a shag carpet. Her roommate was dressed to kill, long hair curled and the Sex/Mex earrings dangling beside her rouged cheeks.

"Let me guess, a date?"

"Well, Monday's a slow day." She pirouetted on four-inch heels, a feat only Renalda, with a couple of decades of experience in trying to be taller, could accomplish.

"Monday's shelf day, so you can work, same as me."

"Come on, Abbey! I got people to do, things to see." As proof, she flashed her wrist mobes, fringed with lace and alive with calls waiting.

"If you're in love again, I think I'm going to scream," Abbey said. Even at thirty-two, Renalda believed each love affair was The One, not so different from her old high school buddy, Abbey herself.

"This guy's different." Their eyes locked for a moment. Renalda backed off first. "And turn up the heat, it's cold."

"It's almost April!"

"I don't care if it's July, it's fucking freezing in here." Harley sat transfixed as Renalda roughed up his face and ears with her fingernails, long as gangplanks.

As Abbey edged by, arms piled high with inventory, Renalda tossed her hair back, highlighting the Sex/Mexes. In the earring displays, Abbey saw a high-reso graphic of herself copulating with a Ken doll.

"You ought to stop that, it looks cheap."

Renalda followed her into the front store. "Somebody's gotta do the marketing! Here, I programmed lots more." She grabbed a cigar box from the counter, rattling the earrings inside. "Come on, they sell great!"

Everything Renalda said came out with a little too much force. Everything was fun or wry or exciting. Well, she was in love. Abbey could remember being in love like that. Especially in winter, when the work dried up, and men went hunting for a warm bed—and free rent—until the growing season brought field-hand jobs. But, make no mistake, come spring they'd rather stand in lines at the gates of farms and shoot the shit with the guys than stick it out with a woman.

She nestled another Barbie doll on the shelf with her prize collection, each doll outfitted for a different dream: ski trips, horseback riding, proms, safaris, beauty pageants, and astronaut adventures, and the greatest dream of all, that 39-22-37 figure. Abbey checked out her butt in the store mirror, glad that the size-ten jeans still fit, even if they were tight, for sure. Her breath clouded in front of her, endorsing her roommate's gripe.

"Store," she ordered, "kick it up to sixty-five."

Harley was whimpering at the mini frig. Relenting, Renalda spread out a leftover bean taco for him on the floor.

"So. Who's the new boyfriend?" Abbey asked, charging back to the storage room for another load.

"DeVries."

"What kind of a name is that?" Behind the Smith-Corona typewriter, still in its hard case and bannered with a "Jerk Dick" bumper sticker, she spied the bread box.

"Help me with this, would you?" She pulled out the typewriter, handing it off to Renalda. Across the avocado-colored roller door a rooster strutted, red crest held high, and surrounded by hearts, as though he were the symbol of romance.

Abbey hauled the bread box forward and slid up the roller door, which grated and clunked into place.

Inside, a small, dark mass. Perhaps a *very* moldy piece of bread. Something gleamed. She reached inside and drew out a black leatherette book with a metal, locking clasp, and on the front, something written in script.

"What is it?" Renalda asked.

Abbey turned the book back and forth to catch the right angle of light to read the inscription. Finally, the words *My Diary* flickered to life. "Oh God," she heard herself whisper.

Renalda reached forward and grabbed the book out of Abbey's hand, tugging at the clasp. "Looks like a diary. Guess you got more than a bread box, huh?"

Abbey stared at the little book, forgetting to breathe.

"It's Vittoria's, isn't it?" But she didn't need to ask, not really. Sometimes when the worst comes for you, your name is carved in its forehead. Abbey looked into Renalda's eyes as though across the ocean. Too far to throw the rope.

"I never knew Vitt kept a diary," her roommate said, scanning the cover as she spoke. "She wasn't the type to keep a diary, do you think?"

"It's Vittoria's, isn't it?" Abbey asked, her mind stuck in the groove like an old 45 rpm. record.

Renalda backed up a pace, clasping the diary behind her back. "Yeah, okay, it has her initials on the front," she answered. "And you know what we're gonna do? We're gonna put it right back where it came from and close that cute little rooster door, and shove it way to the back."

She could hear it coming. Here's the last thing you need, just when you're almost normal again. Whatever *normal* meant. Abbey thrust out her hand for the book.

"No! No frigging diary! No more long goddamn nights with you obsessing about what's dead and gone, talking until I drop dead asleep, and I'm *still* hearing you talk, in my dreams!"

"I'm going to read it," Abbey said. Didn't need to ask herself *why*. It was Vitt's, that was why.

"Ever think that people's diaries are, like, *private*?"

"Hand it over, Renalda."

Backing up another step, her roommate tossed her head, swaying her earrings and bringing on an orgy of activity in the displays. "No, forget it. I can't do this anymore, can you hear me? I can't stand Vitt's dying anymore, night after night. I will go crazy." At the pitch of their voices, Harley slunk to the doorway and parked himself on the threshold, looking like he was to blame.

Abbey conjured up a reasonable smile. It was either that or deck Renalda right here and now. "I'm over that now. Just give me the diary." But even to herself she sounded like a vampire saying "just bare your neck."

"You're over it! I'm going to gag. When's the last date you ever had? Two years. When's the last new clothes you ever bought? Two years. When's the last time we went looking for some guys on a Saturday night? Huh?"

Abbey nodded, yes, yes. But not hearing.

"Huh? You gonna answer?"

Something clicked. Abbey's hands flew wide, her cascade of hair crackling. "Two years! Two years, okay? Think you're the only one who's counting?" She whirled around and slammed the bread box door down with a resounding clunk. The scratch of Harley's toenails on the steps receded toward the apartment. She swung back around.

Renalda looked into her friend's face a long while. "Let the dead rest, for God's sake," she said softly.

Abbey reached for the book. The front doorbell rang. As Renalda let go of the book, a moment too early, it slipped from Abbey's fingers and fell to the floor on its clasp, breaking the lock into two pieces.

She stared at the splayed binding on the floor. "It's a sign," she said, "that I should read it."

Renalda shook her head. "It's a sin. And you shouldn't." She went to the door to deal with their visitor. She turned back. "It's a sin to read someone else's diary, you know?"

Abbey raised an eyebrow at this pitiful tactic. "It's a *sin*?"

Renalda's face crumpled under that hot, hazel gaze. "Okay. It's bad luck, then." She left the storeroom, scowling.

Crouching down and picking up the book, Abbey opened it at random, reading: *"Zachariah knows things. I don't know if he really hears voices from people passed over . . ."* A small tremor shook her hands as she carefully closed the book.

When Renalda came back, she was shaking her head. "Just Outers begging." She threw her arms wide, mobes sparkling on her wrists. "Do I look like I have money?"

"Store," Abbey said. "Screen us Closed for the day. But plug the Barbie special." She wandered over to the multi-lounger and sat down. The chair sighed as her weight forced stale air from its depths.

"You ever hear of Zachariah Smith?"

Renalda pursed her lips. "That guy with the fragged-out followers? Over at the old high school? Vitt wasn't involved with *him,* was she?" Her eyes widened in the ensuing silence. "Vitt wasn't involved with that *freak,* was she?"

Abbey picked up her tea and sipped it, allowing the cold brew to slide down her throat before it swelled into a blockade.

"Because Father O'Conner says they worship the devil."

"Yeah, Father O'Conner sees the devil everywhere."

Renalda opened her mouth to rebut, then reconsidered, retreating to the door. At the threshold she turned and said, "Maybe he is."

Abbey looked up quizzically. "Is what?"

"Everywhere." Her roommate hovered at the door, while Abbey turned the diary over in her hands.

"You gonna be okay?"

"Ask me later." She grasped the small locket hanging around her neck, and even before she heard the front door close behind Renalda, she turned to the diary's first entry, *January 7, 2012,* and began to read.

An hour later, she found herself in the souped-up, double-discount multi-lounger in the apartment, doing a Net probe on Zachariah Smith, downloading his spending patterns, 3-D Web hits, and every other public-access scrap available in the vast digital imprint that he, like everyone else, left in the communal Net.

Lying in wait for Lobo was a bust. Where was a crook when you really needed one? Abbey waited for the TraveLink system to answer her booking, which the real-time display at the LinkStop said would be here in six minutes.

Abbey had staked out Lowell Street at Penburton, Lobo's usual hang, where she had occasionally bought a computer upgrade or game from him, at street prices, mind you, and no questions asked. But no Lobo, not today.

She looked up to see her ride coming. Out of all the linked transport options of buses, maxi-taxis, and mini-cars, here came her luck-of-the-draw, an ancient maxi-taxi, a low-riding, seen-better-days sedan, packed with five other riders, amidst whose grocery bags, pet dogs, and knapsacks she managed to shoulder her way, passing forward her SmartCard, and receiving it back through a relay of hands. As crowded as it was, in truth she didn't mind a little company in the neighborhood she was headed to, where her sources said Lobo could be found.

Out the windows she could see the block-by-block deterioration of this end of town, including metal bars over storefronts, broken windows, and refuse sprouting from gutters and the stoops of once-tidy brownstones. In the distance, anchoring the far end of Defoe Street, she could make out the strutted dome of the old Lowell Street Train Station, once proud, and now, it was said, a palace for rats.

The taxi deposited her, the driver swore, in front of her destination, but as the vehicle squealed off down the street, she saw by the apartment building numbers that she'd have to hoof it another block or two. As she set out, a cadre of old men with paper bags followed her with squinting eyes and a round-eyed Freaker, newly lit with a hit of Xstasy, smiled his Freaker's smile.

She quickened her pace. In this quarter of the city, soot covered the remnants of snow, causing the winter to melt fast, with the runoff spilling over the gutters, pooling the sidewalks in places, and forcing Abbey to splash through and soak the cuffs of her jeans.

As she passed an alley, a small girl jumped up in the middle of a dumpster, eating an orange rind. Even at this distance Abbey could see the girl hadn't seen a bathtub for months. Her long blonde hair was pulled into an off-center ponytail.

Instantly capitalizing on the eye contact, the girl said, "You gotta five?" As Abbey shook her head, the waif backed up and, a moment before toppling off the far end, she cartwheeled off the dumpster into the shadows.

Abbey almost bumped into a reeking old man planted in her path. His face lit up a moment in surprise. Suddenly, it was the face of a man in his twenties; then his youth slipped off again, buried in grime. She swerved away and picked up her pace, finally spotting the etched-in-stone name of the St. Croix. One look at the pockmarked, narrow apartment building, leaning for support on the one next-door, and Abbey began to doubt she had the right address.

The afternoon was failing, and the tall apartments crowded out the remnants of daylight. This was maybe not the best time to come, maybe not the smartest move she'd ever made, coming here alone . . . but the longer she stood here fretting, the darker it was going to get. Besides, maybe she could just call for Lobo. Chances were, with all the broken windows, he might hear her, come out on the front stoop, and make himself an unexpected three hundred bucks.

"Lobo!" she called. And waited. Then called again. Damn, not going to be simple, now, was it? She clomped up the stairs and peered at the roster of names by the doorbell. The names were faded, torn and missing, like the current tenants, most likely. Just as she got ready to knock, the door jerked open. A boy of about eight confronted her. "Nobody's here!" he shouted.

Her hand met the door as he tried to slam it in her face. "Lobo," Abbey said, just as loudly, matching his tone. "I came to see Lobo." She pushed into the foyer, where, beyond the boy's greasy head, a tall stairway climbed into darkness. Not promising.

"Lobo's not here," the boy proclaimed. Something in his eyes made him seem remote, perhaps retarded.

"He's expecting me," Abbey lied. "I'm a friend." Which might be stretching it. But no pint-sized runaway was going to push her off this easy.

At his split-second pause, Abbey sidled by him. The noise of a slamming door several floors up proved *someone* was home. The boy banged the door shut and raced up the stairs ahead of her, blurting out, "It's the Blooos, come for some scrooos!"

Doors creaked open and small faces peered out, sometimes stacked, short to tall, like totem poles. As she passed, the doors pinched shut.

"Where's Lobo?" she asked, shotgun style, hoping to hit something. From the closest door, a lisping, sweet voice said, "Up at the top."

She hesitated, looking at the murky stairway. Maybe this wasn't such a good idea. She *was* carrying a lot of money. What if Lobo wasn't home? Come to think of it, what if he *was*? Lobo smiling on Lowell Street with his sales pitch on automatic might be a different Lobo than the one who retreated each night to the top of the St. Croix.

But she'd come this far. She began the climb. Her sherpa jacket began to feel hot and clammy, but she kept it on, clutching her purse to her belly. On the second floor, a window at the hall's far end provided at least a dim view. She walked to the next flight of stairs, past doors she just hoped would stay closed.

At a noise in back of her, she turned to find a group of four youngsters standing at the head of the stairs as though blocking her retreat. One of them was the ponytail girl from the dumpster. "You got five dollars?" she asked, lifting her skirt and swaying her naked hips. The smallest boy knelt in front of her, demonstrating what the five dollars would buy.

Abbey took a step toward the nasty creatures, edging them backward a notch. "You should be in school! Shame on you!" The girl lowered her skirt, looking doubtful.

"Hey Sooze," one of the boys said, "she ain't your mother!" At this, Sooze turned and jumped on the bannister, sliding into the shadowy depths, laughing raucously, followed by the others like monkeys on a vine. Resuming her climb, Abbey found floor after floor of hollow-eyed children, standing on the thresholds of their respective holes, most scattering as she passed.

On the fifth floor she looked up and saw that the staircase ended at a single door. Like a penthouse. Like an attic. She put her hand on the bannister and looked up at the door, black and far away. Her foot tentatively came to rest on the first step, and then withdrew. Eyes dented her back from the fifth-floor baby dens, eyes daring her to do it, to go up and knock on Lobo's door. And she would. She wasn't afraid of Lobo, or the wild children, or the dark. She could handle those things, she figured. But not the attic. Attics were places you put all the things you didn't want anymore, the things you wished you never had, the dark things. Her foot stayed in its concrete boot.

"Lobo's home," a voice piped from one of the doorways, maybe impatient with her.

"Lobo!" Abbey yelled. It came out a high-pitched mewl. She sucked in a breath and belted out again, "Lobo!"

From nearby came a repeated "Lobo!" and then down the hall, a chant of "LoBO, LoBO, LoBO," and this echo floated deeper and deeper into the building as though the house itself had mouths. Abbey turned to face the pandemonium. These children were pitiful and tragic, and, just now, annoying as hell, calling up the urge to pull a few ears, put someone on a chair in the corner.

From behind her she heard, "Who the fuck wants Lobo?"

Abbey swirled. Lobo had come halfway down the stairs in the confusion. He peered at her in the gloom as though *she* were the strange sight, and not him. He wore his skull cap, with gadgets dangling like insects around his cheeks. A torn, baggy sweat suit hung from his stick frame.

"Shit," he said. "What you doing here?" Silence reigned in babyland. Abbey too felt tongue-tied.

"How'd you get by my guards?"

That snapped her voice back. "These children are living in filth, Lobo. And so are you."

He grinned easily. "Well, we could move in with you, Ab. How'd that be?"

"Ab, Ab, Ab," came the chant.

Behind Lobo, up at the top, his door was open. Beyond it lay his gray den, where Abbey could just make out motes of dust highlighted by some distant window or flame.

"Wanna come up?" Lobo asked.

"Not right now." A trickle of sweat left the nape of her neck and traveled slowly down her spine.

"Somethin' I can do for you, Ab?" His voice took on a prodding, sarcastic tone. He glanced down at the fifth-floor doors, perhaps posturing for his audience.

Abbey straightened. This could get out of hand. "You listen to me, Lobo," she said. "I haven't got time for foolishness. I came to buy something. You don't want my business, just say so."

"SAY so, SAY so," the house repeated.

His hands went up, fending her off. Then a cough shook him and he dug into a pocket, finally pulling out a rag so repulsive that Abbey had to look away. He blew his nose and looked at her over the wad of cloth.

"It's that game," she said. "What do you call it? Nir? Sounds like fun. I'd like to try it. I brought money." She plunged a hand into her bag and pulled forth a crumpled bunch of greens.

Lobo visibly started at the sight of the money. He lunged for her arm and yanked her partway up the stairs, pulling her close to his face. "You're fucking stupid." His breath might have come from a waste vent. He pivoted on the stairs and practically carried her with him down the steps to the hallway. It all happened so fast she didn't have time to react, except she *did* notice he pulled her down, not up, not up to that lair of his.

He was dragging her down the hallway. "Get out of my way!" he croaked at the youngsters who began streaming out from their warrens. "Get out of my way, all of you, or I'll cut you off!" he shouted.

"Money!" the kids shouted gleefully. "Money, money, money," sped through the corridors.

"Fucking stupid!" he whispered hoarsely in her ear. He plunged on, elbowing his way through the crowd of children, now sprinting from doors, up the staircase, down the bannister. There were so many of them, it was a stampede, a swarm. "Money, money, money!" came the refrain from all mouths.

Abbey let him pull her along as his left elbow angled through the bodies like an icebreaker forging a channel. Looking up at her from all sides were little faces contorted with demon energy, screaming, the girls screaming in high-pitched ululations, the boys chanting, money, money, money. She slapped at the insistent hands goosing her from all sides. As they stumbled down the stairs leading to the third floor, a thunderous drumming of feet pursued from behind, threatening to surge over them and pitch them headlong, down, down. And then, for a moment, Abbey saw something glitter, could have been those feral eyes ... could have been a knife. Dear God, just two more floors. Her heart lurched against her rib cage in time with an accelerating storm of Money, money, money, money. . . .